BITTER LEGACY

DAL MACLEAN

BITTER LEGACY

DAL MACLEAN

An Imprint of Blind Eye Books
blindeyebooks.com

Bitter Legacy
by **Dal Maclean**

Published by: ONE BLOCK EMPIRE
An imprint of Blind Eye Books
1141 Grant Street
Bellingham WA 98225
blindeyebooks.com

Edited by Nicole Kimberling

Cover design by Kanaxa

First Edition October 2016

ISBN: 978-1-935560-42-5
Printed in the United States of America

To Josh, without whom this book wouldn't have begun. And to N and J for putting up with me through all of it.

1

It wasn't exactly a usual place to have your throat cut. Not that there were set venues for it, but Cheval Place in Knightsbridge had to be about as far from non-metaphorical throat-cutting country as it got.

James parked his car behind an open-doored ambulance and looked around carefully as he stepped out into the damp London night air.

The quiet, innocuous, very expensive cul-de-sac sat tucked away behind the flashy roar of Brompton Road: on one side, an elegantly painted Georgian mews terrace, on the other, a red-brick monstrosity of doubtful lineage. Now though, two silent blue-flashing patrol cars disfigured the subdued wealth of the street. Garish-yellow crime-scene tape cordoned off a large area of the pavement in front of a shiny, black front door. All very vulgar.

James opened the boot of his Honda and dug into the plastic box of equipment there, full of tools, polythene bags, and a white forensic containment suit which he awkwardly shouldered into. For his muscular, six-foot-one frame, the suits never seemed big enough. The final touches were paper overshoes and a pair of violently lilac, nitrile surgical gloves. Then he pulled up the suit hood to cover his thick, light hair.

James didn't recognize the uniformed PC standing in front of the house, so he flashed his warrant card before ducking under the tape across the entrance, onto the single front step. That was as far as he needed to go to find the reason for the callout.

A woman lay sprawled facedown in the hall, her feet close to the door. Silky, dark, shoulder-length hair obscured most of her face and stuck to the large pool of coagulating scarlet beneath her upper body. Her coat and skirt were tangled at the top of her thighs. But from where James stood, her black tights didn't appear to have been interfered with.

"Evening, Sameera."

Detective Constable Sameera Kaur stood near the head of the corpse, strong, handsome features peering out from her own white paper hood. She'd proved to be one of the best DCs they had, a Sikh girl from Birmingham, desperately in love with the job.

"Evening, Sarge," she returned. "Looking very nifty. You should wear that on the telly."

"Uh-huh. Can't help noticing we have the same stylist. What've you got?"

"There's no sign of forced entry. Seems like she opened her front door, and the assailant subdued her from behind, then slashed her throat." Kaur had a strong Midlands accent, her tone never less than imperturbable. "No sign of a significant struggle. Probably quick."

"Who found her?"

"A neighbor. Wally's calmin' her down. She noticed the door a little ajar around…" Kaur consulted a small black notebook, "…19:30 on her way to Brompton Road, then again just before 20:00 when she got back. She left it for a while then decided to take a nose around."

James nodded toward the corpse on the floor. "Any clue to identity?"

Kaur consulted her notebook again. "The neighbor says the house owner's Maria Curzon-Whyte. Same name on the driver's license and the ID in her bag."

So, James calculated, time of death would have been sometime before seven thirty, and probably after dark. And in London, in February, it got dark by five.

He frowned down at the dead woman, at the huge, bright-red peony of blood sinking obscenely into the pile of her expensive cream hall carpet.

Not a cat's chance now of making his flat-viewing, he thought resentfully. And at once, decent guilt scurried in behind.

From the start he'd sworn to himself that the job would never make him callous. But here he was, annoyed at someone for having the gall to get murdered when he had other plans.

"Robbery?" he asked levelly.

"Haven't seen any signs so far," Kaur replied. "Her bag and briefcase are still there an' they seem undisturbed."

And indeed, both were lying further into the hall, as if they'd been flung there when the woman fell. They appeared expensive, like the woman's clothes, like the house.

Maybe it would be a nice, straightforward domestic. Most murders were.

James crouched lower, careful not to lean too close to the body, in case some of his DNA—a hair or a skin particle—contaminated it. And as he did so, he noticed something—an object—lying close to the woman's head, caught in the shadow of the hallway wall.

"What's that?"

Kaur peered down. "Yeah, I saw it. It's a piece of chain."

Heavy duty. A short length of steel chain with no lock on either end.

James chewed his lip thoughtfully.

It most likely had nothing to do with this. It appeared far too short to have been of any use to strangle or subdue the victim, and too sturdy to have broken without extreme force. But anything was possible in this game; he'd learned that quickly enough.

"Okay." James straightened and sidled round the body to join Kaur, careful to walk on the same thin edge of carpet as she had. "Let's see what we can turn up before Herself gets here."

He found an incredibly narrow house, like a very tall flat, old and quirky and set on three levels. The basement held a study; the ground floor, a sitting room with a TV and a generously sized, scrupulously clear aquarium, a tiny kitchen and toilet; and there were two modest bedrooms on the top floor. In reality, it was cramped, but James knew it would set a buyer back a couple of million pounds at least, in this part of town. You paid through the nose to have Harrods as your corner shop.

Books lined the small basement study, and an open, antique, roll-top desk rested against the wall opposite the door, the top of it laden with framed photographs. Most of them featured a dark-haired girl. Posing with what appeared to be a well-heeled family. Sitting astride an impressive grey horse. Grinning joyfully in her graduation robes.

She looked…interesting, somehow, James thought. Intelligent, challenging. And oddly familiar.

He frowned down at the photographs for some time, wrestling with that sense of vague recognition, but the longer he stared, the further away it seemed to slip.

He began to study the paperwork piled neatly on the desk.

It became evident almost immediately what the woman had done for a living, and with the realization came a needle-sharp stab of apprehension. There were case notes, a pile of opened letters addressed to Maria Curzon-Whyte at her chambers and, now James paid more attention to them, mainly law books on the shelves.

She'd been relatively young to be a criminal barrister, though just leafing through her correspondence, he got the impression of a sharp mind, of extreme competence. But for all they prettied it up with gowns and horsehair wigs, someone wading in the sewers, just like him. There were so many more possibilities now he didn't know whether to feel excited or appalled.

He blew out a tense breath and extracted his phone from his jacket pocket to take some detailed shots of the desk before the SOCO Team arrived. But as he did, he spotted the corner of a small white notepad sticking out from underneath the pile of case notes. He crouched down and edged part of it toward him carefully with a nitrile-covered forefinger.

It was blank, the kind of sticky-backed pad hotels provided for their guests, and sure enough, he could see the edge of a brand logo on it. Ideas and wild speculations darted into his mind as he began to maneuver it out—forbidden liaisons, seedy affairs, murderous consequences. He moved his phone close hopefully, to photograph the pad as it slid out.

Raffles in Singapore.

He sighed heavily and lowered the phone. Definitely a bit far to go for a shag.

But as he moved his head back and started to rise, the light fell on the top page of the pad in a certain way, and he could see an obvious indent. Whatever had been written above it had been written heavily. He didn't even have to rub a pencil over it—just as well because Forensics would have eviscerated him if he'd tried. He just had to squint at it from the right angle…

He copied what he found into his notebook. An address in London.

It could be anything, of course. A hairdresser. A nail salon. The place her murderer lived, with the murder weapon conveniently placed for easy discovery by an enterprising detective sergeant.

He gave a huff of dark amusement and straightened up from the desk.

Maria's excited eyes met his, blazing dark and happy; triumphant at her graduation, her whole brilliant, glittering life laid out in front of her like a carpet of flowers. She smiled at him expectantly, with all the blind arrogance of beauty and youth, daring him not to admire her.

He wanted to smile back. He felt a sudden unwelcome tug of emotion, almost of loss.

How the fuck did you end like that, Maria? he asked those clever eyes.

"Jamie. Anything?"

James drew in a quick, shocked breath and whirled round.

His Detective Chief Inspector—also known as Herself—stood in the doorway, looking exactly like a woman who'd just hurtled halfway across London on a Sunday to attend one murder scene—a stabbing outside a nightclub in Vauxhall—then been required to turn and hurtle back to this one. She wore a white forensic suit too, but the hood remained down, revealing her disastrously disordered corkscrew curls. She raised a mocking eyebrow at James's badly covered startlement, and he could only shrug wryly in acknowledgement.

They got on well, he and Jo Ingham.

She was a small, plump, half-Jamaican woman in her forties from Essex, with a gratifyingly foul mouth, a husband in the force, and no kids. Everyone knew she could easily have reached a higher rank if she'd wished—she had more than enough intelligence and political savvy—but she had no real desire to climb any further up the greasy pole. She wanted to solve crimes.

James knew that, having come up the hard way herself, Ingham could easily have disdained a fast-track recruit like him, but she'd chosen to nurture his potential. In turn he felt a fierce loyalty to her, drawn to her no-nonsense decency like a moth to the light.

"Ma'am. Assuming she's the resident, she seems to have lived alone. And she was a criminal barrister."

Ingham glanced at one of the photographs on the desk behind James, closed her eyes and blew out a despairing breath.

Inevitably this would be high profile. A young, beautiful, rich, professional woman involved in the criminal-justice system, murdered brutally on her own doorstep, and more than that, a woman very probably personally known to crime reporters. Most of all, though, the important words for the front pages would be *beautiful* and *rich*.

"Shit," she spat.

James grimaced in solidarity. Everyone in the South Kensington Murder Investigation Team knew the kind of pressure Ingham labored under, the grinding politics of trying to make a case against budget cutbacks, like every other head of an MIT in London.

Unfortunately though, the argument for any murder team would always be tricky to make. As part of the West London group of MITs, Ingham's unit took a week's turn on call for the whole West London area, and in that week, any unexplained deaths on that patch became their cases. But that meant that, by the luck of the draw, their unit at existing levels—roughly thirty strong—could be alternately worked to exhaustion or stultifyingly bored. Impossible to predict.

Just that afternoon, James and his fellow DS, Alec Scrivenor, had been bitching in their dead office like a pair of adolescents on a message board—all about how fucking unlucky the unit had been with their last turns on call, how the famine in homicide had been telling on morale and much-needed overtime, how bored they were working files on dead cases. They'd been reduced to throwing darts at an ancient board propped against a waste-bin.

Now, on the first night of their on-call week, they had two murders to solve, Ingham had no time, and James understood too well the wisdom of the old warning to be careful what you wished for.

He followed Ingham silently, almost guiltily, up past Scenes of Crime Officers hovering round the corpse and outside, two doors along the damp, now grotesquely busy mews, to the woman who'd discovered the body.

Mrs. Alice Cordiner sat perched at the edge of a pristine Chesterfield sofa in her fantastically elegant, expensively scented lounge. A fine-boned, exquisitely groomed woman of indeterminate age, she appeared to be exactly the kind of person who could afford to live in Cheval Place.

"Mrs. Cordiner?" The woman glanced up from her dazed contemplation of a half-full cup of tea to regard Ingham with large, watery eyes. "I understand you must be very upset." Mrs. Cordiner let loose a snort of desperate amusement. Ingham continued, unperturbed. "But perhaps you can tell us what happened."

"I didn't know her," Alice Cordiner said at once. Her cultured voice sounded thin and high and defensive, as if she were making an excuse for unpardonable behavior. "Well, just to say hello to. You know how it is. I used to see her coming and going."

"Did she have a partner?" Ingham's voice remained conversational.

"I don't know." But then, almost compulsively, "She had some visitors. Men and women."

"But you saw no one around tonight?"

"No! I just saw the door open on my way to Marks…Marks and Spencer, you know? On Brompton Road. There were no lights on, and normally… Well, one doesn't like to be nosy. But it would have been an invitation to theft! Or maybe she'd actually *been* burgled. So I pushed the door, but I could feel something behind it." She lifted a thin, trembling hand to her mouth, breathing becoming more audible; incipient hysteria barely banished and slithering back in at the edges. "And when I put my head round… I have a torch on my phone. There was…so much…blood…and it seemed so bright. I didn't know it would be such a bright…red. On the television it's…"

She visibly forced herself to stop, shaking fingers pressed tight against her lips.

"Did you notice anything?" James put in gently. "Anything unusual? Any detail, however small, that might be of help?"

"*God!* I just saw *her*, lying there, and I ran." She paused, a few shuddering seconds, then she offered to James, tearfully, hopefully, "I did notice she had on Jimmy Choos. New season."

James didn't allow his expression to change. Shock did odd things to people and—he'd asked.

"You've been very helpful, Mrs. Cordiner," James reassured her. She nodded sharply, like a shocked bird, then dropped her eyes back to the safe familiarity of her tea.

As James and Ingham walked back slowly to the now-bustling crime scene, they were both subdued.

"No magic bullet then," James ventured, just to break the silence.

"I stopped believing in Santa when I turned thirty-five," Ingham snapped. "I'm not sure what I'll do if the Tooth Fairy isn't real." She made a hugely impatient sound. "Fuck, we're not gonna get much breathing space on this one."

James nodded wordlessly. But then, as suddenly as if she'd hit a wall, Ingham stopped walking. James, startled, stopped too, a few feet from the scene-of-crime tape.

She faced him full-on, all her focus on him. Her eyes were large and dark, slightly protuberant, and the expectant light in them made James's gut clench nervously.

"How does it feel to you?" Ingham asked. And James realized he'd been waiting for exactly that question, in exactly that tone. How it felt to him.

Because much to his own embarrassment, the leaps of intuition and logic he'd made in the past, which had paid off—had earned James a worrying reputation with Ingham, and Scrivenor for that matter, as somehow...a bit psychic. That unnerved him more than a bit. He appreciated the fact that Ingham took his opinion into account, but even the way she phrased the question felt redolent of crystal balls and communing with the spirits.

All he'd ever done was go with logic and his gut feeling, which had been a new experience for a man brought up to fit into a very tight box. *Feelings* hadn't been welcome in his house.

Still, he tried to give her what he could. How it felt. To him. "Not a domestic... Not at first glance. No sense it's a robbery. As far as we can tell, no obvious sexual motive."

Ingham didn't say a word, just waited.

"Domestic..." James went on. "Well, it'd have to be someone in her life who planned it, someone so full of rage, he, or she, would watch Maria get out of her car and unlock the door, then grab her and cut her throat on the spot. That's a really *intimate* way of killing someone. Unless you're a pro, you'd have to hate her. But I didn't get a feeling of rage. Just the one wound."

Ingham nodded slowly. "So?"

He shrugged, hating that he had so little. "Someone just...needed her dead."

"It could still be domestic. But I take your point. Her job has to be the best lead." Ingham frowned. "Prevention. Or vengeance." A short, tense pause, and she seemed to be bracing herself. "Jamie. I'm going to need you to take the lead on this one."

James stilled, and stared at her blankly. He'd heard the words clearly enough, but he couldn't be sure he'd understood them all the same.

He was a detective sergeant, far down the pecking order. More than that, he was the least experienced DS in their unit. He couldn't *take the lead* on a major investigation.

Ingham grimaced. "Look, I know it's asking a lot. And yeah, I could shift DI Mulligan from the Albert Embankment stabbing, but...I really get the feeling this one's gonna be a bastard."

James gazed at her wordlessly, and her mouth twisted.

"Fuck. Don't look at me like that. I'm not hangin' you out to dry. It's still my case. But I'm not gonna to be able to do the legwork, and there's no one I trust more to dig out the obscure details. You've a copper's nose, Jamie."

"But..." James protested weakly. "Alec..." Because Scrivenor had more than two decades experience over him. In fact, he'd shown James the ropes as a detective.

"I need Alec to manage the office, with two cases going." Ingham said. "I know it's unorthodox, but you'll be a DI soon enough, an' frankly, I've got no options. I *know* you can do it. Just don't go off half-cocked. Come to me with everythin' you get."

She waited expectantly for a second or two, then, with a gusty sigh, she strode off toward the forensics team, working, efficiently silent, in the eerie, winking-blue light.

To James, that sigh felt like a reproach.

He watched her edge inside the hallway, but he found himself slowing deliberately, then stopping, trying to wrestle down his warring emotions.

Had she expected more enthusiasm? That he'd be gung-ho at the unprecedented chance she'd decided to give him?

He'd only been a copper for two and a bit years. And he'd been a uniformed PC for one of them. All his time at the MIT had basically involved acting as Ingham's sidekick—exactly the role detective sergeants were meant to play. Bag carriers. Organizers. Assistants. Sounding boards.

Now Ingham expected him to coordinate a major murder case with no formal acknowledgement and no rank to back him up?

He drew a deep breath, trying to calm himself down. It could be ruinous.

And yet—hadn't Ingham also paid him a huge compliment? She could have moved him to the straightforward stabbing case in Vauxhall, but she'd left that with the senior officer, and chosen *James* to shoulder the hard-core investigation. Rationally, her head would be on the chopping block too.

Fuck! At times like this, James wished bitterly that he smoked.

He gazed restlessly along the mews, noting lights were now on in most of the houses, but then anyone would find it bloody hard to sleep through the aftermath of a murder. All the residents would have to be interviewed anyway, as soon as possible.

Deliberately, he relaxed his shoulders and moved to follow Ingham.

He felt almost comically far from fully engaged now, but even so, as he neared Maria's door, something made him glance to the left, into the deep shadows outside the semicircle of powerful lights shining on the crime scene. It took a second to register it but, as he peered into the gloom, he saw a slightly darker blob a few feet away, almost closer to the neighbor's door. He thought his eyes were probably playing tricks on him, but he strode over to investigate anyway, glad of the diversion.

What he discovered, when he shone his phone torch on it, proved a total anticlimax. A small bag of pebbles rested pointlessly against the house wall—clear polythene, tied at the top with an elastic band, and filled with smooth, white, sea-washed stones.

James frowned almost offended by it, trying to make sense of its presence in a London side street. Maybe someone had left the stones for Maria's fish tank. Or maybe they had nothing to do with her. Maybe they belonged to her neighbor. Or the building work, going on in a house a few doors down.

He told SOCO to document the bag anyway, since this seemed to be his case now. Then the diversion ended.

Grimly, he watched an officer photographing the bag and another dabbing it for fingerprints. And when Ingham reappeared, he managed to find a smile for her before they headed to their respective cars to drive the short distance to the station.

▬ǀǀ▬ ▬ǀǀ▬ ▬ǀǀ▬ ▬ǀǀ▬

James followed Ingham into the station briefing room just after one a.m., and the contrast from the peaceful state in which he'd left it felt staggering—from zero to full, reckless throttle, in just a few hours.

Ingham headed straight for Detective Inspector Mulligan holding forth at the far side of the room to Charlie Brent, his unfortunate DS, and when he saw her, Mulligan snapped to attention before her like a squaddie on parade.

James watched and felt a bolstering stab of contempt. Because—fuck it—whatever the restrictions of leading an investigation with his present rank and inexperience, he knew he could do a better job than Mulligan, a career cop so pedantic and ponderous that James had come close to committing homicide himself on the few occasions he'd worked for him.

The Albert Embankment case—Mulligan's case—rested on CCTV and the hope of eyewitness cooperation. Maria's would be a mystery, James could feel it, real old-fashioned detective work.

And then the remnants of civilian shame tempered that burst of professional excitement—and curdled in with that, realism.

He *had* to get it right. Not just for Ingham, or even himself, but for Maria, for the people who loved her. He didn't want to end up as one of those old cops with a filing cabinet full of the guilty souvenirs of failure.

He tore his gaze away from Mulligan and Ingham and, with a jolt of relief, found Scrivenor sitting off to one side, looking as if he'd been running his hands through his sparse hair for hours. It stood up in tiny tufts now, like the feathers of a pissed-off owl.

Alec was old school—a big, ginger, balding, mustachioed Glaswegian in his late forties, who'd come up through the ranks over twenty-eight years to the plum job of DS in an MIT. He'd spent his entire adult life in London, yet his Glasgow accent hadn't softened by a syllable. He and James were polar opposites, yet they fitted together like puzzle pieces. Within the MIT, they were their own mini-unit.

"Like fuckin' buses," Scrivenor sniffed, as James slid into the seat beside him. "Nothing till yiv given up, an' then two come along at once. An' then it's crazy town."

James huffed a laugh. "It could be worse. We could be Charlie."

Scrivenor grunted with amused malice. "Poor bastard." They sat in silent accord as the rest of the unit shuffled and gossiped in the seats and tables around them, waiting with eager tension for Ingham to begin the show. And as they waited, James worried at how to tell Scrivenor he'd been chosen to lead a murder investigation with just one, single year's CID experience behind him.

It wasn't that Scrivenor had ever showed a molecule of resentment of James and the way he'd been parachuted in from the outside. He'd always been totally accepting of the fact the DS to whom he'd once shown the ropes would be a detective inspector soon, when he'd never had that option. When it had taken *him* sixteen years of hard slog to make sergeant.

James had been in awe of his generosity, but Scrivenor had confided that the endless reforms imposed by the Met since he'd joined had long since left him ready to accept his career could be leapfrogged by an influx of prima ballerinas at any moment.

But still…

"Any joy wi' findin' a flat?" Scrivenor asked idly.

James accepted the escape, though he couldn't call it a restful subject either. "Not so far. There're twenty people after every decent room."

He tried to sound unbothered, but in reality, before this case hit, he'd been manically dedicated to the project of reclaiming a life for himself. Only—London hadn't been cooperating, and now work had kicked him in the bollocks too.

It had all been sparked six weeks before, by one of those epiphanies that usually came in the dead hours of the night. This one, though, had come with James's alarm clock. It had woken him in his lumpy single bed, and he'd stared at the brown-stained paint on the bedroom ceiling, smelled the eternal stink of cabbage, heavily underlaid by damp, and all at once, he'd felt as if he were suffocating.

It'd been a quick, terrifying surge of panic that had sent his heart rate galloping—triggered by one of those too clear-sighted moments no one wanted to have.

The realization that he had no life, any more. No real friends. He had nothing outside of work, because work had become his one refuge and certainty. Being a good policeman provided all his self-belief and pride.

At twenty-eight, he existed and little more, in a rented hovel of a bedsit, furnished with landlord's tat. And he didn't even need to. Poverty hadn't forced him this low. He didn't *have* to live alone like a hermit in a cell. He didn't have to smell fucking cabbage all the time. What he'd done, what he *was*, didn't actually require a hair shirt.

It had been a ludicrous kind of insight—he hadn't even been aware he'd been hiding. But once the awakening had come, his need to get out of that flat had grown manic.

"I've seen fourteen already," James confided gloomily. "I had a viewing tomorrow in Earls Court as well. It looked good."

Scrivenor's bushy ginger eyebrows headed toward his receding hairline. "Earls Court? Ah remember when that wiz affordable."

"No...this one's pretty reasonable," James protested. "That's why I'm so pissed off I'm going to miss a chance at it."

But deep down, he knew he'd have gone for something more modest if the wording of the advert hadn't pulled him in.

Wanted: flatmate for 2-bed frst flr in S Ken. Prkg. Can be M or F. Must be employed, solvent, civil, gay friendly.

Well, he'd thought at the time, excitement beginning to buzz, he fit all of them. Most importantly, he fit the last bit. It had been a major part of James's resolution to change, after all—forcing himself to finally...try. Make his publicly accepted sexuality more than theory. Make some gay friends for a start.

So much for that.

Scrivenor seemed to sense his need to sulk, so they both silently watched Ingham as she finished her finessing of Mulligan, and called the briefing to order.

She rattled through the nightclub stabbing without calling Mulligan to make any kind of contribution. Obviously, her focus lay with the bigger case.

"Right. The second one tonight. Cheval Place—our own backyard. We're treating the house as the primary crime scene until we know different. Going by ID, the victim appears to be Maria Curzon-Whyte, aged twenty-five, a barrister at Blackheath Chambers."

A loud collective groan echoed round the room. They all knew how the press operated.

Ingham ignored them. "She lived alone but she may have had boyfriends, or indeed girlfriends. Sameera and Wally have started door to door. We haven't got a time of death yet, but the assailant used a risky method...body left right in the front hall of a mews house with the door ajar. Jamie...get me a name an' address for next of kin. Barry...find as much info as possible about her chambers." She rattled off more tasks and directions then stalked off to her office.

James realized only at that moment that he hadn't seen her crack a smile in days.

The briefing broke up with a cacophony of scraping chairs and chatter, and everyone trailed down the corridor to the big, open-plan office-come-Incident Room—bleak and grey and filled with ragged furniture and stone-age equipment. James's and Scrivenor's battered chipboard desks were set out face to face in a small island, both half-covered with ancient bulky computer monitors normal people would have laughed at.

James automatically switched on his monitor when he reached his rickety swivel chair, and as he sat down, he pressed the button on a massive, even more elderly computer beside his legs. On a very good day it took just ten minutes to power up, and he had it lucky. Some of the terminals in the office took half an hour to come on. Scrivenor had appropriated this one for James on the quiet, one of the many things he'd done to subtly help him since he'd arrived, though Scrivenor'd be appalled to be called on it.

"Fuck, what I would nae give for a Costa coffee right now." Scrivenor thumped down a pile of files. "An' a muffin." He grinned at James slyly. "All you overprivileged English bastards should come wi' a butler."

James met his eyes expressionlessly.

"Tae go tae Costa for us," Scrivenor finished innocently.

Unfortunately for him, James's attempt at cultivating a "just another copper" demeanor had never quite recovered from the ingratiating gesture he'd made on his first day at the MIT, when he'd made the basic mistake of buying a pair of expensive lattes for Scrivenor and himself, from a branch of Costa on the way to work, rather than grabbing two bog-standard coffees from the vending machine in the corridor. From that moment, it had become a thing between them, proving, Scrivenor claimed, how unutterably posh he really was. James still brought in a cup for Alec regularly, just to enjoy the abuse.

"But…ah gotta go an' see Herself." Scrivenor winked, and he headed for Ingham's office, moving with impressive speed for all his bulk.

James waited for his computer to stagger to life, gazing idly at the hyperactivity around him. Then, for variety, he dutifully studied the all-too-familiar detail of a postcard Scrivenor had carefully sellotaped to the back of his own monitor to "add interest" to James's office land-scape—Salvador Dali's *Christ of Saint John of the Cross*. James had returned the favor by taping a portrait photograph of the Chief Com-missioner of the Metropolitan Police to "add interest" to the back of his.

James would be contemplating that cross for the next few days with not a lot of respite, so it seemed only fair Scrivenor should spend an equal amount of time with the commissioner.

He sighed and stretched, impatient to get going. With any investi-gation, the first hours were the most crucial. Evidence had to be found before the crime scene could be opened, and subsequently destroyed, by inexperienced people blundering about on it. Witness statements must be taken before time blurred memory. Next of kin had to be in-terviewed and consoled before the death became general knowledge.

James rarely saw his own bed for the first forty-eight hours after a murder. In fact, he'd been on investigations where he'd been on duty for four solid days. There had been a collection to buy some camp beds the year before, and everyone kept changes of clothes and toiletries at the station.

He stared at the surreal intricacies of Dali and tried not to imagine what Ingham might be telling Scrivenor until, just when he'd almost forgotten what he'd been waiting for, the monitor on his desk lit up with a discordant clang of chords. He checked his watch. Nine min-utes and thirty-two seconds. A record. Maybe it was a sign.

■II■ ■II■ ■II■ ■II■

It didn't take James long to pull up the information he needed on Maria's next of kin, and as he read, his heart plummeted. If she had any respect at all for career politics, he thought, this should be enough to change Ingham's mind on giving him the lead.

He grimaced and stood up, details in hand.

Ingham had been chatting with Scrivenor when he reached her glass box of an office, but she waved him in.

"Parents, ma'am," he offered apologetically. She caught his tone immediately and her eyes narrowed. "Father is Sir George Curzon, chairman of Grosvenor Properties and Chair of the British Property Federation. Mother...the Honorable Lady Justice Cordelia Whyte." He blew out a regretful breath. "DBE."

Dame Cordelia Whyte.

Every policeman in London had heard of her. A rebellious cornerstone of the criminal-justice system, a constant critic of the Met, a thorn in every government's side.

"Fuck," Scrivenor said succinctly. He spoke, indeed, for them all.

Ingham let her head drop as she ran a hand through her rumpled curls. Then she looked up. "Right. We have at most...thirty-six hours before the suits totally lose their shit. Jamie...you'll do the usual for the press."

James scowled.

Ingham made him do most public-appeal TV appearances with her because, she said, people paid more attention to Pretty, especially Posh Pretty. He fucking hated it. Press briefings, press conferences to appeal for witnesses, and worst of all the BBC's dreaded help-the-police program, *Crimewatch*.

He'd been arm-twisted into that after a TV producer spotted him when he went in with Ingham as bag carrier. And, since Ingham was too nervous to perform confidently on live TV herself, James had found himself in makeup and on the studio floor beside her before he could fully understand what had happened. Unfortunately, thanks to Oxbridge and his father, he'd received solid training in presenting a facade of self-confidence, and his appearance had been seen as a roaring success, not least because the program got a lot of embarrassing tweets from women who fancied him.

"Yes," he gritted. "Ma'am."

Scrivenor grinned at him maliciously through nicotine-stained teeth.

"I've got an address for their London house, ma'am," James went on. "They have a manor house in Oxfordshire too."

Ingham sighed. "Of course they do. Let's try here first."

There would be no question of James making the visit alone, not with people like this. Instead he followed silently as he and Ingham trudged out into the dark, wet car park to her police Vauxhall, leaving Scrivenor behind to coordinate the office. James seriously envied him.

—||— —||— —||— —||—

James loathed first visits to bereaved families—and worst of all, middle-of-the-night visits—more than any other aspect of the job. Hell, who wouldn't? He sat grimly in the passenger seat, staring out at the wet, empty, shop-lit pavements flashing by, dreading what they were about to do.

Eaton Square was one of the best addresses in London, all grand Victorian terraced houses: tall, white limestone, three bay windows wide, sitting across from a splendid central garden. Many of the houses had been converted into flats, each worth a few million pounds in themselves, but this address—the Curzon-Whyte's—appeared to be the original house in its entirety.

The February predawn felt poisonously cold when James emerged into it, and oddly he noticed the lack of smell—no rubbish, no fumes, no flowers, just the scent of expensive neutrality.

It took a good ten minutes of ringing the round brass bell, nerves thrumming in his stomach, before the house could be roused and a disgruntled man in his fifties opened the door to glare at them—of all things, a butler. Scrivenor leapt inappropriately to James's mind.

James couldn't imagine what the man thought could be going on; why anyone would be ringing the doorbell after two a.m. without urgent news. But the butler's lofty aggression didn't diminish until Ingham pulled out her warrant card, and the horror of the visit began in earnest.

The man showed them into a medium-sized sitting room and scuttled off to wake Maria's parents, while James stood with Ingham, contemplating family photographs of happy children and proud adults dotted everywhere. The tension in his gut stretched board tight.

James felt as he always felt waiting to deliver this kind of news: like an emotional mugger, smashing into other people's calm lives, leaving agony and loss behind. The aloofness of his role built his guilt, his distance from their pain. That he could introduce himself to people to deliver news that ruined them, with no wounds of his own to show in solidarity. He was the professional, like a doctor, slicing through their existence then going back to his own clean life.

He'd been studying a photograph of what appeared to be Maria as a child when, at last, a man and woman entered the room, both grey-haired, slender and exquisitely poised, even in dressing gowns, woken in the middle of the night.

Ingham told them as economically as she could.

"But…I talked to her." Maria's mother spoke in clear, cut-glass tones. She sounded firm and reasonable, entirely self-possessed, a woman trained in control. She wore her hair in a stylish iron-grey crop; her eyes were large and dark and hooded. "I spoke to her this evening. She's going to try to come to The Grange. She has a case first, and then…she's going to come."

Her husband already wept silently. He reached out a shaking hand to grasp her upper arm.

"Darling…"

His wife shook her head sharply. "*No.* I was short with her, because she couldn't come tomorrow. That can't be the last time. That's simply not possible."

It felt brutal, watching her try to instinctively hold onto dignity as she fought not to surrender and believe, but all her wealth and influence and worldliness made no difference. She and her husband were simply two people who'd lost a child.

"When you're ready, sir," James said quietly to Sir George. "We'll send a car to collect you." At least he didn't have to say the words; they all knew the body had to be identified.

"How?" Sir George asked suddenly, voice thick with grief. He asked James, not Ingham. "How did he do it?"

James didn't even consider pointing out that they knew nothing as yet about the gender of the killer. He forced himself to meet the man's eyes.

"Her throat had been cut. Sir."

Silence blanketed the room, a layer of shock, torn suddenly by the kind of weak, wounded noise a small animal might make. But it rose and it rose, more and more, in volume and agony, until the uncontrolled screams and howls of Maria's mother echoed unbearably around them, a sound so primal that James felt it in his bones, in his elevated heartbeat.

He didn't know what he'd expected from her, an appeal-court judge who'd heard and seen so much. The continuation, perhaps, of her facade of icy calm? But she'd proved no calmer, no less melted to the heart, than the very first mother he'd had to tell about the death of a child, stabbed through the heart in a gang fight.

There could be no point to this now. He glanced urgently at Ingham, and she nodded as if he'd spoken aloud.

"Please call when you're ready to come in, Sir George." Horribly, Ingham had to shout to be heard over the clamor in the room. "Family Liaison officers will be in touch."

"We don't want Family Liaison!" Dame Cordelia roared, her voice hoarse and thick and venomous.

Every stunned eye in the room locked on to her. Tears poured relentlessly down her ashen cheeks, and she reminded James of nothing so much as a figure in some towering Shakespearean tragedy. But somehow in the midst of her hysteria, she had willed herself, forced herself back to them, alert and present. It felt almost unnatural.

Ingham said cautiously, "Family Liaison officers are there to make sure you're informed of everything that's…"

"Don't patronize me!" Dame Cordelia snapped, and life had returned to her eyes, even as they still wept: fire and steel and outrage. "I know exactly what they're for, and I know how you use them. We don't need people hanging around us, trying to dig for information under the guise of a shoulder to lean on."

Another short, shocked silence followed as Ingham visibly searched for a diplomatic reply to Dame Cordelia's unexpected aggression. She could hardly deny the professional truth of what the woman had said—Family Liaison, otherwise known as FLOs, had an ambivalent role—but in James's experience, most bereaved families at this point greeted a dedicated link to the murder investigation without question. Then again, as a murder detective, he'd never before dealt with a family like this.

In the end Sir George saved the moment. "Darling, I'm sure they'd just be there to help." He held both his wife's hands in one of his, and James noted that he had not stopped shaking. "They'll help."

Ingham made some noise of agreement and tried to hand him her card, but he stared at it as if he'd never seen such a thing before in his life, so she set it on the low table in front of the grand fireplace.

"I'm…terribly sorry," Ingham said, and with a quick, gathering look at James, she headed for the door. Within seconds they'd burst out into the cold night air.

They made their way to the car and fastened their seatbelts in a kind of shocked quiet.

Then Ingham burst out, "*God. This* is going to be a sodding nightmare unless something falls in our laps."

James darted a glance at her frustrated profile as she pulled the car away from the curb.

"It could be something to do with either one of them," he tried. "Their enemies." Then, carefully, "Reacting to having FLOs around like that… Isn't that strange?"

Ingham glowered out of the windscreen. "Maybe. But she isn't exactly a fan of the Met, is she?"

James didn't bother to reply. The reflective lull between them stretched.

James ventured then, "If it's okay with you, ma'am, I've got a lead I want to take a quick glance at. I found an address on a pad on Maria's desk. It's in South Kensington."

"All right." Ingham sounded beyond weary. "Check it out later this morning."

"Right."

"And…pray for a miracle, Sergeant, or we're gonna be poking at a nest of very well-connected snakes."

2

The windows caught his attention as he pulled his car into a parking space, several yards along from No. 22 Selworth Gardens.

They were huge, multipaned, Georgian, and James could tell that they would drench the space behind them in pure, bright light.

No. 22 proved to be part of a terrace, built of yellow-brown London brick. Like all its neighbors, it had three floors of windows, no basement and a painted, paneled door, surrounded by a whitewashed portico. And on the first floor, those amazing windows were decorated with finely wrought mock balconies made of iron, gazing across to the twee, pretty little Georgian houses peering out from behind their privet hedges on the other side of the road.

This would be prime real estate. And, James knew, sadly unlikely to sport external CCTV cameras. They tended to sit on new apartment blocks and commercial buildings. But hell—no one could blame him for dreaming of finding incriminating footage of Maria arriving for afternoon liaisons with an obvious suspect, could they? He still hoped in his heart of hearts that it could be that easy.

James stretched carefully as he slammed the door of the car, a loud, obtrusive noise in the comparative quiet of the street. He felt surprisingly alert given he'd spent the night at the station, but he'd caught three hours of sleep on one of the office camp beds. It would never be a comfortable fit for his frame, but by four a.m. he'd have slept on a bed of nails. He'd even managed to fit in a shower and a shave before setting off here.

On the whole, he'd done considerably better than Scrivenor, who'd resembled an exploded mattress when James left the office. On the *whole*, he thought, he'd best make an emergency visit to Costa for a takeout, before he got back to the station.

He stretched again as he walked along the pavement until he reached the pale-grey front door of No. 22. A brass plate was fixed to the brickwork with three buttons, placed vertically very close together, and an intercom. There was every likelihood that no one would be in at this time of day, but then again, maybe some of the residents were too rich to need to work. James started, methodically, at the bottom. The name beside the button read *Nicholas*.

His phone buzzed in his pocket, and he fumbled for it as he pressed the door button blindly.

He glanced at the screen and sighed. He'd set an alarm a couple of days before, to remind him of his viewing appointment at the Earls Court flat, in half an hour. He'd already phoned that morning to cancel, but the guy had sounded unconcerned; he thought he'd found someone anyway. It didn't ease James's restless conviction, though, that he'd missed out on something good.

Beside him, the intercom crackled into life.

"Okay. You're really early, I'm afraid." An attractive, cultured male voice, which managed to sound, somehow, both friendly and politely accusing. "I'll let you in, but the guy before you's still here. Can you just come up and wait in the hallway? First floor."

James blinked at the brass plate for a confused second. First floor. He'd pressed the wrong bell. But as he opened his mouth to identify himself, the intercom shut off with a loud buzz.

He frowned and pushed the heavy door, which opened at once into a well-decorated, artificially lit hall. A flat door stood to his left, and fresh white paint covered all the woodwork and walls. None of the communal hall smells he'd become used to were in evidence—no stale smoke or urine, and definitely no cabbage. Instead, the place smelled of expensive polish and new carpet. There was no room for a concierge and, as he expected, no CCTV. Obviously, it had once been an old house, converted into flats.

He eyed the door beside him, the one he'd meant to start off with, and deliberated taking his opportunity now and knocking. But the man on the first floor would be expecting him.

His feet made no sound on the bouncy thickness of the dark-blue carpet.

The door on the left at the top of the first flight of stairs appeared identical to the one on the ground floor—paneled and freshly glossed white. But though James knocked on it, ignoring the intercom-man's instructions, and though he definitely heard voices behind it, it remained stubbornly closed. He knocked again. The door didn't open. The man had meant what he said.

James had no real reason to feel as pissed off as he did. The man inside couldn't know he was a detective investigating a murder. He wasn't purposely disrespecting the police. Yet, as James lurked, frustrated, in the plush hallway, stealing irritated glances at his watch, he found himself almost deliberately pushing himself to conclusions.

The visitor in there had an appointment. And the man who'd answered had said there'd be another right after James.

So. What kind of men were most likely to have serial "appointments" at expensive residential addresses? High-end hookers.

He glowered at the pristine door, copper's imagination running with it.

Fuck—the last thing he needed was a vice collar right now, but he couldn't exactly ignore a high-class prostitute operating under his nose.

Or maybe—he could. He really didn't have time for this.

He frowned fiercely, slumped against the opposite wall. Then, without warning, the door to the flat opened with a shocking blaze of light, and a man slipped out into the hall.

James, as he straightened, could hardly fail to notice the guy was flamboyantly good looking—all extravagant cheekbones and pouty lips, like a catwalk model—and to all appearances, extremely pleased with himself. As he strutted past, he gave James a quick once-over and a knowing smirk, then he trotted down the stairs and out of sight.

James stared after him. He didn't look like the kind of man who paid for it, but if police-work had taught him anything, it'd be that people rarely obliged by fitting their stereotypes. Whatever the guy had been there for, he'd emerged appearing very satisfied indeed. James's suspicions solidified.

"Sorry about that, mate. Overran a bit."

James snapped his head back to stare at the figure now standing in the open doorway of the flat, assessing him in turn.

The man was startling. Caucasian, round about James's height, but with a more slender build and thick, dark, shoulder-length hair in silky, loose curls. He had a fine bone structure, straight black brows and large, dark eyes whose color James couldn't determine in the dimness of the hall. If the guy fucked for money, James thought in those first moments, he could fully understand how he could afford to live in Selworth Gardens.

Suddenly James felt very aware that, while he was wearing a very nice Paul Smith suit from his old life, it needed a good pressing. And after only three hours' sleep, he could do with the equivalent himself.

The man smiled brilliantly, which rendered him even more startlingly attractive.

James found himself fighting not to blush. It was his fatal emotional tell and he hated it—a lifetime of self-discipline, and he still colored up like an adolescent.

"Hey," the man said. "Come in."

He backed into the well-lit hallway of the flat, and James followed him inside, turning to close the glossy front door behind him.

"I'm Ben Morgan. And you're Jim, yeah?" the man asked cheerfully behind him. "And in a bit of a rush."

Jim'd be a new client then, James supposed. He sighed and turned round.

"Detective Sergeant James Henderson, I'm afraid."

Morgan stilled, and his smile froze. James gave an almost rueful little moue.

He wanted this accidental collar, probably not much more than Mr. Morgan wanted to be collared.

"Right." Morgan blinked and frowned, but James thought that he seemed more confused and appalled than frightened. "Right. Well. That's...nice. So. Anyway. You'll want to see the room."

Another short silence followed.

"The room," James repeated.

Morgan regarded him carefully, as if he half-expected him to pull a knife.

"That's why you're here," he said cautiously. "Maybe...I could see some ID?"

They stared at each other for another second, then James reached into the inside pocket of his suit jacket to extract the warrant card he should have shown the instant he introduced himself. The card he *always* automatically showed.

Except, not this time.

As the other man studied it, James took the chance to pull himself together.

Morgan had thrown him, he could hardly deny it, and he felt embarrassingly aware of the reason why. *And* he'd jumped to conclusions. Scrivenor had never stopped warning him against that. Yet he found himself unnervingly glad that the guy probably wasn't a prostitute after all, and not, he had to acknowledge, just to save himself the paperwork.

"So, you're renting out a room, sir?" he clarified all the same. He'd check it out later... Search for an advert.

Morgan handed him back the card. He'd stopped smiling. "Yeah. I get the feeling that isn't why you're here, though, Sergeant. I mean, you're not Jim, are you?"

James tilted his head apologetically. "Not as such, no sir. I'm investigating a murder."

Morgan's eyes widened with shock which, to be fair, did tend to be the usual reaction to that statement. He had very thick, long, dark lashes, and James could see now that his eyes were blue. A dark, jewel blue.

"*Murder?*"

"Do you know a woman named Maria Curzon-Whyte?"

Morgan stared at him for a moment longer. "Curzon-Whyte." His voice sounded hushed. "No. I don't."

James pulled out a photograph. "Are you sure, sir?" Morgan took it and studied it with a frown. "She worked as a barrister at Blackheath Chambers," James prompted.

"Wow, she's gorgeous," Morgan said softly, and, irrationally, James felt a jolt of something unwelcome, something like disappointment, at the reverence in his tone. Maybe, James recognized with brutal self-knowledge, his assumption that Morgan might be a hooker had created some sort of unconscious supposition about his sexuality. That must be it, because there had been no helpful stereotypical hints, no breath of campness, nothing. He clenched his jaw as Morgan handed back the photograph. "She looks…sort of familiar. But no…sorry. I've never needed a barrister. You said *worked*. Is she the victim?"

"We found a note of this address at her home, sir."

"*Here?*" Morgan seemed shocked but focused. "This flat?"

"This building," James conceded. Morgan relaxed minutely.

"You'd better come in properly, Sergeant." He turned without waiting for a reply and led the way from the hall through an open door into a huge, bright living room, with a kitchenette tucked at the far end of it. "Can I get you anything? A coffee?"

There were used mugs on the surface of the black-granite-topped breakfast bar, presumably from the last visitor, whose smugness James now entirely understood. Who wouldn't be smug if they had the chance of living in a place like this?

He clocked it all surreptitiously, not just the two huge, floor-length windows complete with shutters and iron balcony, which he'd seen from the street, but the polished wooden floors, the white walls and the bright cushions and rugs; the beautiful, framed, black-and-white photographs on the walls—landscape and still life. It was tasteful and definitely a male space. It even smelled attractive, a clever balance of sandalwood and ginger.

"No, thank you." Though coffee was exactly what he needed. That and a few hours' sleep, to get Ben Morgan and his lovely flat into perspective.

"Take a seat, then." Morgan gestured to a comfortable sofa set back from a large, wall-mounted TV.

James sat and pulled out his notebook and pen. Morgan sank down into an adjacent plumped-up leather armchair, long legs stretched out in front of him, and ran a hand back through his tousled dark curls.

"Can you give me some details about yourself, sir?" James began.

"Me? Right. Well. You know my name. I'm twenty-eight. I'm a photographer."

James wrote it down, but he felt pretty sure most photographers made a living through channeling twee, and it certainly wouldn't be easy to afford a place like this on wedding portraits, and definitely not at twenty-eight.

"Is that your work?" he asked, when he looked up again. "On the walls?" He nodded toward a monochrome still life of a stream, the light caught and twisted, glinting gorgeously.

Morgan frowned. "Yeah." He sounded almost surprised, as if James had wrong footed him somehow, though he continued easily, "Well spotted." But James could sense some nervousness there—some tiny tension. Maybe all artists were like that when their work came up for judgment.

"It's very good. The kind of thing people'd pay serious money for, I'd imagine."

Morgan grinned suddenly, wide and gleeful. "Well, thank *you*, Sergeant! And beautifully done! A compliment and a tasteful probe into my finances in one go. Very smooth!"

James felt his color rise again, like a schoolboy reacting to beauty, but despite himself his mouth twisted into a crooked grin of his own. "Are you the owner of this flat, sir?"

"Yep. And..." Morgan continued primly. "I rent out the second room to help pay the mortgage. Though I make most of my money working on fashion shoots and commercials."

When James darted a glance up from his notebook, the other man's eyes were sparkling, teasing, as if he was actually enjoying this.

"Who else lives in the building? Anyone who might have known Ms. Curzon-Whyte, in your estimation?"

Morgan sobered. "Well...there's Steggie downstairs, but I doubt he'd have known her."

James thought about the brass plate outside. "Mr. Nicholas."

"Yeah. He's a mate. I can't imagine he'd know a barrister, unless he had a lawsuit he didn't tell me about. He's...um...he's an adult actor."

James frowned. "As opposed to...a child actor?"

Morgan barked a delighted laugh. "No! Sergeant. Sorry. I meant... in adult films. I was trying to be tasteful."

"Oh." James knew his instant, mortified flush must be visible from space, but Morgan just kept wrong-footing him.

Fuck. The naive innocent was not a good look on a murder-squad detective.

"And upstairs?" he gritted.

"That's Irina. Her surname...there're a lot of consonants involved. All I really know is she's a model and she's Russian and her father's *really* rich. She's hardly ever here. In fact, she caught a red-eye somewhere this morning...and I know *that* because her driver pressed the wrong bell when he came to pick her up. It's always happening. The buttons are too close together. Hang on, I've got her details."

He extracted his wallet, rummaged in it, and handed a business card to James.

Irina Pozdnyakova. Models Select.

James noted it all down, before he went for the obvious.

"We don't know yet why Ms. Curzon-Whyte had this address, but it may not have to do with her professional life. Is there a possibility you might have met her socially, sir? Possibly in a situation you don't… recall all that well?"

Morgan frowned, then his mouth twisted into wryness.

"Ah. You mean, if I got guttered out of my mind? Did I chat her up, take her here, shag her, then forget all about her? But…she may not have been as casual as me, and kept the address?"

James shrugged carefully, but the fact that he hadn't had to spell it out intrigued him. Or maybe it should concern him.

"Well, Sergeant," Morgan went on calmly. "Possibly I could go with some of that, except for the very *pertinent* fact that I'm gay." He met and held James's eyes. "Not even a *bit* bisexual." As if he were spelling something out to a particularly dense child. "*Totally* gay."

James opened his mouth then closed it again. He wasn't sure what he felt. Awe, perhaps, at the absolute confidence with which Morgan had proclaimed his sexuality. And a disturbing, unwanted surge of pure excitement. He nodded and wrote down the details.

"What were your movements yesterday in the early evening?" He made a show of studying his notebook. Avoidance. Unquestionably. "Between five and seven thirty."

Morgan sighed. "I stayed at my studio until…I don't know…half past six? Then I went to a friend's house."

"Can you give me a name, sir?" He glanced up at last. "Just routine."

Morgan raised a cynical eyebrow, but he pulled his phone out of his jeans pocket and rattled off a name—Matthew Hollister—an address and a phone number, as James wrote.

The door buzzer rang, loud and sharp. They both gave a small, shocked jolt.

Morgan huffed a laugh. "That'll be Jim."

James smiled in acknowledgement, and their eyes locked and held, as if, James thought with a kind of vague panic, they were magnetized. He could feel his stomach tensing, his breath catching in his lungs.

His phone buzzed loudly in his pocket, and to add to the destruction of the moment, the door buzzed loudly again in concert.

They both stood as if they'd been prodded with sticks. James put away his notebook and pulled out his vibrating phone. It was the calendar alarm again. He should have been at the Earls Court flat, at that exact moment.

But instead…fate had brought him here, to the nicest living space he'd seen since he'd been expelled from his own, two and a half years before.

He chewed his lip, all too aware of the odd urgency churning in his middle. When he glanced up, he found Morgan studying him, and he seemed restless too somehow, discontented, as if he wanted to say something but hadn't decided what. Or maybe, James was projecting.

The buzzer sounded again, like a warning that James's time was up.

"Look," he said in a rush, and he hadn't thought it out. "This is a bit…irregular, but…assuming everything checks out…" Morgan's eyebrows rose. *Shit. This is ridiculous!* "By coincidence, I'm trying to find a room myself, in this area. So, if you could tolerate a policeman in the place, maybe I could add my name to the list of…applicants?" he finished weakly.

Morgan's expression didn't change, but James could almost see defensive walls slamming into place around him.

No chance then.

He felt alarmed by the extent of his own disappointment, when he *should* be feeling relief at being saved from his own folly.

"I'm not sure that would work out, Sergeant." Morgan, as expected, sounded coolly apologetic. "If you lived here, I'm afraid you'd inevitably have to deal with The Gay."

He thinks I'm a homophobe! James realized, outraged. And then quickly, reviewing his own external reactions, *Of course he does.*

His heart sped up as it always did at this point. He still wasn't used to being open with strangers. It still felt like a huge leap of courage. But, he managed, "It'd be a bit…hypocritical of me, if that were an issue." He thought he even contrived to sound cool.

Morgan frowned, not getting it for a second, then his eyes widened as he did.

"Oh," he said flatly. "Right." He seemed thrown, but as the buzzer sounded yet again, he smiled, and James thought it had a subtly different quality to it, a tiny, extra layer of warmth.

The buzzer squawked once more, and now it sounded almost personally offended.

"You have a lot of people after the room," James said hurriedly. "So I understand if it goes fast, but…here's my card. I'm a bit busy right now, but maybe you could text me with an appointment or something? If *Jim* doesn't work out."

Fuck. This was so irregular. But…

Morgan took the card, his plump bottom lip caught between even, white teeth. He had an unusually gorgeous mouth, James noticed, full and beautifully defined. It didn't help.

He nodded once then turned without another word and led James back into the hall. He used the intercom to buzz in the new applicant from the street, then opened the flat door.

Definitely James's cue to leave. No question about it. But still, he stood there for another few, tense seconds, eyes on his shoes, waiting for something he didn't understand.

When he forced himself to glance up, Morgan's eyes were fixed on his face. In the poor light, James couldn't see the blue in them any more, and the intensity of his gaze felt just the wrong side of polite.

"I'll be in touch, Detective Sergeant," he said quietly.

James nodded. "Good morning, Mr. Morgan," he returned.

He marched across the small hall to the stairs, self-consciously sure he could feel Morgan watching him as he went. And as he began to descend, Jim—a small, attractive and clearly irritated blond man—trotted past him near the top of the carpeted steps. James couldn't help hoping he'd behave like a total dick.

Despite himself, while he jogged down to the ground floor, he listened to Morgan's voice above him as he smoothed the visitor's ruffled feathers, then the sound of the flat door closing behind them. And he wondered if Morgan's advert had spelled out his sexuality, as the Earls Court one had, and if all the applicants were gay men.

He glanced over his shoulder, up to the shadows on the first floor, fighting an odd, restless sense of threat, a need to act. He felt unsettled, as if something important had been forced out of place.

Bloody hell! You're absurd!

It had only been twenty minutes.

But in that time, he'd come out to a possible witness and suggested sharing a flat with him.

Put like that, he wanted to bang his head off one of the pristine white walls.

Fuck, he'd better hope Morgan came up clean. And he'd also better hope the room got snapped up, and Morgan realized what a stupid, fucking idea sharing a flat with a copper would be.

James firmed his jaw and forced his mind back to business, to the flat in front of him, which he'd intended to visit first, before accident had presented him with Ben Morgan.

He knocked on the door, waited a minute before knocking again, and then again. Just as he began to turn away, it opened.

The man in front of him appeared to be roughly his own age. Caucasian again. Maybe five feet eleven—a couple of inches shorter than James anyway. Though the fact he wore no shoes or socks had to be taken into account. He had a slim build, a thin, clever, pretty face with bright hazel-green eyes and golden-brown wavy hair cut into a careful tousle. He wore sweat pants and a loose black T-shirt, and he seemed tired and out of sorts. But still, there was something stylized about him, James thought…as if every detail counted. As if his appearance was all of him.

Then again, considering his alleged occupation…

The man inspected James, up and down, and his distraction instantly cracked into interest.

"*Well.*" His sculpted mouth stretched into a huge, appreciative smirk. "The day's looking up. *Don't* tell me. I'm not that lucky. Wrong door. You're *either* after Ben's spare room or you're one of his broken hearts. If it's the last one…" He raised his hand to the doorjamb and leaned in, all stagey campiness. "I'd be *very* happy to help you forget your pain."

James opened his mouth and closed it, then reached for his warrant card.

"Detective Sergeant James Henderson." He wondered, again, if he were blushing. "I'm investigating a death."

There was a short, surprised pause, then the man straightened from his pose, and his camp playfulness evaporated as quickly and totally as mist in the sun. His hazel eyes sharpened with a different kind of interest, and James had the irresistible impression that he'd just watched a switch being pulled. From one face to another.

"Well," the man said slowly. "A fantasy cop. Do come in."

He stood back to allow James to enter the hallway, then after he shut the door, slipped round him to lead the way into his bright lounge.

The layout of the room appeared almost identical to Morgan's upstairs; presumably the building had been converted by a developer. But the windows were smaller and less grand, and the style of décor was different—glossy and minimalist, like James's old penthouse flat had been. Somehow it felt like an inferior copy of Morgan's living space. Which, James recognized, was hardly fair.

The man gestured James toward a stylish white leather-and-steel sofa that proved to be less than comfortable. A huge glass-and-metal coffee table lurked threateningly beside his knee as he sat.

"Would you like some tea?" The man sank gracefully onto the other end of the same sofa and draped himself sideways to study James as he spoke, knee up on the seat, pointed toward him. He appeared the epitome of alert relaxation. Quite a trick to pull off, if you knew how. "I have every kind under the sun."

His voice sounded light and pleasant, his accent a kind of posh-Estuary. James thought an elocution teacher might have been involved at some point.

"Er, no thank you, Mr...?"

The man's mouth twitched with politely masked amusement. "Nicholas. Emile Nicholas."

James dutifully checked the spelling and took down the details. Then he remembered. "Mr. Morgan said his neighbor is called...uh... Steggie. Is there also a...?"

"No. Just me. Steggie's a nickname. It's stuck with me since I was a kid."

He smiled sweetly, as if the memories were good ones. James noted his extreme attractiveness, very unwillingly.

It all felt too much, like a sustained assault on his professionalism after the intensity of his encounter with Morgan upstairs.

"Age and occupation?" he asked sharply.

Nicholas's pretty mouth twitched into a smirk. "You do sound *stern*, Detective Sergeant. I'm twenty-eight. And I'm a producer and actor. In film," he finished, and if he didn't intend to mention the adult part, James wasn't going to go there either, unless he had to.

He reached into the inner pocket of his suit jacket and pulled out Maria's picture.

"Do you recognize this woman, Mr. Nicholas?"

Nicholas took the photograph in a slim, long-fingered hand. His mouth pursed in consideration as he observed it. "She looks…rich. Victim or culprit?"

James brows rose minutely. *Culprit?*

He said, "Victim."

"I don't know her," Nicholas returned firmly. "Should I?"

"Her name was Maria Curzon-Whyte. We have reason to believe she may have recently visited this building." Which might be pushing it, but…

Nicholas frowned and dropped his head to one side, intent eyes fixed on James's face.

"Really?" Nicholas sounded thoughtful. "Well, maybe she knew Irina. They seem about the same age. Or maybe Ben? I don't move in these circles, I'm afraid. More of a…self-made man." His sudden grin appeared self-mocking and powerfully charming.

James ignored it and went to the default question. "Could you tell me your whereabouts yesterday, early evening? Between say, five and eight?"

Nicholas's smile faded, and he frowned, but then, that challenge always sounded like accusation.

"Here. I had a meeting in the morning, then I worked at home, going through scripts, which is what I'm still doing in fact. I meant to go out in the evening, but I felt too tired."

James glanced down at the large pile of papers on the glass coffee table. Nicholas seemed in demand all right and probably waiting to get on with it.

"Are you sure you've had no dealings with her, sir, socially or professionally? She was a barrister."

"Then I *definitely* didn't have any dealings with her professionally. I have a contracts lawyer, but that's it. And…we covered socially. Quite apart from anything else you may have gathered, she wouldn't exactly be my type."

Suddenly it felt to James like a perfect echo of his interview with Morgan and, apparently again, a dead end. Nicholas had also, most probably been spot-on. Any connection to Maria in this building would more likely lie with a woman her own age than either of two gay men.

He stood to go. "Well, thank you for your time, sir. I'm sorry to have bothered you."

Nicholas stood too, in a movement of such conspicuously fluid grace that James wondered, in an undisciplined second, exactly how flexible the man might be. Would have to be.

"God. *Please* don't apologize, Sergeant. You've been a very lovely distraction on a dull day." James did his best to ignore his renewed tone of exaggerated appreciation. "They're not exactly *The Godfather*." Nicholas nodded confidingly toward the scripts on the coffee table.

James and Nicholas were both moving around the sofa on opposite sides now, back out into the body of the room, and it struck James again how similar this layout seemed to the flat above; how Morgan and Nicholas had arranged their furniture in much the same order, in an almost identical space, yet to such different effect. It wasn't as if Nicholas's furniture appeared less expensive, or more outlandish, so James couldn't quite work out why the room seemed less attractive to him.

It was only then that he spotted a metal console table set against the wall, just along from Nicholas's TV. But it was the collection of objects arranged on top that held his attention.

There were quite a few of them pointing in different directions—all about nine inches long—bright gold phalluses mounted by their gold testicles on circular golden stands. And at the front of the grouping, like a kind of spokesman, stood an old-fashioned gold carriage clock, small pendulum swinging as it ticked. It appeared unnervingly similar to one James's grandmother had left him in her will, and crazily, comically incongruous.

James couldn't believe he'd missed the display when he came in. Now he couldn't look away.

"SHAFTAs," he heard behind him. "Gay SHAFTAs actually." James turned his head from the small forest of ornamental penises to listen to Nicholas. Somehow he managed to keep a straight face. "Soft and Hard Adult Film and Television Awards," Nicholas went on airily. "You don't get one without...*believe* me, Sergeant...a *lot* of *hard* work."

For a long moment they regarded each other stonily, then Nicholas's facade cracked and he barked an unselfconscious, delighted laugh. James couldn't help but grin a bit wildly back.

"I knew Ben'd have told you. You're all right, *Detective* Sergeant. In fact, if you ever consider a change of career, I'm pretty sure..." he leaned in confidingly, "...I could make you a star."

James puffed out his cheeks and blew out a theatrical breath. "Thank you, sir." He tried for solemnity, but he knew that he'd fallen well short. "I quite like the Met at the moment. Solid career prospects."

Nicholas's hazel eyes sparkled with delight as he hammed up a disappointed moue. "Solid, eh? Well, it's your decision. But if you change your mind, Sergeant Henderson, I really do think you have the potential to get a hold of a golden cock."

As he let himself out the front door into the thin, sharp sun of the February morning, James felt more than slightly stunned.

He'd spent his two and half years as a policeman focusing precisely on the job, on getting every single thing correct—one of the reasons he had no life.

And yet, in the course of half an hour and two interviews in that building, he'd been effortlessly dragged out of his professional comfort zone and inveigled into sliding off the policeman's mask he'd believed solidly glued on. In front of two potential witnesses in a murder case. One after the other.

But as he caught sight of his own reflection in the driver's window of his car, he realized that he was still smiling.

3

Ingham called the next briefing for eleven a.m. in the Incident Room. Already it resembled a thrumming wartime HQ: white boards covered with photographs of the victim and the crime scene; notes with new information; lists of tasks and names allocated against them.

"All right!" The buzz of chatter and shuffling stopped. Ingham, in a fresh navy suit, appeared unsmudged and well rested, yet James knew she'd been fielding political phone calls for hours. The rest of the team, on the other hand, could already pass for roadkill.

"The victim has now been formally identified as Maria Curzon-Whyte," Ingham announced. "Nothing useful initially at the scene. No witnesses so far. The postmortem's set for tomorrow at ten thirty at Guy's. Jamie, I want you to observe. Take Sameera along." Ingham gave the order as if it were entirely normal for her to delegate to that extent in a full-on murder investigation, but James felt a roomful of interested eyes fixing on him. "First things first…we need to track down any partners…ID her friends. Barry. Anything?"

Barry Walsh, the most experienced DC in the unit, waved a notebook vaguely in the air.

"Me an' Ken went to Blackheath Chambers this morning." Walsh was overweight, balding, uncompromisingly Brummie. "The senior partner, Daniel Jackson…he's organizin' a list of her recent work an' he'll let us access as much as he can. Maria's current case is goin' to court today, for a preliminary hearing. She assisted on it. Client is John O'Grady. Charged with importin' three-hundred-an'-twenty-seven kilos of cocaine, extortion, an' rapin' a fifteen-year-old Albanian girl. His legal team're aimin' for a plea bargain to the cocaine to get him off rape an' extortion. Jackson says they stand a good chance. The girl's just a month off sixteen, an' O'Grady's claimin' it was consensual. But her family's not long out of Albania, still settlin' in the scene here. Accordin' to Jackson, they want blood."

Ingham gave a considering moue. "So the family decides to punish O'Grady's legal team for saying the girl wanted it? Getting him off the rape charge?"

Walsh shrugged. The case could be that straightforward.

A multitude of East European crime gangs nesting in Britain were heavily involved in sex trafficking, prostitution and drug running. Contract killing wouldn't be exactly alien to them, revenge and honor killing even less so. James felt sure everyone else would be making the same connections and feeling the same little surge of hope.

"Okay." Ingham certainly looked and sounded brighter. "Barry, follow that up. The girl's relatives'll be at court. See what they're into, and let Jamie know what you find."

Barry raised his eyebrows and turned his baggy, hound-dog eyes onto James, who did his best again to appear unaware of the surprise permeating the room. Because Walsh should be reporting directly to Ingham.

"Jamie? Maria's parents?"

James sat up minutely straighter in his plastic chair.

"They seem to be..." He paused to find the most inoffensive way of putting it, though he was buggered if he knew why, given present company. "Well meaning. But...reasons they may have pissed people off? Legion. Lady Justice Whyte has a reputation for extreme leniency in sentencing, she has strong connections with the Howard League for Penal Reform, and she's made multiple pronouncements that she believes prison doesn't work, and in the power of second, third, fourth chances. Some of her decisions have been seriously controversial. *Countless* potentially aggrieved victims and relatives."

Ingham rubbed an eyebrow wearily. James kept going.

"Sir George is a socialist baronet with vast inherited wealth, which he's substantially increased. He's donated to a selection of left-wing parties, and he gave half a million to WikiLeaks. Rumor has it most of his own millions are safely tucked away in offshore trusts. He's also quietly funded the best defense available for animal rights and anti-globalization extremists brought to court." A collective groan echoed round the room. "Neither he nor his wife seem uncomfortable with their own lives of conspicuous luxury. Seems he's guilty about his background but not guilty enough to give up the money."

"Okay." Ingham sighed into the charged silence that followed. "Plenty in that too." There was a room-wide shuffle at the enormity of the understatement. "Always better to have more leads than too few."

Ingham wrapped up the briefing with a bracing speech about the importance of working fast, which they all knew anyway, just as they knew that, barring a quick convenient suspect, they could be digging through potential enemies for weeks.

"Jamie. You're with me." Ingham gestured with her head toward the door, and James wordlessly collected his jacket.

He had a pretty fair idea they were going back to visit Maria's parents, a visit he still couldn't, politically, make without Ingham. In fact, he thought discontentedly as he followed her out through reception and into the car park, this whole surreptitious-delegating thing had been proving just as awkward and obvious as he'd feared.

Hopeless to think gossips like Barry Walsh weren't already on it and spreading the word. It would only be a matter of time before Mulligan got wind that a detective sergeant had taken the lead on a bigger investigation than his. His ego wouldn't take well to that at all.

James was brooding so intently he almost fumbled the keys Ingham threw to him.

"Buck up, Jamie," she said. James tried for a bucked-up smile. "Anyone questions it, tell 'em to speak to me." She grinned crazily. "After all, we've got plausible deniability."

James slid behind the wheel and started the engine, if only to avoid saying what he really thought.

It took much longer at this time of day to make the journey to Eaton Square.

"I'm giving you Sameera for the duration," Ingham announced, as James pulled the police saloon out into traffic. He could sense Ingham turning to survey him, eyes boring into his profile.

"My own bag carrier," he said dryly. "You shouldn't have."

"She's sharp. And she's ambitious." James understood what she hadn't said; he needed a DC focused enough not to gossip. "Just don't ask her to get your dry-cleaning if you wanna keep possession of your balls."

James smirked, and out of the corner of his eye, he could see Ingham doing the same.

"Anything from that address you found in Maria's flat?" she asked idly after a few moments of harmonious silence.

James's mind flashed back to dark-blue eyes and golden phalluses, and his stomach lurched with a kind of churning, nauseous excitement he couldn't quite understand and didn't much like.

"Nothing obvious."

He'd found himself asking Alec when he got back if he could run the background and alibi checks on Morgan and Nicholas, though he could have done it himself when he got an hour or two's grace. But he'd been instinctively anxious to get an objective assessment, and to get it quickly.

Though, on second thought...

"One of the residents is Russian," he said. "Mega-rich father. She left the country this morning according to the neighbors."

Ingham would follow his reasoning. Russians. Albanians. Operating on different criminal landscapes in the UK, but the various national mafias clashed or cooperated when it suited them.

"Let's try to establish that with Immigration," Ingham said.

"And find out about daddy," James agreed.

Your call, her smile said.

They arrived, for the second time that day, in front of the splendid front door in Eaton Square, to be told that Sir George had gone out to organize *things*, as the butler put it grimly. But Dame Cordelia met them in another gorgeously decorated sitting room. She'd insisted on going to the mortuary with her husband early that morning, to identify the body. Her expression was closed off, ravaged, but her displays of weakness seemed to be over. She spoke to them with a steely, distant dignity, like a queen reluctantly giving time to a couple of importunate peasants.

"She brought joy to all of us from the first. I don't understand how anyone could hurt Maria. She charmed everyone. Everyone adored her."

"I'm very sorry, Dame Cordelia." Ingham paused then pressed on. "From her phone records, we've found that your call would've been the last she took. We think her time of death may have been very close to that."

"*My* call?" Dame Cordelia's chiseled features twisted with a spasm of emotion before she pulled her expression back under rigid control. "We had a disagreement because I felt disappointed. She had a hearing, so she had to delay coming to Oxfordshire...today. It would have been today. But she told me the Crown Prosecution Service might be reasonable, so she may be able to get there on time."

Reasonable, James thought with instinctive copper's revulsion. *What's reasonable for scum like John O'Grady?*

He thought he'd masked his reaction, but even in the extremity of her grief, Dame Cordelia seemed to have a bloodhound's nose for challenges to her ethics. Or maybe she just welcomed the distraction.

"Everyone is innocent until proven guilty, Detective Sergeant," she snapped, and though he'd read about her career, that quick spark of life showed him again some part of who she really was. "We're far too judgmental as a society, never caring what causes crime. Maria believed in genuinely helping people. Unlike the police."

James didn't even attempt a defense—he knew better than that— but he couldn't help but wonder, as Ingham papered over the awkward silence, if, once the first numbness wore off, Dame Cordelia would be up to forgiving whoever left her daughter to die alone, suffocating in blood, on a cold doorstep. If she could really turn away from seeking retribution.

More than that, he wondered just how like her mother Maria had been. Had she been as overbearing in her aggressive compassion? Had she decided to help the wrong person? Or had she succeeded too well and felt the rage of a victim at first hand?

By the time they were walking down the wide, stone steps to the pavement, James and Ingham had learned that Maria had been devoted to her career and the less fortunate, that she had been a perfect daughter and flawless human being, and her parents were unaware of a current or recent romantic partner. They'd also acquired the name of her best friend.

So, as Ingham headed back to the station to attend more budget meetings, James set off to interview Galinda Heywood.

She turned out to be a human-resources manager in the City which, James had always thought, required a heart of steel. But Galinda proved far from steely-hearted when he broke the news to her in her pristine glass office. Somehow, no one had thought to let her know, and her shocked grief dissolved her glossy career-blonde veneer like solvent on paint.

Galinda and Maria had been friends since they'd both been thirteen and at school, and it quickly became obvious that Maria had been the leader, Galinda her acolyte. Yet though she'd clearly worshipped her, Galinda also proved almost innocently perceptive.

"I think she became a defense barrister because they got more money than prosecutors," she confided, when she'd finally sobbed herself to a sort of hiccoughing calm. Her exhausted face wore smears of unselfconscious mucus and black-stained tears. "If you're any good. And she wanted to be the best. She focused really hard on getting to the top. And she *would* have, you know? She had so much drive and…hunger. Like she had a hag on her back sometimes. But she's…she *was* amazing."

James glanced up from his notebook. "Did she have a boyfriend?"

"Oh." Galinda sighed and wiped her nose. "She had loads. She could pull anyone she wanted, if she set her mind to it, male or female." She caught James's questioning glance and produced a wan smile. "Gender didn't much matter to her. She was just…no good at committing. She could be ruthless about it. Really ruthless."

James thought he saw a glint of…something as Galinda stared down at her hands. Something cagey, something sorrowful.

Maybe Galinda had been one of those people Maria had set her mind on. Or maybe she'd wanted to be.

"Who'd she been seeing recently?"

"She didn't really tell me," Galinda said, just too quickly.

James sighed. "We do need the information, Miss Heywood."

Galinda looked at him with betrayed horror. "I don't know!" Then, "I *can't*. She confided in me. She didn't trust many people." Slowly, tears began to tip over again from her swollen eyelids, leaving sad, pale trails in her ruined makeup, and as always when he made a witness cry, James felt uncomfortably like the school bully. "She's my best friend. But I don't know how… I suppose I've always been more… invested in it than her. I never felt she really *needed* friends. Maybe more…people to entertain her. But…"

She closed her eyes and when she opened them, she seemed to have collapsed in on herself, surrendering without warning as if she couldn't see the point any more. "All right. His name's Dan." Her voice was very quiet, almost disappointed. "She worked with him."

A memory clicked. "Daniel Jackson?" James clarified, and he could see he'd got it right. "Her Head of Chambers? Isn't that…?"

"Frowned on?" Galinda sparked abruptly into life again. "Well, that's one reason she told me not to tell anyone, isn't it?"

"And the *other* reason for not telling anyone is because he's married," James pointed out.

Galinda's mouth twisted. "*She* wasn't," she snapped.

James waited until he got into the car to order his thoughts.

If they were to believe Galinda, the Maria her mother didn't know had been ambitious, driven, *and* having an affair with her boss. Not only that, she'd apparently been merciless in detaching from her lovers. So, still more people she might have lethally pissed off.

His car had just edged under the barrier into the station car park when his hands-free phone rang.

Ingham.

"I'm just in the car park, ma'am," he said.

"Perfect. There's a press conference in half an hour," Ingham replied, and James heard grim relish that she could take someone with her into purgatory. "Go and tart yourself up for the cameras, Jamie-boy. You can hold my hand."

Misery really did love company.

At least, James comforted himself while he parked the car, today he just had to sit there, a stuffed dummy in a suit. Unlike *Crimewatch* where he always had to do some talking. At least today he would just be decoration.

At least, he told himself bracingly, he had that.

-ll- -ll- -ll- -ll-

"Hey, Alec. Did you manage to do those checks?"

James slumped into his desk chair across from Scrivenor, feeling the headache of the ages building behind his eyes. Press hell had ended for the time being though. That was something.

"Oh. Aye."

James automatically pressed the button to activate his elderly computer, too aware of his own apprehension.

Maybe he wanted Alec to reassure him that his judgment didn't completely go to shit when confronted by beautiful men. Or maybe, he just wanted the world he'd glimpsed in Selworth Gardens to be as uncomplicated as it had seemed.

Scrivenor squinted at a notepad on his desk. "So…I got their passport details an' I took it frae there. Morgan disnae even have a parking ticket. His dad's some charity bigwig, and his mam's a Liberal Democrat councilor in Peckham." His quirked a cynical eyebrow, which James acknowledged, because you couldn't get much more impeccably right-on progressive than that. "He wiz born in Namibia, but he's UK citizen. An' he owns his own photography business wi' a big turnover. Nae obvious debts. His alibi an' his flat advert checked out. The other fella… Hey!" Scrivenor's face lit up like a child unexpectedly handed a shiny new toy. "Did ye know he's a porn star?"

James smiled wanly. "Adult actor, *please.*"

Scrivenor snorted. "Aye. Right. Well. He's got his own business an' all—Under Milk *Wood* Productions," he pronounced salaciously. "Geddit? Makin' *adult* films. Every appearance of doin' well. Born in Essex. Nothin' on his parents. No convictions. No run-ins. Nothin'." He leaned back in his swivel chair and stretched his large body, his white shirt crumpled and creeping out of the waistband of his trousers, tie at half-mast. "So…is that a total dead end, then?"

James began to explain to Scrivenor the possibilities of the absent Russian model upstairs, but he was all too aware as he did so, that his mood had lifted significantly. He simply chose not to examine it any further.

When they'd finished discussing the possibilities of various East European mafias, Scrivenor gave him the office gossip.

"Mulligan's ran into an epidemic of mass blindness all round Albert Embankment. It's a human tragedy." He smirked. "Just as well Big Brother is always watchin', eh?"

James smiled a slow, pleased smile. "They got it all on CCTV." Of course they had, outside a nightclub.

But Scrivenor scrunched his nose and waggled his hand. "Aye. But nae facial ID, *and* generic clothin'."

"Shit."

"Aye."

They both scowled into middle distance in a shared moment of disgust because, much as neither of them wanted Mulligan free to meddle in Maria's case, a quick result would have been a result for the unit. And it might have given Ingham more ammunition in battles upstairs.

"*Talkin*' of Big Brother," Scrivenor said suddenly. "An' human tragedies... Ah almost forgot. Media and Communications wiz lookin' for you. Maybe they need a nice, new photo."

James scowl melted to despair, and he slumped forward until his forehead thudded gently on his desk.

"Fuck *me*."

"Well, that's nae the language I'd expect from the poster boy for the new Met."

James raised his head off the desk to catch Scrivenor's prim smirk, and dropped it again with a thud. They both knew he could run, but he couldn't hide.

From the moment he'd joined the Fast Track Initiative, the media team had descended on him like twinkly vultures, using him shamelessly and ruthlessly as the program's PR face.

A Double First from Oxford, a 4th Dan black-belt in aikido, a slightly-more-than-basic knowledge of a group of Asian languages thanks to the family business, all cherry-topped by ticking the inclusivity box through declaring his sexuality—to the Powers That Be, James had Fabulous Public Image written through him, like a stick of rock. He'd been earmarked for the top. And that, to be fair, had won him assignment to this MIT, replacing a DS with twenty-six years behind her, rather than having to work a divisional sergeant's post like other inexperienced recruits.

"Pretend you didn't tell me," he mumbled against the chipboard.

He could hear Scrivenor sucking his teeth gloatingly. "The PR lassie wiz very insistent. *Georgia*, she's called. She wants you tae 'pop down' tae her office." He waggled his eyebrows salaciously. James shook his head. Scrivenor knew his sexuality perfectly well, but he fucking loved watching James trying to wriggle out of situations like this one.

James rubbed his eyes and glanced down at his mobile phone lying stubbornly silent on the desk.

He couldn't block the thought any longer or the inconvenient feelings that came with it. Morgan had said he'd be in touch about the flat, but James knew he wouldn't call. The room had probably already gone, and even if it hadn't, that first reaction to James's profession had been familiar and telling. He'd sat through so many interviews for rooms since his flat search had begun, and it always ended there. No one wanted a copper living with them, except, maybe, another copper.

Anyway, going to live with someone he'd interviewed in a murder case would be insane. It had just been a mental lapse.

He wouldn't see Ben Morgan again, which had to be—definitely—for the best. But James still felt unaccountably glad that Morgan and Nicholas had turned out to be as they'd seemed.

He stood abruptly, grabbed his phone and his coat, and strode toward the door.

"Oi!" he heard called indignantly behind him. "Whit aboot Georgia?"

James ignored him, just as he intended to ignore Georgia.

"First I'm going to Costa," he announced, to piss off Scrivenor. "Then I'm going to rumble up Maria's boyfriend."

━♦━ ━♦━ ━♦━ ━♦━

According to the receptionist at Blackheath Chambers, Daniel Jackson had been sent home by his doctor and could see no one.

And I wonder why that would be, James thought cynically. But he determined that his trip would not be allowed to go to waste. Jackson's partner, Peter Gill, was in, and he'd do as the afternoon's target. Though, from the sound of the verbal tussle James could overhear between the flustered receptionist and Gill's secretary, Gill didn't like the idea at all.

Peter Gill looked, James thought sourly, when he finally got shown into his office, like a Casting Agency Queen's Counsel, with a thick silver mane, brushed majestically back from his forehead and a handsome, craggy face. His eyes were deep-set, cold and dark and clever. He exuded irritation, and James had a feeling that he operated on a factory setting of "staggeringly patronizing" when dealing with the police in the course of his job as a defense barrister, and he seemed disinclined to alter his view of them as the enemy just because one of his colleagues had been murdered.

He gestured James impatiently toward a chair set in front of his large desk. James countered with an unruffled smile.

But as James sat and pulled out his notebook, Gill demanded querulously, "I know you, don't I?"

James glanced up with an automatic frown of denial, because he'd never seen the man before. But before he could utter a word, Gill's expression transformed with dawning revelation.

"Well," he pronounced. "Yes, I do. *Sergeant* Henderson. Good God! Magnus Henderson's Prodigal Son."

James hesitated for the tiniest fraction of a second before unhurriedly extracting a pen from his jacket pocket.

Gill laughed with delighted mockery. "I've seen you on television, haven't I? In fact, I remember now... The business pages were agog when you left it all behind. And here you are." He grinned, a huge shark's smile. "Still *playing* at being sheriff and wearing a big. White. Hat."

James's narrowed eyes were the only external reaction he allowed. Because if his father had taught him nothing else of use, it had been to never leave blood in the water. Never let anger distract him. He clicked open the pen, ready to begin.

"The Met are *actually* trying to sell you as a *typical* copper, aren't they?" Gill gave a loud, provocative bark of derision, but his expression pretended that he expected James would share the joke. "So, how're you enjoying slumming it?"

James smiled as if no one had spoken since he'd entered the room.

"I just have a few questions for you, Mr. Gill. I'm sure you're anxious to help with our inquiries."

Gill's mask of chummy good humor slid off him, like a snake shedding its skin. He made a sound of sarcastic disgust. "Oh, naturally, *Sergeant*. But I have no new information for you. You're wasting my time."

James opened his notebook, deliberately ponderous. *I'll decide that*, the movement said.

An extended verbal scuffle followed. Yes, Gill gritted, with the exaggerated weariness of a man humoring a stupid but persistent child, he'd known Jackson had been having an affair with Maria. No, Jackson could not have killed Maria, because Gill had been at Jackson's house with his girlfriend on the night, and at the time, in question. Yes, Jackson had seemed perfectly normal.

James doggedly ignored Gill's aggression, though he allowed himself vivid imaginings of punching him in the face. But as they slogged through their cat-and-mouse game of question and sneering, minimally helpful answer, James's refusal to either rise to the bait or be driven off in anger finally seemed to wear Gill down.

"God! All right!" he exclaimed, and with a theatrical sigh to signal surrender to the forces of idiocy, he flopped back in his large leather desk chair. "I can tell you have hundreds more inane questions scribbled in that little *note*book, so let's spare us both the tedium. This is all I know. Maria was a piece of work. She seemed genuine. But I could see her game." He wrinkled his aquiline nose. "I went for a drink with her once and I almost fell for it myself. But she let slip she'd had a thing with a professor at university, and I knew she'd got close to her pupil-master when she arrived here. There were rumors of a fling with the chief clerk... That's who advises solicitors which barrister to choose for their cases."

"Yes," James said imperturbably, though his attention remained riveted. Galinda hadn't come close to this kind of gloves-off frankness. "So you're saying she slept her way up."

Gill shrugged, unruffled. "That's one way of putting it. It's a brutally competitive line of work, but let's say...Maria got on fast. She got pupilage at her first try, then a tenancy, and God knows that's hard. Then getting the cases to get noticed, to work up to taking silk..." He made a dismissive sound. "She used the assets she had, and if that included playing people, well...I doubt she agonized about it."

"And you weren't tempted?"

Gill met James's eyes. He'd finally, unselfconsciously engaged with the interview, James realized, caught in his own tale.

"I suppose it'd have been easy. Knowing it'd be a transaction, getting some good sex in return for using a bit of influence. But..." Gill's mouth twisted. "There was something about her. Something...damaged. Driven. It would have been too tempting to try to be the one to fix her. That's what happened to Dan, and rumor has it, that stupid bastard of a pupil-master never got over her. She seemed...*disarming*. Always mocking herself. She used it on everyone, even the bloody receptionist. It made her appear harmless...soft. Totally untrue, of course. I got the feeling she'd never settle. Nothing…no one would ever be enough. There was a kind of emotional disconnect there."

"Are you saying she was sociopathic?" James asked.

Gill gave a noncommittal moue. Yes, then.

"You certainly seem to have studied her," James observed.

"She'd started shagging our Head of Chambers, who also happens to be a friend! Naturally I kept a close eye."

Yet James had a strong sense that Gill, himself a cynical cataloguer of the lows of human nature, had been fascinated by the ambition and emotional unavailability he'd seen in Maria. Drawn to it, even. But he'd had the basic sense of self-preservation to stay away, and that, James could understand.

"Did people resent her? The men who fell for her? The colleagues she leapfrogged?"

Gill snorted and smoothed a hand back over his thick silver hair. "I don't know. Probably. Like I said, it's a dog-eat-dog profession. But I doubt that's enough to literally cut her throat."

Smartarse, James thought with renewed dislike. "Names, Mr. Gill? The pupil-master? The chief clerk?"

Gill's glare became arctic. "Is it really necessary to embarrass them? Their indiscretions are in the past."

"It's a murder inves…"

"My *God*! Are you people trained to utter only clichés?"

James raised his eyebrows in a deliberately poor attempt at surprised censure. Rattling Gill felt like a deeply positive thing to do.

Gill huffed an angry breath through his nostrils. "Simon Peake," he spat, pure resentment. "John Caudwell."

"Thank you, Mr. Gill." James smiled, like a teacher who'd made a breakthrough with a recalcitrant pupil. "Does the name Irina Pozdnyakova mean anything to you?"

Gill's chin pulled back minutely at the change of pace. "Should it?"

"She's not one of the firm's clients?"

Gill glowered furiously, but to James's surprise he pulled his mouse and keyboard in front of him and checked for himself on his state-of-the-art iMac.

"We have no record of anyone by that name, client or witness."

"And the John O'Grady case? Did any of your team feel threatened?"

Gill's expression soured further. James thought he might be deciding whether to go through the expected dance of protesting about confidential case details before James countered with the it's-a-murder-case gambit. Thankfully, after a short internal struggle, Gill opted not waste more of their time.

"It's messy," Gill bit out. "Obviously. The girl's family aren't pleased, but I'd imagine their rage would be directed at Mr. O'Grady rather than his legal team."

"You'd imagine?"

Gill rolled his eyes. "The firm has a policy of reporting all such things to senior partners through our secretaries. I did *check*, Sergeant. I'm not an imbecile. Maria hadn't logged anything." He'd omitted something, James could feel it. He held Gill's eyes steadily until Gill closed his, searching for patience. "In the interests of full disclosure, then, she mentioned something to the team in passing, a couple of weeks ago. She said she'd had one or two silent calls to her mobile phone. But she'd had them before, and nothing came of it. Everyone gets wrong numbers."

"And that's all?"

"The only *actual* phone call came to me. It's not unusual in a sensitive criminal case, you know. People letting off steam. This one... I don't even know if it might have been an attempt at intimidation, the man's English was... Frankly, he sounded like Igor in a very poor production of *Frankenstein*."

"But you're sure nothing else came to Maria?"

"She acted as junior counsel. They might as well have threatened the tea-lady. I'll have my secretary send you the details of everything logged for the past year, but I assure you, you'll find nothing reported by Maria. Your *minions* already have names and contact details for everyone involved in the case." He expelled a dramatically impatient breath. "Now, Sergeant, I'd appreciate it if you could *finally* let me get on with my schedule. Oh and..." A last, vindictive smile. "Do give my regards to your father."

James met his eyes without emotion. "Thanks for your help, Mr. Gill."

Gill didn't get up to see him out.

James thrashed through it as he walked to his car, grip too tight on the keys in his hand.

Gill might be an obnoxious dickhead, but James had found that people like him, people who searched out the worst in others, often turned out to be the most useful witnesses after a murder. Sentiment and respect and *decency* never held them back.

"The business pages were agog when you left it all behind. And here you are...still playing at being sheriff."

James grimaced viciously as he pushed the button on his key fob and watched the indicator lights of the disconnecting alarm blink a sick orange on his dark-grey police saloon. It was an ugly car, a car he wouldn't even have considered getting into, once upon a time. Back when *things* had compensated for everything else he'd been missing.

But maybe...that's how people really did see him, people who knew his background and heard the gossip. Just as Gill had implied: that he had some sort of sad, superhero complex. A wannabe white knight.

His mind caught on his last image of Gill, sitting behind his desk, face a mask of urbane malice.

He slid grimly into the driver's seat and switched on the engine.

Fuck him, he thought furiously.

"Give my regards to your father."

Fuck. Him.

■¶■ ■¶■ ■¶■ ■¶■

For most of that evening, James worked doggedly on locating Maria's ex-boyfriends to interview the next day, using a list compiled by a reluctant Galinda. Finding the unnamed professor Gill had mentioned would be hard, but Maria's personal life still felt to James to be a fruitful area to search.

Barry Walsh had been supervising the exploration of the O'Grady link—investigating the family of the girl allegedly raped by O'Grady, and probing the affairs of O'Grady's business associates. But so far, no link with Maria had been unearthed. Other officers had the backlog of Cordelia Whyte's more controversial decisions to slog through, plus Maria's old cases and Sir George's possible enemies. The sheer volume of possibilities had only increased, but anything had to be better than no leads at all.

James succumbed to exhaustion at almost four a.m. and grabbed a few hours of cramped sleep on one of the office camp beds set up against a grim foam-tiled partition wall. Then, after a quick shower and shave in the gents at seven, and a sent-in cardboard breakfast, he spent a couple of hours slogging through Walsh's reports until Kaur came to get him to head to Guy's Hospital for Maria's postmortem.

He thought she appeared unnaturally bright-eyed, all things considered. He hadn't the energy left to resent it. "Morning, Sameera."

"Sarge." Her coat draped neatly over her arm. "You look surprisingly chipper for a dead badger."

He didn't bother pretending not to be amused. "I'm pretty sure that's..." His mobile jumped and buzzed on his desk. "Very insubordinate. Though sadly, also true." He pressed the answer button. "DS Henderson."

"Oh. Hi...um...Sergeant."

James's smile dropped, and his whole midsection tensed as if he expected to take a punch at any second. He shouldn't be able to recognize that voice after such a short meeting.

He met Sameera's eyes, and his own must have been showing shock, because she appeared suddenly almost as wary and alarmed as he felt.

"Uh. Yeah." He waved her away and moved toward the office door, hoping she'd take the hint and allow him some privacy. Maybe she thought it was bad news. "This is...is that?" He could feel the familiar red heat of embarrassment surging over his skin.

"Ben Morgan. From the flat in Selworth Gardens." The voice sounded amused and totally self-possessed.

"Oh. Yes." James shoved open the office door into the stark, badly lit corridor outside and strode along it for a few yards until he could lean against a grimy magnolia-painted wall, safely away, he hoped, from observation. He waited in an agony of tension.

"Well," Morgan went on at last. "You said you wanted to view the flat as a potential tenant. And I promised I'd call, so..."

He had. But James hadn't actually *expected* him to, and he would never have made the call himself, not in the circumstances. He'd obviously hoped though, deep down; he could hardly deny it, with his guts in knots.

"Yes. That's…" Fuck, couldn't he manage more than one-word sentences? "Thanks."

"Right." Morgan sounded careful now, awkward, as if he thought he'd made a mistake. "Well, I just thought…in case you were still interested…"

"Yes!" James blurted though he hadn't thought it through. Not properly. But he couldn't stand the idea that Morgan would think he'd rejected his kindness. "I am."

"Right," Morgan said again, but he didn't sound convinced. "Good. Well. You could come for a viewing this evening if you like, after I finish work. Maybe six-ish? There's someone else scheduled for seven."

And that reminder of the competition prompted a very firm, "Yes. That sounds great. I'll see you then."

Morgan's tone was unreadable. "See you around six then, Sergeant." He rang off.

James let the hand holding his phone drop limply to his side, staring straight ahead at the opposite corridor wall.

A nauseous mix of excitement, nerves and apprehension swirled around his abdomen.

He didn't know how long he stood there, staring at magnolia blankness, before Kaur emerged into the corridor and raised her eyebrows at him. "Ready, Sarge?" she asked cautiously.

James straightened up, and the emotion that surged to the surface felt like the kind of exhilaration that came from taking a mad risk.

He said, "Ready."

⬛⬛⬛⬛

James hadn't felt critically squeamish at a postmortem since his first attendance, when he'd heaved up his guts over the pathologist's extremely expensive trousers. They'd been a fine navy pinstripe. He'd never forget them, and the pathologist had never failed to wear his scrubs again.

Familiarity had bought James some immunity, but the smell got him every time. No matter what the state of the corpse, at every event like this, it felt as if the stench of death sank into his pores.

He stood with Kaur now, beside Maria's empty, dummy-like remains, and watched and listened as her body gave up its last dignity and its secrets.

The wound on her neck looked obscene on the unblemished porcelain of her skin—bloodless and frayed with rubber flesh. But her cold, youthful, startled mask of a face seemed the most obscene image of all. The last memory her parents would have of her.

James stared down at his shoes, obnoxiously shiny in this dull, dead room.

The small, plump middle-aged doctor had been new to him, and unlike their usual pathologist, he didn't indulge in any banter, didn't say a word not pertinent to the case, as he started work, cutting and pulling and muttering into a recorder as he went. He treated the entire encounter with cold respect, and James wasn't sure if that made it worse or better. He usually felt both guilty about, and grateful for, the distraction of a pathologist who showed no regard in the presence of gruesome, undignified death.

The murderer had been right-handed, the doctor pronounced, and apparently the culprit watched *CSI*, because he or she had left no trace at the scene, not a finger or footprint, not a hair or a flake of skin on the body. They'd worn gloves, the pathologist said, and probably a hat and possibly a mask of some kind. "Forensic aware", the term would be.

"There are no abrasions from struggle underneath the killer's body, so we can assume the killing blow would have been almost immediate." The doctor leaned over Maria's ruined body to demonstrate. He had a fringe of black hair trimmed carefully around his bald head, and James could see the enlarged dark pores on his pale scalp. It didn't help settle his stomach. "It would've been quick, or at least as quick as it takes to die from a cut throat. There's evidence of a blow initially to the side of the neck...an old-fashioned brachial stun. Possibly it rendered her unconscious...certainly it would have disabled her. Then, I would suggest, the victim was pulled back against the killer's body, allowed to slide down toward the floor, and her own weight on the blade provided the force to kill her. It's an old army technique...requires little body strength from the perpetrator. A little old lady could kill with it."

James blew out a despairing breath. He'd hoped, at least, to be able to rule out little old ladies.

The doctor went on. "There's some evidence of relatively recent sexual intercourse, possibly the night before. No traces of semen.

Some old, heavy scarring on the back and thighs, but nothing recent. I'd put the time of death between six p.m. and seven."

"Scarring?" James asked sharply.

The pathologist raised an eyebrow. "When I say old, I *mean* old, Detective Sergeant. Early childhood injury according to her medical records. Anyway…the murder was efficient. From the physicality of it, I'd say the perpetrator would probably be male, though as I pointed out, a woman would have been capable of it."

James worried at it, as he and Kaur strode back to the car through long, busy, antiseptic corridors. They had an appointment to see Daniel Jackson next, and then James needed to get back to the station to get a grip on the other ongoing lines of enquiry. The postmortem had told them nothing they hadn't already surmised. But…

"It was brutal," James mused as they walked. "But…just to get the job done fast. Does it remind you of…I don't know…the slaughter of an animal? 'Nothing personal. You just need to be dead.'"

Kaur threw him a sideways glance. Neither of them slowed down.

"You're thinking a pro then…a contract? That army technique?"

James chewed his lip. Yes. That *should* be it, the O'Grady link maybe, though it would be a sodding nightmare nailing the culprit if it turned out that way.

"Maybe. There's no feeling of hot blood. Premeditated, almost certainly. Someone who didn't pause to gloat. No sense of killing just for the enjoyment of it…watching the victim realize what's happening… struggling to get away…"

They dodged past a porter wheeling along an old man attached to a portable drip. Kaur shot James another wry glance.

"Well, look on the bright side, Sarge. At least we can discount a serial psycho beginning a spree on our patch."

"It's like…" James went on as if she hadn't spoken. "Like someone taking payment for her sins. Or someone else's sins. Maybe, someone she helped escape punishment."

"And doesn't that just fit every scenario we have?" Kaur remarked, with horrible, dogged perkiness.

James didn't even try to deny it as they emerged out of the main hospital doors into the grey winter light.

4

James darted into Ingham's glass-box office the moment he saw her blinds open.

She had less than an hour to take lunch at her desk before her next meeting, so he sat down and rattled out the postmortem findings as quickly as he could. Then he went over the interview with Daniel Jackson.

Like all of them, Ingham hadn't had a proper night's sleep for days, and she looked grey with exhaustion, but her grooming remained impeccable, corkscrew ringlets gleaming darkly against her strong jaw. James wished to hell she'd let them all know how she managed it.

She scribbled a few notes, but for the most part she tapped a pen rhythmically against the tattered blotter on her desktop as she frowned at him. Because none of it could be described as particularly promising.

At six that evening, it would be forty-eight hours since Maria's murder, and that would be like…missing a deadline, like the first intimation of defeat. Every detective knew that if they hadn't found anything substantial, any solid lead or prime suspect in those first couple of days, the likelihood of a quick end to the case—the likelihood of finding the culprit at all—diminished hugely. It was a copper's touchstone.

But James had nothing solid to offer Ingham, nothing but maybes and perhapses. He'd even established that a step-by-step guide to the technique used to cut Maria's throat could be found on the Internet. Complete with drawings.

Rationally, James knew he couldn't be blamed. Rationally he knew that Ingham would have done exactly the same things he'd done; she'd trained him after all. But in his heart, she'd appointed him the team leader. And he felt as if he'd failed her.

"You believe him? The boyfriend?" Ingham asked.

James rubbed a finger roughly against his mouth, forcing concentration. Did he?

A romantic partner always became the automatic first suspect, as a rule of thumb.

But Jackson?

James had accepted he would always struggle to genuinely understand what made men like Jackson tick. James didn't understand infidelity, any more than he understood crazed love. He simply couldn't comprehend the level of selfishness or desire required to drive the betrayal involved.

James's last ex-girlfriend, Ellie, had once called him—fuck, he still winced from the humiliation of it—she'd called him *an emotional innocent*. As if he were two years old, clinging on to Father Christmas. She'd said...he shouldn't judge what he'd never experienced, because he'd never personally felt any of the messy, clawing desperation of intense passion, or need, or love. So he couldn't hope to understand why people did insane things because of it.

It had hurt to accept that she'd been right. Even now James recognized himself to be outside that human experience, uncomprehending of that kind of pain, and as a policeman, maybe that had to be a major flaw. He could only imagine it, like someone reading a book.

So, with Jackson's two small children playing outside, James had tried to listen as neutrally as he could as Jackson confirmed that he'd had protected sex with Maria the night before she died. That he'd been totally in love with her. That, yes, he'd known he felt far more for her than she'd ever felt for him. That he'd helped her career nonetheless. That he'd been grateful for whatever she'd chosen to give him in return. James found he'd been able to understand Jackson even less after that interview.

How could the man knowingly risk all he had, those kids, to be with a woman he *expected* to hurt him. What kind of reckless emotional masochist would he have to be?

He couldn't deny, though, that Jackson's devastation had felt real, as if the lights had been turned off for him. In fact, James wondered how his wife could avoid noticing that the guy seemed to be in extreme emotional shock.

Even so, he felt compelled to say to Ingham, "He seemed obsessed by her, but he knew she was using him. That could create an explosive kind of bitterness."

"And...you think now he's traumatized by having slashed the throat of the woman he loved?"

"It's possible." But James could hear the lack of conviction in his own voice.

"Lots of things are possible, Jamie," Ingham returned. "Ancient aliens are possible. But is it likely?"

Ancient aliens? James carefully directed his smile down to his shoes. It broke him out of his postmortem-induced funk at least. "No, ma'am."

A moment of silence followed, then, "Which one are we talking about? Jackson or the aliens?"

"Either, ma'am. On the balance of probability."

"I wish I hadn't asked."

"Yes, ma'am."

"One more 'ma'am' and you're cleaning all the toilets."

"Yes, m..." He shot her a wicked glance up through his lashes as she stared stoically at the ceiling for patience. "I could call you guv?" he offered.

He didn't tease her often; he respected her too much to risk it. But she seemed so tired, and he felt a certain sense of achievement in amusing her.

"You don't sound right saying guv, Jamie. It's like the Queen saying guv."

"Yes, ma'am."

They both grinned wildly, then the moment passed. Ingham rubbed her eyes wearily.

James hadn't known he planned to ask her until he opened his mouth. "Do you remember the address I went to in Selworth Gardens? The one I found in Maria's study?"

Ingham's gaze sharpened. "You found something? The Russian thing?"

"No," he said quickly. "It's just...one of the flats. It had a room available."

Ingham appeared puzzled, clearly searching her memory for a link to the investigation. James could tell that her thought processes were sluggish with tiredness, like his own. Then her expression cleared. "Oh. Alec said you're still looking for a place."

The confirmation that Ingham and Scrivenor gossiped about James came as no surprise. In a strange way, it felt almost comforting.

"Yeah," he pressed on. "So I wondered… Do you think it'd be… appropriate to check it out, with a view to renting? I mean, since I interviewed the landlord?"

Ingham raised her brows then rubbed her palm across her eyes.

"Fuck, I could use a few hours' kip." She focused on James, as if by an act of will. "I'm assuming he came up clean. The landlord."

James nodded and stood up. "Alec did the check."

She seemed ready to put her head down on the desk and pass out. "Okay then."

"I kind of planned to view it this evening. At six. But it's probably far too pricey. And I won't go if anything comes up in the case, of course, or…"

"*Jamie.*" James snapped his mouth shut. "For fuck's sake. I've heard about the shithole you're staying in from Alec." She waved a limp hand at him. "Just *go.*"

James drew a deep breath and let it out, and suddenly the pall of apprehension that had hung over the prospect of his appointment that evening seemed immeasurably lighter with her blessing.

"Thanks, ma'am."

"Right. Oh. Hang on…" Ingham said, as if she'd just remembered something unpleasant. "I meant to mention…" And that sounded far too casual. James braced himself. He wasn't going to like it. "Your father called today."

James blinked. Blinked again. He felt sure he'd misheard.

Ingham took in his expression and cleared her throat. "Yes. Alec picked up the call and he…um…he thought it best to forward it to me." There, proof again of Ingham and Scrivenor acting like the parents he should have had. They both knew his history.

James choked out. "What did he want?"

Ingham appeared very awake now and extremely uncomfortable. "He said he wants you to sign some documents, and he doesn't have your contact information."

James swallowed. It felt like one of the universe's little fuck-you jokes after Gill's taunts the day before.

He straightened to attention. "What did you say to him?"

"That you're a credit to the team," Ingham answered. "Honestly, Jamie—I don't think he called just to get you to sign some papers." She scrabbled on her desk and came up with a yellow sticky note. "He said this is his new private number."

The number Magnus had changed after James left. As James had discovered when he'd tried to get in touch.

"Look…" She hesitated. "Maybe you should call him. Maybe you should grab the olive branch, Jamie. You're too old to sulk like a huffy teen."

James stared at her. *Olive branch?* He felt sick with a wild confusion of betrayal and excitement. But it vanished beneath the knee-jerk defensive anger thoughts of his father always aroused in him.

"Right. Perhaps I'll do that, ma'am." He wondered if he sounded as insincere to Ingham as he did to himself. "Thanks, ma'am. I'll send someone in with some tea. Ma'am."

He had the door closed behind him before she could say another word about his father or his petty insubordination, and for once he didn't care that he probably showed everything he felt as he walked to his desk.

—||— —||— —||— —||—

James very carefully didn't think about his father or Selworth Gardens as he worked through the mass of preliminary files he had to check out—Gill and his girlfriend, Daniel Jackson, and Galinda Heywood had no record of police involvement, neither did Daniel Jackson's wife. Gill, Jackson and their partners were each other's alibis.

From there James dived into the family background of Irina the model, but he found no obvious issues there either. Her father turned out to be a Russian industrialist who may have been involved in dodgy dealings in Moscow but seemed, to all appearances, as clean as a whistle in his businesses in the West.

James forced focus fiercely, refusing to let his personal concerns reach his conscious mind. But as the afternoon wore on, he found his body letting him down, stomach skittering with a kind of blind apprehension. It reminded him of the way he'd felt before big rugby matches at university, or before his first major interview at the Met.

Because when he let himself remember his conversation with Ingham, he couldn't smother the dark suspicion that he knew exactly why his father wanted to contact him after two years of radio silence.

And on top of that, the very real probability that going through with the planned visit to Selworth Gardens would be unutterably stupid.

Perversely his determination to ignore his nerves about the flat-viewing appointment meant he left his desk later than he should have, so he had no time for last-minute second thoughts. And only his local knowledge of the side streets in South Kensington got him through the rush-hour traffic to stand at the front door of No. 22, just ten minutes late.

As he rang the doorbell, James felt off balance, unprepared, heart beating too fast from the stress of the race through dark, rain-greased streets. But he'd thought at least he'd have time to gather himself, if only the distance of a flight of stairs to the first floor. He did not expect Morgan to open the street door for him in person.

James had convinced himself he'd remembered Morgan's impact well enough to brace for it, but if anything, it felt more powerful the second time around. Worst of all, Morgan didn't appear to be trying.

He leaned, hand on the top of the open door, effortlessly spectacular in a loose plain white T-shirt and faded blue jeans. His dark curls brushed his shoulders, and his skin seemed to glow a pale, smooth gold, even in the harsh, white electric light of the hallway behind him.

James felt an almost physical jolt of alarm as he took him in, his subconscious yelling at him, again, that this could be a terrible mistake.

"Evening, Sergeant." Morgan grinned, all perfect white teeth.

James somehow produced a smile in return. "Good evening, Mr. Morgan." He sounded horrendously reserved, but he'd managed calm. "Thanks for making time to let me see the room."

"Ben. Please. And I promised I'd phone. I always keep my promises."

Fuck.

"James. Then. My name's…"

Ben's grin widened. "You said. It suits you. Pull the door closed behind you, yeah?"

James nodded and obeyed, heart still pounding a bit too fast for comfort as he followed the other man up the carpeted stairs. And he noted against his will the breadth of Ben's shoulders; his small waist and long legs; the splendid little arse encased in light-blue denim.

The flat door lay open when they reached it, golden light spilling out into the more conservatively lit first-floor hall, and the impression of elegant welcome only increased as James ventured inside.

"How about I show you round first?" Ben asked, already moving. "Start off with the room for rent?"

James followed. They moved down the long whitewashed hallway, and James noted a bathroom, door ajar, more than halfway down to the right, and at the end, two doors, set opposite each other. Ben opened the door on the left and flicked on the light.

The bedroom turned out to be almost as big as the entire bedsit in which James had been living for the past year. The walls were painted white, it had a large, white-curtained window, and it smelled of beeswax and honey. The bed appeared to be queen-sized, and the room also had a large wardrobe, a small desk and a set of wooden bookshelves which made James feel weak with longing. His books had been stored in boxes for more than two years.

"Okay?" Ben asked, smiling, and James could only nod again, feeling, abruptly, almost ready to beg.

The bathroom shone white and perfect too, with a slipper bath and a big walk-in shower, incredibly bright and clean and damp-free.

"And that's it, apart from my room and the lounge." Ben hovered in the bathroom doorway, half in the hall, watching James pretend to scrutinize the glories of the power shower to give himself time to work out a strategy. Though, now that he'd seen it properly, James felt doubly convinced he wouldn't be able to afford it anyway.

"It's great." He tried to sound casual. "How much would the rent be?"

Ben's hesitation was barely noticeable, then he named a sum so far below the figure James expected that he turned from his fake inspection to gape at the man now leaning, arms folded, against the doorjamb.

"That's...isn't that...quite a bit below market levels? For South Ken?"

Ben let out an amused breath. "You're *supposed* to be bargaining me down. The room's been empty for a few months and…honestly…I just want to find someone…normal to share with. Not some trust-fund baby. I'm not greedy."

James opened his mouth then shut it again. No point pretending to himself any more that he didn't desperately want that room, but perversely, he felt even less optimistic. Anyone who'd heard the low figure set for the rent, anyone who'd viewed the flat, would be ready to do anything to get in. He'd seen a couple of the guys who'd looked at it.

He frowned at the floor, teeth chewing at his lower lip, then back up again, ready to start serious bullshitting. But the expression on Ben's face silenced him.

Ben still leaned in the bathroom doorway, but his fascinated eyes seemed fixed on James as if he'd never seen anything quite like him before, as if James were some strange new creature deserving serious study. The intensity and stillness of his expression were unnerving after the animated confidence James had seen in him until then. They gazed at each other for a few beats of oddly breathless, absorbed silence, and James didn't know what to make of it. Then Ben blinked and snapped himself out of it.

"Right," he said. "I meant to ask if you'd like a bite to eat? While we talk."

Another startled silence.

"Well…" James began awkwardly. But his ingrained manners kicked in to remind him that one always turned down invitations made purely from politeness. "That's really kind of you, but I couldn't possibly put you to so much trouble."

Ben's mouth curved into a winning smile, confounding James again. "It's just lasagna. I make enough to freeze, so there's loads of it."

Without waiting for an answer, he turned and disappeared into the hallway, and James, perplexed, set off after him.

James had loved the lounge at first sight, but at nighttime it took on a different charm, lit by table lamps and a pattern of recessed spotlights over the kitchenette. The wooden shutters at the huge windows were folded open onto the night sky, and the lovely sandalwood and ginger scent of the room, which had fixed treacherously in James's memory, now subtly mingled with the smells of cooking—onions and garlic and tomatoes. The entire effect was delicious, sensual and welcoming.

"Did you come straight from work?" Ben bustled behind the breakfast bar at the kitchenette. "You must be exhausted."

James glanced down at his suit, crumpled worse than ever. He must appear freshly dug-up by now.

"It's a busy time," he said weakly. "In fact, I really should get back."

"Oh. But it's ready." Ben unleashed a hopeful grin, and he managed to give the impression that James would be doing him a huge personal favor by accepting his kindness.

It was unnervingly endearing, impossible to refuse gracefully. Even if James had wanted to.

"Well, I...yes. Thanks," he muttered. He could feel himself blushing. "That's...really very nice of you."

And as if he'd known he wouldn't be denied, Ben tentative smile transformed to a satisfied beam. He bent down and opened the oven door, unleashing a hot cloud of mouthwatering steam. The undeniably large dish of lasagna he set on a trivet on the breakfast bar looked incredible, like a photograph from a cookery book.

"Take a seat." Ben shoved two sets of cutlery and some tablemats into James's hand, and gestured toward a dining area between the kitchenette and the living room. James laid everything out on the rectangular wooden table and sat on one of the padded black-leather chairs set round it.

"Do you feed all your prospective tenants?" James ventured as he watched pasta, meat and sauce being ladled onto two large plates.

"I was taught to be hospitable," Ben replied primly. "But not *everyone* gets my lasagna."

James smiled down at the plate Ben laid in front of him, then back up into thick-lashed navy-blue eyes.

He felt ridiculous. Tongue-tied. Fourteen years old. He managed a shy, crooked grin. "This really...this is great."

Their gazes locked, and James could feel his heartbeat quickening again, like an idiot.

"What did Jim get?"

Ben laughed, grabbed two glasses and a carafe of water from the breakfast bar and sank into his chair across the table. "Ah, Jim. Jim got nachos, complete with plastic cheese. But everyone's gotta die sometime."

James's smile widened. "I'm honored to have escaped the plastic cheese."

"Actually, it's a rite of passage," Ben confided, smirking, as he poured water into James's glass. "But if I'm being honest, you don't look in any condition to handle it."

James picked up his fork. "You really know how to make a man feel warm inside," he said dryly.

"Wait till you try my plastic cheese."

They grinned at each other until James felt that traitorous adolescent blush rising again and quickly turned his focus to his food.

He'd never actually found himself in this position before: flirting, sober and in his right mind, with an attractive man. Whereas, with women, once upon a time, he'd been able to overcome his basic shyness with little effort. Mainly, he supposed, because he hadn't really cared if they fancied him.

He shoveled in a large mouthful of lasagna, and the intensity of the combined flavors burst brilliantly against his tongue.

"This. Is. Amazing!" he announced when he'd swallowed, and he hadn't exaggerated his enthusiasm either. After days of canteen slush and prepackaged sandwiches, it genuinely did taste like one of the best meals of his life, as good as anything he'd encountered in a top restaurant. He was dimly aware that he might have lost perspective, but he didn't care. "Really. Did you make this yourself?"

Ben glanced up, mouth twitching with pleased amusement.

"Yeah. But I'm sensing anything would taste good to you right now. Even the nachos. Have you been home at all since I last saw you?"

"Not yet," James replied, though *home* currently felt not a lot better than the station. "How did you guess?"

"You're wearing the same clothes."

James glanced down at his suit. "I *have* changed," he protested. "I've just had to...recycle."

Ben snorted. "That's reassuring. So. Tell me a bit about yourself?"

"This is the interview bit then." James threw him a small, pained smile. "Softening up the subject with unfairly delicious food?"

"Oh. Flattery. Very good. So have I softened you up enough to come clean about any nasty habits?"

Well, his job would hardly come as a shock, would it?

"No nasty habits." He took a bracing sip of water. "I'm twenty-eight. I'm a DS at a Murder Investigation Unit, and I'm on a fast-track program, which means that I get to detective inspector in ten months time, if I don't cock everything up."

"Well." Ben sat back in his chair. "That sounds…yeah, that sounds…really…impressive."

He didn't seem impressed, more as if the information unnerved him. James didn't even know why he'd mentioned his career prospects, other than perhaps to reassure Ben he'd be good for the rent.

"I should…I mean…can I ask…?" Ben ran his fingers back through his long curls. "Do you um…" He squinted at James. "Bring your work home?"

James eyed him uncertainly. Had that been a try at a joke? Or not?

"As in…work on cases at home? Or bring home suspects to interrogate?"

Ben gave a wincing smile. "As in…how would you react…*hypothetically*…if you saw someone…smoking a bit of weed? Or…something."

James put down his glass.

Well? How would he react?

He knew how he *should* react. When he'd first gone to Hendon to train he'd had the newbie's stick of righteous zealotry lodged firmly up his arse—evangelical about the law, determined he would never condone any skirting of it. Zero tolerance.

But working in homicide, he'd realized it sometimes became necessary to bend a bit, use minor infractions as a lever, even, to extract information to solve a bigger crime, or to build trust. He'd become practiced, in fact, in keeping his eye on the bigger picture. And in this case, the bigger picture was this flat, and the first step toward a life that involved more than just being a police officer.

So, Ben smoked some pot. And he'd *hypothetically* told a copper about it. Not exactly a big, bad villain.

Those windows really were beautiful. And so was Ben Morgan.

The sharpness of that thought stilled him, unease surging again, almost like fear.

"I suppose. If it were only pot, occasionally," he said calmly, nevertheless. "And…if no one were dealing. I just wouldn't realize anything had been going on. I can be really thick."

Ben laughed, but James worried that it seemed too careful maybe. Then again, it would be quite a risk to take in a policeman as a flatmate if you were into recreational drugs.

They both turned back to their food, James trying urgently to think up a way to negate his career in Ben's mind. He'd been drilled to wield social skills for fuck's sake. Why were they failing him now?

"So, is that the kind of photography you do?" James gestured pleasantly at the framed art on the walls. "They're really good."

Ben appeared almost startled that the tables had been turned. "Thanks. I think I told you I mainly do fashion. Magazines. Adverts. A few portraits. But I'm hoping to get the chance to disappear up my own arse, by doing my own exhibits of…" He waved at a framed photograph. "That kind of thing."

James raised his eyebrows. "Sounds glamorous." But he found himself asking, because he remembered all too well what those first would-be tenants looked like, "So do you primarily work with models?"

Ben stared at him for a long, surprised second, then his face split into a delighted grin.

"Is that you living in hope, Detective Sergeant?"

James's eyes widened. "*No!* No! I was just…" He flushed violently in the face of Ben's shit-eating smirk. "Asking," he finished with a weak sigh.

Ben's grin widened, if anything. "Yeah, I do work with models actually. And designers, and journalists, other photographers, assistants… All kinds of people."

"Mainly beautiful," James added, because his hang-ups were not going to defeat him.

"Mainly beautiful," Ben agreed indulgently. "I get to travel too. That's my favorite bit. I worked in Wales last week, and the North of Scotland before that." He fiddled with his fork while the silence stretched comfortably. "Um. I hope I'm not being rude here, but you seem a bit…"

"A bit…?" James asked apprehensively.

"A bit…*posh*. For the Met?" Ben finished. "Like one of those gentleman detectives you see on telly on Sunday evenings. Like…Inspector Lynley."

James made an outraged sound of protest.

Ben's grin widened manically. "Or who's that PD James one… With the poetry? Are you a secret aristocrat?"

James huffed in delighted affront. "Fuck off!"

"But you went somewhere *very* posh for school. Eton!"

"No! Of course I bloody didn't." Then, sheepishly, "Westminster."

Ben's huge bark of laughter was joyful and infectious, and suddenly it didn't seem a hard story to tell.

"Westminster and Oxford," James confessed it all. "Economics and History."

"But something like seven prime ministers went to Westminster!"

"Yeah. But…not all at once. And at least I didn't have to wear a hat."

Ben laughed again, leaning forward on his elbows. "An intellectual cop." He shook his head, eyes sparkling with glee. "You must stand out like a duck in a hen house. Did you *always* want—I mean you could have done anything, right? Why did you want to become a copper?"

And maybe because that last conversation with Ingham hovered over James like the Sword of Damocles. Or maybe the odd sense of connection he felt with Ben, the exhilaration of Ben's attention, weakened his defenses. But without conscious decision, James told him.

"After Oxford, I expected to take over my dad's company. I mean, I'd trained for it pretty much since the womb, being the only heir. I hadn't really thought there could be an alternative."

Just as he hadn't thought there might be any alternative to the beautiful, cultured wife he'd take on in a few years, the two, possibly three, children he'd have. A boy first, of course.

He'd driven an Audi R8 once upon a time, had a huge wardrobe of designer clothes and a penthouse flat in Canary Wharf, in which he fucked some of the gorgeous, skinny rich girls he'd pulled to please his father.

His life had been gilded; he'd been told always how lucky he was, and objectively he'd known it to be true. Even after his mother died, before he'd reached seven years of age, and took all the love in the house with her. He'd felt ashamed of his own unhappiness, so he'd buried it beneath just enough alcohol, the judicious use of coke, and a lot of mediocre sex.

"So what happened?" Ben asked, intrigued.

James drew a deep breath through his nose and let it out again in a hard sigh.

"It…I'd been to a lunch. A business lunch with my father. And as we were getting out of the car I saw a woman a few yards away, falling from the pavement into moving traffic, and a man running away from her, with a…a big shoulder bag in his hand. I didn't even think about it. I ran after him."

Past the blaring car horns, the shouting, screaming people gathering round the shocked woman, weaving through the crowds after the fleeing man.

"It didn't take long to bring him down, then I sort of marched him back. I gave my statement, and waited for the ambulance to take the woman, and a police car to take the guy…and I realized…I'd never had the feeling before that I'd done something that actually mattered."

James looked up nervously at Ben then back down at his glass of water.

His father had been furious—gave him a lecture for risking injury and becoming involved in such a messy situation.

But James had gone home that night, sat on his enormous leather sofa gazing out at his spectacular city view, and allowed himself to face the truth about his life. The fact that he'd spent his entire twenty-five years existing only to please his father. That he could never truly be the man his father wanted him to be. That what he *did* with his life would be the important thing, not the things he had.

"So I decided to do something about it. I told myself Father would respect my choice when he thought about it, which…well, actually… maybe if I'd known how badly he'd react, I wouldn't have had the guts to go through with it."

When James had told him he'd been accepted into the Met's elite fast-track program, his father had at first refused to believe he could be serious, then coldly told him his mother would be ashamed of him. Which had been the first time he'd mentioned James's mother to him since the month after she'd died, just before James's seventh birthday.

"Plus I had a final 'screw you' moment and also told him I'm gay, so...well, when I didn't recant, within twenty-four hours he'd closed my bank accounts, removed my company flat and car, and changed his private number. His PA told me only a full and groveling return to the firm will ever gain his forgiveness. And...I haven't heard from him for over two years."

Until today.

"Fuck," Ben breathed.

James kept his eyes on his glass.

Now he existed on his sergeant's salary and interest on the sizeable inheritance left to him by his mother, which he didn't want to touch, just in case. And somewhere on the other side of London, there was a huge storage container, bursting with furniture and art and books, things he'd extracted from the flat before he told his father his plans— as a precaution. It all sat there, waiting for the time he got properly back on his feet, when he could afford his own place and have his own things around him. He drove a secondhand Toyota. And he had never been happier.

He still felt a bit of a fish out of water, of course, trying to integrate himself into normal life with normal people after the strange, idealized existence he'd tripped through before. But he fit in with the police brilliantly. Life with his father had made him, professionally and psychologically, as tough as hell.

"Yeah," James agreed. He forced himself to glance up, to radiate unconcern. "So now I'm...inconveniently poor, but free."

Ben regarded him with open fascination. "That's really...that's *amazing*. You should be so proud of yourself."

James flushed, this time with gratification as well as embarrassment. He took a concealing gulp of water. It occurred to him what a good listener Ben had been, how he'd just let James talk.

"Are you out at work?" Ben asked. "I didn't think…coppers liked that kind of thing."

"Times have changed." James gave a one-shouldered shrug. "They love diversity. Well, the PR department does anyway. I mean, I haven't stood on a desk and made an announcement, but the people I work with know. So far, it hasn't been an issue."

But he hid so much more he couldn't admit. The fact that he had no more clue now, than he'd had over two years ago, how to find other men who might want more than a quick fuck. That he'd never slept with anyone he actually, truly wanted. That he had no idea where, or how, to start, and still keep his dignity and professional integrity intact.

That his father's generational prejudice toward homosexuality had laced through his childhood and adolescence like dripped poison, and it had stunted him. That a childhood filled with expectation and little affection had stunted him.

His entire experience, apart from girls, came down to a couple of rushed hand jobs and a guy who'd pushed him into a toilet cubicle at the Students' Union when he'd been too drunk to object, and blew him to heaven. But at least he didn't have to hide any more. He preferred nothing at all to the dishonesty of pretense, or more meaningless fucks.

He hadn't expected the touch of Ben's long fingers on his bare wrist, a gesture of solidarity, or sympathy. It took all of James's concentration not to stare at them, not to shake them off. The easy, casual touch felt alien to him.

Ben's voice was quiet. Intense. "If your dad has any sense, he'll see you for what you are. Noble. And *honorable*."

Somehow, the words sliced through every defense James had.

James showed strong emotion to no one. His father had taught him that.

Yet, out of nowhere, tears were prickling in his eyes, the lump in his throat thickening to choke him. He looked away sharply, appalled. Somehow Ben Morgan had got him to this point by saying the exact fucking things he hadn't even realized he'd been aching to hear.

At that moment, the door buzzer shattered the delicate silence, an ugly shock of sound, and—James remembered with a kind of hysterical relief—a perfect echo of their last meeting.

Saved by the fucking bell.

"Shit! Sorry," Ben murmured. "That's the seven o'clock."

James nodded and gathered up his plate and cutlery to take to the kitchen sink, dimly aware that Ben did the same. By the time he'd turned to face him, James had himself under control.

"Well." He smiled politely. "Thanks for dinner and showing me the flat."

Ben's expression of mild concern melted into a grin.

"You're welcome." He seemed entirely at ease. Perhaps he heard other people's awkward life stories on a regular basis. The buzzer sounded again, and Ben laughed. "God, we've been here before. I'd better let him in."

As James followed him to the door, it really did feel like déjà vu—as if it were yesterday and they were back to being Detective Sergeant Henderson and his interviewee, except now James had lost his dignity. The buzzer sounded with comic familiarity, and James forced a grin.

Ben waggled his eyebrows and pressed the door release. "Come on up, mate," he called into the intercom. "First floor." Then a sigh to James, "Impatient bastard."

"It's not Jim again, is it?" James tried.

"Nah. He's probably been hospitalized by the plastic cheese."

James directed his strained smile at the floor. Escape was imminent.

But all of a sudden, a queasy feeling of imminent loss surged up to overwhelm his uncertainty and embarrassment. The realization that the price of his own vulnerability might be worth paying in return for this incredible feeling of affinity.

"So," he said quickly. "Are you just going to call the successful—?"

"I'll call everyone," Ben interrupted. "I've got manners, remember?"

Their eyes met, and on cue, James's heart began to thump too hard, pulse fluttering with nervous tension.

A loud, rapping knock sounded at the flat door.

Ben gave a rueful, conspiratorial eye roll and reached for the latch.

James found that he'd so believed in Ben's reluctance that he expected the visitor to get, at best, an unenthusiastic response for turning up at the wrong moment. He might even have expected coolness for the man's impatience.

Instead, he watched Ben produce the same happy, welcoming, breathtaking smile he'd used to welcome James.

Exactly the same smile.

"I'm really sorry for keeping you waiting..." Ben said. "Greg, right? There's just been a bit of a backlog."

James cast his eyes down to his shiny black lace-ups, concealing everything.

A bit of a backlog.

He felt far too keenly the sharp punch of humiliation and disappointment, the understanding that he'd badly misread the situation.

What had he thought anyway? That someone as spectacular as Ben would be as affected by James as James had been affected by him? That James, in all his embarrassing inexperience, would somehow stand out to him?

Ben had the ability to make anyone feel that they were the most important person in his world at a given moment—the definition of charisma. Galaxies out of James's league.

James eyed the newcomer at the door, taking in his smooth auburn hair in a super-fashionable short cut; crotch-throttling trousers; a carefully-too-small green jacket; his generic model face, symmetrical and chiseled.

"Oh, *no* problem," Greg the Interloper drawled to Ben. "I love the view already."

James drew a deep breath. He hoped his face was stone.

"Well, thanks again," he said with a pleasant nod to Ben, and without waiting for a reply, he walked smartly toward the stairwell, a stiff in a suit, leaving the beautiful people to flout the Misuse of Drugs Act with their class B cannabinoids.

He heard Ben call a casual farewell behind him then the sound of a closing door.

He felt oddly naked, ridiculous, as if his exhaustion had cost him all his judgment. He'd essentially stripped himself of his own privacy and dignity to try to impress someone else, for whom it had been, at best, a moment's diversion.

All he wanted to do was forget it.

5

In the early hours of the following day, James contrived to grab five hours' sleep on a camp bed, then showered and shaved as usual in the gents. He put on his last clean shirt, and when he looked in the bathroom mirror, the bags under his eyes were the size of suitcases.

That morning in Ingham's absence, he held the debrief for the team on Maria's case, to red-pencil the possibilities already closed off and dole out the next set of leads. Ingham's office blinds were stubbornly shut, and DCs reported to James as a matter of course, as her proxy. It amazed him how quickly necessity had wiped out custom. Or maybe no one had the energy to take umbrage.

James worked doggedly on locating Maria's ex-boyfriends and setting up interviews while Kaur ploughed through Maria's phone records. Barry Walsh and his partner were out digging on the O'Grady link. But nothing had taken, and James couldn't shake the ingrained belief that they were running out of time, that without a quick lead, the killer would slide through their fingers for good.

"Here you go, laddie."

James glanced up from the pile of papers on his desk, realizing that his hand, propping up his head, had clenched tightly in his thick hair. He felt as if every molecule in his body was quivering with tension.

Scrivenor slid a polystyrene cup along the desk to him, like a zoo-keeper pushing meat at a dodgy lion. "It's nae the posh stuff, but ye need somethin' to distract ye from rippin' the hair outta yir heid."

James gave a wan smile. The liquid inside the cup was a watery grey-brown and hot enough to scald the membrane of his mouth, but James didn't care. It helped keep him awake, either through caffeine or pain.

He peered at Scrivenor around their monitors as the other man sat down behind his desk.

"You cannae keep goin' without a break, Jamie." Scrivenor's voice remained deliberately low. "Ah know this is yer first case as lead, but it's nae gonna be a quick one. We can a' see that. Yiv gotta pace yersel', lad."

"I'm fine," he gritted, but he had to force himself not to bite back, to remember that tiredness could make friendly concern feel like a personal attack. Hidden beneath one of the piles of paper on his desk, his mobile began to buzz and jump, and his tension upped another notch. He clawed for it irritably.

A withheld number. Of bloody course.

"DS Henderson," he snarled.

"Oh. Hi. It's…Ben Morgan?"

James's straightened in his chair. Exhausted frustration popped out of existence, and a burst of startled pleasure replaced it.

Then he remembered. *The backlog.* His eyes closed tight against a tide of mortification.

All he fucking needed—a reminder of baring his underbelly to a complete stranger.

He opened his eyes and manned up.

"Oh, yeah," he said casually to Christ on His cross. "You said you'd call everyone."

He even found himself impressed that Ben had kept his word, though he'd have preferred never to hear from him again.

"I did. But I'm calling you first. To see if you still want the room?"

James's face slackened.

"You're offering it to *me*?" And his incredulity must have been so huge that he could see Scrivenor, in his peripheral vision, stop and eye him worriedly across the desk. Maybe he thought it was Media and Communications.

"Yes," Ben laughed. "Why not you?"

"Well, I didn't think…"

I spilled my bloody life story all over you. And there were models.

He couldn't help himself. A frisson of hope fizzed in his gut, that maybe he hadn't imagined the connection between them after all. That maybe—somehow he'd stood out to Ben.

"Common sense, mate," Ben said airily. "If you're gonna invite a complete stranger to live with you, the best bet's probably a policeman."

Right.

"That's. Well...thanks," James returned weakly.

"No problem. When d'you want to move in?"

"When's convenient?"

"Anytime at all." Ben sounded indulgent. "Do you have to give notice?"

"It's not that kind of place." Even through James's exhaustion, a kind of sluggish excitement began to overwhelm his ambivalence about the wisdom of more contact with Ben. He wanted new friends, didn't he?

That flat. The bookcase. Those windows. Models.

"The sooner the better," James blurted.

"Tonight then?"

James blinked and opened his mouth, aware of Scrivenor's blatant curiosity.

Why not? "I'll have to check, but I should be able to do that. It could be quite late though."

"No worries. I'll be here. I'll have the documents ready to sign."

When the call ended, after a few more details exchanged, James couldn't quite believe he hadn't dreamed it.

"You got a perch, then?" Scrivenor asked.

"Yeah..." James grinned, though his belly felt like a ball of knots. "Selworth Gardens."

Scrivenor gave an impressed moue. "Wooh. That's... Hang on. Wizn't it Selworth Gardens I checked out the other day?"

"Yeah." James preferred not to hear the defensiveness in his own tone. "But it's okay. I ran it past Ingham. And you said the guy was clear."

Scrivenor's bushy brows reached new heights. "It's nae the porn star?" he asked with scandalized delight.

"No!" James protested. "And anyway...adult actor."

Scrivenor seemed extremely let down. "So the photographer guy, then?"

James rubbed his eyes. He registered how tense he felt, probably even tenser than he'd been when Scrivenor had decided to relax him. "He's the owner. There were a lot of people after it."

Scrivenor met his eyes for a long, narrow moment and James felt an incriminating flush surfacing, just from that knowing gaze. Scrivenor had, after all, witnessed James's flustered reactions to the call.

The big ginger moustache bristled. "Well. Good luck, ay?"

James couldn't help but see, though, that he looked concerned.

◼◻◼ ◼◻◼ ◼◻◼ ◼◻◼

When Ingham heard about James's intended move, courtesy of Scrivenor that lunchtime, she told Alec to order him to take the rest of the day off. So, in the early afternoon he legged it to his car and drove out to the bedsit he'd been renting by the month.

His rent had been paid for the next fortnight, so he called the landlord to cancel his short-term lease, packed his modest belongings into a few boxes and bags, shoved them all into the car, and he found himself standing, ringing the doorbell at No. 22, not long after seven p.m.

Ben opened the street door for him almost at once.

"Your last place that bad, then?" he said, grinning. He wore light-blue jeans again and a loose black tank top that showed off lean, well-muscled arms, broad shoulders, gorgeous collarbones and a lot of smooth, pale golden skin.

Each time they met, James felt sure his attraction would have diminished and he'd see Ben only as the potential friend for whom he'd been hoping. And each time it felt as if Ben upped the ante. Even if he didn't know the guy, if he'd just seen him pass by, dressed like this, on the street, James knew he'd have stared after him, weak at the knees.

Without waiting for a response, Ben slid past James to reach the open boot of the car, and lifted out the largest box, the muscles of his arms flexing deliciously. James stood, inwardly salivating, on the front door step as Ben strolled back toward him with his burden.

"Well, come on then, Detective Sergeant! I'm not doing it all for you. It's bloody freezing!"

James snapped out of it, abashed, and it took them only fifteen minutes to get all his cases, boxes and bin bags up the stairs—a pretty pathetic commentary, he acknowledged, on twenty-eight years of life and two careers.

Still, he'd landed here, a brand-new resident on a different planet.

When he closed the door of his new bedroom behind him, he pulled off his wrinkled suit jacket and put away his clothes and toiletries. Then he sat cross-legged on the floor and gazed, with barely leashed joy, at his empty bookshelves. In an odd way, it felt like coming home, only on his own terms.

His box of books had remained taped up since he'd packed it two years before in his Canary Wharf flat; all through the months he'd camped at his ex-lover Ellie's, then more months at a friend's, then finally at the last dump. And okay, these shelves wouldn't come close to housing the books he had in storage, but they could take his work stuff, his home copies of *The Police Investigators' Manual*, and the *Police and Criminal Evidence Act*, and a collection of tomes on forensic medicine and the law. He had his inspector's exams coming up in a few months, and to be able to unpack even that much of his stuff was incredible.

"I knocked, but I don't think you heard. You about ready?"

James looked up, startled, from his automatic filling of the shelves, to find Ben hovering in the open doorway, smiling, hand pushing back through his long, silky curls. It seemed to be the closest he had to a nervous gesture.

He smiled a lot too, James observed. In fact, cheerfulness seemed to be his natural state.

"Yeah. Sorry. Just the rest of these books."

"It looks good already," Ben approved warmly. "I've made spag bol. Should be ready in ten minutes or so. You look like you need an early night though."

James gazed up at him wide-eyed. "You cooked for me again? You shouldn't have bothered."

"I was going to eat anyway. I just made it a bit bigger."

"But..." James protested, but Ben made shushing movements with his hands.

"It's your first night! And anyway I like cooking. I'll probably force random food on you as a hobby."

James smiled, because he couldn't help it. "Okay then. But I'll have a go too. I can do non-poisonous." A skill learned relatively recently, out of desperation. Ben laughed and closed the door behind him.

James returned to filling his shelves.

It felt surreal to be here in a bright, warm flat with a real bed beside him, when just that morning, he'd woken in the grey light of the office, trying not to accept that the chances of solving Maria's case quickly had vanished.

When James emerged, he found himself shepherded to the dining table, and again Ben's food tasted excellent—rich and flavorful. They cleared their plates then loaded the dishwasher together, and James, when he sat on the large, squishy sofa with his second glass of red wine, genuinely couldn't remember when he'd last felt this replete and relaxed.

"That tasted amazing," James said lazily. "Why do your flatmates ever leave?"

Ben fiddled with Netflix settings from the other end of the sofa. "I make them into Bolognese sauce when they bore me. Honestly, I just like to cook. And you looked as if you could use some spoiling."

James chewed his lip for a second or two. Having caught sight of himself in a mirror, he did have to admit he looked fucking awful. But he didn't want to go to bed yet; it was only half past eight.

In short order, he and Ben discovered they shared a taste for cheesy reality TV shows, classic comedies, crime drama, science fiction and fantasy. In fact, they agreed on almost everything, viewing-wise. So they settled in for a watch of the rebooted *X-Files*. It all felt so easy, James couldn't even remember why he'd been worried about moving in; at that moment his only real concern was falling asleep on the sofa and snoring. He put down his wine on the coffee table, just in case.

"James?" Ben sounded thoughtful.

James glanced up, realizing the TV screen was frozen. Gillian Anderson looked out at him, as if she had something important to tell him. He got the definite feeling he was about to be sent to bed like a schoolboy.

He turned all his attention to Ben, trying to look alert.

"D'you ever think of contacting him?" Ben asked. "Your dad, I mean?"

James felt as immediately wide-awake as if someone had slapped him. His expression must have reflected his astonishment.

"Look. I'm sorry," Ben hurried on. "I know it's none of my business but…maybe he regrets what he did. Maybe he can't make the first move." He shrugged, and for the first time since James had met him, he looked awkward. "Maybe he has regrets."

It had to be James's turn to speak, but he seemed to have lost any mental agility he possessed that could allow him to cope with such painful personal questions with any social grace. After Gill's malice, and the threat implicit in the phone call, and then his own humiliating confessions to Ben, he'd very deliberately not thought about his father.

Ben sighed and dropped his eyes, and James found that, even more than he wanted the subject to go away, he wanted to wipe that look of embarrassed discomfort from Ben's face.

Happy seemed to be Ben's default setting. And James had already made him sad. Yet equally, there could be no point in letting him believe a miracle ending would ever be possible for James and his father.

"He doesn't have regrets," James explained softly. "*Regrets* are for the weak."

Ben's gaze darted up to meet his, and his face twisted with an emotion James couldn't read; or maybe he could just recognize a direct quote when he heard one.

"Your parents…you're really close to them, aren't you?" James asked.

Ben regarded him with an odd expression James couldn't place. Caution, or suspicion perhaps. Then he nodded. "Yeah. That's why I thought…if there's any way you can have your dad in your life…you know?"

Briefly, James debated telling Ben about the phone call, the *documents* he had to sign, but he couldn't face a dissection of what it meant. What he felt about it.

He fixed his eyes on the TV screen. He thought now that Gillian looked sympathetic.

"There isn't a way. Not if I want it to be my life and not his."

"Okay." Ben frowned at the glass he'd been twirling restlessly in his hand. His hair looked like skeins of fine black silk in the lamplight, his eyelashes thick and dark against the pale gold of his high cheekbones. "I'm really sorry I interfered. God, you just moved in!"

James picked up his own glass of red wine and took a necessary gulp. But all he cared about in that moment was making Ben smile again.

"It's okay. Really. And I'm glad you were lucky. It's good to know they're out there somewhere… Parents who don't fuck you up."

Ben's gaze shot to James's face, searching for dishonesty, perhaps, or a social lie. But James smiled and reached out his glass for a makeshift toast.

It took a few seconds for Ben to relax in turn, to trust his mood, but he reached out his own glass to clink solidly against James's.

"To parents who don't fuck you up," he repeated softly. He held James's eyes for a beat then he looked away, pushed a button on the remote control, and the screen burst back into life. Gillian resumed her investigations, her sympathy, it transpired, entirely imaginary.

–‖– –‖– –‖– –‖–

"Jamie. I've been meaning to say…just let me know when you want to bring someone over, okay? So I can make myself scarce."

James looked up blearily from his buttered toast and tried to focus. Though he'd never mentioned his office nickname, Ben had started calling him "Jamie" spontaneously, as if it were his own invention. James couldn't pretend to dislike it.

His first couple of days and nights in the new flat had been pretty much perfect. He had a space of his own to retreat to, a comfortable bed, and a flatmate who cooked dinner, left some for him when he came home late, and had coffee and toast on the go before he left for work in the morning. Not only that, it was so much closer to work than the last flat that he got forty extra minutes in bed. His decision to take the place now seemed a moment of genius, rather than an insane compulsion.

"Someone over?" he repeated.

He pondered whom he might invite. Scrivenor? Mac from aikido? Maybe a couple of the lads he still saw from uni? Ellie?

No. Too soon.

But Ben should meet his other friends. He already felt like a great mate. Their schedules didn't always match, but then James worked very unsociable hours and Ben seemed to work at insane times too.

For example, though Ben had been working late on an evening shoot the night before, James was pretty sure he still hadn't been home when he staggered in from the station himself, after two a.m. In fact, James had no idea if Ben had been to his own bed at all, and he didn't want to ask.

But—when James and Ben did get time together, they seemed to be on the same wavelength in almost everything. They happily took the piss out of each other, they enjoyed the same kind of things, and, like James, Ben did a martial art—savate, in his case—which kept him…very fit.

When he'd accidentally seen Ben clad only in a towel, before his shower on the first morning, James had felt physically winded, though he still believed familiarity would dull the shock of Ben's beauty. That had to be how these things worked.

It made it a bit awkward, though, that Ben had one of the nicest male bodies James had ever seen in real life, even in the hundreds of changing rooms he'd been in over the years—lean and smooth and beautifully muscled. Entirely masculine. It made James feel self-conscious about his own broader frame, even though he knew his body to be, ob-jectively, more than acceptable.

And here James was, fanning the flames of his crush, doing the very fucking thing he'd ordered himself not to do.

He surfaced to find Ben looking at him with ill-concealed amuse-ment, leaning back in his dining chair, mug in hand.

"Jamie." Ben's voice sounded rich with indulgence. "Even Inspec-tor Lynley takes it out for a quick spin sometimes."

"A spin?" James asked blankly.

Ben rolled his eyes. He looked particularly good that morning, in a light-blue Henley and tight black trousers, hair a dark, elegant mess. James wondered again when he'd come home.

James, as always for work, wore a tie and dress shirt, suit jacket ready on the back of his chair. He felt five hundred years old.

"Have some more coffee." James obediently took a large swig from his mug. "I *mean* a shag, Posh Boy. Or…a boyfriend?"

James swallowed more coffee, but that was not the reason he sud-denly felt very awake indeed. He couldn't hope to halt the old treacherous rush of embarrassed blood flooding his neck and face, and yet again he cursed his self-consciousness with this.

"I'm..." *Pull yourself together you stupid wanker!* Which was pretty much the perfect description, he thought hysterically. "I'm not seeing anyone at the moment."

Ben, alarmingly, had stopped grinning. "Yeah, but...you don't... I mean don't you need to let off steam? Have a good fuck?"

James's flush deepened—like a Victorian virgin rudely confronted with the facts of life. He'd have sold his soul for the fire alarm to go off.

"I'm not really into...you know...casual..." The heat of his face could fry an egg by now. "Hookups."

"Oh." Ben raised his eyebrows, then frowned down at the table. "I suppose you'd have to be extra discreet, being a policeman and all. Still..." He grinned wickedly. "It's probably as well for public safety. You'd have to taser them off you, down The Admiral Duncan, looking like you do."

James met his eyes steadily, though his mortification was still so intense his skin was actually prickling like a heat rash. But he wanted to ask, *Looking like I do? Do you like how I look?*

"Anyway..." Ben went on. "You won't mind *me* getting on with it, will you, mate? Not having your Roman stoicism and all."

James regarded his half-eaten toast. He'd been hungry when he sat down.

"No, of course not. It's your flat."

Though the idea made him feel stupidly threatened, as if he'd just okayed an invasion.

"No, Jamie! It's *our* flat, which is why we should set out ground rules. How about...if either of us has someone over, the other leaves them to it, if they're in the living room. Okay? And...a closed bedroom door with a sock on the handle means—"

"I get it," James interrupted. He took an unwanted bite of toast.

"Great," Ben said, but though he smiled, he looked awkward, and James had a horrible feeling that he hadn't hidden much. "So...what's with the Armani today? Impressing someone?"

James didn't know why he felt surprised Ben had noticed. He seemed to see everything.

"My boss and I have to go to a victim's funeral." He stood and shouldered into his black suit jacket. "And I have to give evidence in a court case." There was no escape from those, even in the midst of full-on investigations. "It's from a few months ago. Man beat his wife to death. Vicious little dickhead tormented her for years." He fiddled with the knot of his silk tie. "Allegedly."

Ben gave a snort of fond amusement as he stood too, but James didn't expect him to lean across the small table to straighten the tie knot himself.

"If I were on the jury, I'd hang anyone you told me to. Just for how you look in that suit."

And there it came yet again, that fucking flush.

"For the sake of British justice, let's hope you're never on jury service."

"Do you blush when you're reading them their rights?" Ben asked evilly, and that proved a mortification too far.

Don't fucking talk about sex and flirt with me at breakfast then, James wanted to say. To show his irritation at being teased like this.

Instead he blurted, "Got to go," hurried out to the hall, grabbed his briefcase and barreled out the front door.

He hadn't expected to encounter another body, so he literally knocked the person standing directly outside off their feet.

He heard an outraged screech, and then he could only gabble profuse apologies as he tried to help the victim, sprawled on the communal hall carpet. It took a second to recognize the downstairs neighbor.

The porn star, Scrivenor crowed, inside James's head.

"Well," the man camped breathlessly when he righted himself, holding James's supporting hand in a firm grasp. "Detective Sergeant Henderson. This is a lovely surprise. I see Ben's...helping you with your enquiries. I want to ask about 'taking down his particulars.'" He grinned wildly. "But I never like to push a metaphor."

James didn't bother to worry about blushing. The guy had excellent reason, after all, to believe James had been doing the walk of shame.

"Mr. Nicholas." He tugged at his hand, but Nicholas didn't let go. "I'm actually Ben's new flatmate."

Finally Nicholas released his hand. His clever, pretty face seemed alive with interest. "So, we must all be off the hook, then, if you've moved in."

James kept his face carefully blank. What could he say? *You are, but your upstairs neighbor's still in the frame?*

"You coming in, Steggie?"

James jerked round to find Ben in the still-open front door looking impatiently at Nicholas. He held his phone, apparently mid-conversation, from the tinny sounds issuing from it.

"Our *very* hot policeman just swept me off my feet." Nicholas smirked.

"Yeah, they do that," Ben said dryly. "If you want a coffee you'd better come in now. Let Jamie get to work in peace." He disappeared behind the door, talking into his phone.

There was a short silence.

"Well, it's been a pleasure to meet you again," Nicholas said. "And please, call me Emile." Then a second later, "Though actually…" His mouth stretched into a tense smile, and just like that, the man's brittle facade blinked away and an ordinary guy peered out at James instead. "My *friends* call me Steggie," he said carefully. "I expect…that's what we're going to be, isn't it?"

His smile didn't diminish, but there seemed to be something guarded there, as if he fully expected rejection or worse. James thought he must be very used to being judged.

And James was a policeman after all, who might not want to socialize with a man who made a living winning Golden Cocks.

"Steggie, then," James said.

Their eyes met, and Steggie's smile relaxed into genuine warmth.

At that moment, Ben stuck his head out the door and waved his phone.

"We're all going out to tonight. The Trafalgar," he announced to the hallway. "Time you met the rest of my mates, Posh Boy," he said with a grin and ducked into the flat again.

"*Posh Boy?*" Steggie hissed, mock-scandalized. "*He* can talk! He went to private school, you know. *Don't* let him take the piss just because you speak like Lord Grantham. *You* just remind him…*he's* no Mr. Bates."

James blinked, nodded and backed away toward the stairs, wondering what signals he gave out that made other gay men want to mother him, or mock him.

"Work," he explained weakly.

But as he looked at Steggie still beaming at him through his retreat, James felt an insane tug of excitement.

Ben. Steggie. Pub tonight.

A whole new social life could be starting up around him, with new friends who weren't scared of being gay. People who possibly wanted to get to know him in the real world, apart from money or job. People who might even accept the person he was.

The day proved to be hellish. And as if to stick a throbbing red cherry on top, James's route back to the station from the Old Bailey had gridlocked with rush-hour traffic.

He'd spent six hours sitting, waiting for his turn to testify in the trial; the actual testimony had taken less than twenty minutes. Then, right in the middle, there had been Maria's funeral.

Kaur's updating phone calls through the day hadn't helped his mood: no new breakthroughs in any direction. Now she had to tell him that her own investigation into Maria's phone records had drawn another blank.

"There *was* one number I couldn't tie in to an ID." Kaur's apologetic voice sounded tinny and thin over the hands-free car microphone as James edged the car slowly forward, yard by yard, but James could hear her perfectly. Unfortunately. "It turned out to be a pay-as-you-go. Unregistered."

Of course it fucking had.

At last the car reached the opening to a side street, and James indicated and accelerated in. Under the glow of sodium lights, pavements lifeless, buildings looming, the road looked like a stage set waiting to be used. He didn't care, as long as the car moved forward.

In truth he had no idea if all his ducking and weaving through traffic got him to his destination any faster, but he far preferred to drive a longer distance and keep moving than to sit still and wait on the direct route. At least this way, he felt in control.

"I ID'ed every caller up to three months back," Kaur went on. "I can go further if you like, though?"

"No." James changed gear. "Three months should be enough for now. Move on to her caseload. Thanks, Sameera."

"Bye, Sarge."

The call cut off and James hit his palm hard off the steering wheel.

The frustration of endless dead ends ate at him on this case, worse than it ever had. The sense of personal responsibility. Of looming failure.

Just one break—one tiny chink of light to guide them the right way... But luck wasn't with them. With him.

What are you waiting for? A magical entity to fly in? Wave a magic wand? You make your own luck, boy.

James clenched his jaw tightly and glowered at the windscreen.

Magnus Henderson's contemptuous voice. It never quite left him.

With a blaze of cleansing malice, he'd made the decision that morning to take the situation with his father into his own hands. He hadn't used the number he'd been given by Ingham—the private number. Instead he dialed his father's secretary and told her to send any documents to his new address: the one with the gay flatmate and, he assumed, the equally gay, porn-star neighbor.

His mood improved when he reached the office and learned that the Crown Prosecution Service were almost certain they'd get a conviction in the case for which James had just given evidence.

"Yer like a secret fuckin' weapon, son!" Scrivenor gloated, by way of greeting. "Should be deployed tactically. It's they bonnie *suits* an' that posh accent. Juries wet their knickers."

James dropped his briefcase, complete with case notes, onto the floor beside his desk and tried his utmost to ignore Scrivenor. But the DCs in their part of the office, who were doggedly slogging through background files on Maria's case, jumped on the distraction by sniggering and hooting, and then sniggered and hooted even louder when

James gave them all the middle finger, turning in a circle for maximum coverage.

"You're just in," James complained when he sat down. Scrivenor, after all, had drawn a night shift. "How the hell did you know?"

Scrivenor tapped the side of his nose smugly. "*Sources*, laddie. Oh…an' I've some news. Ah finally managed to speak to Irina's father. He says *he* did nae know Maria, an' Irina spent the evenin' with him before she flew out—the time of the murder. Irina's nae due back in London for a coupla weeks. She visitin' her granny in the Caucasus."

James huffed a desperate laugh. It sounded farcical. It felt farcical.

Scrivenor went on. "I'm tryin' some numbers an' email addresses an' social media an a' that, but they're nae comin' up wi' anythin.'"

Three desks along, the red HAT phone began to ring.

Activity stopped, as it always did, even though everyone knew phoning the HAT line from across the office was the prank of choice on bored days.

But this could never be said to be a bored day, and incredibly, it was still their unit's week on call. It felt like so much longer than five days since he'd been dispatched to Cheval Place.

"There cannae be a third ane," Scrivenor muttered. "I'm never moanin' about nae overtime again."

James chewed his lip as he watched the face of the officer taking the call.

Not a joke.

The three officers assigned to the Homicide Assessment Team were the ones sent out first to a call, to decide if a death appeared to be murder or an accident. An accident would be given to borough detectives; otherwise the on-call unit got it.

Details were yelled out as the HAT team left—a man found dead, facedown on his bed in an Earls Court bedsit, with an obvious head wound. Normally, the whole team would be primed and ready, but with Maria's murder still only days old, a call to Ingham had DI Mulligan, though still embroiled in his nightclub stabbing, sent to meet the HAT boys. And James, for the first time since he'd joined the MIT, got sent home after a genuine HAT phone call. He didn't even feel disappointed about it.

When he reached the flat, he found Ben had left some food for him, ready to heat up, because, an attached note said, James would have no time to eat otherwise. And as he looked, nonplussed, at the note and the cling-wrapped plate of chicken casserole, he couldn't help a frisson of pleasure at the gesture. There could be no question of backing out of the pub trip then, for all he'd had a few moments of inventing tortuous excuses to avoid going. But all in all, he felt his gung-ho optimism of the morning had held up pretty well, despite the day he'd had.

He got ready quickly, pulling on a faded lemon-yellow cotton shirt, old light-blue Levis, boots and a black wool peacoat. Then he grabbed his keys and racketed down the stairs.

He found Steggie letting himself out of his front door.

"Ooh, I'm in luck! It's The Bill!" he exclaimed. "And you won't often hear me say those two sentences in quick succession, I can assure *you*."

Steggie had a coat over his arm, and he wore tight red trousers and a black sleeveless T-shirt—even tighter—exposing a kind of armband tattoo inked round his biceps. He had an air of challenging sexiness about him, of intelligence and confidence, which made James feel incredibly conservative and boring in comparison. Still, he appreciated the consolation once-over Steggie gave him.

"Fancy a lift?" James asked.

"Oh yeah, please! So have you just come from work too, then?" Steggie asked as they headed for the door.

"Court Appearance. How about you?"

The front door swung closed behind them as they trotted down the steps to the pavement, and James took a second to wonder what it would look like, if anyone knew who they were, a policeman and a porn star out on the town together.

"Oh, just a straightforward shoot," Steggie said, campness all gone. "Nothing complicated." James gestured to the right, and they walked toward his car parked a few hundred yards away.

He tried not to imagine what a "straightforward shoot" would entail in porn, even as he groped for a way to show Steggie that James found his profession as acceptable as any other. As acceptable as... dentistry. Or...

"You must be really good at it," James said very casually as they walked side by side. "To own a flat here." And as his brain finally caught up with his mouth, "At acting. At acting, I mean."

Steggie shot him a disbelieving glance. "What a fabulous compliment, Inspector Clouseau."

"Sergeant." James grimaced. "Clouseau."

Steggie snorted. "Well the thing is…my fan base is very…*devoted*." He made the word sound filthy—echoes of rubber, whips and sponge baths. "And I produce as well as perform. That pays the mortgage more or less, and if I need to, I travel a bit, work in different studios."

"That'd keep your hand in," James agreed, grateful for Steggie's show of mercy, but the moment the words were out, he realized he'd done it again. He darted a wild glance sideways.

Steggie met his gaze with wide-open eyes, clearly trying to keep a straight face, but it was hopeless. They both started to laugh, and they were totally out of control by the time they reached the car.

"Do you know where to park?" Steggie asked, with lazy amiability as they set off. "It's not a car anyone's gonna bother keying."

James tried and failed to appear offended.

"But you never know," Steggie continued. "There's a street not far from the pub where it'd probably be safe overnight."

James changed gear smoothly. The roads were slick with the same fine rain that coated the windscreen. "No need. I'm still on call. No alcohol." Though he hadn't intended to drink anyway, with a group of people he'd never met before. Those days were past.

"Well, you're gonna get some serious stick for that, Detective Sergeant," Steggie warned.

James glanced at him then back at the road. He should have thought of that. The first impression Ben's friends were going to get of him would be "stereotypical uptight copper".

"Ah, don't worry, Jamie." Steggie seemed bizarrely able to read his mind. "Leave it to me."

They made easy conversation for the rest of the trip to the pub, as if they'd been friends for years, and James actually felt quite relaxed when they made it to the door of the Trafalgar.

Inside, the pub proved to be nicely decorated, with a blue-painted bar and decor hovering somewhere between minimalistic and twee. Somehow, it worked. Friday-night London crowds were out in force— but James could still see floor.

Steggie led them toward a large table set against a red-brick wall, with a curved, bright-blue leather bench built in at the back, and wooden stools and chairs around the front.

And there they were: Ben and his friends.

Ben had only reached the point himself of taking off his jacket and setting down a leather bag. James thought, with a pang, that he looked lithe and young and disturbingly beautiful in simple black jeans and a black rugby shirt.

Gratifyingly, his face lit up when he saw them. "Jamie! Steggie!"

"You play rugby?" James asked, surprised, as Ben hugged him in greeting. The shirt felt as soft as it appeared.

Ben pulled back to shoot him a disbelieving stare. He gestured to the logo on his chest. "For the Stella McCartney XV?"

James really hoped he hid his embarrassment. "Oh. Thought it looked a bit poofy."

Ben laughed. "Bet *you* played," he said provocatively, as he slid onto the bench. "At *Westminster*."

He patted the seat beside him, and James eased his way in as Steggie trotted off to get drinks without further consultation.

"Oh *yeah*," James returned, all remembered revelation. "You didn't mention you went to a fee-paying school yourself."

"Steggie." Ben sounded utterly betrayed.

James hid a grin and scanned the table. Everyone seemed unnaturally attractive and dressed edgily. In fact, they looked like what they were—a group of people who worked in some of the trendiest industries in London.

"This is Jamie," Ben introduced him grandly. "My new flatmate." James fixed a smile and tried not to feel surplus to requirements.

Beth, a model, lived with Gareth—something in fashion. Glynn, also a model, sat beside Naomi, Ben's lighting assistant. Steggie had given him the vital information in the car that Glynn and another guy called Oliver were gay, the others more or less straight. Given his useless gaydar, James had needed the heads-up.

"So," Glynn drawled, "you're the copper. Murder Squad, Ben said."

"Yeah. Well, a Murder Investigation Team," James replied.

"We thought Ben had lost the plot, letting a policeman move in," Beth threw in helpfully. "But now we see you, it all makes sense."

Ben put his head in his hands.

"It must be *such* a tough job though," Beth went on with great conviction.

"What must?" A new voice. James glanced up to see a tall, slim man shouldering off a clearly expensive leather jacket.

"Olly!" Ben shouted happily and the man grinned back at him. "Jamie, this is Oliver. He's in PR, so everything he says is a lie."

James couldn't help but wonder wanly if Ben had any ordinary friends because Oliver was even more attractive than Glynn, who was attractive for a living. He had short brown hair and careful stubble, a wide mouth and pretty green eyes. His features were even, regular and masculine. He could have represented a media stereotype of the ideal gay man.

"It must be so *awful*," Naomi took over from Beth. "Arresting people. And telling people someone they love died."

James sighed inwardly. Still his turn then. Aloud, he said, "Yeah... yeah it is. That's by far the worst part of the job...telling relatives. But someone has to be there to do it. Arresting people's okay though," he finished provocatively.

A short silence descended. Naomi held his gaze, and James wondered if everyone was considering their own legal status. Then he recognized that Naomi's regard appeared less interested than avid.

He cleared his throat.

"You have the most amazing *eyes*," she said finally, voice a dreamy singsong. "They're sort of...silver. And with that dark ring on the outside..."

James looked sharply away, horrified. But as his color rose relentlessly, she became even more complimentary about his bone structure and his coloring, insistent that he should do some shots for an agency. *Really* he should.

He could feel Ben beside him vibrating with laughter, and Steggie, who'd arrived with their drinks, began to make encouraging noises about a modeling career. James felt sullenly sure it had to be revenge for his own blundering earlier on, or possibly his early refusal to do porn.

"Test shots!" Ben exclaimed.

For a second, James thought he meant liquor, but Ben grabbed the leather bag from the floor at his feet and slid rapidly backwards up the leather bench dragging a large Nikon camera from the bag as he went, until he sat perched on the back of it, boots on the blue seat cushions. Once there, he snapped off the lens cap and pointed the lens straight at James. The whole fluid sequence of movement took only seconds.

James opened his mouth to protest even as he heard the first loud, spastic clicks of the shutter. He flinched and turned his face away to profile, but the camera shutter kept chattering. He knew his expression would be as carefully blank as he'd learned to make it from boyhood, but he could do nothing about the heat of violent embarrassment radiating off his skin.

"Best get it over with, love," Glynn advised with apparent sympathy. "He's fucking relentless. Voice of experience here. If he doesn't get you now, he'll get you when you're hurling your guts up. Or 'aving a shit. So you do it on your own terms."

The group grinned at James as if they expected him to perform somehow for Ben's camera; only Oliver appeared detached. But James didn't have a clue how to "do it on his own terms". Simper? Glower, like models did? He hated having his photo taken at the best of times, as Georgia and her colleagues in Media and Communications had good cause to know.

He felt a hand squeeze his wrist briefly in solidarity. Steggie.

"Jamie. Here!" Ben snapped. James's gaze shot around at once, to obey.

Ben appeared entirely serious and professional, as if he really were directing a model. James's wide eyes met the gaping black eye of the lens.

"Beautiful," he heard Ben say softly from behind the camera. "Just…do that. Focus on me. Forget everyone else."

And James did, as the shutter whirred and clicked over and over again. Even in the hubbub of the pub, surrounded by people watching them, it felt intimate. Private.

When Ben lowered the camera, he smiled, radiating satisfaction, and without comment, he slid back down into his seat.

Conversation continued at the table as if nothing had happened, much to James's relief, but when he glanced around, he noticed that Oliver's attention hadn't wavered from him. He contemplated James as if he'd discovered a new species.

Or perhaps, a new, startled thought, *perhaps he fancies me.*

The unexpected possibility hit him with a lurch of unease. Because…he hadn't come searching for it, but…hell, it was well past time he tried. Even if Oliver could probably eat him alive.

"How're you settling in?" Oliver asked. James shifted with nervous anticipation.

"Settling in?" James parroted.

"To Ben's flat."

Shit. Of course. "Oh. It's great."

Oliver took a sip of his drink, something clear, like gin or vodka, and made a noncommittal sound.

"Yeah. Did you know there were thirteen other people after it?" he asked pleasantly. "And yet…here you are."

James frowned. "I was lucky."

"You were. Still…interesting choice. I saw a couple of the others."

Their eyes met and held. Oliver's were full of a challenge James didn't understand. Except he could be pretty sure now that it wasn't attraction.

"Oliver's a bit touchy about the police," Ben confided loudly beside him. "Since he got done for possession."

Oliver's cat eyes turned toward Ben. He didn't appear amused.

"I'm not trying to—" James began.

"We *know*," Steggie put in quickly from James's other side. "Off-duty's off-duty, yeah?" He gave James a comradely nudge. "Don't be a wanker, Olly."

Oliver's expression barely changed, but James could hardly miss the charged undercurrent between he and Steggie. After a moment or two of silent communication, though, Oliver turned back to the others, leaving James feeling out of his depth and stupidly deflated.

Maybe it just wasn't possible to be a policeman and successfully gay.

"Ignore Olly," Ben said quietly. Then, tone still gentle, "Hey, I hope I didn't embarrass you. I get carried away behind a camera."

James turned to find Ben closer than expected, close enough to make out strands of lighter blue in his irises, the first dusting of evening stubble on his fine-pored skin, the insane thickness of his lashes.

And James felt familiar, unwanted excitement thud into his gut, the unique, visceral reaction he had to Ben that he just couldn't seem to divert himself from or talk himself out of.

"I love watching people through the lens," Ben went on innocently. "You see deeper that way." His full pink lips pressed together and he raised his eyebrows comically. "And don't I just sound like a pretentious tit? Anyway. I am sorry, Jamie."

James frowned at his low-ball glass of sparkling water. Steggie had done a sterling job of disguising it as a gin and tonic, even down to the hunk of lime.

"So…" He gazed up again at Ben, challenging. "Private school?"

"It was progressive!" Ben protested.

James grinned. *Open goal.* "Yeah? Progressive enough to let kids in without paying?"

Ben kept his face straight for a few seconds, then his mouth began to quiver. "Okay, Posh Boy. Bloody touché." James raised a quelling eyebrow, and Ben let himself laugh out loud. "That's brilliant. You do that in interrogations?"

"So how *progressive*, exactly?"

And Ben happily began to tell James all about his schooldays in Hampstead, with no uniform and no homework, and no pressure from his rich, liberal parents. No one interrupted them.

Were they flirting? It felt to James as if they were flirting hard, focus never leaving each other, smiling helplessly, animated. Butterflies thrummed beneath his breastbone: hope, fear, elation.

By the end of Ben's account of his childhood, James was zinging in mocking one-liners, and Ben didn't even try not to find them funny.

Finally, they began to quieten.

"Naomi's interested in you," Ben murmured, warmly conspiratorial. "I can tell."

James sighed. "She's not exactly my type, is she?"

"Well..." Ben shrugged and loosed a shit-eating grin. "I don't know if you're bi, do I? Or...whatever. I'm just trying to get you some action."

Get him some action? Fuck, he must seem pretty pathetic.

"I had a girlfriend when I came out to my father," James volunteered. He remembered with painful clarity the exact expression on Ellie's face as she'd sent him off on his great adventure, the grief of hopeless, unrequited love. "If I were bi...I'd probably have been in love with her."

Ben regarded him carefully. "But you're not?"

James's mouth twisted. "No. I'm not."

He took a sip of his drink, sensing Ben's frowning attention fixed on him. He glanced up, and their gazes locked and held for too long. Too long to be comfortable. James's pulse began to speed up, then to pound.

"She's right, you know," Ben murmured almost absently into the breathless silence between them. "You really are something."

Somehow James found a smirk to paste on, to show he hadn't been taken in at all, but he became aware of something, some last wary defense, slipping away, and he felt like a tiny ship caught uselessly in the tractor beam of Ben's charm.

James's phone, lying on the table in front of him, screeched through the moment, and James jolted in place as if someone had shaken him awake.

It took him a second or two to fumble it into his hand. He stared at the number on the display with apprehension.

"Alec?" James checked his watch. It read just before ten thirty.

"You're on, son. There been another one."

James blinked twice, sure he'd misunderstood. "You mean...a *fourth...?*"

"Aye. That's what I mean. It's like the fuckin' twilight zone. They're comin' in twos."

James sucked in a heavy breath. "Where?"

"Ah just got a heads-up on a 999. A woman found in a car in Flood Street. Severe blow to the head. She's hangin' on though."

"That's a few minutes from here. I'm on the King's Road." James could feel the adrenalin rush hitting, shooting through his veins.

"Well, get yer arse down there then. The HAT boys are at Earls Court wi' Mulligan. I've sent Barry an' Ken to this ane, tae set things up, but they're still on the way. I dinnae think even the response car's there yet. Look...you get there as soon as you can, aw right? Get the lie of the land. Herself is on the way too."

"Okay. Thanks, Alec." James closed off the call and turned to Ben, who'd been staring at him with frank fascination.

"Call out," James said, already on his feet and shouldering into his jacket.

"Ooh...has there been a murder?" Steggie stood excitedly to let him out. Glynn and Naomi were gazing up at James with the same awe as if he'd just whipped off his clothes to reveal a superhero leotard beneath.

"And you have to go." Oliver made no attempt at regret.

James ignored him and focused on Ben.

"I don't know when I'll be home. Could be a couple of days." It occurred to him only as he said it how domestic it sounded.

"I'll keep your slippers warmed," Ben said. Then, more urgently, "Hope it works out, Jamie."

Steggie gave James an encouraging pat on the back as he moved away. "Good luck," he called, echoed by the raucous good wishes of the rest of the table. And James, for the first time since he became a policeman, found himself heading for work like a hero going off to war, warmed by an insidious sense of friendship.

But that didn't stop him from elbowing his way brutally through the crowds packing the pub, until at last he'd fought his way to the door and shoved out into the freezing night air.

The moment he stepped out onto the pavement, he began to run.

The ground was damp from a day of drizzle, but no rain fell now. The air hung damp, and cold, and still.

The King's Road bustled and heaved in full Friday-night mode.

It was mainly a shopping street, so calmer in the evening than the tourist madness of Covent Garden or Piccadilly. But still…too busy. The two-storied red-brick wall of shops and bars and restaurants spilled customers idly onto the pavement: huddles of smokers; girls in tight, short dresses and teetering heels; packs of laughing young men. At just the wrong time a cinema had disgorged a slow mob onto the road, chattering, comparing notes, blind to James's urgency as he carved his way through them.

He darted, then, through the slow-moving traffic to the other side of the street, racing along the gutter until he reached the entrance to Flood Street.

James could see it at once as he reached the opening—impossible to miss—the silent blue pulsing light of an ambulance, double-parked halfway down a long, otherwise deserted road. He didn't pause; he propelled himself round the corner and ran toward the scene at the same desperate pace, belting past a couple of cars, a long rack of Boris Bikes.

On one side, James vaguely registered the brick facades and white porticos of old warehouses converted into flats and offices; on the other side, smaller red-brick buildings which might be homes. He saw a few lit windows, but after the bright roar of the King's Road, the dingy-orange light of the street, the emptiness of the pavements, felt shocking. All he could hear was the thud-thud of his boots, the gasping efficiency of his own breath.

He skidded to a halt beside the ambulance and reached for his warrant card, but no one paid attention. The only onlooker, a well-dressed white woman, stood to the side and sobbed quietly, holding two, small, struggling spaniels on their leads.

Two male paramedics knelt, working on a girl lying on her back on the wet road beside the open door of a soft-top Mercedes. And all James could make out at first were impressions as the surreal flashing light of the ambulance came and went, back and forth—startling blue to the dull orange of the street lamps then back to blue.

Long, silky dark hair spreading out on the tarmac like a pool of oil round a white oval. The woman's skirt, riding obscenely high on her stockinged thighs. The medics, working without cease—one small and wiry, with a full head of grey hair, the other big and half-bald and bulging out of his uniform.

"Detective Sergeant Henderson, South Kensington MIT," James identified himself, if only somehow to make himself part of their effort. "A blow to the head?" It struck him how little blood there seemed to be.

The larger medic glanced at him for a second, no more, then back down to his work.

"Not a blow. She was shot." He had thick London accent, uncompromising. "I think she's been 'ere quite a while." He rapped out to his colleague, "Pulse is thready and rapid."

James moved sideways cautiously until the oval resolved into a pretty blank face, upper lip smeared with blood, wide-open eyes. The girl looked obscenely young, almost a child.

"Shouldn't she be dead, then?" James asked stupidly, because gunshot wounds to the head were fatal ninety percent of the time. To have any chance, victims needed fast treatment.

"She's hangin' on, aren't you, darlin'?" the medic said. "You don't wanna go. You're gonna be my miracle." He pressed an oxygen mask to her face, concealing her pert nose and full, slack mouth, leaving only those agonized eyes. "Gunshot wound behind the right ear but not a lot of bleeding." He whipped out a penlight and shone it into her eye as the smaller medic attached an IV line to her arm. "Pupils are sluggish but do contract. Let's load!"

The smaller man darted into the ambulance and slid out a stretcher, which James helped manhandle to the ground, then he watched uselessly as the paramedics skillfully lifted the woman onto it.

Fuck! A bullet through her brain. How much longer can she possibly have?

"Where are you taking her?"

The medics didn't pause. They lifted the stretcher into the ambulance and immediately began to attach wires and tubes. Without thought, James climbed in too. A machine was bleeping loudly and far too fast.

"I said…"

"The London," the larger man snapped, hands moving automatically, checking bags of fluid and the monitors above her head.

"But that's in Whitechapel! She'll never last till there. There's a hospital just up the fucking road."

"No Accident an' Emergency. An' the London has a neurosurgery department. They're prepping for her... Fuck fuck *fuck*! She's seizing!"

James sat down quickly, out of the way, on a low bed on the opposite side of the ambulance, watching, horrified as the girl's body stiffened and her arms and legs jerked violently. The unmistakable, sharp, meaty stench of urine filled the ambulance.

James could barely take in what was happening, but he recognized that, and his heart ached with compassion for her.

The paramedics turned the girl on to her side, an airway now shoved into her mouth. Then began, what seemed to James, a kind of frantic dance around her, to a horrible soundtrack of beeps and whines, shouted instructions about Valium and Phenytoin, oxygen saturation, atropine...

From where he sat uselessly, gut roiling, James could see her bloodied doll's face, mouth stretched and distorted around the tube, as her body convulsed and convulsed until at last she stilled. Her large, dark, mascaraed eyes were at a level now with his own, and he could almost believe, as he stared at her, that they were holding each other's gaze.

He felt again that desperate pull of human recognition as he sat helplessly, witness to her terror. He knew he must be projecting, that the likelihood she retained consciousness had to be vanishingly small, but somehow the brutal cacophony around them faded, and he felt such pity, such grief for her.

He was dimly aware that she'd been turned to her back again, that the medics were shouting, pushing a defibrillator to her chest, but her head lolled toward his as if she were searching for him. Her body jerked in a spastic arc, then relaxed. Her wide eyes still held his.

"Hang on, sweetheart," he murmured. "You're being so brave."

She blinked.

James let out a soft sound of shock. Without thought, he reached between the medics, pushing and shoving and fighting for her life, and grabbed hold of her hand, dangling limply over the side of the cot bed. It felt cold and small, with little bird bones.

"Heyyy!" The disbelieving relief, the shock of euphoria he felt, was indescribable. "Hello there! You're gonna be..."

"That's it," the larger medic said shortly. "I'm calling it at...22:53."

James frowned up at him, bewildered, until he registered that the only sound remaining in the ambulance was a relentless, ugly, single note.

Her hand felt warmer in his though, and her eyes were still wide open.

—‖— —‖— —‖— —‖—

"Romilly Crompton. Twenty-three. Lived alone." James held up the evidence tape and let Ingham duck under it, until she could peer inside the open driver's door of the car around which white-clad forensics officers were humming and hovering, like ghostly bees in the sodium streetlights.

James, peering over her shoulder, couldn't distinguish the blood on the dark leather seat or the carpet of the footwell, but he knew it must be there, melded in after the best part of a day, camouflaged by the shifting shadows.

His watch informed him it was just after midnight. Saturday morning now.

He felt detached from everything; nothing felt important enough to impact his emotions. He could barely comprehend that just a couple of hours ago he'd been worrying about who fancied him in the pub.

Eric, the larger paramedic, said he was probably in shock, which didn't sit well with him at all. He might not have seen someone die in front of him before, but he'd seen more than his share of dead people.

As had the medics, of course. But still, after the machines had been turned off, the three of them had waited in the ambulance in silence, like a vigil, listening to the sirens of the police response car getting louder and closer.

Eric had told him it was unusual for a patient's eyes to remain open during the kind of seizure the girl had endured. "Tonic-clonic," he'd called it. In James's mind that read as one more proof of how desperately she'd fought for every minute she had left in the light, before she'd been forced into the darkness for good.

He'd managed to snap out of it, to pull his head out of his own arse, when the first uniformed PC had poked her head inside the open doors. And when his own MIT team, in the form of Ken and Barry screeched up moments later, he'd briefed them and dispatched them to do some preliminary questioning door-to-door.

Then, standing apart from the gathering knot of spectators, he'd noticed the woman who'd been there when he arrived, still hovering with her dogs, makeup grotesquely streaked with tears and snot.

As he'd suspected, she'd first spotted the girl slumped across the passenger seat of her car, tried to get some response from her, and dialed 999. It had been pure good luck—terrible luck for her, James supposed—that one of her Cavalier King Charles spaniels, on their evening walk, had stopped to shit beside the Merc, and she'd had to crouch down to bag it up.

Without that, the girl would have died quietly and alone, and very possibly her corpse would have lain where she'd been abandoned for an indeterminate time, until someone started worrying about her. After all, how many people really looked inside parked cars?

When Ingham arrived, shortly after Ken and Barry, James had felt as relieved by the sight of her calm face as he'd felt the first time his mother had come to fetch him home from school.

"You all right?" she asked.

James swallowed and nodded curtly. He could see uneasy sympathy in her eyes, but he didn't want to talk about *how he felt*, especially when he'd rather not feel anything at all.

She headed for the ambulance, followed, like a loyal Labrador, by James.

"I'm assuming she didn't say anything before she died," she called over her shoulder.

James bit the inside of his lip hard. "No."

The back doors of the ambulance hung wide open, and inside, the elegantly patrician divisional surgeon crouched on the ambulance floor to work.

The victim lay on her back as she had died, head to the side, but someone must have moved her slightly, because her long hair had slipped down over her face like a shroud, to cover her. As they watched, the doctor pulled some of the dark, silky mass back gently, like a lover, or a father, and tucked it tenderly behind her ear. A police camera flashed with bright violence over his head.

Both paramedics were getting their boot and fingerprints taken by SOCO, and their DNA would be swabbed there and then, for convenience. James's boots had been done as well. None of them had considered the sanctity of the crime scene in the desperation of their fight, but now it had to be all about the cold aftermath.

The pathologist glanced up and let out an audible breath, mouth pursed with unprofessional sadness. His first job was always to officially declare life extinct, however obviously dead the body. This one was very dead.

"Just a guide at this point, Detective Chief Inspector, but as you can see, cause of death would appear to be a close-range gunshot wound to the head. Two, in fact. It's hard to ascertain how long ago the attack took place, but my guess is she's been here since yesterday morning."

James rubbed a hand over his mouth, and he didn't know how to process what he felt.

All day. All evening. Lying there alone.

That was even longer than he'd imagined or feared or believed medically possible. She really had clung on to her life for as long and as fiercely as she could.

It meant too that they were well on the back foot with this case already...twenty-odd hours gone since the attack happened. And still, Maria's case—*his* case—reproachfully unsolved. Fuck—he'd watched her parents bury her only her hours before. The unit couldn't slacken their efforts for her. Yet James had no clue how they could cope with all this—with four murders in a week.

At least they had one crumb of consolation—according to Alec, Mulligan's second case seemed straightforward, the lucky bastard. An argument, a fall, a suspect already in custody. Manslaughter, most probably.

"What do we know, Jamie?" Ingham asked, as she always did.

James rubbed his fingers across his aching eyes. "Apart from name and address, not a lot yet, ma'am. No witnesses. No official CCTV in this street." So far, so familiar. James watched her head drop in despair.

"The victim lived round the corner, in a block of flats on the King's Road."

Ingham nodded slowly. She looked small and exhausted, James thought with a pang of worry. He could only imagine the pressure of final responsibility for all of this.

All around them, blue squad-car lights winked and flashed in silence. The ambulance light had been extinguished.

"I've sent Sameera to trawl for any private CCTV tapes," he went on. "The night concierge at her building said Romilly usually left for work at about four thirty a.m., and he last saw her yesterday morning. She works in breakfast TV."

"TV?" Ingham repeated sharply. "How do you know?"

"The concierge knew." He held up a plastic evidence bag containing a Chanel wallet. "Name, date of birth, address and place of work. That's all we've got at this stage."

"Gunshots," Ingham said. "But no one heard anything?"

"A silencer presumably. Maybe a pro. Victim left neatly out of the way so she'd be unlikely to be found quickly. That took some thought. Except... They weren't killing shots."

"You think that was deliberate?" Ingham eyed him narrowly. "Make her suffer?"

James pressed his lips hard together. He found himself heavily invested now in the hope that the girl had never achieved any real consciousness, whatever he'd brought himself to see at that last moment. He told himself over and over that her mind had to have died with the bullets, leaving only her body trailing behind, ticking through the motions.

"Or the victim struggled and he—or she—muffed the shot," he said.

Ingham shrugged. "Not so professional in that case. Though I suppose even pros fuck up."

"I've been thinking, ma'am..." He fucking hated to be the bringer of all the bad news. "We should possibly brace ourselves for a feeding frenzy on this one."

Ingham regarded him without expression. They both knew the press would be interested. But he could tell she hadn't got it yet. He drew a deep breath.

"Pretty girl working in TV? Killed by a gunman?" he prompted.

Ingham frowned, still not quite there.

"The Jill Dando thing?" he continued.

And then she was. Dando had been a TV news presenter killed on her doorstep by a shot in the head, one of the most memorable murder victims in modern Britain.

Ingham closed her eyes and let out a despairing sound. "Sometimes I wish you'd stop thinking, Jamie."

James grimaced in sympathy as the full implications of the mess they were in hit him, just as he knew they must be striking Ingham.

The miasma of a stalled major investigation hung around a squad and the officers involved, like dogshit, subtly infecting morale and career prospects. And seriously focused press interest made failure infinitely more damaging. Now they had two simultaneous high-interest cases to potentially cock up, and not enough manpower to deal with them.

"*Shit!*" Ingham almost visibly pulled her determination around her. "This is... I'm going to have to go hands-on again and fuck the budget meetings. This is out of control."

James nodded. *Out of control.*

It came treacherously close to his own train of thought: if he'd been able to find a quick way through Maria's case, use that supposed intuition; if he hadn't fucked up the first investigation he'd been trusted to lead; if he hadn't let Ingham down...

"We can't run one each," Ingham went on. "We don't have enough people to share out. I need Alec to stay as office manager. Mulligan can deal with his two. But Maria and this one...you and me...we'll have to duck and weave between them."

It took a few seconds for James to fully accept that there was no trace of reproach in her voice. Nothing like his father, at the slightest whiff of failure.

She knew him too well.

"*Jamie.*" She shook her head impatiently. "You have to stop beating the fuck out of yourself. You've covered every angle on Maria. I *have* been keeping track." She sighed and seemed to deflate again. "Let's just hope this one's...*simpler.*"

=||= =||= =||= =||=

Back at the station, Ingham called the team together in the briefing room, now set up for the new case. She looked grim, pared down. James sat near the front, arms folded, beside Scrivenor, and willed her on.

He had to force himself to study the board of photographs behind her, because each image brought back too many unwelcome emotions. Too close, too soon. He felt only impatience at his own weakness.

"Settle!" Ingham rattled quickly through the basic details, then she waited for a second or two, mouth thin, as the implications sank in around the room. That in terms of a media feeding-frenzy, apart from a member of the royal family or a movie star, the case couldn't get much worse.

Ingham continued doggedly. "The victim's father is Anthony Crompton, a senior investment banker at Goldman Sachs. Mother is Faye Ralph, a criminologist, campaigning author and commentator. We have some tape of Romilly in the lobby of her building heading out to work at 4:26 a.m. yesterday morning. And that's it so far."

James stretched his weary frame as Ingham handed out tasks: various DCs were dispatched to seek witnesses and any CCTV at all; others were assigned for that day to working through the multiple possible avenues that remained open in Maria's case. James was to oversee both, assisting Ingham.

James made himself examine the images on the board as she spoke—the interior of Romilly's flat, the car, the gutter beside it. Romilly's vacant, dead face. He felt a nudge of loss and familiarity, as if someone he'd known had died.

He and Ingham still had to face the drive out to Holland Park to notify the Cromptons. He tried not to dwell on it.

He focused on Ingham instead as she launched into her final pep talk: the traditional "Aragorn at the Black Gate go and get 'em" speech, to a group of people who were more than capable of adding one and one and getting a very unfortunate two.

They were working a second high-profile case while they still had no whiff of a solid line of inquiry on the first one. Not even Aragorn could have pumped much joy into that.

8

"Well, I'd say she looked good on camera, loved acting the part." Clara Daley, Romilly's Deputy Head of News, sat behind her tidy desk, in a room made up mainly of windows, bathed in dull, white February light. The room reeked of stale coffee and stale cigarettes.

Clara was a thin, brittle blonde who'd been landed with James and Ingham because her boss declared himself unavailable. James suspected she probably wouldn't see fifty again, but she appeared well-preserved, well-exercised and ruthlessly well-groomed, radiating the kind of amused cynicism James had found many journalists worked to cultivate. She hadn't even tried to pretend grief.

"Acting?" James repeated, tone chilly.

He realized that his impartiality had probably been compromised, but to him the Romilly this woman had described seemed nothing like the dying child whose hand he'd held.

Clara smiled at him. In fact, she'd been smiling at him since she'd laid eyes on him. "Every decent news presenter's a bit of a showpony, Sergeant," she declared sweetly. "I mean, no one behaves like that naturally, do they? Romilly adored it."

"Adored journalism, or being on camera?" Ingham asked.

"I don't think she gave a toss about journalism, frankly. She just did whatever it took to get to the front of the scrum, to get her face on the telly."

A tiny pause. "You didn't like her," Ingham observed.

Clara regarded her sharply. James could see it had struck a nerve, and he fully accepted, then, that the mild hostility he'd been feeling toward Clara sprang from her clear disdain for Romilly.

Fucking hell. He needed to get a grip. He should be using Clara's obvious reaction to him, not pissing her off.

Clara leaned back in her chair, glaring at Ingham. "How did you get there from what I said, Detective Chief Inspector? I just described eighty percent of the up-and-coming talent in TV. Romilly used sharp elbows, like the rest of the crowd. But she seemed okay. I mean, narcissistic as all hell and totally in it for the attention, but she wasn't nasty."

"So how did she get to the front of the crowd?" James asked.

Clara turned to him, and her wide, red, lipsticked mouth tilted upward, as if she couldn't help it.

"Well, I suppose this isn't relevant," she began, still eyeing him. "But I know you're going to hear it. Geoff—my boss—he's a good friend of Romilly's mother. They used to be colleagues. Anyway, the rumor went round that he got Romilly in here because of that. A bit of nepotism. Everyday stuff in this business."

"The rumor went round?" James even managed a smile.

"All right, he *did* get her in as a favor to her mother," Clara twinkled back at him. "There might have been some resentment once the gossip started. But Geoff genuinely seemed to see star quality."

"And you didn't?"

Clara seemed momentarily surprised to have been asked.

"Well." She pressed her bright-red lips together. "Okay. Romilly was one of those rich girls who can pick and choose careers like this as an ego boost. Geoff rated her more highly than I did. He's going to be devastated when he hears. I *mean*," she corrected herself quickly. "Of course. *Everyone* will be really upset."

James raised an eyebrow and wrote some more. He glanced up. "Was there anything romantic between them?"

Clara bristled like a startled cat, and James could sense Ingham still beside him. But then, she had to pay more attention to political sensitivities than he did.

"Between Geoff and Romilly?" Clara scoffed. Her smile had vanished. "He has daughters older than her!"

James didn't allow his expression to change.

Clara flushed. "Look. I don't know." Then, "All right! There were rumors...*again*. I put them down to resentment that she had the inside track with him. He was obviously fond of her, but she turned on the charm with him. You've heard of the cliché...a man's woman?"

No, Clara really *hadn't* liked her. Only death had earned Romilly any leeway with her.

"She had a lot of boyfriends, then?" Ingham asked.

Clara's large, hooded eyes swung to her. "You could say. She liked to brag a bit."

"Brag?" Ingham encouraged.

"Well…she used to joke about it at news meetings, though I'm not sure the men were laughing," she said dryly. "Let's just say, the way she talked, they were smitten and she could take them or leave them. They tended to be rich…gave her a lot of gifts she didn't need…I don't know any details…though I think I heard her describe the last one as a bit of a silver fox." She mused, "Hard on Geoff."

A tiny beat of silence, then Clara's eyes widened in obvious alarm.

"Did you get a name? Anything that could identify him?" Ingham asked, as if she hadn't heard any implications at all.

"I'm not sure," Clara rushed on. "Something like George or Charles or Arthur… Something…upper class. She dumped him before Christmas anyway. I think she said he was getting too intense."

James's phone buzzed loudly in his pocket, and he grimaced an awkward apology to Ingham as he pulled it out.

A text from Ben.

You didn't get home. Hope you got some kip. Eat breakfast. Or lunch. Preferably both.

James stared at it as if it came from another world.

━╫━ ━╫━ ━╫━ ━╫━

James turned on the ignition of their car before Ingham finally let her stolid mask drop.

"It's not gonna be simple, is it?" she fretted. "Unless Forensics comes up with something, or the *silver fox* is conveniently violent, what're we left with? A deranged fan? A resentful colleague?" She blew out a hard breath. "Let's hope to God something came from her flat. And where did the thing about Romilly and her boss come from anyway? Talk about a leap!"

James supposed he should feel flattered that Ingham expected him to produce a solid reason, when in reality, as so often, it'd been nothing more than gut instinct.

"Just…something about the way Clara talked about her. Romilly. It reminded me of Gill about Maria." He put the car in gear as he caught Ingham's frown, and reversed out of their parking space. "There *are* parallels, ma'am," he ventured, "between them. Romilly and Maria. They both seem to have been exceptionally charming and ambitious.

Emotionally unavailable, maybe. And…" He tapped the steering wheel absently. "Both killings have possible signs of a contract."

Out of the corner of his eye, he saw Ingham glaring at him. "You're making wild assumptions, Jamie."

"I know. It's just a feeling." He pulled up beside the guard hut, on the way out of the TV station's car park, and waited for the barrier to rise. Then he couldn't help trying: "But there are similarities."

He edged the car out onto the main road and the heavy afternoon traffic, waiting for retribution.

"Jamie," Ingham gritted out. "Don't even *go* there unless you have something solid. You're trying to link them because they both happened on our patch and they were close together in time. *And*…okay, they're young professional females. That's it. The connections are superficial. They have *totally* different MOs for a start. Say one had happened *next* month, would you be pushing a link? No."

James nodded tightly. Message understood. No one wanted a serial.

But the press would ask. They made tenuous links and insane leaps of logic as a matter of routine.

Ingham sighed impatiently, as if she could read his mind. "*Fuck.* Okay. I'll put Sameera onto it, *just* so we rule it out. But it's a waste of manpower."

A short, tense silence fell. James knew he should feel pleased, but he found little satisfaction in her concession. He wanted her to see the possibilities, not just try to close them down.

"I'll take the postmortem on Monday," Ingham announced out of the blue. "You can get on with things at the office."

James glanced in shock at her then back at the road. "But—"

"Jamie," Ingham cut him off. He could tell she'd prepared for his resistance. "Our whole fucking job's about death. But it doesn't hit home till you see a life go out in front of you." Her voice softened. "Maybe you should talk to someone."

James pressed his lips together, keeping all his emotion inside. "Ma'am, I don't need a counselor. And I can handle a PM."

Ingham made a restless movement, but whatever she wanted to say, she reduced to a simple, "She's real to you. You don't have to watch her being cut apart."

James swallowed, suddenly unable to say any more. He couldn't understand why he'd been reacting so dramatically. He'd believed himself to be tougher than that. He'd been *raised* to be tougher. But the visit to the Cromptons that morning had been beyond hellish, and James felt as if he'd watched Romilly's mother die in front of him too. When he considered what he'd see at the postmortem, he understood the gift Ingham had given him.

By the time they'd arrived back at their desks, James felt distanced by fatigue and suppressed emotion, as if he were watching life go by on TV rather than being personally involved. It almost felt like a good thing.

That night he caught a few hours' kip on one of the office camp beds, but he could allow himself no more because he had to sift through the list of Romilly's friends which their FLOs had managed to coax from the Cromptons. Plus he needed to review work on Maria's case.

So he worked from the early hours and through the rest of that day—Sunday—but it proved to be a slog of disappointing forensics and distraught friends and useless interviews with Romilly's neighbors.

There were moments it felt as if he were on an endless journey through a morass of weariness and human misery, and the only bright spots were the sprinkling of encouraging, concerned texts from Ben— messages from the outside, where things were good and normal.

James texted back when he could, and perhaps it was the vulnerability of exhaustion, but he allowed the evidence of Ben's interest, his worry for him, to thrum away safely inside him, a low riff of excited hope.

▬ll▬ ▬ll▬ ▬ll▬ ▬ll▬

At lunchtime on Sunday, when James walked into Ingham's office to collect her for the inevitable press briefing, she looked stony, braced for a battering.

"The Chief Super's attending," she said by way of greeting, which proved that the top brass were well aware of the potential shitstorm gathering around Ingham's MIT. "By the way, the Cromptons' FLO just called in. According to Romilly's dad, she'd been getting fan mail through the post he didn't like. Anonymous, and in mirror writing."

James blinked. "I thought that went out with Twitter."

"This is an old-fashioned nut. He, or she, sent letters in actual envelopes, with actual stamps, but the thing is, the last two were sent to Romilly's home address not the newsroom. Romilly's father wanted to report it, but she wanted advice on the PR implications, apparently."

"Right. The career boost of being seen to inspire crazed fans, as against prosecuting them."

Ingham gave a wry grin. "Yeah. Well, her dad's blaming himself now for not pushing her to report it."

"I've something for you too, ma'am," James said quickly. "The foxy boyfriend's turned up, through Romilly's phone contacts. His name's Charles Priestly. Sameera arranged an interview for us the day after tomorrow."

Ingham nodded, marginally more relaxed. "Nothing more from SOCO in the flat?"

"Ken's going through all her documentation, and Barry's onto her laptop."

"Okay then." Ingham sighed. "The mother's still totally out of it, and the father's not much better."

Remembering the state in which he and Ingham had left them, James couldn't be surprised. He chewed his lip for a second then decided to go for it.

"I've been thinking—that's actually another parallel with Maria. Both sets of parents are extra-liberal about criminal punishment."

Ingham regarded him with weary patience. "You don't give up, do you? Well, for your *satisfaction*, I asked Romilly's father. And no, the Cromptons didn't know Maria. And Maria's parents say they didn't know Romilly."

"Right," James returned. So much for his bloody intuition. Yet something inside him couldn't seem to let it go. "Faye's books on the criminal-justice system, though, they're like listening to Dame Cordelia. Big on alternatives to jail. No one is naturally evil. All that kind of thing."

"You read her stuff?" Ingham looked startled.

James rubbed his nose. "Read the reviews on Amazon."

Ingham rolled her eyes and stood up. "Just focus on something a bit more tangible. Priestly. And the letter writer." She pulled down her top and straightened her suit jacket. "Right. Time to face the scum. Or did I mean scrum?"

"Maybe it won't be that bad, ma'am."

But it was.

Timed deliberately to hit the evening bulletins and the next-day papers, the press conference heaved with journalists and TV cameras—far more than usual for a briefing like this.

As he waited behind Ingham, ready to take their places, James's phone buzzed: *Are they ever letting you home?*

His pulse leapt slavishly. Annoyingly. Still he couldn't resist tapping a surreptitious reply as the conference began to settle around him: *Maybe tonight. Probably not.*

An instant response: *You must smell.*

And his own, as he tried to hide his smile: *You better believe it.*

Ingham took her place beside the beautifully groomed Detective Chief Superintendent in the ruthless white glare of the TV lights, and relayed the basic facts. Then the DCS took over the mess that followed, batting off questions like the consummate politician he was.

There were the inevitable, excitable Jill Dando comparisons. Could Romilly's murder be linked, since the Dando shooting remained unsolved? The same team was dealing with the second murder of a young woman in a week, in the same area. Were they connected? Were there any solid leads? Any suspects? Why weren't there any suspects? Any bone to throw the public, or were the team foundering? Were the Met considering launching a higher-powered investigation with a stronger team?

James sat beside them at the top table, barely able to resist covering his eyes as the Chief Superintendent unleashed all his oleaginous skills to flannel the hacks and underline Ingham's appeal for witnesses and information. But James knew the DCS would take out every second of embarrassment on Ingham's hide. He did not have the reputation of an understanding man.

When it ended, a grey-faced Ingham disappeared into her office with the DCS like a human sacrifice, slatted blinds closed, and James slid behind his desk across from Scrivenor, switching on his computer to begin the long wait for his monitor to light up.

"Bad?" Scrivenor asked. James gave a woeful grimace. Bad would be a flamboyant understatement. "She'll be a' right, son. We can cope wi' both cases." But James thought even Scrivenor looked worried.

At least with Romilly, there were still some active leads. But Maria... Alec had been unofficially supervising the small group of detectives currently focusing on her murder, overseeing the continuing slog through old files on her own cases and her parents' potential enemies; still trying to locate ex-boyfriends; still pursuing the Albanian link.

But everyone in the office sensed Maria's case slipping away, and irrational as Ingham might feel it to be, James felt that failure like a dagger to the heart.

—||— —||— —||— —||—

James didn't manage to leave the station and head for home until almost one a.m. on Monday morning.

He wasn't in the best shape to drive; he should have just requisitioned one of the camp beds again and put his head down there, but... *but*—he found himself desperate to get some straight hours on his own mattress before he had to be back on duty at eight thirty. Or— face it—he might as well admit that most of all he couldn't wait to see Ben at breakfast.

He could only muster up a kind of dazed relief when he turned in to Selworth Gardens and found a parking space a couple of hundred yards along from their front door. But he was so tired he took two tries at parallel parking to get the car in. He could only be grateful no one saw him.

Blearily, he fumbled out the computer bag he'd taken from work, his peacoat from the evening at the pub and a bag of dirty clothes, then he trudged to the front door and on up the stairs.

He was running on the dregs of his endurance, fuelled by coffee, Red Bull and Pro Plus tablets. But as he reached the front door of the flat, anticipation had begun to cloak his exhaustion. It was more than just animal relief at being home.

He could hardly deny the idiocy of forcing all this extra effort on himself, but somehow, it felt worth it. The hope he felt about this thing with Ben felt worth it—like a neon-bright spot in his mind—new and exciting and full of limitless possibility. The kind of thing other people had.

At some point over the past couple of days he'd realized that the only person he wanted to talk to about Romilly's death was Ben—what he could tell him at least. Not a counselor. Ben. He wondered if that classed as "bringing work home".

The buzz of optimism revived him; sufficently to realize that he should make as little noise as possible. But as he silently opened the flat door, he heard the murmur of the TV in the lounge.

The remnants of exhaustion dropped off his shoulders like a tattered coat, stomach skittering with elation and new confidence. Because Ben had obviously stayed in and waited up, on the off-chance that James would come home.

Ben wanted to see him. Ben wanted to see James, as badly as James wanted to see him.

He carefully hung up his jacket and dropped his bags onto the hall carpet, smiling crazily as he crept along to the lounge for a surprise entrance. The lounge door lay slightly ajar, lamps lit, but it still took him too many seconds to process what he saw when he pushed the door open a further inch or two.

From where James stood, partly in the dim hallway, he had a good view of someone—a man—sitting on the sofa. His hair appeared even longer than Ben's and a much lighter brown.

And as James registered that, he accepted the rest of the scene.

That the man's trousers and underpants were clumped around his ankles; that his shoulders and chest were bare; his head thrown back, neck stretched, eyes closed.

That another man—Ben—knelt between the seated man's legs, dark curls brushing his naked back, jeans halfway down his thighs, giving the stranger on his sofa a very enthusiastic blowjob.

James stood numb with shock in the doorway, listening to the man's moans—the soft, wet, obscene sounds of suckling. He saw Ben's dark head bobbing expertly over the man's groin; the man's fingers twisting and playing in thick, silky hair; the movement of lean muscle in Ben's back under flawless skin.

James backed away silently, not least because the man on the couch would spot him if he cared to open his eyes. He fled quickly and quietly to his own room, taking his laptop and his bag of laundry with him, and when he slipped out to brush his teeth and wash sketchily in the bathroom, he did it as silently as he could.

He doubted that Ben and his friend would notice a car crashing into the flat, but he felt thankful he didn't need to flush the loo all the same.

He lay in his bed at last, wide-awake and ridiculously out of breath, and fought to ignore the jagged lump of hurt lodged in his throat, the bizarre betrayal he felt. And when that failed, when he heard low, laughing voices in the hallway, and the door of Ben's bedroom closing, when *ignoring* didn't work, he argued himself down.

He reminded himself over and over that it had all been in his own head, flagellating himself for his own stupidity and the ludicrous extent of his pain and embarrassment. It wasn't Ben's fault.

Fuck...how had he convinced himself Ben had been missing him? Waiting for him to come home? The fucking *naivety* of it.

James had totally misread the signals. Ben didn't see him as anything more than a flatmate. At best, a new friend for his circle. James really, really had to remember that from now on.

And what the fuck did it matter anyway, he asked himself fiercely, in the greater scheme of things?

The *job* mattered. Justice for Romilly, and Maria. That mattered.

He closed his eyes tight in the darkness, and at last, he permitted himself to let go. To allow in vivid sensory memories of Romilly's death: the feeling of her small hand in his, those frightened eyes. The smells and sounds and terror of her death.

Her postmortem would be at ten. Would he be letting her down, by not being with her? Would she want him there for that too?

He lay there alone and allowed himself grief and irrationality and guilt, until at last he felt the truth of his exhaustion tugging him under.

Still, when he finally slid into sleep, the sharp lump of disappointment and rejection was there, digging into his heart, as solid as if it were made of real tissue, and not just emotion.

9

James got up deliberately early the next morning. And yes, he knew it was avoidance.

He dressed in one of his best suits for that day's press conference, a light-grey Hugo Boss, with a white shirt and a dark-red tie, and when he examined his reflection in the full-length mirror on his wardrobe door, he supposed he passed muster. But as he looked at himself, he felt no pleasure.

Whatever good looks other people insisted he had, they didn't seem to attract men, or at least not ones he wanted.

Maybe he looked too broad, he thought restlessly. His shoulders were pretty wide, and though he had quite a narrow waist and hips, his muscular arms and chest gave him a solid build, which he supposed suited his height all right. But he wasn't lean, like Ben, or sharply cut, like the gym bunnies he saw on the websites he visited. Maybe he had the wrong haircut as well... He had thick, fair hair, but it wasn't... edgy. Or maybe his mouth was too wide. Or maybe...

He closed his eyes, took a deep breath.

It wasn't meant to be like this. Accepting his sexuality...that should have been liberating, rejuvenating, confidence-building. But instead it felt as if his limited self-belief as an out gay man was being slowly chipped away. It felt pretty devastating to accept that he'd been infinitely more successful, infinitely more desirable, straight.

He clenched his jaw, grabbed his laptop bag and went out into the hall.

The smell of coffee and toast hit him at once.

Escape was his first and most powerful instinct. He headed quickly for his coat hanging on its peg, but before he could reach it Ben appeared in the open door of the lounge, sexily disheveled in a white toweling robe, sleepy eyes taking in James's finery.

James froze like a cornered rat.

"Hey," Ben said with a swift smile. "I was starting to think I'd imagined you."

James swallowed the sour taste in his mouth. *You too,* he wanted to say. *Until I got home.*

"I got up when I heard you in the shower," Ben went on. "I thought you could use some breakfast."

"You got up to make me breakfast?" James repeated stupidly. *After screwing all night?*

And suddenly James didn't just feel trapped, off balance, he felt furious. Furious that Ben could throw him like this, make these…*gestures* that misled him, that made him hope for so much more. Want so much more.

"I thought you could use the boost," Ben said kindly. "You must be fucking knackered."

Like wet cardboard, James's protective rage collapsed.

How could he resent the guy for being thoughtful? Being sweet? Just because James had developed an ill-advised crush, because he'd read everything wrong…that couldn't justify fucking up the first friendship he'd made with another gay man.

"I don't have much time," James conceded, but for all his resolution, he couldn't quite look at Ben, eye to eye. And he couldn't bear to look at his mouth.

"Morning!" And there, relaxed in the doorway behind Ben, stood the man from the night before, bare-chested and clad only in clinging boxer briefs, mug in hand.

He looked magnificent, face chiseled into symmetrical Hollywood perfection, six-pack and pecs tanned and waxed, groin bulging. He might as well have manifested in their living room directly from an online porn site.

"Jace," he said in a cheerful Yorkshire accent, grinning widely and whitely at James. "You'll be the reason we're up at the crack of sodding dawn then."

James manufactured a practiced smile in return and shook Jace's offered hand. "I'm James."

Jace. He wanted to sneer. *Who calls their kid Jace?*

"Well, you didn't have to get up too, did you?" Ben protested. "Did I make you?"

Jace snorted. "I'm gonna ignore that blarin' innuendo, an' go back to bed." He slid past James with a flirty wink and headed up the hallway toward Ben's room. "If you're lucky, I may be *up* when you get back," he called. "Nice to meet you, Jamie."

James's stomach felt hollow, but hunger had nothing to do with it. Jace had seemed disappointingly nice. Of course he had. *Ben* was nice.

Why hadn't Ben mentioned him before?

James trailed reluctantly after Ben into the main room and over to the dining table.

His toast sat, already buttered, on a plate, alongside a mug of coffee prepared as he liked it, with milk, no sugar. He stared at the plate and the mug, and his heart hurt.

"How did you know I made it home?" He thought he hadn't left any evidence; he thought he'd been quiet. Unless—he felt a cold flush of horror—unless Jace had seen him watching. Thought he'd got off on it, like some Peeping Tom…thought…

"I saw your jacket hanging up."

James skittering panic hit a wall of relief. "You noticed that?" *Between orgasms.*

Ben seemed surprised he'd asked. "Course."

James frowned. They sat down in their usual seats, facing each other across the table.

Ben had a red bruise on his throat, ringed by the faint imprint of teeth. He looked content, replete.

James focused on his toast and braced himself for small talk, the usual civilian curiosity about his cases. After all, he knew bitterly, that's what he must seem to Ben, a curiosity. He'd even have reveled in the attention, before Jace.

He juggled conversations in his head, what he could say and what he could stand to say.

"Jamie."

He glanced up and found Ben grinning at him, camera in hand, just before he heard the unmistakable artificial click of the phone camera.

"Photographer," Ben said unapologetically as if that explained everything. But James's stunned expression must have begged more.

He grinned. "I couldn't help it. You look amazing. What's that anyway? Armani?"

James blinked at him, then he couldn't help but laugh. Because it seemed so obvious now what all of it had been. What this must be. His friendly, early-morning ego boost.

"Hugo Boss," he said.

"Oh." Ben smirked. "Well, it could be a new concept in law enforcement. Detectives who look like GQ covers. No one runs away."

Despite everything, despite his new understanding of his place, James felt a reflexive flush of pleasure, reacting to Ben's teasing like Pavlov's fucking dog. And then, just like that resentment surged back in to swamp it—that Ben could play with him so easily, patronize him.

In seconds though he'd wrestled it under control. Ben was just showing friendship. Supportive friendship.

"It's because we have a televised press conference today," he said quickly, loathing the volatility of his own emotions.

"Yeah?" Ben seemed innocently fascinated. "So you may be on TV?"

"Doubt it. I'll be in the background. I'm just a tailored dummy. The DCI'll do all the talking. We'll have to do *Crimewatch* though," he added with gloom.

"*Crimewatch?*" Now Ben really did seem impressed.

"You watch *Crimewatch?*" James asked doubtfully.

"Well…no. But I will now. So will everyone else once I tell them. The audience figures'll quadruple!"

James gave an insincere half smile, took a last swallow of coffee and stood up. "I'll warn them about the extra nutters calling in then. Thanks for breakfast."

Ben stood too. "So when'll you be back?"

"No idea," James said shortly. Escape beckoned. But as he headed for the door, he noticed Ben give a small frown, finally registering, perhaps, James's lack of warmth.

And James forced himself to absorb his lesson again. It wasn't Ben's fault he'd had his hopes dashed. He could only blame himself for building up the hopes in the first place.

"It depends how things go," James amended. "But the first couple of days are usually the most intensive until we start to close in."

Ben lifted his chin in acknowledgment, but James could see more caution in him. James sighed inwardly. Fuck, he was such an arse. He really was.

"Well…" Ben ventured. "If you get away, we'll probably be at the Trafalgar tonight. I've got a magazine shoot this afternoon. But after that."

It hit James then that he hadn't asked about Ben's schedule, or how things had been with him. That the friendship seemed to be all generosity from Ben and brooding from him, and it might not be long before Ben had enough of that. The revelation shocked him into a deliberately warm grin. "I'll do my best."

And he realized that he'd have to mean it.

10

It'd been shaping up to be quite a bright morning when Ingham dropped a copy of the preliminary pathologist report for Romilly on James's desk as she passed. Weak rays of February sun had managed to penetrate the office, briefly illuminating the beige plastic of their monitors, the Chief Commissioner, and Christ on the Cross.

James had just been about to leave, in fact, to interview Romilly's boss, but now he braced himself to review the postmortem photographs and notes.

Carefully, he went over all the details on the gun and entry wounds, deciphering the jargon as he went. It took a certain expertise to place shots above the ear rather than to the temple, as TV shows usually had it. He'd learned in Hendon that a bullet in the temple just as likely severed the optical nerves as killed the victim. Romilly's murderer had the knowledge of where to place the bullet to allow no chance of survival, but it seemed Romilly had moved in the last split second, which explained why she'd lasted as long as she had.

James noted the significant details. The killer had been forensic aware; he or she had left no helpful traces. Romilly had been shot twice at close range by a small-caliber pistol with a silencer, outside her car, then her body shoved inside. Most gunshot victims bled to death, but by a fluke both rounds had lodged in Romilly's brain and allowed her that extra time.

The first bullet had embedded against the temporal artery resulting in a slow bleed; the second had sheared a bridging vein resulting in a slow leak. Between the two, intracranial pressure had built for hours until the swelling finally caused cardiac arrest.

Nothing surprising, nothing new. But the next paragraph had him leaping to his feet and heading straight for Ingham's office.

She looked at him, as if she'd been expecting him.

"Circular scarring, approximately two millimeters in diameter," he read aloud, "in a rough pattern on the lower back and buttocks. According to medical records these are the result of shrapnel from a gas-canister explosion when the victim was three."

Ingham's head dropped theatrically. "Jamie—"

"Maria had scarring too."

"Maria fell out of a tree onto a pile of branches, on holiday in Antigua, aged five," Ingham recited. "Not to mention *her* old lacerations were nothing like the marks on Romilly. Hell, I've got a childhood scar on my back from falling on a branch that looks like a stab wound."

"It *is* another connection though," James insisted. "Along with the possibility of professional killings. And complete forensic awareness. And *both* these accidents happened abroad. The Cromptons were expats in Mauritius at the time of that supposed explosion."

"So what're you suggesting?" Ingham snapped. "That the Cromptons were stubbing out their fag ends on Romilly's backside while the Curzon-Whytes were thrashing Maria?"

James gazed at her wordlessly. What *was* he suggesting?

Ingham sighed. "Jamie, you know I respect your intuition, but come on. Both the families have denied contact with each other, and Sameera hasn't been able to find any link between them or the victims."

"Yes, ma'am," James said sullenly. But his irrational sense of frustrated resentment must have been obvious.

He excused himself and headed for the car park, well aware of the seething volatility of his mood. And on his own in the car, with no bells and whistles and no distractions, he could no longer deny the feeling of depression sinking into his bones.

He'd always remained calm, in control, able to rely on absolute focus and self-possession. Since he'd joined the Met he'd tried to retain his compassion, but he'd also carefully held his distance.

But...*but*, there was just...something about these two cases that pushed every emotional button he had. Maybe he could blame the sense of personal responsibility he felt for failing to find Maria's killer. Maybe he should have listened to Ingham and seen a counselor after Romilly died in front of him.

And maybe he should admit too the ridiculous impact of his dashed hopes over Ben, for all he tried to convince himself it didn't matter. That factor in his depressed mood horrified him most of all.

He owed it to these women to give everything he had, and instead he'd allowed himself to become diverted by personal disappointment.

He drove and forced himself together again, and wondered if he'd made the wrong choice after all, in moving in to Selworth Gardens. Perhaps having no life outside work had actually been the right path for him to do this job to the very best of his ability.

Maybe he couldn't cope with the insanity of strong emotion. Maybe he needed a really long sleep.

By the time he reached the TV studios, his policeman's mask had been glued firmly back in place. But Geoff Leadbetter gave him nothing new. Just as Clara'd hinted, Leadbetter had obviously been unrequitedly besotted by Romilly. But James found that he felt an unwilling, visceral pity for him, which probably wouldn't have been there before he'd seen Romilly die, or before he'd begun this pathetic, pointless crush on Ben. Before Ben, he wouldn't have understood at all.

He drove back to the office, mind churning over the interview, and he felt restless, sure something vital must be escaping him, just out of his line of sight.

He tried to articulate it to Scrivenor when he arrived back, since Ingham wouldn't want to hear it—that nagging, inchoate sense of familiarity between the two cases.

"The way Leadbetter talked about her...Romilly...she sounded...I don't know...not the *same* as Maria. Not as subtle. But they both seemed to have a sort of charm they could switch on. Like...like a light bulb for a bunch of moths."

"Oh, very poetic." Scrivenor snorted. "I would nae try it wi' Herself though. The DCS is in wi' her."

He and James exchanged a meaningful stare, and James decided the better part of valor would be to stay at his desk and write out his report on the Leadbetter interview without the poetry.

It didn't take long, and as he happened to glance up when he finished, he saw the DCS emerge from Ingham's office with the air of a man who'd just taken out his professional discomfort on his subordinate.

James looked away and grabbed of a set of prints lying on his desk, copies of the latest scene-of-crime photographs, and spread them out haphazardly to study, somewhere to hide from his own irrational guilt.

He stared at them for long, blank seconds, then he found himself focusing. And once he saw it, it couldn't be unseen.

No. It was fucking *stupid.*

Yet…his gut told him otherwise. Hadn't something been propelling him this way from the start?

"Alec, mate," he said. Scrivenor looked up from his keyboard. "Got a minute? Ingham's office?"

Scrivenor raised his brows, but he followed without a word.

"Ma'am."

Ingham appeared less than thrilled to see both of them in her open doorway, but she gestured them to come in and close the door. "What?"

James laid the photograph on the desk in front of her, and Scrivenor leaned over to peer at it. All three of them gazed at it for silent seconds.

But as James waited for a reaction, it became clear that, of course, they weren't seeing what he had.

The image showed a view of the passenger side of Romilly's car, taking in the gutter and part of the pavement. James took a deep breath to control his butterflies.

"What's that?" He pointed.

Ingham peered down, frowning. "A few stones?"

She sounded uncertain, as if she knew it had to be the wrong answer and she must be missing the obvious. She looked at him suspiciously.

"A *pile* of stones?" he prompted.

Ingham looked down again. "I…suppose?"

Scrivenor bent closer to the image on the desk, eyes dark as flint.

"And there…just beside the stones?" James asked.

Ingham narrowed her eyes. "A neck chain," she said with an impatient frown. "We have it in Exhibits. No prints…no DNA traces. It's just a cheap nickel-alloy chain. Must have been there for a while."

Both Ingham and Scrivenor stared at the photograph, then back at him, waiting for his moment of genius. James bit his lip, now quite sure they were about to be disappointed.

"Maria's front hall. There was a piece of chain lying near the wall. And…"

"A bag of pebbles beside the step," Ingham finished, getting it at last. She studied the photograph again. "But that's… I mean these are just random *stones*. You'd find them in any street. And…I dunno. Someone's chain broke. I mean, Jamie…there's thinking outside the box, but this is… We *discussed* this. There's no evidence of a link."

"There are some parallels. We know that," Scrivenor said suddenly. He stroked his moustache in thought. "And *maybe*… Well, I canna think many of us would've seen a link in this…but ah can see Jamie's point."

James threw him a look laced with gratitude and relief. But in truth, he'd ended up trying to force the theory on them. The idea was credible, or not.

Ingham watched him expressionlessly. He could almost feel her calculating the odds, balancing what could only be seen as a huge intuitive leap against the knowledge that James's instincts had, at times, been shown to be extraordinary.

"So you're suggesting this is a signature. A serial. A pro wouldn't leave a calling card," she said.

James grimaced, hating to say it out loud. He felt adrenalin draining from him like water from a wrung-out rag.

"Well…it takes three killings to make it serial but…yeah. It could be a coincidence, ma'am. Of course. But I think it's a line worth looking at, even if we're not overt about it."

Ingham held his eyes for a moment longer, then she nodded stiffly.

"I'll allow a line of inquiry," she said. "But we're keeping it to ourselves for now. We'll get crucified if it gets out and it turns out to be puff. Which means it's down to you two, on top of the other stuff. And talking of the other stuff—Jamie, I need you to look at Romilly's ex before the interview tomorrow. Now...bugger off."

Scrivenor left with an encouraging wink to James, but James didn't move, unwilling to leave until he got Ingham's real reaction, given he'd just landed her with an outlandish theory which could potentially draw down even more flak on her head from above.

She sat back in her chair and contemplated him standing to attention in front of her desk like a schoolboy before the headmistress.

"You'll be quite a copper someday, Jamie," she said finally, almost absently, before her mouth curved into a wicked smile. "Actually now I think of it, I could go a latte. No sugar. I like Costa. And a chicken sandwich. Maybe a doughnut."

James opened his mouth, closed it again. There were worse ways of being put in his place.

11

After his punishment coffee run, James returned to digging into Charles Priestly.

Priestly's background check put him at forty-four, not as old as the words *silver fox* had led James to expect. He'd been born in Kent, had no criminal convictions, no run-ins with the police, no unpaid debts. His name appeared in only one piece of official documentation—the DVLA record of the purchase and sale of various cars: the first one, thirteen years before. Late, James mused, for a first car. But then the man may have just preferred to use a bicycle.

He seemed impeccably clean and upstanding. And because he was clean, only chance led James to stumble on his employment history. Once he read it, he went straight back to Ingham's office and knocked on her open door.

"Ma'am. Priestly is Chief Financial Officer at JWLC Entertainments."

Ingham's brow creased then cleared. "He works for Joey Clarkson."

James grinned. "The very man."

Clarkson could be classed as a bit of a celebrity to most coppers in London, a businessman as far from the level as it was possible to be and still remain outside police custody. He owned a series of nightclubs, bars and massage parlors throughout the city, and the police knew that they fronted for drug-dealing, gun-running and prostitution. Unfortunately, they could never quite manage to hang anything on him, and his very expensive lawyers made sure any overt police attention quickly led to claims of harassment.

And Charles Priestly helped run his empire.

Ingham stood and pulled her jacket off the back of her chair. "I think Mr. Priestly's interview just reprioritized itself."

They headed straight for the car park, and as Ingham drove, James called Priestly's secretary and told her they wanted to see him immediately as opposed to the next day as scheduled. The woman huffed and puffed but when James suggested they could invite Priestly to the station instead, she crumbled.

He didn't have to be psychic to see Ingham's optimism that this could be their breakthrough at last—a clear link to a world where ordering a woman to be executed might not be such an unusual thing to do. The O'Grady mafia lead might have come up cold in Maria's case, but that didn't mean this one couldn't be the answer for Romilly.

James and Ingham had to flash their warrant cards to get past the muscle on the front door of Tina's—Clarkson's first and most successful strip club, and named unironically, legend had it, after Clarkson's dead mother. Inside though, they seemed to be alone, save for a cleaner.

They walked down a few wide stairs into the body of the club.

Everything—walls, carpets, furniture and wall-to-ceiling poles—appeared to be unimaginatively black with a few accents of red and silver. In the evening through an alcohol haze, it probably oozed sex; but empty, with the house lights up and a vacuum cleaner wailing in the background, it seemed tawdry and sad.

"Officers? If you'd like to follow me?" A deep, cultured, accentless voice behind them.

James and Ingham turned sharply to find a man descending the steps they'd just come down.

Charles Priestly—silver fox—didn't disappoint. He appeared roughly James's height, slim and fit, with tanned skin and expensively cut silvery hair. James got the odd impression of weary knowledge that added years to him. James had seen it before in serving military, but Priestly's record showed nothing like that. Maybe it came from working with Joey Clarkson.

They followed Priestly through a concealed black door close to the bar.

He led them along a lushly carpeted corridor, stinking of stale smoke and air freshener, then through another door into a large anteroom where a secretary's desk sat unoccupied. The sudden brightness of the afternoon sun felt physically shocking after the dimness of the club, but Priestly seemed unaffected as he took them further, into an even larger room, where at last he stopped beside a big glass desk covered with papers.

He strode to a large leather chair behind the desk and dropped heavily into it in a movement that could never be described as relaxed. "So," he said. "How can I help you?"

And finally James identified what, other than Joey Clarkson's patronage, rang alarm bells about Priestly. For all his urbanity and experience, the man was deeply nervous.

James took out his notebook as Ingham made cursory introductions. They both took chairs in front of the desk.

"We've been told you were Romilly's last romantic attachment, Mr. Priestly," Ingham began.

Priestly blinked and blinked again. His eyes were pale blue, striking against his tan. "I don't know if that's correct. We split up a couple of months ago, as I said on the phone to the officer. I'm sure she'd seen other people since."

Which sounded to James, not so much hopeful other boyfriends might catch police attention, as bitter that they might exist.

"Why did you split up?" Ingham asked.

Priestly looked down at his desk. "Romilly didn't want to get serious with anyone. She was too young and too...too restless to get involved. I knew that."

"But?"

"*But...*" he returned with unmasked resentment. "We can't pick and choose where our emotions take us, can we, Chief Inspector?"

"You *were* significantly older than her," Ingham said.

"Yes." Wearily.

"So how did you meet?"

"I met her in the club." He paused. "She worked here."

"Worked as what?" Ingham asked, and from the sudden, pained look on Priestly's face, James thought he could guess.

Priestly bit out the confirmation. "She worked as a dancer. A... stripper."

Out of the corner of his eye, James noted Ingham's theatrical surprise. "There's no record of that on any employment history."

Priestly barked a laugh. "Of course there isn't, Chief Inspector. It's not as if she declared it to the Inland Revenue. She didn't do it for *money*. She used an assumed name. She just...she loved the attention."

"The kind of attention she'd get taking off her clothes?" Ingham said, tone deliberately unpleasant. James had always admired her serious talent for rattling people's cages. "Did she work as a hostess as well?" Which in Clarkson's clubs meant having sex with the clients.

Priestly leaned back in his chair defiantly. "Yes. But she stopped when she got a chance of the TV job. She wouldn't risk tarnishing that for a bit of fun."

"She was a thrill-seeker then," Ingham goaded. "She didn't need the money, and yet she chose to do...that."

Priestly's false ease vanished. "Don't you *dare* judge her." His hands clenched on the arms of his chair, as if only that stopped himself from launching across the desk at them. "She wanted to push her own boundaries, all right? She loved life and she wanted to *live* it. Romilly never just...existed."

James clenched his jaw, seeing again those desperate dead eyes.

"Did you start seeing her immediately after you met?" he asked. Priestly blinked at him as if he'd forgotten James existed.

"We were friends for quite a while after our first..." He floundered, then recovered. "Before anything romantic began."

"So," Ingham put in again, as if she were trying to get something bizarre straight in her own mind. "You paid for sex with Romilly, you waited for her to agree to start a romantic relationship with you, you had a little time with her. And then she dumped you."

Priestly flinched as if she'd punched him.

"Yes," he said. "And that's life. She broke my heart, and, yes, she could be ruthless. The young often are. Is that a good motive for murder in your world, Chief Inspector? Because I've found unrequited love just makes you sad and miserable and tired."

There was a beat of almost startled silence when he finished, as if that blast of pure emotion had shocked everyone. But Ingham moved quickly on to gather the usual details—where Priestly lived, where he'd been at the time of the murder, if he had any corroboration for his alibi.

He had been at home, in bed, he said, with a lady friend, for whom he provided a name and contact number.

James and Ingham stood to leave when Ingham delivered her last zinger.

"Would you happen to know of anyone in Romilly's circle who has routine access to firearms, Mr. Priestly?"

Priestly flushed violently. "I know what you're trying to imply, *Chief Inspector*, and I've never handled a gun in my life. I would never cause Romilly harm. I loved her. I hoped one day she'd learn to love me back."

James and Ingham walked back through the club, past the howling vacuum cleaner and out into the sharp, cold air. There were tasteful green-painted boxes of crocuses and snowdrops on the windowsills beside the door—gaudy yellow, purple, white—heralding spring. Time moving on. All James could smell was petrol and smoke.

"If that was all shit, he should be on the stage." Ingham sounded disgusted. "But by the sounds of her, a crime of passion wouldn't exactly be a shocker."

James's jaw clenched. "I'll keep digging."

But, despite an afternoon of phone calls and computer searches, he could find nothing on Charles Priestly.

As far as tax records were concerned, Priestly had simply appeared in Joey Clarkson's employment from nowhere, thirteen years before. His passport was up to date, and he'd used it once every year for holidays on the Continent or in the United States. He'd gone to France, Belgium, Germany and Estonia. Once, he'd gone to Kenya. It got no more exciting than that.

James put in calls to Vice and to Drugs to ask them to keep an ear out for any talk of a recent execution contract emanating from Clarkson's operation. Then he had nowhere else obvious to go on Priestly.

He should have gone home at six, but he and Scrivenor put in some extra hours on "Jamie's pet theory" as Ingham called it, looking through the General Registry—the Met's records of murders and deaths by violence in London—for any mention of stones or chains at a scene.

"'S nae gonna be easy," Scrivenor muttered, as he rubbed his face. "I mean *we* didnae think to input *chain* or *stones* as keywords, so why would anyone else, if they were nae obvious?"

James sighed and shrugged. Scrivenor's patience frankly amazed him, sticking it through with him, with only the bribe of the odd fancy coffee.

But something in James couldn't let it go. He planned to spend as many hours as he could squeeze in at the Method Index in New Scotland Yard, to look through records of unique, memorable crimes for any hint of a similar signature—stones and chain. But he'd begun to lose most of his initial messianic confidence in the idea. Only stubbornness kept him going.

"We could try HOLMES," he suggested.

"You think the killer's operatin' outside London too? It's been pretty local up tae now if it's linked."

"Fuck...it's worth a try, Alec."

HOLMES was the much-improved computer system supposed to enable major inquiries across the UK to access and exchange information, and it had been designed to allow for sophisticated searches, and throw up patterns and coincidences. But, as Scrivenor had pointed out, someone had to judge the information as important enough to input.

James added the details into the case notes on HOLMES anyway, then he launched a search on as many variations of *chain* and *stones*

as he and Scrivenor could think up. They got a slew of quick responses, most of which looked obviously wrong, but they divided them up
anyway for scrutiny the next day.

His phone buzzed on the desk. *We're at the pub if you fancy coming
along.*

He frowned down at it, unconsciously worrying at his bottom lip.

"Bad news?" Scrivenor asked.

James looked up guiltily. "Just my flatmate. They're all at the pub."

"Well, why the fuck are you hangin' around here?" Scrivenor
asked, as if it were the stupidest thing he'd ever witnessed from a sen-
tient being. "There's nae miracles tonight, laddie."

12

All day, James had efficiently buried any thoughts about Ben, but
he'd made the decision that morning to try to be a good friend, and he
wouldn't go back on it now. So he drove past the road that would have
taken him to Selworth Gardens and headed instead for the Trafalgar.

He wanted to normalize things between them and hope like fuck
that Ben never ever found out about the insane crush James had been
harboring. It had just been unaccustomed proximity to a very attractive man, who was as friendly as a puppy. No more than that.

When he walked into the pub, he spotted Ben and his friends
seated at the same table as they'd used on the night of the call-out for
Romilly—and he felt embarrassingly relieved to see Steggie there too.

"Jamie!" Steggie camped, apparently equally pleased to see him.
"You look scrumptious!"

James fixed a smile on his face, noting Oliver in the group, along
with a number of unfamiliar faces—more glamorous fashion people
by the look of them.

Steggie took no prisoners. "This is Jamie," he announced to the
table. "*Only* the hottest detective sergeant in Central London."

A new man and girl, who'd been snogging at the right-hand end
of the semicircular bench, stopped at once and turned to eye James
with suspicious alarm, as did the three new men, all dressed in clothes
James couldn't even contemplate trying to wear.

James kept his smile fixed in place.

"Also my flatmate," Ben threw in diplomatically from his position next to the once-snogging couple, and with that, the alarmed staring, at last, eased. The new people, James learned, were from Ben's shoot that day. He saw no sign of Jace.

James took a stool beside Steggie, who submerged him in questions about the latest murder, most of which James doggedly refused to answer, no matter how Steggie pouted or pleaded. It felt like a game.

But Steggie wasn't alone in his interest. An imminent appearance on *Crimewatch*, reported to the group at some point by Ben, had given James a kind of celebrity status, which Glynn, his unexpected boyfriend Graham, Beth and Naomi were happy to buy in to. In no time, James felt as if he were giving a career talk on being a detective, because in their world, he seemed the exotic one.

Through it all though, he remained infuriatingly aware of Ben, happily engaged in what looked to be a full-on flirtation with one of men from the magazine—a nice-looking guy with fashionable, and probably unnecessary, glasses, and a small goatee.

James joked and chatted, and worked to ignore the lump of stupid disappointment in his stomach and told himself it would all help. It helped to see the type of men that Ben actually wanted.

"I didn't realize how much work detectives do," Naomi breathed with touching horror after James had recounted a typical investigation timetable. "It's never like that on TV. You never see Inspector Lewis on a camp bed."

"You must be the ideal flatmate," Oliver drawled, the first thing he'd said. "Never around enough to get in the way."

James met and held his eyes, and Oliver smiled a cool, pleased little smile, as if he'd just realized James wasn't worth his hostility.

"Your round, Jamie." Steggie reached out a surprisingly strong hand to grasp James's wrist. "I'll help."

James, having known Steggie only a matter of hours in total, still understood enough not to argue, so he let himself be led to the bar, where he and Steggie found enough space to lean side by side and wait to catch a barman's eye.

"So. That felt like an intervention," James remarked after a minute of amiable silence. He shot a sideways look at Steggie, and Steggie grinned back.

"Well. You're not as much of a virgin sacrifice as you seem, Detective Sergeant. Excellent." Steggie's campness had dialed down to almost zero.

"Steggie," James said wearily. "Tell me."

"Oliver used to be Ben's flatmate. The one before last. I moved in about seven months ago and Olly came just after."

"Okay," James said cautiously.

"He has a bit of a thing for Ben. And he may be a bit jealous you're Ben's flatmate now. He's usually really charming. PR man, yeah? Only actors are worse."

James eyed him thoughtfully, then nodded his thanks. If nothing else, Steggie seemed to have his back.

They carried the drinks back to the table together, but when they settled James couldn't help fixing on Oliver, observing him through the prism of this new information.

Now he could clearly see Oliver's distraction when talking to the others, the direction his eyes always drifted, his repeated efforts to involve himself in conversation on Ben's side of the table, and James realized that, yes, *obviously* Oliver was hung up on Ben. He could barely believe he'd missed it, he'd have seen it immediately if he'd been observing these interactions for a case. But when it finally mattered to him personally, it felt as if every single skill he had in reading people slid into neutral, and he found himself second-guessing himself on everything.

In any event, Oliver had nothing to be jealous about. James was a guy with his nose pressed against the glass, just like him.

James sipped at his pint until he realized that, with the fuel of adrenalin-nerves and anticipation spent, he didn't want to be there any more. He'd done what he'd come to do, and exhaustion had begun to crash down on him. He swallowed another couple of swigs of lager then stood to go.

"Sorry, I'm knackered," he announced apologetically to the group. He got a chorus of polite nothings, though he thought Ben's friends had started to warm to him. Ben though, looked startled, as if he'd only just remembered James was there. That would please Oliver, James thought with rush of reluctant resentment, maybe get him to ease off the pointless bitchiness.

"You get some sleep," Ben called across the table, like a mother sending a small boy to bed. So much for unresolved sexual tension. "I'll see you in the morning."

James gave a polite, noncommittal smile. He'd already turned for the door when he felt a hand on his arm. Steggie. "I'll come with you. Bum a lift, okay?"

And James felt less of a loser walking out with a friend than as a lone workaholic.

They talked about nothing much on the way home, but James needed all his remaining attention to drive in any case. Then, once he found a parking space, they walked in easy silence through the light drizzle to No. 22, a blessedly peaceful end to the night. James just wanted to get to bed.

But Steggie had different ideas. "You're coming in for a nightcap," he declared grandly as they walked in the ground-floor hall. "I have the *best* bottle of red, just waiting for a police presence."

James could have moaned with despair. He'd managed to find a second wind to go out, socialize as necessary and get home. But he couldn't face any more.

"I really am shattered, Stegs. Another time?"

Steggie produced an understanding smile, but James felt as if he'd really disappointed him. Still, "Another time," Steggie said gracefully.

James said his good-nights feeling a definite pang of guilt.

But the following day, Romilly would be going to her grave, and James wanted to give her the only tribute he could. With his last dregs of awareness he'd remember her—the few minutes he'd known her, in whichever way he'd known her—his own personal wake for the dead.

■II■ ■II■ ■II■ ■II■

James rose early the next morning, dressed in his best Armani black suit and left before Ben could emerge for breakfast. Assuming he'd come home at all.

James couldn't be sure what impelled him, but he decided to circle back to the King's Road before the funeral, parking, ironically, on

Flood Street. And just after eight, he found himself donning purple nitrile gloves and ducking under the yellow scene-of-crime tape across
the door of Romilly's flat to enter her long, elegant hallway for the first
time.

Everything obviously pertinent to the investigation had been removed to be forensically examined, leaving Romilly's home almost as
she'd have known it.

It appeared to be an extremely expensive property, with a state-
of-the-art kitchen, large windows that let in the morning light, and
upmarket furniture; the kind of flat a designer might have put together.
In fact, a designer probably had put it together.

But Romilly had left behind small, human details—a half-open jar
of Nutella chocolate spread and a packet of Frosties on the breakfast
bar; a bowl with a spoon and a small ring of milk beside the sink; a
hair slide and a flyer for a concert on the coffee table. Grey fingerprint
powder lay everywhere, like a dusting of volcanic ash.

Romilly's bed sat rumpled and unmade, as it had been when she
got up for work on the last morning of her life. James noticed a mirror
fixed on the ceiling above the bed and beside a pillow a small brown
stuffed bear, so forlorn and tattered that it had to be a childhood memento. James bit his lip and sighed.

He moved to slide open one of the mirrored doors, which took
up a whole wall of the sizeable room, and what he found inside didn't
surprise him. It was an enormous walk-in wardrobe: rails of designer clothes, rows upon rows of handbags and shoes in every possible
color—hundreds of them. It was a collection to which Imelda Marcos
would have nodded with respect.

James had noted Clara Daley's idle remark: *narcissistic as all hell.*
And the more he heard about Romilly, the clearer it became to him.
This was just one more piece in the jigsaw—a classic sign of Narcissistic Personality Disorder, spending obsessively for control and comfort. Yet, as he looked around him at the obscene excess of Romilly's
hoard, he only felt sadness.

He backed out into the bedroom and slid the door closed until
he could see his own weary eyes in the huge mirror. The bed stood
behind him in reflection, and only then he noticed that a tripod and

a state-of-the-art video camera were positioned at the far end of the mirrored wall.

The contrasts were dizzying, disorientating—the childlike food for breakfast, the well-loved teddy bear, the mirrored ceiling and the sex cam ready to go.

He picked up a framed photo on a bedside table.

Romilly smiled at him at last, beautiful and alive and loving every second of it.

It felt to James as if everything he learned about her was calculated to crush the romanticized image of innocence that he'd burned into his own brain as he'd shared her last moments. He didn't know why he found it so hard to let that picture go. But in the end it changed nothing. She was still the girl whose hand he'd held as she died. She still deserved justice.

He put the frame down gently. But as it kissed the surface of the table, he heard behind him the faintest sound of a clicked lock.

He didn't pause to think he might be mistaken, he simply belted out into the lounge. He found it empty. But he didn't slow his pace out into the hall.

The front door he'd left slightly ajar now stood half-open, and a man, with his back to him, ducked under the police tape, back out to the hall.

The moment James's hard-soled shoes hit the wooden floorboards of the hallway, the intruder froze. But it took only a split-second glance over his shoulder before he began to run.

James burst through the police tape after him like a gold-medal winner, and he had momentum behind him while the intruder had to make do with a standing start. But the man had the huge impetus of fear.

He slammed through the door at the end of the hallway, leading to the emergency stairwell, and by the time James burst through it too, the intruder had begun to bound down the stairs—three, four at a time, plunging toward the street door. Through his own gasping breaths, the hard sound of his shoes clattering on the stone stairs, James could hear the repeated impacts of the other man's thudding leaps, and he could see the back of his head repeatedly disappearing as he rounded each landing to the next short flight of steps.

James bellowed "Police! Stop!" in case this was some misunder-standing, but that propelled the man to take increasingly desperate jumps, move even faster. James vaulted one banister, from one set of steps to the one below, gaining a little ground, but the intruder had already hit the grey concrete of the bottom floor, nearing escape onto the street.

There was no time left. On impulse, James launched himself from the top of the final flight of stairs, arms flailing—one last desperate leap. He landed with jarring force on the concrete floor, but he managed an aikido roll on his shoulder and somehow came up gracefully on one knee, grabbing the back of the man's short jacket. He heard a startled yelp and panted out again, "Police. You're..."

Blinding white force seared through his skull as the man slammed an elbow into James's temple. He felt the reverberation of the blow in his eye socket, and the shock knocked him onto his back.

He lay stunned for only seconds before crazed, blind stubborn-ness drove him to his feet, barely aware what he was doing, staggering and dazed with pain. But it was pointless. His quarry had crashed out through the exit door.

James stumbled across the small lobby and burst out onto the pavement after him, but the man was nowhere in sight, lost in the milling crowds.

He turned, head throbbing, and screamed his frustration, "Fuck!" right into the face of an elderly lady pulling a bulging tartan shopping trolley. But after he'd calmed her down, called in the incident, and gone back upstairs to check for any evidence of disturbance, all he could do was sit and seethe, and nurse his headache while he waited for uni-forms to arrive.

When he got back to the station he had to try, with embarrassingly limited detail, to describe the man: IC1—Caucasian—medium height, medium build, thin, cropped mousy-brown hair, wearing a short blue nylon jacket. James was certain he'd seen a glimpse of metal-rimmed glasses. And that described tens of thousands of men in London.

By the time James slumped into his office chair, his huge high of adrenalin and anger had seeped away into misery. His temple throbbed, his shoulder and hip felt badly bruised, and he had no one in fucking custody. At least his suit had emerged miraculously unscathed.

Scrivenor dutifully listened as James ranted away his disappointment. "I can't believe I let him go!"

"You didnae *let him go*, Jamie. He smacked you in the skull, an' he escaped. It's nae as if you helped him out of the buildin', is it? An' believe me…that's happened before." Scrivenor's phone rang. "Oh by the way…that Irina bird…"

James looked up, wide-eyed, as Scrivenor picked up the receiver and put his hand over the mouthpiece to delay the caller. "She called her dad. She's nae back in London till next month but she says she never met Maria."

James's mouth opened and closed again as he tried to take that in, with all its implications—the opposite of what he'd casually expected. He'd *expected* to hear Maria and Irina had been at least acquaintances.

And now? He felt an unpleasant swooping sensation in his abdomen—a kind of incipient panic.

"But," he asked uncertainly. "How did that address get on Maria's notepad then?"

James's own address now.

Scrivenor gestured with his head. "Barry's got somethin'." He turned to his caller.

James made immediately for Walsh's desk. He found Walsh hunched over, oblivious, under headphones, as he trawled through video on his monitor, logging every detail. So James forced himself to stand back and let him finish taking his notes, watching restlessly over his shoulder. It took a short time to register, with a punch of shock, what and whom he was looking at.

He couldn't hear any sound, of course, and it wasn't exactly full HD, but still—clear enough.

A naked man and a naked woman, on a bed, in a familiar room. The man crouched on his knees, side to the camera, with hands bound at his back and face partly visible against the surface of the duvet as he tried to breathe. The woman roughly shoved a large dildo, with a long, stylized horse's tail flowing from it, mercilessly, in and out of the man's backside, her breasts jiggling with effort.

James must have made some movement, because Walsh stopped the tape and turned to him, smiling humorlessly as he pulled off the headphones.

"Mornin', Sarge. Shit, that eye looks sore." Barry never looked the picture of health, but now he appeared ready to collapse. He gestured tiredly behind him at his screen. "Feels like she taped every fu...every *encounter* she had. There's some seriously kinky stuff in there, an' I'm not even 'alfway through. Never thought I'd be beggin' for a break from porn."

James's eyes slid unwillingly to the frozen screen—Charles Priestly's agonized profile, Romilly smiling with complicit wickedness straight into the camera lens.

James nodded tightly. "Alec said you have something on Irina Pozdnyakova."

"Oh yeah. I found this in Maria's work emails last night." He swung round in his chair and flipped a page on his screen; the image of Romilly and Priestly vanished, and an email appeared. "It's a group email from a junior counsel at Blackheath Chambers to a bunch of people in the office, *including* Maria, tellin' them about this party Irina had at her flat on January 31." He pointed at the screen. "It says Irina's parties are a free-for-all...free champagne, free coke, and he's not talkin' cola. It says they can all get in by mentioning his name. Ken spoke to the guy who sent it. He was drunk and coked up at the party—and it was packed, but he thinks he saw Maria there. Can't definitely swear to it though. Her work emails went to her home computer as well her office one, so...that's why she had the address in her house."

When he finished James could have snogged him. He should have been gutted to lose one more lead in Maria's failing case, but this one—Selworth Gardens? He felt only huge relief that it had turned out to be nothing. Somewhere inside, he realized, perhaps he'd still felt unease that he'd pursued the room in the circumstances.

He'd solidly believed, though, that Irina had been the connection. But now to discover that it had just been a random address, scribbled down and left by chance by Maria for James to find and change his life... Weird that it had meant nothing to her, yet so much to him.

"Good work, Barry. Keep asking round, though, to see if we can definitely place her at the party." He took in Walsh's horrified expression and added swiftly, "When you get the chance." They hadn't the manpower to tie up every loose end in an impeccable bow. What Walsh had done had been commendable enough.

James kept digging uselessly around Priestly, until, at three p.m., he set off with Ingham for Romilly's funeral.

It seemed less grand than Maria's, as if no one could muster the energy to keep up appearances, but it had the added horror of a press contingent, complete with TV cameras camped outside the church. Neither of Romilly's parents seemed to notice. They both appeared to be in a fugue state, the kindness of tranquilizers perhaps, until the small, pale coffin passed the front pews, to be set by the altar, and Mrs. Crompton began to wail—an ululation of intolerable agony, a biblical sound. It reminded James of Dame Cordelia's breakdown the night they'd told her about Maria, and it held relentlessly and unbearably throughout the service, through the readings and the hymns and the prayers, lowering at times to a moan then rising grotesquely again, as the woman's pain swamped her in waves.

By the time she was led out, stumbling like a child behind her daughter's white casket, the atmosphere felt febrile with grief, and most of the congregation were sobbing hysterically. James didn't feel that far away from it himself.

As he and Ingham moved into the aisle, he spotted Charles Priestly, sitting, frozen still, in an empty pew, tears coursing down his face unchecked. And right at the back, Eric the paramedic and his small, thin colleague, grim-faced and unfamiliar in suits.

James and Ingham returned to the station in near-silence. They'd been to too many funerals together, all of them desperately sad. But this one—James felt as if he'd been emotionally mugged.

Scrivenor took in his expression when he returned to the office and offered consolingly, "We found Maria's professor."

James slumped into his chair, rubbed a hand over his face, and forced himself to focus.

That had been one of his projects, before Romilly. Find the professor. "Uh-huh?"

"He'd heard about the murder. Think he'd been waitin' for the call but hopin' it would nae come. He claimed he hadnae had any other affairs in twenty-eight years of marriage, an' Maria dumped him cold after he helped secure her a pupilage. He sounded pathetic tae be honest. Said he'd have done anythin' to keep her."

"Sounds familiar," James said. Scrivenor raised a bushy, ginger eyebrow.

Jackson. Leadbetter, given the chance. Priestly. Even Galinda. It felt as if every interview confirmed both victims' ability to create some kind of near obsession in the people on whom they focused.

A narcissist. And...a sociopath? Was it going too far to shove that label onto Maria? She fit a lot of the markers. And the rest? He ticked it all off compulsively in his head. Both women, both with old, different scars. Both magnetically charming and emotionally ruthless. Murdered within days of each other in the same patch of London.

Yet, as Ingham said, those could all be coincidences, because the fact remained—no one could find one solid link between their lives.

"Aye...well..." Scrivenor broke into his frustrated introspection. "I will say he sounded like he hated her guts. An' he's still crazy about her. Anyway, he checks out in Ireland the night she died. *But...*" Scrivenor went on. "The good news is Wally's come up wi' Romilly's fan letters. They're off for prints."

James nodded in acknowledgement, but his insides were a churn of the frustrated restlessness which had haunted him all day. Failing to catch the intruder. Finding more of who Romilly had been. Burying her.

The physical pain left after his morning's useless encounter felt like nothing to the pressure of emotion in his head.

13

James got back to the flat after eight to find it lit but quiet. He thought Ben must be out, until he heard a faint rhythmic noise from the end of the hall and he realized it came from behind Ben's bedroom door. A large, red football sock adorned the doorknob.

James stared at it for whole seconds before he let himself accept what it meant. As always he felt infuriated by his own persistent gut sense of betrayal. And yet, tonight of all nights, he realized, he'd needed Ben. Just to talk to—not even to talk about the shit that had happened. Just...to look at his face and see his smile.

He stared at the red sock and listened to the noises of sex, and it felt like the last, hellish straw piled on top of a head fuck of a week.

Without conscious decision, he dropped his bag where he stood and slammed loudly out of the front door, totally aware and unashamed of his own passive aggression.

He thundered, grim-faced, down the stairs, intending to head for the nearest pub, but when he reached the ground floor, he found himself staring at Steggie's door. He hesitated. But he remembered Steggie's invitation the night before, how genuinely Steggie had seemed to want his company—and he'd seen lamplight in his window when he'd come in from the street.

He had another brief moment of pause—he shouldn't inflict this mood on anyone—but he went ahead and pressed the bell. Gratifyingly, Steggie, when he opened the door, seemed thrilled to see him.

"Jamie!" He eyed his coat. "Are you on the way out?"

James went for his patented puppy-dog look. He didn't do it often, but he'd been told it was very effective. "I just got home, but Ben's um… busy."

Steggie rolled his eyes, which James found unfairly satisfying.

"So," James continued. "I just wondered if your offer of a drink still stands? I mean I know you're probably busy…"

"Jamie." Steggie took a half step nearer. "Did someone punch you in the face?"

James grimaced, but now Steggie had reminded him, even that movement hurt. "Something like that. But I'd rather not talk about it."

"Get your arse in here and take that coat off."

James grinned and complied.

"Have you eaten?" Steggie asked as he hung the coat on a peg in the hallway.

"Yeah. At the station." A limp sandwich and some powdery soup.

"Okay. So…a beer?"

He led the way into his lounge—just as James remembered it from his first visit—neat and tidy and sterile, other than the surreal shrine of golden cocks.

"Yeah. Thanks, Stegs." James sank onto the uncomfortable white leather sofa with a sigh of relief. He had no clear idea why he'd searched out Steggie, other than the need for distraction, a refuge from the noise in his own head.

Steggie handed him an ice-cold bottle of lager and sat beside him on the sofa.

"So. You look fucked. And not in a good way."

Straight to the point as usual. James didn't reply, but he thought his expression probably said everything. He pressed the cool glass bottle against his puffy eye.

Steggie frowned. James had become so used to seeing only blithe good humor on his face that it looked all wrong on him, like another mask. Or maybe, James thought vaguely, his constant geniality was the illusion.

"Just a hard few days," James said. Avoidance and dismissal. His special skills. He stared at his hand, holding the bottle, and he saw Eric's sad, understanding bloodhound eyes; Romilly's elated grin to the camera as she fucked her slavish lover with a piece of silicone; the small, white coffin, a child's color, ready for the cold ground; those huge child's eyes dying in front of him; the man he could have caught if he'd just been quicker.

He jerked his gaze up to meet Steggie's open concern. "I just… The case I was called out to," he blurted. "The victim died in front of me."

Steggie's hazel eyes widened with horror. "Oh, Jamie," he murmured.

From there it felt easy, unstoppable, spewing out of him like sickness. He told Steggie none of the details, but all of his confusion and sense of failure, all he'd wanted to confide to Ben. And Steggie listened silently until James finally ground to a halt, exhausted by the catharsis of expelled emotion.

"Jamie." Steggie heaved a huge sigh. His elegant features had softened. "I can't believe how much you care." He laid a tentative hand on James's wrist. "It's…shit. Life is *shit*. But if all coppers were like you… You're incredible."

Steggie blinked suddenly and huffed a little laugh, as if he'd embarrassed himself, and James shook his head, denying it. But perhaps because he'd never seen Steggie take anything seriously before, his gravity touched James as few things could have done.

Then the moment blinked away.

Steggie sprang to his feet. "We need something stronger!" Mood flipped, just like that. "If we're going to wallow, *we* need..." He waggled his eyebrows at James and headed for the kitchenette. "The grown-up booze."

From behind the counter, he produced the unmistakable shape of a brandy bottle.

James groaned, but he didn't protest. The inevitable headache tomorrow could go fuck itself. Somehow he felt lighter already—shriven.

"So," Steggie chirped as he came out of the kitchenette, carrying two huge measures of brandy. "Since we're doing true confessions... You're never gonna ask, are you? You're just too bloody polite."

He handed James a glass and flopped down onto the sofa beside him. The steel legs creaked ominously.

"Ask?"

Steggie grinned. "Yeah. *Ask.* How a nice boy like me ended up in porn."

James cleared his throat. "Well...it's none of my business."

"God, don't worry. It's really boring. I was in care, that's all."

James frowned with incomprehension, and Steggie rolled his eyes, as if James were being purposely dense. "So I hit the streets." He widened his eyes meaningfully, waiting for James to catch on, and then he did. Steggie gave a sympathetic smile. "I'd been there about...six months maybe, when it happened the first time. A member of staff. And *he* told his mate, who had a go too, and word got around..."

"*Christ!*" James stared at him with wide, appalled eyes. He felt as if he'd been punched awake.

Steggie leaned forward to put his glass down on the coffee table. He seemed surprised, almost scornful. "Come *on*, Jamie. It wasn't exactly unusual. I decided I may as well get something out of it after a while and started charging. I did a few years on the game, got some regulars who became friends, and one of them got me into movies. Which got me *off* the streets and..." He waved his hand at his surroundings—*hey presto!* "Eventually, into a very nice lifestyle." He picked up his glass and slumped onto the firm leather back of the sofa with the satisfied air of a tale well told.

James stared at him as if he couldn't look away. "How...*shit*. How old were you?" Though maybe he didn't want to know. "When it started?"

"Nine," Steggie said nonchalantly. "The first time."

"*Steggie!*" Of *course* James knew it happened, but Steggie's matter-of-fact acceptance of it seemed worse than self-pity. "Did anyone get charged?"

Steggie turned his whole body toward James, the better to direct his look of total incredulity. "*Charged?*" He hooted. "Very funny, Detective Sergeant. They all retired on a nice pension, I'd imagine."

"Stegs! It's not too late. You could..."

"Press charges now? Seriously? The word of a porn actor, an ex-rent boy, against reputable local authority employees?" Steggie gave an icy smirk, and for those seconds, the veneer of detached amusement had vanished. "I don't think so, somehow, do you?"

"Yes. I do!" James protested. "It's *not* too late. Just...give me the name of the home. The names of the abusers. You can still get justice. I mean, what if they're still doing that to kids?"

Steggie rolled his eyes dramatically. "And there he is. The White Knight. Look, I appreciate your concern, but it was almost twenty years ago for God's sake. The home's shut down. And they were fat old bastards then. They're senile or dead by now."

"But there *are* ongoing investigations into historic..."

"And you know what?" Steggie went on relentlessly, as if James hadn't spoken. "I have zero interest in putting my life on hold to trip down memory lane with a bunch of *caring* coppers. Go through all that to try to get back at a few nonces too old to get it up any more? No way. It's too fucking *late*, Jamie."

There could be no question he meant it. His expression, his body language, screamed at James to let it go, to stop cutting open old scars. But the copper in him couldn't stop.

"Steggie," he coaxed. "They could have recruited younger members of staff. They could still be operating in other—"

"If they did, it was after I left. And do you know how many homes out there *could* have abusers operating?" Steggie's mouth thinned; his nostrils flared. "Jamie, I mean it," he warned. "Back off. I told you what happened to me as a *friend*, not as a policeman. It's. Too. *Late.* I'm not giving you the name of the home, or any of those old cunts. And I'll deny it, if you try to drag me in."

Their gazes locked for whole furious seconds. James pleading, Steggie relentlessly, icily, absolutely determined.

"Anyway," Steggie said, suddenly all airy unconcern, as if their battle of wills had never happened. "As I was saying. It's all water under the bridge. I took control. I actually get fan mail now, you know that?"

James managed a weak smile, fighting to go with the flow and show his understanding even as his copper's instincts yelled at him to push on and insist on justice and punishment.

He knew on one level that Steggie might be right. That it *was* too late, and James shouldn't be asking him to expose his underbelly to the world on the off-chance they could dole out retribution to someone, somehow.

He should be relieved that Steggie'd coped so well. That he'd made it easier on himself, rather than swimming in bitterness.

But Steggie's rock-solid fatalism dug at him like a splinter under his skin. Something in him urgently wanted Steggie to *fight*, not bend before the wind.

"But…don't you ever think about what else you could be?" he blurted, and he didn't appreciate until the words were out how judgmental they were, and not just of the adult-movie industry.

Why did you give in to it? he'd asked, really. *Why won't you stand up and accuse them, even now? Why did you have to become what they made you?*

Steggie's good humor disappeared again as completely as if a cloth had wiped it from his face. He looked almost betrayed.

"There's not much point, is there?" he bit out.

And James had to shove down the urge to tell Steggie that there *was* a point. That he was young and bright and lovely, that he could still make something brilliant of his life. He shook his head, pity and outrage a churning mass in his abdomen.

"What about your parents?"

"They died." No questions invited. A short, horrible silence, then he went on distantly, "I used to think I'd have a house like theirs one day, though...an' a wife...to bake me *cakes*. Kids of my own. Like all good Catholic boys."

James felt the shock of that in his heart.

"You're...aren't you gay?" he breathed with horror. And yes he knew sex workers and adult performers were generally hardly in it for the sex. But God, if what Steggie had done since childhood also went against his own sexual inclination...

Steggie pulled a wide, cheeky smile. "Who bloody knows? I mean...let's face it—I didn't exactly get much chance to find out."

He seemed to be urging James to join in with the joke, to stop making a fuss. But James couldn't understand it—why Steggie wasn't raging against the world?

Steggie's eyes locked with his, and the cheerful facade faded again. Behind it, Steggie looked bleak, somehow, very young.

"I am what I am, Jamie," he said.

They stared at each other for long agonized seconds, then, as James watched, Steggie's game face slid back firmly into place.

"*Anyway,*" Steggie camped. "Your turn. Why aren't you with someone who's spoiling you rotten, gorgeous fella like you?"

James looked down at his hands, away from those determinedly bright eyes, shaken, moved. Then he pulled it together and forced out his own truth, if only because he felt he owed it. His turn. It felt indescribably trivial now.

"I just don't have a lot of time. And...I've never...done it."

Steggie's eyes widened comically.

"No...not...*it!*" James clarified quickly. "I mean...*men.* I slept with a lot of girls. But I'm not...experienced at all. With men. I mean... pulling...men. The gay scene."

He felt hot and flustered when he finished, amazed Steggie hadn't laughed at him outright, but Steggie just had some quality about him that he trusted—some wise, kind core to him. Perhaps it came from having lived the sort of life he had.

"Well," Steggie said, with slow consideration. "There's an easy answer to that. And you're looking at him."

It took James a shamefully long time to catch on.

"Steggie!" he protested. But he could see, with a sinking feeling, that Steggie actually meant it.

"Why not? It'd be between mates. You know. Friends with benefits."

James wondered too late, how much of his instinctive revulsion showed on his face, because Steggie flinched. Then that concealing smile had returned. "Or maybe not."

"No! I just…Steggie, you've been exploited enough."

"Oi! I do the exploiting now, thanks."

"And you don't even know if you're gay!" James steamrollered on as if he hadn't spoken, because that revelation had hit him stupidly hard. "Your life's been…men taking advantage. I don't want to be another one of them."

Perhaps his genuine belief shone through because, though his smile didn't alter, something brittle eased in Steggie's expression.

"All right then, Sergeant," he said. "Have it your own way. But it'd be no hardship, and I don't say that often."

James managed a sad laugh. He couldn't read Steggie now at all; couldn't tell if he'd upset him, or pleased him, or made a total arse of himself.

"I'm not…"

"It's *okay*. I get it. I'm too damaged for a pure heart like yours."

"No. Steggie!" But in essence, wasn't that what he'd said? "That's not true. I just…"

"You're holding out for someone…bright and shiny. For Ben."

The pronouncement silenced James's bluster as abruptly as a slap across the face.

Steggie's words had sounded almost bitter, at last. But James felt too humiliated to think about that. Somehow, he'd imagined his feelings were private, that no one had sussed. Now he wondered, mortified, if they all knew.

"The thing is…" Steggie went on softly. "He'll break your heart."

The silence held for long, charged seconds, and James didn't know what he felt beyond a kind of sick depression.

The shrillness of the flat doorbell sheared through the moment.

Steggie took an instant to gather himself, then he trotted out into the hall.

James sat frozen on Steggie's sofa and took a huge swallow of brandy, welcoming the shocking chemical burn on the back of his throat. He heard the muffled conversation at the front door moving closer. Then Ben's voice from the lounge doorway, talking to him, tone almost anxious. "I heard the door. And your bag was in the hall." Then, "What the hell happened to your face?"

"He doesn't want to talk about it," Steggie answered for him.

After the conversation he'd just had, James felt horribly unnerved to see him, but Ben appeared too annoyed and ruffled to notice.

"I just decided to come down and see Steggie." James didn't know why he felt apologetic about it. "What about...your...um?"

Ben shrugged dismissively.

"I wasn't in the mood for an overnight." He sounded short, almost defensive. He looked defiantly at Steggie, who'd raised his eyebrows in extravagant surprise. "Small dick."

"In that case, you'd better have a drink...to get over the disappointment," Steggie said dryly.

James snorted, high with exhaustion. He slouched down as best he could on the shallow sofa, cradling his glass and watching as Ben dropped into one of Steggie's uncomfortable modern armchairs.

It felt easy, then, friends relaxing together with no pretenses, and James felt bewildered by how quickly he had come to feel such complex things for both of them.

—¦¦— —¦¦— —¦¦— —¦¦—

Life in the flat seemed to get easier for James, if only because work got harder.

Activity on both cases became a continual, methodical, unrewarding slog, so when the red sock materialized on Ben's door two days after the first time, James felt tired enough to accept his disappointment philosophically.

Steggie's friendship felt simple to him by contrast, existing without the tension and magnetic pull James felt around Ben. But it had changed after that night of mutual confession. It felt deeper. Real.

Ben though... A large part of James—the sensible part—groaned at the huge stupidity of allowing himself to get in any deeper with a friend on whom he had a kind of...crush. But he just couldn't force himself to turn away from a friendship like Ben's when he'd never had anything like it before—such an overwhelming connection, with so much in common, thrumming with underlying attraction and excitement. At least, on James's side.

For the past week, when the red sock didn't appear or when Ben wasn't working—or, James supposed, fucking someone somewhere else—they'd spent their free time together in the flat, discussing everything from martial arts to politics to movies and music, and they got on incredibly well, even when they disagreed.

Ben, for example, loved Arsenal; James loved Chelsea. They playacted mutual loathing and watched TV football matches together hurling happy abuse. They just...fitted.

It didn't seem fair.

Meanwhile, twelve days after Romilly's murder, and seventeen after Maria's, the team was desperate. Every avenue of possibility collapsed when touched, like card castles.

The O'Grady line had fizzled into nothing, and Dame Cordelia's caseload continued to raise a paralyzing number of so-so possibilities which were flickering out one by one. Priestly's dominatrix lady friend had corroborated his alibi, and they were still trying to find some forensic evidence from Romilly's anonymous fan letters.

They needed a miracle. A break. Just...luck.

And that meant appealing to the public. An appearance on *Crimewatch* became inescapable.

James got off work early the night before he and Ingham had to head for the TV studios in Cardiff, half-expecting to be faced by the red sock and the rhythmic battering of a headboard against the wall. But to his huge relief, he found the flat empty, and a note to say Ben had gone to savate.

James changed into a loose, faded red shirt and battered jeans, pulled out a stack of takeaway menus and decided dinner would be on him.

He thumbed a text to Ben: *Nipping out to pick up food. Vietnamese, Indian or Thai?*

But after ten minutes and a repeat text, he realized there would be no quick reply.

He chewed his lip for a few seconds then picked up his car keys, grabbed his black wool jacket and headed for the car.

Ben had mentioned where he trained, but James hadn't expected the typical boxer's gym he found when he went in—nothing like the upmarket fitness club he imagined Ben would use. This was purely functional—all about fitness and combat—a large brick-lined room with a battered wooden floor, training equipment and, off to the side, a boxing ring, in which two tall men were sparring, no holds barred.

The combat caught and held James's attention, lunging into a vicious, grunting exchange of gloved punches and powerful high body kicks. The speed and intensity of the bout seemed spectacularly athletic and graceful while also wincingly brutal. Savate combat.

After the flurry, the men pulled back and slowly circled each other, assessing.

Later James could blame lack of context, but he shouldn't have felt so stunned to realize that the taller of the men in the ring was Ben—hair tied up in a bun, dressed in a black singlet and track pants, sweat glistening on his sculpted muscles. The scraped-back hair, the expression of cold, fierce focus—both rendered him unfamiliar. He seemed nothing like the Ben James knew. This man was a fighter and sexy as all hell.

James knew only the basics about savate—that it had formed as an amalgam of English boxing and French street-fighting. He understood that Ben had reached an expert level—silver glove. But he had not been prepared for the shock of these quick bursts of pure, balletic violence.

He hated the arousal fluttering in his middle as he watched, because, *fuck*, how could he be turned on by a fight? Yet he found this alien warrior Ben horribly arousing.

Without warning the battle erupted into a flurry of punches and kicks, almost too fast to distinguish until, with spectacular fluid speed, Ben whipped his body round on one leg and used the momentum to deliver a merciless roundhouse kick to his opponent's head. Neither man wore protective headgear, so it came as no surprise to see Ben's opponent collapse like a stringless puppet.

James didn't even look at the man on the floor; he stared, mesmerized, at Ben, so he had clear sight of the icy, merciless triumph on his face as he looked down at his vanquished challenger. The expression held for no more than a second or two before it vanished behind a polite smile directed at the man on the ground. Yet James was sure he hadn't imagined the ruthlessness there.

In the ring, though, all the civilities were now being observed. Ben thumped his fist to his chest, in what appeared to be a ritual salute, and held one gloved hand up to white teeth to worry the lacing open, apparently trying to get a hand free to help the dazed man get up. His fallen adversary made a poor attempt at a return salute, and James could hear Ben making some commiserating "Good fight, mate. Hang on and I'll give you a hand" remarks as he fought with his glove. The other man seemed unable to reply.

But just as Ben managed to get his laces free, about to reach down to the other man, he spotted James, and his attention fixed on him with almost comical astonishment. James felt the shock of the connection like a blow.

He flushed guiltily, feeling like an intruder, a discovered voyeur, because his cock had chubbed-up to tumescence in his jeans and his pulse was still hammering—and all from watching Ben in the unconscious intimacy of battle. He felt ridiculous, like a fan gazing up at some idol so far out of his league...

Ben, though, after his moment of surprise, showed no awareness of James's turmoil, only innocent delight at his presence, and the sweet, happy smile he sported now contrasted dizzily with the image of his savage expression in victory. They seemed to James like two entirely different men.

Yet, while James felt both confused and ashamed by his wild attraction toward the merciless fighter, he felt no less in thrall to the friendly, familiar Ben walking toward him.

"Jamie!" Ben exclaimed. "What're you doing here?" With his hair pulled back, his cheekbones and eyes stood out with stark beauty.

Behind him, his adversary struggled to his feet forgotten, and wove over to slide under the ropes then down to the gym floor.

Ben stayed in the ring, gloved wrists resting on the ropes, laces dangling, grinning down at James. "Beats the hell out of aikido, eh?" he teased. "Literally."

Fuck... James thought miserably. *His arms. Those collarbones...* His skin glowing gold with sweat...

"Let's say I'm not planning on pissing you off you any time soon." James could only be grateful his voice sounded normal, given the hungry, breathless churn of lust in his stomach. "I nipped in to see if you fancy a takeaway. I'm going to pick it up."

Ben's reaction to the offer held all the astonished relief and gratitude of a man who'd been handed a winning lottery ticket at the door of debtor's prison.

"*God*, Jamie, that's brilliant! I know you're off to do the TV thing tomorrow, but I didn't want to cook if I could help it. I had a shite day till this."

James looked toward the door into which Ben's opponent had limped. "Looks like he had a worse one."

Ben's gaze followed his. He grimaced, a kind of sheepish guilt.

"Grudge match," he confided. "We beat the shit out of each other, any chance we get. He gets his own back every time his wife leaves him."

James shook his head like a put-upon parent and left after Ben had put in his food order. He needed time on his own to get himself back together.

He arrived back to the flat before Ben, because the Indian restaurant he'd chosen had been relatively empty and Ben had needed to shower at the gym. So James had plates and cutlery on the table, and their curries warming in the oven, when Ben came in the door and fell ravenously upon the food.

James had spent every minute since he'd left the gym castigating himself for his reaction. Now he found himself desperately eager to prove to himself that he could be a friend. That the rest didn't matter.

"So, what went wrong with your day?" he asked.

Ben made a disgusted sound. He must have shaved his evening stubble in the shower, James noticed unwillingly, and his hair was loose again, thick and shining with health. "Just...models. Egos in inverse proportion to their brains. Nothing important." He gestured to the food. "This is magic!"

"A lot of your friends are models," James observed with amusement.

"And that just goes to show how shallow I am." Ben finished chewing and took a sip of red wine. He sighed. "I couldn't get the shots I wanted. I pushed them and fucking pushed them but…" He shook his head and some troubling thought seemed to hit him. He put down his fork. "I dunno. Naomi said they were fine. But I didn't feel it."

"Show me," James urged. Not that he'd thought it through, but glum depression didn't sit right on Ben.

Ben hesitated, as if he didn't want to bother him, but after a second or two he went to extract his laptop from its case by the sofa. He opened the lid and clicked on the touchpad.

"I couldn't get either of them to show anything but…vacant, you know? I needed some *hint* of intelligence for this brand. But they're both such difficult shits. He's a cokehead, and she lives on vodka and fags which does nothing for her temper." He swung the laptop round to display a screen of photo contacts.

A man and a woman, both hollow cheeked and full lipped, dressed in dark high-fashion clothing. Ben hadn't lied about the sullen vacancy on their faces. But James thought the decayed urban setting, the clothes, the lighting, the composition, did more than enough work in suggesting rebellion and danger.

"Seriously," he said. "They're beautiful. Just like all your stuff. Don't let the way you feel about the models spoil your view of the work."

Ben frowned uncertainly and rubbed a cheekbone. "You really think they're okay?"

"*Better* than okay." James's small smile was entirely genuine. "Really."

Ben eyed him suspiciously, then he looked away. His lips slowly curved upward. "Right then. If the picture editor hates them, I'll refer her to you. And you can arrest her."

By the time they were standing side by side at the sink, rinsing dishes and filling the dishwasher, Ben had snapped back to his usual relaxed, sunny self. James watched with wry affection.

"Nothing gets you down for long, does it?" He handed Ben another plate to stack. "It's like you only see the bright side of life."

Ben shoved the plate in its slot and straightened up, scowling. "Fuck *you*! You make me sound like…Pollyanna."

James grinned and handed him yet another plate. "Compared with me, you are. Own those pigtails, sweetheart."

Ben took the wet plate, but he didn't bend down to stack it. His eyes sparkled with mischief. "So that's how you see us, is it?"

James shrugged provocatively. "Pretty much."

"Well...you just needed a bit of jollying along."

"Nope," James said. "I'll be a miserable bastard to the end."

"Well then, *we* are going to cheer you up!"

James shook his head, watching Ben smiling like a fool, still holding on to the plate. "Oh yeah? How're you going to do that then?"

"For a start..." Ben reached into the sink, hoisted a huge handful of wet suds and splatted them into James's face.

James didn't move a muscle in reaction. "Put the plate down, sir. And step away from the bubbles."

Ben grinned manically. "I know my rights. As an officer of the law, you can't—"

James lunged and grabbed the plate, trying to wrestle it out of Ben's soapy grasp before dousing him in the sink, but it took a good ten seconds to get it away and get rid of it, though Ben was laughing hysterically. They were both giggling like little boys as James tried to manhandle Ben into a dunking position, even as Ben fought back with his own considerable strength and savate skills, and finally he used low tactics to cut James's feet from under him, until they both ended up on the wet tiled floor of the kitchenette, rolling around, whooping with mirth as they struggled, exhilarated.

Breathlessness got to them eventually, both laughing so much they finally called a wordless, mutual halt, going limp, still cackling. Ben had ended up half on top, James flat on his back, shaking with ridiculous mirth, beneath him. He couldn't remember when he'd last let go like that.

"See?" Ben panted. "You just need a bit of jollying along!"

James wouldn't have been able to say what did it. The stupid, childish fun they'd had, the smug triumph on Ben's face, the well-buried Fuck It All streak in him that had finally broken him out of his father's straightjacket.

Something in that moment gave him the insane courage to hook a hand round the back of Ben's neck and pull him down. To press that lush, pink mouth against his own.

It lasted only a second, maybe two, before Ben jerked back, eyes wide. He wasn't laughing any more. He looked as shocked and appalled as if James had punched him.

They stared at each other for long, gruesome seconds, James feeling just as stunned as Ben appeared to be, barely able to believe what he'd done.

A huge stone pressed down brutally on his chest—rejection and disappointment and humiliation, and he wanted more than anything to get his feet under him and run. But he had to stay. Rescue this somehow. Make amends.

Even so, he couldn't help but close his eyes and turn his face away, no longer able to bear Ben's horrified embarrassment.

"I'm...I'm really sorry. I got a bit..." He swallowed hard, ready to choke on the lump in his throat.

Strong fingers grasped his chin and turned his head back.

He squeezed his eyes tighter shut, hiding like a coward.

He heard, whispered, "Oh, Jamie." Then soft, soft lips pressed against his own.

He froze, just as Ben had frozen, and he didn't kiss back, because he knew that this was pity, consolation, and that felt unbearable.

But Ben moaned thickly against his mouth. "C'mon, Jamie."

His lips moved coaxingly, fingers still holding James in place. And at last, though he knew it had to be Ben's kindness, James responded to the first proper kiss he'd ever had from another man.

It felt different from the kisses he'd had with women, chemistry perhaps, but the feel of Ben's mouth pressed against his own, the slow, liquid, confident lick of his tongue, the light prickle of evening stubble, sent a shuddering, uncompromising excitement through every cell. He'd never had a kiss that affected him so overwhelmingly, as if every hair on his body were rising to stand on end. His heart pummeled against his ribcage like a crazed bird. Everything felt unreal, distant.

Ben pulled back and cupped James's face with the hand at his jaw, as if it were something precious. And James opened his eyes to meet Ben's, velvet black, enigmatic, in the dim light of the kitchenette.

"Come to bed." Ben's voice sounded odd, almost shaky.

When he rose to his knees and reached out his hand, it didn't even occur to James not to take it.

14

The light was low in Ben's bedroom, dependent on the table lamps Ben put on as James watched from the doorway. Until now, this room had been for other men, and seeing it at last felt important somehow. As if James had reached a goal he hadn't realized to be vital.

The room seemed slightly bigger than James's, and so did the bed—a king-size, made up with white linen and a stylishly masculine, grey-checked flannel duvet. It was a bed made for more than one person, more than sleeping.

James hovered uncertainly just inside the open door, until Ben turned to him. He looked somber but there was more there—resolve, determination and James couldn't help but flash back to the dominant fighter in the boxing ring. He moved toward James and reached his arm over James's shoulder to push the door shut behind him with a decisive click. Then he slid his hand down to grasp James's wrist and pulled him firmly toward the bed.

When they reached the foot of the mattress, he turned James round, and James went with all of it, putty in his hands.

Ben's eyes were hot under straight, dark brows, intense, predatory, holding James's gaze effortlessly.

Slowly he slipped out the top button of James's shirt. James's breath caught, but he stood mannequin-still, until that knowing hand slid tortuously further down to open the next button, and the next, and James's shirt hung open, his chest bared.

Ben didn't break his gaze. James felt as if his heart were about to hammer out of his throat, and he could hear blood thundering in his ears, his whole body feverish and desperate.

"You have no idea," Ben murmured, and words seemed almost shocking in the hushed tension of the room. "How often I've imagined this...*exact*...scenario. You just...standing there and letting me do what I want to you...stripping you out of one of those sexy suits..."

James let out a heavy breath. Shock. Relief. Because...Ben must have wanted him too then. Perhaps James hadn't been alone after all, in some unrequited crush.

James's confidence roared back giddily from nowhere, though he wrestled it down to a cocky grin. But it seemed Ben didn't want him in control of himself.

His expression edged to wickedness, and his hand whipped down to the button of James's jeans, slipping it open and pulling down his zip, all deft, fast movements that left James gazing stupidly at his exposed underpants. And even as he took that in, a firm shove in the middle of his chest toppled him backwards over the end of the divan bed, landing half sitting, half lying on his back, propped on his elbows.

He gave an *oof* of surprise, but Ben was already on his knees between James's spread thighs and leaning in to kiss his naked chest. Any concept of protest blinked out.

It had been so long since James had been intimate with someone else, so long since he'd been touched sexually. And it had never felt like this—hot and possessive, arousing beyond belief.

James tried to watch as Ben kissed slow torment down his belly, but too soon he had to shut his eyes to fight the huge surge in arousal the image created, combined with the silk scald of Ben's lush mouth on his skin. James knew he was already far too close to humiliating himself.

He squeezed his eyes even tighter shut when Ben's mouth reached his boxer briefs and began to kiss over the cloth, and he didn't make the mistake of opening them, even when the tormenting pressure of Ben's lips moved inexorably down to mouth at the leaking bulge of his erection through stretchy cotton. He moaned at last.

"Sssh, sweetheart," Ben said. "It's been a while, hasn't it?"

The kissing stopped. James made himself open his eyes.

Ben still knelt on the floor between his open, jean-clad legs, and he looked debauched, his pale skin flushed, mouth swollen, blue eyes black with lust. But even through his own urgency, James thought he saw more than desire there. He thought he saw understanding.

"Why don't we take the edge off, ay?" Ben murmured. "Level the playing field?"

James knew he should be feeling embarrassed by his obvious desperation, but he couldn't muster it up. He nodded dumbly.

Ben smiled, slid a confident hand into the opening of James's boxers and casually pulled out his erection.

James drew a knife-sharp breath, but he couldn't take his frantic gaze off Ben's face while Ben looked thoughtfully down at James's red, swollen cock, now gripped in his palm.

An aching pause—and James found his mad, confused arousal vying now for supremacy with ingrained male insecurity.

Ben glanced up and met his eyes. But he seemed strange, almost off balance. Though…when would Ben be off balance in the bedroom?

Ben said wryly, "You never disappoint, do you, Jamie?" James blinked back at him, uncomprehending. "I had a fair idea from when you were parading around, doing your Greek-god-in-a-towel thing but…"

And that broke through James's daze. "I don't *parade* around in…"

"*But,* you can never *quite* be sure until it's…standing right there in front of you," Ben finished, as if James hadn't said a word. He grinned and with no warning, bent and sucked the head of James's cock into his mouth.

The world whited out. James had been given blowjobs before of course from girlfriends, and that one brutally fast one from the guy at the Students' Union, but this… Ben didn't rush it with too much suction or try to cram too much into a too-small mouth. He knew precisely what to do.

His soft, velvet tongue felt perfect beneath James's rigid shaft, and his mouth felt languid and wet and relentless, bobbing and sucking gently until all James could feel was the build of sensation in his gut and thighs and arse, tension rising and rising, as if his heart were about to splatter open inside his chest.

He wanted to unlock his elbows, fall backwards flat onto the bed, but he couldn't bear not to stroke and grip the silky curls he'd obsessed over for so long. He couldn't bear not to see that this was Ben. *Ben* on his knees for him. That his cock was sliding in and out of Ben's mouth.

He wanted relief so badly, but he couldn't bear for it to end, so he held on as long as he humanly could.

Ultimately, the visual finished him. He surrendered when Ben threw him a wicked look up through his long, sooty lashes, mouth stretched and distorted round James's swollen, red shaft. And James came as if he hadn't orgasmed for months, emptying his balls blissfully into Ben's mouth, trying and trying to keep his eyes open to watch it all.

Ben pulled off after accepting a few long, gut-clenching spurts of semen into his mouth, but he let the rest hit his cheek and neck, letting James watch its slow, obscene slide down to drip onto his chest, as Ben licked his lips and smiled.

James gasped through it like a landed fish, but Ben, after a few panting seconds, had his own breath back. He smiled as James collapsed flat onto his back.

"Got a bit carried away there," Ben said, as chattily as if he were discussing a round of Xbox. "We should've used a rubber."

James, still struggling to focus, tried to squint down the length of his own body to look at him. Then the sense hit him.

No condom. He'd come in Ben's mouth. And Ben had swallowed. *God!*

The memory, in all its glory, brought a slavish twitch of renewed arousal to his exhausted groin, and he stifled a groan.

"I'm clean," he managed.

He watched as Ben levered himself easily to his feet, not a button out of place, towering over him while James lay sprawled, jeans round his ankles, his cock deflating on his thigh.

"I know," Ben said indulgently. "Which is why I did it." He moved to a bedside table and used a tissue to casually wipe the spunk from his face. James frankly he wished he had a camera. "But that's not the point. Being safe's vital, Jamie. *All* the time. I did a stupid thing."

In the circumstances, James thought it sounded jarringly didactic—instructions in sexual etiquette from an expert. But equally, he could understand that with Ben's current lifestyle, he was totally correct.

"Yeah. I know," James agreed, still boneless, eyes glued to Ben. "Until you can trust someone."

Ben, standing by the bed, holding the crumpled semen-stained tissue, stared down at James as if he'd just declared all politicians were honest. His skin glowed smoothly golden in the lemony lamplight; his eyes looked black. The front of his jeans bulged obscenely.

"Jamie!" He laughed and it sounded disbelieving. "You can never trust anyone that much."

James considered the implications. "You mean...you've never done it...you know...bare?"

"*Bare?* I've never felt that suicidal, mate."

James blinked. *Mate?* And Ben had *never* been in a relationship he trusted?

Then Ben asked cautiously, "Have you?"

James levered himself up a little on his elbows.

"Yeah. With my last girlfriend. We trusted each other...I mean I knew she was on the pill." Ben gazed at him as if he couldn't believe his naivety, but James could also see the unspoken question there. Intense male curiosity. James answered it as best he could. "It's different. A lot more...sensation, you know? It's impossible to describe really, just...a lot better. For me anyway."

And it had been...the clinging, liquid softness on his shaft had helped him to quite a few less-than-inevitable orgasms with Ellie, whilst condoms had distanced him enough to allow him to think about what he was doing and that he didn't really want to be doing it.

Happy days.

He tuned in again to find Ben looking at him with near fascination, as if James were describing some arcane custom from a different world. Then he seemed to come back to himself.

"Guess I'll never know," he said airily. "It feels plenty good as it is, anyway." He pulled his T-shirt up over his head and off his arms in one smooth motion, revealing a glorious, leanly muscled torso. James found it surprisingly difficult to swallow.

"Go on then..." Ben urged, working on the fastening of his jeans. "Strip and get in."

James rolled to his feet and began to comply. But he'd only managed to get his jeans halfway down his legs before Ben wrestled his own jeans and underpants to the floor, and unveiled his big erection, red and bouncing.

James froze in place and shamelessly gawped at it, relieved that it seemed roughly the same size as his own, though it appeared bigger with Ben's thinner frame. It was a gorgeous cock, far nicer than any James had seen in online porn.

Ben laughed when he noticed where James's wide eyes were fixed, so James tore his gaze away to quickly remove his own clothes. He felt hugely self-conscious, standing there stark naked, sure his body must be far from the gay man's ideal. But Ben's hungry, wolfish stare felt more than reassuring.

They slid under the duvet from different sides of the bed, and Ben wriggled over to press his body against James's and it felt…totally new and absolutely right.

A body as long as his own, as flat and muscular and strong as his own; miles of smooth hot skin, hair rubbing the hair on his legs, aroused male genitals kissing and pressing in a stunningly delicate rush of pleasure.

For a few seconds, they simply lay there and hugged, as if Ben realized what the moment must mean to James, then Ben pushed him onto his back, rolled on top, and that was it.

He felt for the first time, the shocking delight of another cock rubbing against his own. The glorious friction between their bellies as they rolled and writhed and rutted in their own sweat and precome. Ben's mouth all over him, sucking covetous marks onto his throat, shoving his tongue between James's lips and taking his breath, as if he were greedy for everything about him. As if he really had wanted this as badly and as long as James had.

They peaked so close to each other that James couldn't tell who went first, but for him it had become a blur of ever-escalating pleasure and then blinding, bursting release, as his cock rubbed and blurted in Ben's hot slippery come. As Ben's did the same in his.

Afterwards he lay there, exhausted and stunned, ecstatic under Ben's weight, and smiled like a fool at the ceiling.

"Fuck," Ben breathed. He rolled off and flopped down beside James, arms and legs still touching. "It's insane that was your first proper try. You could've had a mile-long queue, any time you wanted."

"Nah." James felt replete and unguarded enough to admit it out loud. "Girls fancy me, but men don't."

He felt the bed heaving as Ben pulled himself up to look at him with as much disbelief as if he'd just announced he was actually Robert Mugabe. "Are you serious? Jamie, I wanted to fuck you the moment I saw you. Complete with little notebook."

The warmth in James's chest could have been satisfaction or pleasure. Maybe both.

Ben, by contrast, seemed almost thrown by his own confession. He hurried on. "Look, if you haven't been getting offers, it's because you don't put out any signals. You're fucking *beautiful*, but…well *I* thought you were straight till you told me different. Maybe you're too intimidating for most men to take a chance on."

That hit home. The possibility that he'd hidden for so long that he couldn't stop.

"You're incredibly sexy, Jamie," Ben went on softly. "You have no idea. With that face and that body and that whole strong…superhero thing going on. Like Steggie says…hunting down the bad guys."

James stared at him, overwhelmed, because he'd felt unsure of his place for so long, undermined by the conviction that he couldn't fit in the world he wanted to join.

Ben cupped his jaw. "You're amazing."

"You're inflating both my heads," James managed.

"Someone needs to, Jamie," Ben returned. "Somebody needs to make you see you're incredible. You're wasting who you are."

And later, James would wonder if that was the moment he slid into love.

15

James woke the next morning to the screeching clamor of an electronic alarm, a sound unfamiliar enough to his instincts to jack-knife him instantly upright, wondering for a panicky second where the fuck he could be. Then his mind woke up too, and he remembered.

He was in Ben's room. In Ben's bed. Being woken by Ben's obnoxious clock.

But Ben wasn't there. James let himself flop back onto the mattress.

The sheets were expensive white cotton, a high thread count, like the ones James had been used to at home, and they smelled of the fabric softener Ben always used in the machine when he did the laundry, often including James's things. Overwhelming that though—the heavy scent of male musk and semen, of both James and Ben combined. To James, it smelled fantastic—a sensory ghost of the most erotic and overwhelming experience of his life.

He'd had sex with Ben Morgan. How lucky a bastard was *he*?

He grinned at the ceiling, feeling just as crazily optimistic as he had when he'd fallen asleep, but a glance at the clock told him he couldn't afford to indulge himself a moment longer if he wanted to shower before heading for the train station. And God, did he need a shower.

He wasn't sure what, other than his usual reticence, made him slip on his boxers to go and get his toilet bag before heading for the bathroom, because for once *he* was the man emerging from Ben's room, and there was no one else to worry about, no one to play James's role of uncomfortable, envious flatmate.

He smiled at the thought and strolled out into the hallway, hearing the muted sound of TV voices in the lounge. All his instincts urged him to go in there, to see Ben.

But an insidious thought slid in for the first time: *What if it's awkward?*

James had made the first move, after all. What if it had just been a one-off because James had been there, and desperate? Because Ben hadn't wanted to reject him cold. Why the *fuck* hadn't he considered that, instead of lying there gloating, making *assumptions*?

He clenched his jaw, nostrils flaring, and strode along the hallway to the lounge door, because he might as well get it over with. Know the worst.

It wasn't until he'd opened the door and walked into the lounge that he realized the TV wasn't on. The voices came from actual people. Ben, bustling in the kitchenette, was chatting with Steggie, sitting at the dining table, holding a coffee mug and a piece of toast. And although Ben hadn't noticed him when he entered, Steggie had a grandstand view, taking in James wide-eyed, in all his wrecked, near-naked, post-sex glory, covered in hickeys and with flakes of dried semen matted in his sparse chest hair.

James stared mutely back, beetroot red, waiting for the first screech of mockery. But Steggie seemed almost frozen, stunned—as if he hadn't expected this at all. Then the strange moment broke.

Steggie laid down his toast with exaggerated care, and when he looked up again, he was smirking lecherously, the way James had first expected.

"*Well*," Steggie said loudly. "That's a sight to raise anyone's truncheon."

Ben turned round from his place beside the cooker. It took him a moment or two, eyes popping, to get a handle on the situation, but then he began to grin like a maniac, as Steggie was grinning. And for all his mortal embarrassment, James felt something—some steel-wire ball of tension in his chest—ease and release because Ben was smiling.

That had to be a good sign, didn't it? No discomfort between them?

Or—maybe this was just what Ben did. Had sex with friends and moved on. Like Oliver. James's stomach clenched.

Ben strolled out of the kitchenette, plate of toast in hand.

"I'd offer you coffee but…" He stopped a few inches in front of James. "You need to shower first. You smell like a tart's boudoir."

James flinched. But Steggie seemed to find James's predicament as hilarious as Ben did.

Ben loosed a short, delighted laugh. "Ah…seriously, Jamie. Gorgeous as the view is, you have to go and get ready right now. Then I'll give you breakfast. You've got a train to catch." But as if he couldn't resist, he leaned in and began a gentle, delving kiss that threatened to weaken James's knees.

All that kept James centered was the uncomfortable edge of the cold plate digging into his abdomen and the even more uncomfortable knowledge that Steggie watched them.

When Ben pulled back, his eyes were dark, and he raised his free hand to rub James's lower lip gently with his thumb. "Go on then. Before I embarrass you some more."

James snorted a laugh. *How much worse could you do?*

"You think this is pretty, Stegs," Ben said, without breaking eye contact with James. "You should see his cock."

James accepted defeat and fled the room. He found himself unable to stop grinning like a lunatic, though, when he stepped under the shower, and all his worries seemed thin and pointless. Ben hadn't brushed it off as a one-night stand or pretended it hadn't happened, even with Steggie there.

He'd acknowledged it openly and been his usual funny, sexy self, but with a new, very welcome edge of open lust.

James couldn't remember ever feeling so blindingly happy before.

—ıı— —ıı— —ıı— —ıı—

When he'd thought of it idly, in a theoretical way, James had wondered whether getting involved in a genuine romantic relationship would distract him from the focus he needed to do his job well. A genuine relationship—not like his old ones.

And in a way, as he sat in the train carriage to Cardiff with Ingham and a small posse of DCs, he had to accept that it did.

He answered when spoken to, engaged in appropriate discussions, but every minute he could gather to himself, he stared out the window, countryside flashing by in front of his unseeing eyes, and his mind drifted, compulsively, to the evening with Ben—the gym, the meal, the kiss—and like a besotted boy, to the night and the morning, and what it all meant.

Yet James also found that his restless happiness helped the day pass more easily. His optimism made even tedious things more bearable.

The train journey into the gloriously art-deco Cardiff Central took only two hours, but the fuss of taxis at either end, and connecting rail links, meant the team didn't arrive at the TV studios in Llandaff until lunchtime.

The building had gone up in the sixties—a bland monolith of concrete and glass—on death row, apparently, once it gave way to a shiny new TV center in the redeveloping city. Steggie had been devastated to discover all BBC Wales's drama programs were already filmed elsewhere, so James stood no chance of getting him Dr. Who's autograph.

But this elderly, unglamorous building suited the unglamorous reality of live TV very well, in James's opinion—a lot of boredom and waiting, punctuated by concentrated flashes of terror.

The day at the studios trotted through its usual, predictable routine—producer briefings, checking the reconstruction VTs, makeup, mic-ing up, and rehearsals on the blue-lit studio floor. James surfed through it all on a kind of euphoric wave, smiling at everyone. That day, nothing seemed boring. Nothing seemed too much trouble.

His mood jacked up even higher when he got "good luck" texts from Ben and Steggie, confirming that, for the first time, James's TV appearance would be a bit of an event for people who cared about him. He hadn't experienced that before, and he found himself snapping a surreptitious selfie on the studio floor to send to both of them.

The knowledge he had his own personal audience at home, though, also hit James's nerves as he waited in position with Ingham for the presenter and cameras to circle round to them. Until now his sole concern had been ensuring he and Ingham said everything important. Now, for the first time he actually had people he wanted to impress.

As always, though, once it started, the live program went by in a blur. Time seemed to speed to nothing, and while, on the downside, any mistakes were out there for good, James loved the fact that no one could tell them to do it again.

James and Ingham finished their two interviews—one, standing up, for Maria; one, sitting down, for Romilly. Then they joined the DCs they'd brought as props to man phones in the studio; James did another short chat from the phone set, and the end credits rolled in no time. The team were off air by ten p.m., but the aftermath of pat-on-the-back wind-down, and checking calls from the public, meant none of the them reached their hotel until almost one, mentally exhausted but buzzed wide-awake by adrenalin.

James had a peaceful nightcap with Ingham at the twenty-four-hour hotel bar, but he waited until he reached his room, stomach tight with tension, to check his phone. There were two new texts, one from Steggie: *You looked hot! But find Dr. Who.*

And one from Ben: *You were brilliant. Proud of you. X*

He lay in bed, waiting to calm down for sleep and wishing he had the guts to call, afraid to wake Ben up, wallowing in happiness and hope.

■||■ ■||■ ■||■ ■||■

"Nice *going*, Sarge!" The catcalls began the instant he entered the office.

"The mascara did wonderful things for yir eyes, son," Scrivenor called from across the room.

James glowered, but it made no difference. Ingham had gone straight to the Chief Superintendent's office when they arrived back, so James had to face the wall of mockery alone. The office appeared full, most officers busily manning phones, the inevitable aftermath of a *Crimewatch* appearance.

"Twitter timeline was interesting again." Kaur grinned as she plonked a cup of canteen coffee on his desk. She held a sheaf of paper, pretending to be shocked.

"*Definitely reconsidering my attitude to police brutality,*" she read. "*#Crimewatch #arrestmesergeant*"

James let his head drop to his desk, his signature signal of despair, forehead hitting chipboard with an audible clunk. He could hear a lot of people laughing.

"*Wooh! Hot Cop's back on Crimewatch! Wish he'd take down my particulars. #crimepays #Crimewatch #hotcop*"

"*Just off to shoplift in Knightsbridge #Crimewatch #arrestmesergeant*"

James didn't move his head from the desk, just groaned loudly and piteously. The *arrestmesergeant* and *hotcop* hashtags had been coined on Twitter after his first *Crimewatch* appearance, and they'd hounded him ever since. The office fucking loved it.

He raised his head at last, a few inches from the desk, to glare up at Kaur. "I don't suppose anything came of it?"

She grimaced with rueful apology and sucked her teeth. "Nothing that stands out yet. Sorry, Sarge."

James manned the phones in the office with the rest of the shift until six p.m., talking to the people the program had somehow galvanized to get involved, whether to try to help, or hoax, or in a couple of instances, ask James out on a date.

He felt exhausted by the human race when he clicked off his last call, and his insides were swirling with all the frustrated, pressured restlessness that had become more and more the norm at work. The day in Cardiff, flying high on the developments in his personal life, felt now like a bit of a holiday.

Still, he put in a couple of extra hours on the General Registry, looking for a match to a stones-and-chain signature. In case a miracle happened.

But it didn't.

Just before nine, he headed home, overnight bag in hand.

Darkness had fallen, miserably cold, though the evenings were lengthening slowly as spring advanced. The rising hopelessness he felt about both cases was, he knew, spreading through the team. But though he felt like shit as he left the office, the moment James slid behind the wheel of his car, the nervous eagerness he'd been suppressing since he woke that morning in his Cardiff hotel burst back into life, wiping work from his mind.

As he put his key in the lock of the flat, his guts churned like the drum of a washing machine, because now he was actually back—what if he'd got it wrong, what if he'd just imagined how much Ben had seemed to want him?

But when he opened the flat door, overnight bag in hand, he could smell garlic and onions cooking, and Ben emerged from the lounge door to greet him in shirtsleeves and worn Levis.

"Hey...you're back!"

And it felt...easy. Better than James could have dreamed.

He didn't have to second-guess himself at all, because Ben pounced instantly to kiss him a devastatingly hungry hello. And then James got changed, they ate, and watched TV and snogged, and then they went to Ben's room again and Ben eagerly taught him by example how to give a blowjob.

James had never taken another man's cock in his mouth before, though he'd imagined it so often. And it was Ben's cock. That, in itself, made the experience stellar.

James thought his performance was terrible—awkward, clumsy and too keen. He hadn't understood just how sore it could be on the jaw, how difficult not to gag, his respect for the girls who'd done it for him rocketing by the second. But Ben seemed gratifyingly turned on by everything he did.

He writhed and groaned, pulled at James's hair, restless hands touching everywhere.

"God, your mouth, Jamie... You have the *sexiest* fucking mouth."

James couldn't help wondering how much of Ben's extreme arousal came from the knowledge that his was the first cock James had ever sucked. But it hardly mattered.

James found he loved the hot, twitching weight on his tongue. In fact, he became almost as turned on as Ben, though he hated the taste of the latex Ben insisted on. At last he could experience sex the way he knew was natural for him—and that meant everything.

After they'd both orgasmed twice, they lay side by side in Ben's big bed. Their bodies touched along their full lengths, relaxed and languid, drowsing idly in the exhausted quiet.

Ben broke the sleepy silence just as James began to tip over into a doze.

"Was so determined I wouldn't do it again." He sounded barely awake himself, as if he were talking in a dream.

It took James's sleepy mind a second or two to properly register what he'd said. And then, he felt very much awake.

He forced himself to keep his body deliberately loose and relaxed, but he felt the exact opposite. He felt devastated. Bewildered.

Ben hadn't wanted to have sex with him again? Then why had they just come all over each other twice?

"Do...what?" He managed to sound merely amused, but his gut felt hollow.

Ben gave a sleepy snigger. "Do my flatmate. Was gonna be *so* good. Shoulda known though." He snuggled in closer, and his body relaxed even further against James, sliding into sleep.

James lay in the gloom and made himself think it through calmly.

He could hardly blame Ben for thinking a relationship with a flatmate might be risky. He had the messy precedent of Oliver to warn him, after all.

Yet, Ben had broken his rule for James, hadn't he? Despite himself?

Out of nowhere an undermining idea careered into his mind—that Ben might have chosen him for the room because he'd seemed the least-tempting option out of the many attractive men who'd applied for it. Hadn't Oliver implied exactly that, when they first met?

But as he stared blindly into the darkness of the room, James forced himself to be rational.

Ben had chosen to let him into his bed, and to keep him there. Ben had proved he wanted *James*. And James would not let his own insecurity ruin it.

16

"We got prints!"

James and Scrivenor looked up in synchronized surprise from their desks at a triumphant Ingham, resplendent in purple, grinning crazily down at them.

"Romilly's fan mail! He used gloves. No prints on the letter or the envelopes, *but* they got a partial on one of the stamps. Must've been when he bought it."

"And they're on file," James confirmed. The letters had been with the lab for the best part of a week, and the team had pretty much given up hope.

"They certainly are, Sergeant," Ingham said happily. "Richard Burnett. Sentenced to two hundred hours of community service, thirteen months ago, for trying to break into a TV presenter's garage. *And* currently under a restraining order for stalking and threatening an actress. Or should that be 'female actor'?"

James whistled soundlessly. "So…"

"*So*… Off your arse, Jamie. We're off to PC World."

James jumped to his feet as if she'd stuck a pin in him.

"He's a computer nerd," Ingham went on gleefully as they walked. "About as stereotypical as you get."

James kept trying to get his head around it as he dutifully guided the car through the busy afternoon traffic on Camden High Street, past the garish, brightly painted two-story buildings lining it; the bustling tourist stands; the shops selling vintage clothing, goth and punk fashion, tattoos and body piercings. It was one of the most vibrant streets in London, and James had always loved its quirkiness. Today though, he registered none of it.

Could it really be as simple and tawdry as this for Romilly? No contract killing. No link with Maria. No signature. Just a pathetic stalker who'd snapped and killed?

James felt almost sorry for Richard Burnett when he and Ingham swept into his place of work demanding to see his manager. Because, guilty or not, Burnett would be tainted. Burnett's boss had certainly been unaware that Burnett was anything other than another counter drone.

When he allowed himself to be ushered into the manager's office, Burnett looked ill with apprehension—a bespectacled man in his midtwenties, with thin, cropped, mousy-brown hair, medium height, medium build, medium everything. And, the residual ache in James's cheekbone told him, very familiar.

His heartbeat picked up with stunned excitement.

"Ma'am." He pulled Ingham to one side. He kept his tone quietly conversational. "I'm ninety-nine percent sure that's the guy from Romilly's flat the other morning."

Ingham stared at him, eyes wide, then turned that gaze on Burnett. She didn't smile, but James could see her surging satisfaction.

"Well," she said levelly. "Go and do your thing then, Jamie."

James nodded and walked over to the manager's desk where Burnett hovered. On the whole, James thought, it wasn't really worth the time inviting him to sit down.

He met Burnett's gaze and smiled, catching the instant the man recognized him, in the fixing of his stare.

And he could barely believe that this could be the face of Romilly's killer. This banal, lifeless little man.

"Mr. Burnett." James kept his voice as pleasant and level as if he were remarking on the weather. "Would you care to explain why you were trespassing on the premises of Flat 1, Kings Mansions, Chelsea on the morning of February nineteenth?"

James waited. He'd found that a tone of absolute certainty went a long way.

Burnett's brown eyes began to water behind his glasses.

"I *didn't*...I was just...I just wanted to see..." He stopped, close to hyperventilating, gazing pleadingly at James. He hadn't even tried to deny it.

"You wanted to see?" James prompted.

"Where she lived."

James gave a slow nod, and Burnett relaxed minutely, as if he believed that had been all he'd needed to say.

James pursed his lips, almost apologetically. "Richard Burnett, I am arresting you on suspicion of assault with intent to resist arrest, and assault on a police constable in execution of his duty. You do not have to say anything..."

Burnett whimpered. James almost felt sorry for him. Almost.

Behind him James heard the delicate chink of metal, and Burnett's eyes swung from him, as he finished reading him his rights, to fix on something over his shoulder.

"Do you understand?" Burnett's eyes were still caught by something else behind him and James felt pretty sure it had to be Ingham's set of handcuffs. "Mr. Burnett. Do you understand?"

Burnett's attention swung wildly back to him. "Yes! But you don't need those. *Please*. Not at my work!"

Now James *did* feel a twinge of pity, but..."I'm afraid we have to, Mr. Burnett. We can't risk you resisting arrest again. My eye couldn't take it."

Burnett eyed him for a moment more then slumped in surrender. From there they marched him out through the shop to the car and headed for the station.

And at last, for the first time in either murder investigation, they had a suspect in custody.

Burnett appeared sunk in depression during the drive in, and he spoke only to confirm his name to the custody sergeant and refuse the offer of legal advice because: "I haven't done anything wrong."

James thought too many people equated a request for a lawyer with a tacit admission of guilt, but he couldn't exactly urge them to reconsider.

In the interview room, Burnett sat on one side of the table, looking small and alone. Ingham and James sat on the other.

"You understand you're under arrest for assaulting a police officer, Mr. Burnett," Ingham began.

"It was an accident!" Burnett blurted. "I didn't know he was a policeman. He was chasing me!"

"I did identify myself, Mr. Burnett," James replied. "Loudly. Twice."

Burnett flushed. "I didn't hear you."

Ingham sighed. "What were you doing in Ms. Crompton's flat?"

Burnett looked down at his hands, locked tightly together on the surface of the table. "Like I said…the door was open and…I just wanted to see it. Maybe get something…a memento. Nothing valuable," he rushed on. "Just…something tiny of hers. And when I heard someone behind me, I panicked."

"You sent Romilly a number of letters," Ingham began.

Burnett's eyes widened to an almost comical degree. Had he really not seen this coming?

"Those letters suggested that you and she were 'destined to be together' but…" She paused to hone a suitable tone of ridicule. "'Society was keeping you apart.' Is that correct?"

Harsh patches of scarlet bloomed on Beckett's sallow cheeks.

"You don't understand," he said weakly. Then, "How did you know I sent them?"

So, again, there would be no tedious denial. James caught Ingham's cordial, crocodile smile out of the corner of his eye.

"You left a print, Richard. Do your friends call you Richard?" And with that, Ingham smoothed into full interrogation mode. The use of a first name signaled a subtle reduction in respect.

"Rick. I'm Rick."

"Why did you send the letters, Rick?"

Burnett's flush deepened to crimson. "She was *special*. A star in the making."

"But you went further than her other fans, Rick. You found her home address, and you sent her anonymous letters."

"There was no harm," Burnett defended. "I'd have told her my name eventually. I wanted to intrigue her. Show her a bit of mystery."

"Like mirror writing," Ingham said. "That's mysterious. Where did you get her address, Rick?"

Burnett's mouth tightened. "I just...I waited outside the studios till she came out, and I followed her home. Her name was on her doorbell, so..."

Ingham sat back, satisfied. Burnett displayed exactly the dodgy behavior she sought.

James took his cue. "You know Romilly was murdered."

Burnett's eyes swiveled behind his glasses to look at him. Fear radiated off him now like the stink of sweat.

"You have a conviction for breaking and entering, and you have a restraining order," James went on. "You have a record of obsessive and intrusive interest in young women in the public eye. You're a stalker, Rick."

"I'm *not* a..."

"You've just admitted criminal trespass, breaking and entering and assaulting a police officer, in an attempt to get..." he chose his terminology carefully, "...a trophy of Romilly's life. It's not that hard to believe you might have gone further, is it?"

"Do you possess a firearm, Rick?" Ingham asked.

"A *firearm*? Me?" Horrified. "No! *No!* I sent her fan mail, that's all! And I liked to watch her sometimes, but just on the street."

Ingham sighed as if Burnett were being entirely unreasonable. "All right, Mr. Burnett. This is what's going to happen. I'm going to charge you with assault on a police constable in execution of his duty. You can think yourself lucky. That's the lesser charge."

And the one more likely to stick, Jamie added silently.

Ingham continued, "I'm not going to keep you in custody..." *Because she doesn't have sufficient grounds.* "But I want to see you back here for an interview at an appointed time. Do you understand?"

Burnett's eyes looked ready to pop from their sockets with terror, but he nodded.

When two uniforms came to take him to the front desk, Burnett appeared shell-shocked while Ingham exuded the determination of a bloodhound on the trail.

—ıı— —ıı— —ıı— —ıı—

Ingham called an informal briefing to introduce their new Person of Interest, and as she detailed the case against him, the general lifting of gloom in the unit was tangible. Ingham left most officers to pursue their own continuing lines of inquiry, but five DCs were drafted on to digging into Burnett alone—his movements, his past and his connections—with Ingham overseeing them.

James could hardly fail to share the sense of euphoria that they had a lead at last, yet listening to the chatter around him as they all made their way back to their desks, he couldn't help feeling uneasily as if the team had now decided this man *had* to be the answer, the way to grab some victory from a pit of failure. That Burnett was not only guilty, but they needed him to be guilty, and that could be a dangerous point for any investigation.

He sat down, about to raise that with Scrivenor, when his phone began to jump and buzz on his desk.

A text from Ben: *Trafalgar tonight?*

He grinned unconsciously down at the screen.

For the past week, James'd felt as if he and Ben were sharing a sort of blissful cocoon—so domestic, it seemed like a dry run for living together in official coupledom. It'd been so easy, so natural, to fall into a routine of waking with Ben; breakfast with Ben; snogging voraciously at the front door on the way out; work; home to Ben; then falling into Ben's bed for copious amounts of sex. James found himself avoiding Steggie, because he'd suss at once how besotted James was.

Every night James or Ben hadn't been out working—or in Ben's case, work-socializing—they spent together in the flat, and sometimes James found himself, at work, having to drag himself out of a haze of recent glories, reveling in Ben's interest and warmth, and in his own now fully awakened sexuality.

James had finally found a real relationship, with someone he wanted beyond reason. Things he'd come to believe would never be his now were, and as his belief in the relationship grew, he could sense the bow-tight tension which had always been a part of his identity beginning to loosen.

Tonight though, it seemed Ben had decided their private cocoon should be breached, but Ben's other friends had to know sometime.

By seven p.m., James had arrived home to be kissed, fed, and chivvied into getting changed, before he and Ben fought through the Friday-night pub crowd together.

Oliver, Naomi, Gareth, Beth, Glynn and Graham were all at the usual table, with full drinks in front of them, so James went straight to the bar, leaving Ben to head for the table alone. It was easy to see, from the welcome he always got, how much Ben's friends loved him.

Ben and Glynn had sunk into deep conversation when James reached the table, so he slid Ben's pint in front of him and eased onto the bench beside him ready to chat with someone else. But as he sat, Ben, still distracted by Glynn, dropped his hand onto James's left wrist and rubbed a thumb there in absent thanks, a small, unthinking gesture between two people who were in the habit of touching a lot.

James knew from the sudden silence around the rest of the table that the others had spotted it. Even Glynn stared down delightedly at that incriminating finger as Ben continued to regale him with some scandal about a fellow model. Still, James made the choice to go along with it, to sip his pint with his right hand, and leave his left where it was, as Ben kept chatting.

He felt a bit embarrassed—no avoiding that—but he also couldn't help a sense of pride at how subtly Ben had showed his friends how the land lay now, without having to make a big deal of it.

He'd thought no one would say a word, just gossip after they left, but Glynn surprised him.

Ben had barely finished his story when he crowed with delight. "Morgan! You horny fuck! You *swore* you weren't gonna go there."

"Go where?" Ben asked blankly.

James's eyes were locked on his glass, but he felt intimately the moment understanding hit Ben. The hand on his jerked minutely, then whipped away, as if James's skin were acid. Everyone at the table laughed.

James took a slow, unwanted swig of lager, fixed his gaze on the table and considered the evidence.

First, Ben had discussed with his friends whether or not he'd bed James. Second, Ben had not intended the others to suss their relationship. Third, Ben had meant every word of what he'd muttered on the verge of sleep. He really hadn't intended to start anything with James, to the point of jokily pledging it to his friends.

It took all his willpower not to flinch when he felt Ben's arm slide around his shoulders a moment later. He wouldn't give the others the satisfaction. But he wondered if Ben could feel his tension—how badly he wanted to pull away.

"C'mon, guys," Ben protested laughingly. "You know…there comes a point when you have to be the bigger man and admit defeat." The table hooted with mirth. "Ah, give me a break. Even Steggie knows it was impossible. He's seen him in his boxers."

James kept his gaze trained on the surface of the table as more hilarity ensued, an easy, false smile glued to his face.

But—how the fuck was he meant to react to that? Talking about him like he was easy meat…some bimbo, begging to be had?

He couldn't exactly flounce off—that would make him an even bigger figure of mockery. He had to sit there and take it. So he did what he did best; he hid behind an inscrutable mask.

He sat and seethed and riffled mentally through responses that might restore some dignity without showing how much he cared, but his stomach felt leaden, heavy with the sludge of stunned disappointment and betrayal.

Despite himself, he jumped minutely when Ben leaned over and nuzzled his ear.

"I'm sorry, Jamie," he whispered. "They're like sharks. Never let them smell blood."

It took a second to process, a second to understand, and suddenly he saw it wasn't Ben and the group discussing him as a new conquest; it was Ben and James, against the rest. The friends, James realized, that Ben might love, but could also, apparently, see clearly.

The squeezing ache in his gut began to ease and relax. And as Ben had predicted, given no signs of embarrassment to feed off, the others accepted the new landscape with no more fuss.

James deliberately didn't look at Oliver, and Oliver didn't say a word.

By the time he and Ben walked into their flat, James had buried his moment of disillusion and reveled in his own contentment. They were already living together so easily, he and Ben. It had all slotted effortlessly into place.

His father had been matchmaking for a year before James had broken away, trying to get him to settle down. He'd ranted regularly, in fact, about James's juvenile insistence on playing the field.

Careful what you wish for, Father, James thought, with malicious contentment.

17

"Fuck! About time!" Scrivenor exclaimed when James arrived at his desk on Monday morning. "Come an' take a shifty at this." He appeared oddly agitated as he gestured James round to look at his monitor. "It came from the stuff we put in HOLMES."

James eyed Scrivenor, bewildered by his unusual excitement, then peered at the screen. It displayed an email addressed to both himself and Scrivenor from a DI Buchan based in Aberdeen, who'd noticed and recognized their search parameters.

"I called him already," Scrivenor said.

James nodded and pulled up a chair. "Tell me then?"

"It's a cold case. The victim wiz a fifty-one-year-old male, IC1, worked on an oil rig, passin' through Aberdeen on his way home tae London. Seems he went to savor the delights of the local ladies of the night, an' got a knife in the back and his heid staved in wi' a rock."

"A rock?" James frowned. "Is that the link? Because that's—"

"He had fifteen wee stones in his pocket."

James let his breath go in a whoosh of hope. "And?"

Scrivenor grinned, nicotine-stained teeth glinting beneath his voluminous, faded moustache. "*And,* Buchan thought the stones were weird, but till he saw our HOLMES alert, he did nae think to wonder..." he paused for dramatic effect, "...aboot the chain-link bracelet in the other pocket."

Their eyes met and held, and James unleashed a grin as wide and manic as Scrivenor's.

"Fucking *yes!*" Then, "Who was he?"

"Ah, well." Scrivenor rubbed his nose and suddenly he appeared almost shifty. "That's the other thing. Gary Drake. Address in Croyden. Lived alone, nae family. Name ring a bell?"

Gary Drake? James scoured his memory, idly scratching the back of his head. It meant nothing to him.

"Bit before your time." Scrivenor hit a button and pointed again at his monitor screen, at a page he'd called up in the background, ready. James had to lean over him to see. It took him a few moments to understand what he'd just read, so he read it again to make sure.

Gary Drake, sentenced to fourteen years in 1996 for assisting... *Christ!*

He stared at the screen disbelievingly, then at Scrivenor, and back at the monitor.

"*Eve Kelly?*"

And that was a name impossible not to know.

One of the rarer types of criminal—a female serial killer, not in it for gain or control, just, apparently, for kicks. The papers had feasted on it. "The Holly Golightly Killer" they'd called her because she looked like Audrey Hepburn in her heyday—elfin, beautiful, big-eyed and mesmerizing—while she'd gleefully tortured and slaughtered five men, and severely maimed another, with no obvious motive she'd ever explained.

James'd been a kid when it happened, but still he knew about her. He even saw her image sometimes, on alternative art. She'd achieved notoriety in the same way Rose West and Myra Hindley had—a pop-culture mass murderess, and only the fourth woman in British history to receive a whole-life term.

James looked up at Scrivenor, stunned. "How the fuck does that fit?"

Scrivenor grimaced. "Coincidence? The killer decided to practice on a drunk who'd just had his end away wi' a hooker...an'it...happened to be Gary Drake?"

James rubbed a hand over his mouth. It was facile, but what else had they got? Coincidences did happen.

"I suppose some people would say it was karma," he said.

Scrivenor gave a cynical snort. "More like one last run o' bad luck for the poor bastard."

James raised his eyebrows, because Alec had never been one to sympathize with the lowlifes they caught.

Scrivenor shrugged. "A pal uv mine worked the case. He said Drake and they other two muppets wi' him were like putty in her hands. They'd'a done anythin' for a glimpse uv her tits."

James huffed a disbelieving sound. "C'mon, Alec. You don't do what Drake did for a quick feel."

"I dinnae think they even got as far as a feel. They were like they... vampire servants. In thrall."

James grinned at him. "*Vampire servants?*"

"Aye well." Scrivenor shifted awkwardly, almost, but not quite, embarrassed. "The missus is into a' that...Buffy an' stuff."

James let it go on compassionate grounds.

"Is it enough to show Herself though?" James chewed his lip absently. "She won't be happy. She's got Burnett in her sights."

Scrivenor frowned at the screen. "We cannae ignore it."

But Ingham, when they shuffled into her office, very clearly wished they'd done just that.

"What the *fuck* have you two been smoking?" she howled. "Kelly's serving life with a recommendation! How the hell could she be involved?"

"A wannabe?" Scrivenor suggested imperturbably. "Someone wantin' tae touch the Kelly glamour."

"Alec, the MOs are totally different from Kelly's! The *targets* are totally different," Ingham retorted. "Kelly killed *men*."

James drew a deep breath. "Is it worth asking her?"

"Asking who?" Ingham snapped.

"Eve Kelly?"

Her eyes bugged. "*Eve Kelly?* Are you *serious*? Do you *know* how many cocks we'd have to suck to get the go-ahead for that? And you expect a diagnosed sociopath like her to help us? Why? Civic duty?"

James stared stoically ahead. He hadn't seen Ingham this upset for quite a while.

He said calmly, "She's the only link to Drake we can reach, ma'am. Buchan picked through his life and came up with nothing."

"Drake's not our case, Jamie! You said yourself that Buchan's investigation concluded it'd been a run-in with a pimp. *No* evidence someone wanted to make a name by offing Eve Kelly's sidekick."

"Yes but...Buchan was never really convinced."

"Tough shit. Kelly didn't help the Aberdeen investigation, did she? And I can just imagine how much fun *their* SIO had justifying an interview, and *they* had reasonable cause."

"She met them though," James countered doggedly. "It's *possible* something might come of it."

Ingham glared at him, eyes stony, then she let loose a huge, calming breath and ran a palm over her mouth.

She was considering it, James knew, for all she didn't want to. For all she wanted them to be wrong, she'd give them a fair go.

"*Fuck!* All right. It's an insane stretch but…" She looked at James. "*You* can look into it. Don't bother me with it unless you get something solid. And if nothing comes up by the end of the week, I'm pulling you off. Alec, you stay in the real world."

They both nodded smartly, "Ma'am," and left.

"A week's nae long," Scrivenor pointed out as they walked back to their desks.

But James was grateful even for that. Ingham was right. It *was* a mad stretch. But he'd pushed her because deep down something still told him Maria and Romilly could be linked, though he had no idea how.

He worked late, scouring everything he could find about the Kelly case.

There had been three accomplices—or more like disciples, as Scrivenor had pointed out. William Frederick Smith had been the most involved, sentenced to life in prison with a minimum of nineteen years. He'd only lasted four, before being knifed to death in the showers. Gary Drake had gone down for fourteen years for assisting an offender and three counts of preventing the lawful burial of four victims. He'd served eleven. A third man, Stefan Karol Ksiazek, got ten years for assisting an offender and preventing the lawful burial of two victims. He'd got out on license in five.

When he left that evening, James had a headache of epic proportions and his mind was racing like a mouse on a wheel, trying to grab on to any connection at all between Kelly and her gang twenty years before, and the murders of two young professional women now.

He was still preoccupied when he quietly unlocked the front door of the flat, so it took him a few seconds to recognize that the muffled voices coming from the lounge weren't from the TV, but a real-life conversation. For a moment, paranoia gripped him—the scars of that first time, stumbling on Ben servicing a lover. And though he told himself it would just be Steggie, still, some instinct had him on edge.

He hung up his coat automatically, took a breath, and opened the lounge door.

His worst-case scenario had been walking in on Jace, or any of Ben's faceless lovers; the last person in the world he expected to find sitting in an armchair was his own father.

Magnus Henderson had taken up residence in their lounge.

Through the enormity of his shock, James registered that Ben, seated on the sofa, and his father, in half-profile to the door, were holding a civil, even a cordial, conversation. That both had mugs of tea in front of them, and that, of all things, there was a teapot. Ben had even cracked out the biscuits.

His mind skittered blindly back and forth, bouncing off disbelief and anger and fear, but he had no alternative but to accept it.

Magnus had arrived to disinherit him in person, rather than through lawyers.

Perhaps for something this final, his father's sense of honor required that he look James in the eye.

James had been quite sure, ever since Ingham had told him about his father's call, what those *vital* documents had to be.

His hopes that his father loved him deep down as a son, rather than tolerating him as an heir—those had been annihilated in that last pitched battle before he left. But he realized now that he must have still clung to some remnant, hidden so deeply that he hadn't even acknowledged it to himself. That last seed was gone.

His father desired so definitely to end their relationship that he wanted to engrave it in law. And he wanted that so much, he'd turned up here to ensure James signed on the dotted line.

James didn't want to walk forward, but he could hardly run away, so he stood there numbly for the seconds it took for Ben to notice him, and for Magnus to turn and stand up too.

For the first time in over two years, father and son looked at each other through identical silver-grey eyes and took each other in.

His father hadn't changed much—he was gaunter, perhaps, but still a very handsome man with thin, fine, patrician features. He'd reached his late fifties now, tall and fit, because self-indulgence had always been foreign to him, and his hair was cut in its customary short, elegant style, though grey had almost overwhelmed brown. Everything about him, from his handmade Savile Row suit to his polished Italian shoes, spoke of money, discipline and attention to detail.

For long, tense seconds, neither man spoke, and if James hadn't known him, he'd have sworn his father felt as much at a loss as he did.

Finally, James's ingrained manners and pride overtook him. After all, he was the host.

"Father," he said coldly. Bitterness tasted sharp and metallic in his mouth. "This is an interesting surprise."

He saw a flicker of something unidentifiable in his father's eyes, then Magnus said with equal coolness, "James. You look well."

It sounded as casual as if nothing remarkable had occurred between them. As if they'd only seen each other that morning; as if their final vicious argument had never happened. As if Magnus hadn't cut off his own son. As if he weren't here now to finish the job.

Well, *fuck* him. James had done fine without his money, and he'd never had his love.

"Thanks," James said with calculated disinterest. "So do you."

He felt ferociously relieved that his father hadn't found him existing, alone and out of place, in a dump stinking of piss and cabbage. In fact, he realized that, to Magnus, he must appear exactly like his old self, the James that Magnus had molded, with his designer suit and neat haircut. Now some juvenile part of him wished fiercely as his father scrutinized him that he still walked the beat in uniform, complete with pointy helmet and truncheon, just so Magnus would be forced to acknowledge his son's choice to become a public-sector drone.

The pause stretched as they continued to stare at each other, and now James could take in small changes—some new lines, deeper old ones, a harder mouth.

"Would you like some tea, Jamie?" Ben asked, as if the atmosphere weren't treacle thick. "Why don't you both take a seat?"

James forced his gaze away from his father and over to his lover.

Ben had somehow retained the air of a relaxed host to two charming guests, as opposed to an onlooker to a pissing contest. But then, Ben probably believed that Magnus had come to make amends, as he'd once predicted. Hadn't Ben made it clear he believed reconciliation with a parent was worth any effort? Ben's faith in the parent-child bond had been created by his own easy, loving childhood. And as he looked at his hopeful smile, James found he couldn't bear to be the one to disillusion him.

Let Magnus do that.

So, purely because he knew Ben wanted it, he sat down on the sofa and joined the tea party.

When Ben picked up the teapot and began to pour, the weirdness of the moment struck James again. Neither he nor Ben ever did anything other than dunk a teabag in a mug of hot water. James hadn't even known Ben possessed a teapot. Yet somehow Ben had assessed Magnus as a man for the niceties, who didn't believe in stinting on effort. And making an effort with tea for a guest would be something of which his father would approve.

Because James said nothing, Ben smoothly took up the conversational burden, continuing, apparently, where he and Magnus had left off—chatting about Ben's photography business and the state of the markets.

James only half listened at first, seething with a toxic ferment of shock, rage and pain. But gradually he tuned in, and he saw that somehow Ben had found exactly the right tone to connect with Magnus. There was no hint of the artist as he talked with James's father—he was all businessman. A very straight businessman.

James sat and observed and sipped unwanted tea and brooded, feeling like a sulky adolescent watching how real adults behaved, man to man. He knew his resentment to be partly impatience to be done with the niceties and get on with the bloodletting, but he also had to acknowledge that some of it was a kind of hurt that Ben conversed so easily and amiably with his father when, deep down, James unfairly wanted him openly on his side, full of defensive outrage on James's behalf.

And maybe…maybe too, James had once wanted his father to talk to *him* like that—as if he were someone he might consider worth respect.

He didn't know how long the other two men had been talking when Ben put down his mug and rose gracefully from the sofa. His smile was startlingly charming.

"I'm afraid I really have to deal with some urgent emails," he said. "It's been a great pleasure meeting you though, Sir Magnus."

It was very obvious Ben judged that James had been finessed over the first shock. Now he was graciously withdrawing to let he and his father have privacy. He could have aced a career in the diplomatic service, James thought resentfully.

Ben reached out a hand and James's father took it. Both their handclasps looked firm and manly. But, when he let himself look closely, James realized that Ben was masking displeasure, and by his lack of eye contact with James, that displeasure had to be directed at him.

He sighed inwardly. Ben had every reason to feel pissed off. After all, they were in a relationship, yet James had never told him who he actually was. He'd lied significantly by omission. And yeah, James had *meant* to say, but he'd learned to treasure not being seen as the one-time heir to Henderson Oil.

Magnus murmured, "Likewise, Mr. Morgan. Thank you for tea."

Ben didn't so much as glance at James as he left the lounge.

James eyed his father, and waited. His father returned his stare. Ironically, Magnus had been the one to teach James, long ago, how to use silence to intimidate the enemy.

Finally, Magnus's stern mouth tipped up in an icy smile of acknowledgment. "Isn't it rather overdramatic to hide who you are from your friends?"

Overdramatic. His father used that word on the rare occasions James had ever displayed any kind of strong emotion in front of him. So—battle rejoined then, and no holds bloody barred.

"We *homosexuals* do tend to drama," James said. Magnus's gaze flickered for just a second. *One-nil*, James gloated inwardly. "In any case, Ben's more than a friend." He paused provocatively. "He's my boyfriend. We live together."

Magnus pursed his mouth, as if he tasted something sour. "So I gathered."

James was almost certain his father hadn't had a clue that Ben was gay, but Magnus never admitted ignorance if he could help it.

"I understand from your Detective Chief Inspector that you're doing well," Magnus went on, as if James hadn't just blatantly stuck his unwanted lifestyle in his face. James's eyes narrowed—a battle-hardened rabbit confronting a suspiciously disengaged wolf.

"I enjoy the work." He sounded defensive, though he desperately wanted to manage disinterest. "It's very rewarding." *Unlike my old career* went unsaid.

Magnus, though, gave a slow nod. He was ignoring all provocations, refusing every invitation to battle, every goad to lance the boil and let the poison out into the air.

"I brought this," Magnus announced instead, and held out a large envelope, a rectangle of thick, creamy paper.

James, after a beat, took it. He didn't look inside. He didn't want to give his father the satisfaction of showing that much interest.

He'd actually fully intended to sign the documents on the spot, then hustle Magnus out, but now he had them in his hand, he found he needed time to accept that his own father really did despise him that much. Perhaps he needed to hear Magnus *say* it, give his reasons. Burn their relationship to the ground for good.

"I...the company that is..." Magnus clarified, as though they weren't one and the same. "As you know, we donate to many charities."

For tax breaks, James sneered inwardly, though what the hell that had to do with anything...

Magnus continued stiffly, "But this year, we've decided to run our own fundraising event. In your mother's name."

James stared at the envelope and then at Magnus with as much shock as if he'd just donned a red nose and a clown wig.

He wondered briefly if the memory of their last confrontation—what had been said about James's mother—had also just struck Magnus. But most of all, he didn't understand what was going on.

Magnus cleared his throat. "*So.* If you wish to take part, you may inform my secretary. Or call me on my private line. You have the number."

James looked down at the envelope again, then back, stupidly, at his father. Magnus nodded curtly and stood to go.

"But..." James called, bewildered. "Don't you want me to sign something?"

Magnus frowned at him. "All the details are in the envelope," he snapped. Suddenly he sounded querulous, as if he were being held back from a vital appointment. He moved away to the lounge door. "Let me know your decision. I'll show myself out."

James stared at empty space and heard the front door slam.

Tentatively, he looked down at the envelope. Jaw set, he opened it and slid out its contents, as if they might transform and go for his throat.

Not legal documents, but an expensively tooled card which, when he studied it, proved to be an invitation to a charity art showing and ball on the first of June, in aid of…the Rose Henderson Trust. The inscription read: *James Henderson plus one.*

James stared at the card, uncomprehending.

From what he remembered of her, his mum had loved painting and loved art. The accompanying leaflet spelled that out and included a rare photograph of her.

There had to be a reason.

His father wouldn't have come here for anything other than the furthering of his own agenda. And being of interest to Magnus Henderson again could only mean pain, despite all James's comforting assurances that he didn't care any more. Yet he couldn't deny that, along with bewilderment, there was relief. Unwanted, but vast and powerful.

He felt as if the card might vanish in his hand like a hallucination. But it remained—the gold company logo, the list of beneficiary charities running in gilt lettering across the bottom. They were familiar to him and covered most of the bases: two cancer charities, a children's charity, another for the elderly. But the benevolent fund for artists hadn't been on the old list. And—

James's eyes fixed. Perhaps this *would* all turn out to be a hallucination brought on by stress and tiredness. Typed in gilt: an emergency switchboard to help LGBT+ youth.

An alarming swell of emotion hit out of nowhere, lodged under his breastbone like a solid ball. Suppressed grief, probably. Fear. Longing.

"Jamie?" Ben stood frowning in the doorway, looking as if he couldn't settle on whether to unleash anger or concern. But, being Ben, concern won out. "Did it go okay?"

James gave a choked laugh and ran his free hand across his mouth. He sniffed hard. "I have no idea." He'd been so certain that his father had been about to cast him out, once and for all. He'd braced for it for days, and instead...had that been some kind of awkward try at rapprochement?

"He invited me to a ball."

Ben's mouth opened and closed, as if he didn't know which response to go for. But then he said, "*Henderson Oil*, Jamie! Why didn't you *say*?"

James sighed. "You knew my family is rich. What difference does it make?" Though he knew too well.

"What difference? That you're...a billionaire playing at being a policeman."

And that stung badly. James had enough people accusing him of being some sort of dilettante, idling away his bored days at the Met. He hadn't expected to hear it from Ben.

"I am not *playing* at being a policeman. I *am* a policeman. And I'm not a billionaire either."

"Henderson Oil?" Ben scoffed. "Yes, you bloody are!"

"No. I'm not." James kept his voice level. "Magnus is a billionaire."

"A future billionaire then." But Ben's expression shifted minutely and anger drained from it. He let out a heavy sigh. "I'm sorry. It just... caught me off guard. I mean that's a different level. That's...yachts and supercars. And I didn't expect *Sir Magnus* on the doorstep."

"Seems like you did pretty well anyway." James felt wrung out. "I'm sorry too. It just...it's not my life any more."

"It *could* be, Jamie. I think he wants to build bridges."

James considered the card in his hand. Just ten minutes ago, he'd have laughed hysterically at that.

"Maybe," he said slowly. "But I can't be who he wants me to be. I'm happy with my life now."

"Are you going then? To the ball?"

James shrugged and blew out a breath. "It's a couple of months away. I don't know." He tried for cheerfulness. "Hey, you can be my plus one."

Ben gave a thin smile. "Yeah...I don't think I want to piss off your dad that much. I'll stick with his first impressions."

"Too late," James admitted. "I told him we're together."

Ben's eyes widened. "You're joking."

"I wanted to shock him," James returned lightly, though he couldn't help notice that Ben didn't appear remotely amused.

"Fuck." Ben blinked. He seemed to force himself to relax. "And here I was trying to show him you had nice, trustworthy, manly mates. I even got the fucking teapot out."

And that finally made James laugh. "That's not very manly. It made the whole thing even more surreal when I came in."

"The Mad Billionaire's Tea Party." Ben laughed too, though he still appeared a bit unsettled. Understandable, James supposed. None of this was his problem.

"It was nice of you," James said affectionately. "To entertain him like that. And, you know…try to make a good impression."

Ben ran a hand back through his hair. He looked rueful. "He's your father, Jamie. Even if he's turned out to be Magnus bloody Henderson. I want you to be happy. To make up with your dad."

James's stomach turned to goo.

"You want everyone to be happy." But hearing Ben say he cared for him gave him just what he needed, so badly, with the ground shifting underneath his feet. He felt battered, his emotions minced. "D'you mind if I don't go out tonight?" They'd planned to meet the others, which James quite enjoyed now, and the group seemed to have accepted he and Ben were an item.

"God! No, Jamie. That's fine," Ben said earnestly. "Actually, how about I stay in too? That must have been a hell of a shock."

But after they'd had dinner and cleared up, Ben clearly decided to allow James as little time as possible to brood. James had just finished filling the dishwasher in fact, when he found himself backed up against the fridge freezer, being snogged ravenously.

He could taste wine and tomatoes on Ben's tongue, and he loved it. Loved feeling so desired when he desired so much in return.

"So…" Ben murmured sexily against his mouth. "What d'you say we widen your horizons?"

James gave a giddy smile. "What're we looking at then, hot shot? Cannibal fantasies? Pony play?"

Ben pulled back warily.

"It's amazing the things you encounter as a copper," James finished.

Ben huffed a laugh. "You'll have to tell me. I was actually thinking something a bit more..." His hand trailed up to tangle in James's hair. "Old school though. I was thinking...*maybe*...you'd like to fuck me with that lovely big cock of yours."

James's smile dropped as if he'd been stuck with a fork.

At once, his pulse began to gallop. His prick, which had been chubbing up lazily to the sweet, seductive atmosphere, surged in an urgent swell, filling with impatient, hungry blood. Apprehension, though, put a definite brake on the proceedings. He'd never got *close* to having anal sex with another man before. But God...he'd thought about it. Imagined it.

Then the understanding hit him that he could actually have this, and with the guy he loved. It broke through his eternal reserve, and like a wellspring, excitement, gratitude, adoration gushed up through the cracks.

He grinned wildly. "I think I could see my way clear to giving it a go."

The reality though wasn't just sex, not for James.

The intensity and intimacy of what they were doing; the slow intense preparation Ben led him through; James's fingers inside Ben's body; the moment Ben slid the condom onto James's aching erection; watching Ben smile up at him with uncomplicated affection...James knew he would never allow himself to forget one brilliant, terrifying, sweaty second of it.

His girlfriends used to accuse him of emotional distance, of being cold, unavailable. If they could see him now. If they could see every defense he'd ever had being leveled, all his life's armor laid at the feet of this beautiful man, a man who cared enough to share his burdens. Happiness swelled like a tide in his chest.

"How would you like to...?"

Ben stretched luxuriantly, his long body on wanton display in the gilded light of the bedside lamps. "Like this," he decided, settling on his back among the pillows, hard cock bobbing against his flat stomach. "I want to watch the virgin's deflowering." James grinned back.

Casually, Ben pulled up his legs to expose his crack and the glistening pink hole that James had so diligently loosened and lubricated. All ready for him. Lust wiped the smile from James's face.

It was really going to happen. James didn't know why this act seemed so much more significant than the other things they'd done. Why should it be any more intimate than sucking someone else's cock, even if latex got in the way of flesh every time now? Or coming, rubbing up against each other, panting into each other's mouths?

But somehow this did feel...*more*. Like a confirmation of something. James knew it to be objectively ridiculous, but to him, doing this for the first time with someone who meant so much... It felt like a consummation.

His eyes, hot with feeling, stared into Ben's for long beats of charged silence.

"God, Jamie," Ben breathed. "What you do to me." He huffed a little laugh, but to James it sounded strained, and his eyes weren't smiling. Then he seemed to catch himself and haul himself back from whichever emotion had struck him. He broke the moment with a wicked grin, familiar Ben. "You're so fucking *sexy*, you bastard. I'm a lucky man getting at you first."

James wanted to protest, but he knew better. Now was not the time to make the point that *Ben* was all he wanted. But Ben would learn. He'd prove it to him.

He shuffled forward on his knees and leaned down, latex-clad erection in hand, aiming it at its target. His heart hammered in his chest, his gut swooped with empty nerves.

And then he pressed the head against the glistening, pink-brown dimple of Ben's anus and pushed forward, still holding his fat, swollen shaft as if it would fail otherwise. He felt the dip of tight muscle, resistance, and then, with a slippery shock, the head of his cock slid through into clenching tightness, the sphincter muscle contracting around it. He froze for a second, shocked by the magnitude of pleasure, then he let his weight carry him forward and his shaft glided deep into the sweet, dark heat.

He heard Ben gasp. "Oh God, that's nice. That's lovely..."

James's arms were braced, straight, on the bed on either side of Ben's shoulders, and he felt Ben's long, slim, muscular legs sliding around his waist and clinging there. He pulled out an inch or two, but he couldn't help shoving back at once into the perfect tightness, trying at least to angle his cock to rub against the tiny, spongy nub of nerves

Ben had taught him to find. The perfection of that hungry clench stunned him. He could hardly comprehend that another human body could give such pleasure.

He began to thrust, to fuck, and fuck hard, though he'd meant to be gentle, pumping his hips between Ben's spread legs into the hot, velvet clutch. And Ben pushed up to meet every shove and pull, writhing on James's prick, moaning, panting in concert with James's desperate, gasping breaths.

Eventually, Ben began to claw at James's biceps. His rigid cock bounced obscenely between their bodies as they fucked. But he made no effort to touch it, apparently getting off just fine on James's cock pumping in his arse.

James tried to hold on, but the sight of Ben arching up, pushing in to the fuck, and the sensation of tight, gripping heat, were edging him beyond his endurance.

He reached down and rubbed Ben's rigid erection, and with a kind of wail, Ben arched up, at once rammed his arse down hard one final time onto James's prick, and erupted, shooting long gushes of semen up over his chest and belly.

The spasming massage on James's shaft became just too insanely sweet then. Pleasure rose and rose to an unstoppable crescendo, until he felt as if his heart were stalling in his chest, blood pressure about to blow his skull open, and he came so hard he thought he must have burst through the condom with the force of it. But it was illusion; familiar hot wetness trickled snug against the head of his cock as he shot and shot, and he found himself wishing fiercely that the rubber weren't there.

He collapsed, finally, onto Ben's relaxed body, and they lay tangled for minutes, panting and sweating until Ben groaned, "Condom," and James forced strength back into his spaghetti limbs to pull himself up and ease his fast-deflating cock out of Ben's arse before the rubber began to leak.

He knotted up the full condom, looking down at his own semen-smeared chest; at his exhausted reddened cock; at Ben, lying, eyes closed, still breathing heavily, and he couldn't help but lean down to kiss him hard on his bitten lips, putting all his gratitude and happiness into it.

Ben kissed back for a while, slowing down, sensuous, almost dazed, while James reveled in the feeling that they hadn't only fucked, they'd made love.

When James pulled back, he let their foreheads rest together for a second or two, then he slumped away to lie on his back beside Ben, beaming at nothing.

He sensed Ben's turning his head on his pillow to look at him, but nothing could dim that huge, besotted, euphoric grin.

"Well, fair guess you liked it." Ben laughed. James didn't move or stop smiling, but he made a sound to suggest the redundancy of the comment. There was another satisfied silence, then Ben said, "Fancy trying it the other way next time?"

James flopped his head sideways to look at Ben, trying to blank his own expression.

Well…did he fancy it?

A knot of apprehension had formed under his breastbone again, nibbling at the afterglow. But fuck—he'd thought about it that way too, often enough, over the years, alone in his bedroom. Imagined what it might feel like. Not just doing it to another man, but having a man do to him. The reality of it though… Putting that much trust in someone else…

But hadn't Ben done just that? Didn't he owe him the same kind of trust in return?

"Okay," he replied, trying for casual, though his pulse rabbited with nerves. "Yeah."

"It's about the only thing you haven't done now…'cept kink," Ben commented, with a yawn. "God 'm knackered. That was one helluva fuck."

James frowned. He felt unsure whether to feel be flattered by the review or disappointed at hearing the experience reduced to that.

Christ! He lashed at himself. *It's just a figure of speech, you stupid wanker! You're turning into a little girl. What next? Justin Bieber on the wall?*

"Yeah, it was," he said, suitably cool and unconcerned, but still he found himself adding waspishly, "Glad I passed the exam."

"Flying colors," Ben drawled sleepily before visibly sliding over the edge to unconsciousness.

18

The next day, all the talk around the MIT appeared to be fixed firmly on Burnett.

"Herself wants tae bring him in an' roast him," Scrivenor advised. "But she wants somethin' solid on him first. There's nothin' unless we get in an' search his place though, an' we cannae do that without serious grounds. Or chargin' him wi' somethin' more serious than smudgin' your mascara."

James found himself peering around to make sure the coast was clear before he said, "I'm still not sure I like Burnett for the killer."

Scrivenor didn't look annoyed. He merely asked, "Why?"

"Because..." *It's a feeling.* Fuck he couldn't admit that, even to Alec. "Only two percent of stalkers kill their victims."

Scrivenor frowned. "Aye. Maybe he's in the two percent. The mentally ill."

"Does Burnett seem like the kind of man who could stage a killing like Romilly's? I mean we're talking balls of steel doing that in a partly residential street, even in the early hours. It'd have taken clever planning. Efficiency. And...I don't know if I see that in Burnett. I mean... the chase... He went into the flat impulsively and he didn't have a backup plan. He's a panicker."

"Still brought you down though." Scrivenor waggled his eyebrows, then he said quietly, "You're still determined Maria's case is tied in to Romilly's, aren't you?"

James didn't answer but beckoned Scrivenor over to look at a police mug shot on his monitor. It showed a young man, six feet, according to the police height chart behind him, dark haired, and significantly overweight. An overgrown beard and thick glasses did nothing to boost his appeal. They both regarded the image for a second or two.

"Stefan Ksiazek." Scrivenor's tone sounded neutral.

"Yep. Polish family, but born here in the UK. He's the only one of Eve Kelly's gang still alive. Apart from her, of course. Did your mate say anything about him?"

Scrivenor scrunched up his face in thought. "Gimme a minute." He slid round to his own desk and picked up his phone, engaging in a conversation that sounded equal parts jovial and grossly insulting. He disconnected a few minutes later.

"Pat says the guy wiz obsessed. Young in the heid. I mean…hard to tell by lookin' at him, but he wiz only in his early twenties an' he wiz a stereotypical geek. Nae idea about wimmin. All Kelly's gang were under her control but…Pat said Ksiazek wiz slavish. He'd've jumped aff a tower block if she'd bothered tae ask him."

"DI Buchan said they tried to find him when they were looking at the Kelly link," James said. "But he left jail, did his probation, got a job, then he disappeared. They got a track on his passport…he entered France, then Holland, but nothing else. Interpol had no trace."

Scrivenor stroked his moustache and leaned back in his chair. "You think he's abroad?"

"Could be. *Or* he could've got back into the UK with a new passport."

"You think he could be a possible then?" Scrivenor gave a surprised frown and proceeded to echo Ingham. "Ah mean, for Drake, ah can see it. But Maria? Romilly?"

"Yeah, I *know*, Alec. But if there's a link, apart from Kelly herself, he's all I've got. And *she's* inconveniently locked up for life."

His frustration didn't leave him until that evening when he reached Selworth Gardens, to find the flat warm, lit, and smelling of cooking food.

"It'll be ready in ten minutes!" Ben called from the kitchenette when James peered in the lounge door. "Go and get changed."

But James could no more have obeyed than walk out of the flat. Instead, he strode over and pulled his lover into a deep, delving kiss, full of lust and gratitude. Ben froze for a surprised second, but then he gave as good as he got, as if he couldn't help it either. When he pulled back, James thought smugly that he looked a bit dazed.

"Mmmm…do I get one too?"

James held Ben's rueful eyes—but there was no escape. He'd done it again.

Steggie sat behind them, twisted round on the sofa, positioned to chat to the cook, and James had entirely failed to notice him in his single-minded focus on Ben.

"You want one?" he asked, as casually as he could.

Steggie looked ready for a film shoot, eyes subtly lined with kohl, wearing a sleeveless black mesh T-shirt, exposing his sexy tattoo. He looked, James thought reluctantly, like what he was. Beautiful public property.

"Oh, you *know* I do, sweetie, but I wouldn't like Ben to get jealous." Steggie threw a provocative glance at Ben, who gave him stiff, narrow-eyed look back. A *behave* look. James glanced down to hide a smile. He enjoyed the idea of a jealous Ben, after his own early agonies.

Steggie stood and stretched his long body. "Well, *much* as I'd love to sit here gazing at Ben's fabulous still lifes..." He gestured with panache at a photograph on the wall—the stream in sunlight. "I've got to go and get fucked for money." For a second, James thought he might have heard bitterness, but Steggie produced an evil grin, as if he'd anticipated James's frozen reaction to the mention of the realities of his job. "Anyway," Steggie went on. "All this cooing leaves me feeling *very* green and hairy."

James did everything in his power not to flush, but beside him, Ben had already pulled away.

"Don't be so fucking stupid," he said with contempt and marched back to the kitchenette.

Steggie's eyes followed him, but he didn't seem shocked by Ben's rare show of temper. He appeared almost satisfied to have got a rise out of him.

"I make it a rule *never* to play gooseberry," he declared as if Ben hadn't spoken. "*Never* get in the way of true love." He winked at James, "Bye, sweetheart," and exited with a flourish. The front door slammed shut a second or two later.

A peculiar silence followed, broken only by the quiet background muttering of the TV. Ben stirred the contents of his saucepan fiercely, head down.

"Hi," James tried. He hadn't a clue what had just happened, but he'd never seen Ben react like that before.

There were a few more silent seconds of concentrated stirring before Ben spat, "He can be a serious pain in the arse sometimes."

James frowned uncertainly. "He was just teasing," he ventured. But something *had* been mildly off in Steggie's demeanor. Perhaps James had walked in on a bit of an argument.

Ben stopped stirring and turned round.

"It doesn't bother me." But he seemed tense, even flustered.

Perhaps it *did* bother Ben to be teased about being in love. Maybe he got embarrassed at being called on it.

"You know he loves winding people up," James coaxed with a grin. "He doesn't mean any harm."

Ben drew in a deep breath and let it out in a gusty sigh. "You and Steggie," he mocked, shaking his head, and just like that, his cheerfulness returned, fully restored. James loved that about him. It could also be why Steggie baited him, come to think of it.

They ate dinner, plates on knees, in front of the TV, but soon the combination of red wine, good food and relaxation began to send James to sleep.

"C'mon, Jamie." Ben stood and turned off the TV, then switched off table lamps too. "Bedtime."

James looked up at him dopily, about to protest, but remembered what bedtime meant tonight. Somehow, the run-in with Steggie, and his own weariness, had sidetracked him.

He stood too, abruptly wide-awake. "I should shower."

Ben turned off another lamp. "Do you need to?" He sounded sultry. James couldn't make out his face in the new dimness.

"I don't know," he said.

Ben walked toward him switching off the last lamp on the way. "Tell you what. Why don't you get into bed and I'll let you know."

James swallowed. "Okay."

"Hey." Ben's voice sounded softer, gentler. "If you're not up for this, we can do something else, you know." There could be no more doubt they were talking about the same thing: James's final loss of virginity. "Or nothing. Since you're knackered."

For a second James toyed with the idea of escape then rejected it.

He wanted it. He wanted to give Ben this, and to experience it himself, with Ben. He wanted it to be about love. He caught Ben's hand and didn't say anything at all, just turned and led him to the bedroom.

James hadn't allowed himself to obsess about it…how the idea of doing might make him feel, not just physically but emotionally. A man who'd trained himself to never give in, rolling over and letting someone fuck him.

Ben sensed something, though, and he talked him through it with a mixture of gentleness and filth.

"It's easier on your belly first time," he murmured. As James turned over nervously to obey, he gave a long, possessive stroke to his backside. "And I get to see my dick, pumping in and out of your incredible arse."

Ben turned out to be as good at topping as he was at everything else in the bedroom, and he took an eternity to prepare James, working him until James had got over the oddness and embarrassment of someone else's fingers in his arse, and frankly writhed on them. When at last, Ben mounted him, he vocalized all the time, as he eased his erection inside, letting James hear his pleasure.

"That's it just…oh God, Jamie…that's it. Just…you feel so fucking good…"

To James, it felt like an assault, emotions up and physical sensations bombarding him—panic at first as it started to happen, then forcing discipline. Fullness and invasion. Gradually feeling that rigid, alien rod of flesh inside him. Ben began to move, to push and pull, his cock gliding past nerves that stunned James with pleasure.

Overwhelming the physical, though, for James—the significance of letting someone else inside his body for the first time. The staggering intimacy of it.

Ben encouraged him constantly, stroking his cock, never losing patience, and he sounded euphoric when James began to respond in earnest and moan and lose his inhibitions.

Soon after, Ben pulled back and had James turn over onto his back. He pushed in again, staring down into James's eyes, and it became a blur of new pleasure and more intensity. Ben told him over and over again how good he felt, how amazing, until it all reached an unbearable peak and James shot over his own belly, a different kind and quality of orgasm to any he'd felt before as he spasmed and clenched around the steel length lodged inside him. He watched Ben greedily as he took his final desperate thrusts, gazing at James as if he could barely believe he existed, until at last he let go in a rictus of ecstasy. And then it was done.

Ben took a minute, perhaps, to recover, but he didn't lie and bask in the afterglow as James had when he'd topped. Instead, he pulled out almost at once to dispose expertly of the condom, trotted to the ensuite for a warm cloth to clean them both up, then slid back into bed and pulled James in for a cuddle.

To James it felt again unnervingly like a master class—this time in the proper etiquette of postcoital care after deflowering a virgin. But there were undoubtedly times it could feel like Master and Student, if James let it. And he felt pretty sure, as he lay, held close in Ben's arms, that there had been more than a few virgins before him.

He tried not to think about it, because jealousy of Ben's multitude of previous lovers was ridiculous and out of line. But it was an instinct, primal possessiveness, rooted somewhere in the lizard brain.

What Ben had done with his other men though—that had been sex. Whereas James only had to recall the intensity of their joining, the way Ben had looked at him as he moved inside him, and he knew he and Ben had made love.

19

The next day, James went in to work riding a new wave of euphoria and exhaustion. He'd taken breakfast with Ben, and they'd smirked at each other like two kids who'd done something they shouldn't and got away with it. He found himself picking up a coffee for Scrivenor, just because he felt that good.

His arse was definitely tender, and emotionally he recognized an odd vulnerability that bit when he dwelt on the night before. But it didn't feel bad—he didn't feel weak or threatened. Instead, he felt... renewed.

Scrivenor eyed his surprise latte with exaggerated suspicion, but he took it without verbal question. James even beamed at Kaur as she dumped a huge mountain of files on his desk, and began to sort them into smaller hills in front of him.

"Mulligan's got a bloke in the cells," Scrivenor announced, as he sipped blissfully. "The Vauxhall-nightclub thing."

James nodded, though Mulligan's case felt like ancient history. Before he could say that, Scrivenor scrunched up his nose and leaned closer.

"D'you get a haircut?" he asked accusingly.

James's reactions were definitely delayed by tiredness but, "What?"

"A haircut. When d'you get the time?"

"I haven't had a haircut," James protested. He could feel Kaur studying him too.

"Have ye no?" Scrivenor took a long sip of his coffee, leaving a fringe of froth on his moustache, but his eyes remained fixed on James, as if he were trying to place a suspect. "There's just…I dunno. There's somethin' different. Is that a new tie?"

James rolled his eyes and mocked Scrivenor's attention to James's appearance, and his off-beam observational skills. He wondered if he were actually still asleep in Ben's bed, having a particularly quirky dream.

But…he'd already accepted that today he did feel a bit different. Could there actually be…something other people sensed? Perhaps allowing…that…really did affect something profound. Or, *perhaps* that was just James. Overthinking everything.

"Ah know whit it is," Scrivenor pronounced. "Ye look glaikit."

James bridled. "What the fuck is *glaikit*?"

"Bet he has a new boyfriend," Kaur put in. "That's why he's smilin' into space."

"Aye. That," Scrivenor approved. "Smilin' in tae space. Glaikit."

James knew too well that his complexion would be approaching pulsating crimson. But with beautiful simplicity, it struck him that he had no reason to deny anything. He had nothing to hide, nothing to be embarrassed about. For the first time in his life, he had a happy relationship with someone of whom he felt incredibly proud, a relationship they'd just taken to a new level.

It felt like a huge moment, indescribably liberating, when he said casually, "Well, I am seeing someone."

"I knew it!" Kaur said triumphantly. "What's he like? Is he good looking? I bet he's good looking."

"Um. Yeah, he's…good looking."

"Oooh!" Kaur grinned. "How tall is he?"

"About my height." James was aware that somewhere along the line, the chain of command had disintegrated into girly gossip but he didn't stop it. Scrivenor seemed struck dumb.

"What's his name?"

"Ben." He felt a rush of pride saying it out loud. That the amazing, elusive Ben Morgan had chosen him.

Scrivenor waited until Kaur had drifted away to ask, "Is that your flatmate, then?" Who James had asked Alec to investigate. James nodded, hoping he hid his sheepishness.

"You kept that quiet." Scrivenor sounded careful. Maybe Ben looked like a decadent media badass on paper. Or maybe it offended Scrivenor's flatmate rule.

James beamed at him anyway, touched by his protectiveness. "He's a really nice guy, Alec. You'll like him."

They would get on well, and James decided to broach the idea of introducing them with Ben that evening.

As it turned out, James didn't get his key into his front door until after eleven, and though Ben had texted to tell him he'd be out at the pub with that day's clients, and maybe even be forced to go on to a club, it still felt like anticlimax.

But Ben had left some lamps on in the lounge, and when James looked in the kitchen, he found a note stuck by fridge magnet, telling him about a portion of shepherd's pie in the fridge. The physical evidence of Ben's care for him always touched him, but he didn't feel hungry, so he poured a glass of wine from a chilled screw-top bottle in the fridge and went to slump in front of the TV.

The ringtone of his mobile sounded shockingly loud in the nearly silent room. James felt proud that he hadn't jumped upright. He was nervy as fuck, he knew.

He looked at the phone screen and smiled ruefully as he answered, ready to take some pressure. "Hi, Stegs. You in the pub?"

"Hey! No such luck. I'm in the flat. Just finished a shoot."

James sighed inwardly. "Just got home myself." He braced himself for the inevitable.

"Great. I'm just off out, and *you're* giving me a lift."

"Steggie," James groaned. "I'm knackered, mate."

"Then unknacker yourself. You're coming." Then, like a carrot waved in front of a particularly weak donkey, "*Ben'll* be happy if you turn up."

James considered for a moment. He didn't want to go, and he'd braced himself for a short squabble to resist. But Steggie being downstairs, as opposed to already at the pub, would be banging down the door in minutes if he refused. And he felt far too wired to sleep yet.

"Okay." He sighed. "Give me fifteen minutes."

When they reached the pub, the wall of noise from the surprisingly large Wednesday night crowd didn't allow for anything other than yelling, but they got through to the bar, thanks to Steggie's vicious elbows, then fought their way out again toward the usual booth.

They found it packed with unfamiliar people, but James barely noticed anyone else in the group. All his attention fixed on Ben holding court at the left of the table. He wore a black sleeveless tank, arms on display and sexy as hell, and he seemed deep in laughing conversation with three youngish, generic, overstyled men—presumably the clients. They all looked much the same to James now.

"Stegs! Jamie!" Graham sounded happily drunk from the back of the table. "You're fucking late!"

"And we're fucking hammered!" Glynn added cheerfully. Oliver ignored all four of them.

The bench being full, James sat on a stool beside Steggie, but he didn't know whether to interrupt Ben's conversation, or wait for him to surface and come to him.

Steggie had no such qualms. "Oi! *Ben!* We're here! Your boyfriend! And your mate!"

James tried not to laugh. But…*boyfriend.* He'd been teased about it all afternoon by Sameera. It was only when he met Ben's hazy eyes that he realized sinkingly that his *boyfriend* appeared to be half-plastered.

"Jamie!" Ben pulled a sloppy, charming grin. "You're here!"

James smiled back, amused and stupidly pleased. Ben was a puppy-like drunk.

"Ross!" Ben turned happily to the man beside him. "This is Jamie, my flatmate! And this is Steggie. He lives downstairs. Ross is ad exec on the shoot."

Ben beamed, first at James and Steggie, then at Ross, a pretty blond guy in his twenties, apparently as blurry round the edges as Ben. But Ross said something inaudible to Ben, which caught his attention completely, and he turned back to their conversation as if they hadn't been interrupted. James took a face-saving sip of his pint. He did his best not to glance in Ben's direction again, determined not to show any insecurity or possessiveness, though, despite himself, "flatmate" had stung.

As time went on it became clear to him, even with just the odd glance and peripheral vision, that Ross had begun to lean closer and closer to Ben while Ben chatted on oblivious. And whatever they were talking about, neither of them seemed interested in including anyone else. For all his determined internal lecturing, James couldn't help the tug of disappointed tension in his gut.

He'd made it partway down his second pint of shandy when he registered that Ben had risen to his feet, edging his way out toward him. James looked up at once—like a dog at his master, he rebuked himself, irritated—and met Ben's eyes.

"Jamie." Ben gave him a huge affectionate smile, as if James were one of his very favorite things, then he bent down, arm braced on James's shoulder, to press a soft, alcohol-flavored kiss to his open lips. "I'm glad you came."

He gazed at him, still smiling, for a moment longer then he patted his shoulder absently and headed off, making—James established after twisting round slightly—for the gents. He moved reasonably steadily though, and James thought he might be less plastered than he'd feared.

James turned back to the table, annoyed with himself for feeling relieved by their interaction, annoyed by his own flashes of insecurity. But when he started talking to Steggie again, a fair part of his attention remained focused on waiting for Ben's return, in the hope he could be persuaded to go home.

It felt like a long time. In fact, he realized, as he confronted a third pint Glynn slid in front of him, it it *had* been a long time. More than ten minutes. Maybe Ben'd nodded off in there, he thought with impatient worry. Booze tended to make him sleepy eventually.

He twisted his head round to check behind him, in case he'd somehow missed Ben's return, and he noticed only then that Ross had gone too. He turned back, pouting thoughtfully, but as he did, he caught Oliver watching him, an expression of eager, satisfied malice on his face. And without really understanding why, something cold began to form in James's belly.

He blanked his face of all expression and looked calmly away from Oliver's gloating green eyes. But still, he stood, because he couldn't ignore it, and without looking at any of them, he made his way through knots of laughing, chatting people to the gent's loo.

The room seemed shockingly quiet after the noise of the pub— large, covered with white- and burgundy-colored tiles, and surprisingly, not full. Three unfamiliar blokes were using urinals, and of five floor-to-ceiling stalls, two were occupied.

James felt numb. He used a urinal and washed his hands, and behind him he could see in the mirror that one of two closed stall doors was opening. His stomach clenched like a vise.

A tall, balding, bespectacled man emerged and headed for the washbasins. James dried his hands mindlessly, feeling the desperate naive optimism still clinging on inside him beginning to shrivel and curl up, like paper in a fire.

He had no way now to pretend he wasn't waiting, so he slid into one of the cubicles and left the door very slightly open. They were private, these cubicles, almost soundproof. Perfect, he supposed, for getting off with random twinks.

I'm going to look back at this and I'm going to feel like a jealous arsehole, James told himself.

But still, he sat on the closed toilet seat for almost exactly seven minutes, listening to the traffic to and from the urinals, and it felt like much longer. At last, he heard the unmistakable metallic snap of a cubicle lock opening.

He waited for a second or two, then walked out.

Ross stood at the washbasin, rinsing his hands. He looked skinnier and smaller than James had thought, shorter by several inches than either James or Ben, and he seemed flushed. He met James's eyes in the mirror, and after an instant of surprise, he gave a kind of conspiratorial smirk—all boys together—which slid slowly away in the face of James's blank stare. He frowned and blinked, as if he realized he'd misjudged, eyes darting furtively toward the cubicle he'd just exited. And when James followed his gaze, he saw that the lock was red again; that someone, still inside, had thrown it, until, presumably, a decent period of time had elapsed. James was impressed they'd managed that much discretion.

He felt his face twisting into an involuntary grimace of distress. There really wasn't any denying it any more.

He could wait until Ben came out, play the whole scene as cuckolded lover in front of the small audience at the urinals. He could go back out to the table and pretend to be none the wiser. Or he could just...go.

He smiled blindingly at Ross and walked out.

He was barely aware of how he got his coat or got out of the pub, now busier than ever, or how he drove home, but somehow it all happened. He was throwing his keys on the lounge coffee table by half past midnight.

He went straight to the kitchenette to extract the bottle of wine from the fridge. The shepherd's pie sneered at him from the middle shelf. He poured a huge glass of alcohol and downed it in two gulps. Then he stood, braced against the counter, head down, and refused to think.

His bedroom, when he opened the door, felt cold. He hadn't slept here for almost two weeks.

He undressed quickly, pulled on some pajama bottoms and slid beneath the duvet. The sheets were freezing. In his imagination, they smelled stale. He set his alarm, switched off his light and lay in the dark, not caring how cold it was, because he felt colder inside. He tried to sleep, but he managed no more than a kind of alert dose. It felt as if he were lying in someone else's bed, or waiting for some disaster.

A key turning in the front door lock woke him as efficiently as a klaxon in his ear. His luminous clock read 3:22.

James, eyes wide in the darkness, listened carefully, stomach a hopeless lump of dread, expecting to hear two voices, low and seductive, or laughing.

No one spoke. *Maybe they're kissing*, his mind supplied treacherously.

After a few minutes though, spent, presumably in the lounge, he heard movement in the hall again, Ben opening his bedroom door and closing it. He didn't come near James's room.

—||— —||— —||— —||—

When his alarm rang the next morning, James came to instant alertness. He'd fallen asleep with his nerves churning, and he'd woken the same way. His eyes felt full of sand; his stomach was acid.

He got up at once and slipped across the hall to the bathroom, though switching on the shower filled him with dread. If Ben hadn't woken already, the shower noise would probably do it. Even after full nights of boozing and sex, Ben rarely slept in.

But James felt confident he would at least pretend to, today. From all he knew of Ben, he'd avoid unpleasant confrontation.

He found himself glad of that, because he didn't know what to say. He just knew what he felt—a sick depression, the feeling of having misjudged everything important.

He washed quickly, wrapped his waist in a towel, and got out of the bathroom as soon as possible.

The sounds of normality coming from the lounge stopped him, horrified, in the hallway. Breakfast TV, crockery clattering.

Well. It seemed he'd misjudged Ben again.

He dressed in grim daze, and when he used the mirror to comb his hair and knot his tie, he thought he looked like a man about to go to war, jaw clenched, eyes stony.

Eventually, he had no option but to go out there.

Ben sat at the dining table in front of the kitchenette, dressed in his toweling robe as usual before he showered, hair an elegantly tousled mess. He sipped a mug of coffee and watched the TV and a huge plate of toast lay in the middle of the table, with another steaming mug set out for James.

And since James was a grown man, a civilized adult, what could he do but sit down in his place and accept the terms of battle?

"Hey. I didn't want to disturb you last night." Ben beamed at him. "Did you have a good sleep? I didn't get in till after three."

And that normality James really hadn't expected. Hadn't the others told Ben anything? Hadn't Ross?

"Yeah." James's voice sounded cool. "I heard you come in."

Ben blinked very quickly and looked sideways. And just like that, James knew.

That tiny second of…what? Guilt? Discomfort? Disappointment? Impossible to tell.

But enough for James to realize that Ben was faking normality. Giving him the chance to let it go.

It told him something about the other man…he'd chosen to face the music immediately, rather than wait and hope the issue would go away. He had guts at least. And he was very good at pretending.

"You could have slept in my bed," Ben said mildly, but it sounded hopeless.

"I didn't know if you wanted it for Ross." And there it was. Even to his own ears, his voice sounded thick with poorly suppressed pain.

Ben's eyes locked with his, and James thought he saw turmoil and guilt there, then regret and defiance.

"I didn't know you were still having sex with other men," James managed. Ben didn't reply. The words hung like icicles in the air. "Why didn't you just *say*?"

"Jamie…"

"Was he the first? *Ross*. Since we started?"

Their eyes locked again, then Ben slowly, regretfully shook his head.

James's face twisted, and something, some last hope he hadn't acknowledged he'd clung on to, expired like a soap bubble in the air.

"Why didn't you say anything?" he demanded again, and anger arrived at last, to fit alongside the killing disappointment in his gut. "*Why* did you let me think it was just me?"

He half-expected Ben to deny it, to point out he'd never said anything of the sort, but there seemed to be too much honesty in him for that. He'd known what James had believed.

"I *should* have told you. I put it off because…maybe I'm a coward." He sighed heavily. "I shouldn't have let it start in the first place. And…I just let it go on too long." He sounded gentle but firm, like a doctor explaining the bad news to a patient in denial. An adult, forcing the truth about Santa Claus onto a small child. "I'm sorry. It's my fault. I should have told you."

And James knew that this was going to be just as bad as he'd feared. Just as messy and destructive.

"Well," he snapped. "I'd say your fucking someone else in a public toilet got the message across nicely."

Ben refused the provocation. He looked sad and worried.

"You fought so hard to be who you are, Jamie, " he said. "But it's like…you think you have to run right back to what you escaped from. The whole heteronormative…romance…monogamy thing. It's… We don't need to do that." He shook his head, apprehensive, careful, earnest. "I didn't want to hurt you. I meant everything I said. You're…lovely."

James took in a deep breath through his nose and clenched his jaw hard, and he didn't know at that moment which was greatest: his anger, his disappointment or his humiliation. He let the breath out again loudly. It hadn't calmed him.

"So there's a political imperative for fucking around, is there?" His voice dripped contempt. "Well. I fought to be who *I* am. *Me!* Not to have to buy into some kind of—"

"*Most* men aren't into monogamy," Ben interrupted. "If they admit it to themselves." He finally sounded impatient, yet James could see, even through his own rage and pain, that he was still trying to keep the exchange civilized, though he must be feeling unjustly under siege. After all, their *romance* had all been in James's head. "*That's* what's different with us. Two men don't need all that *only you forever* stuff most women hold out for. We can be honest. But you're like…fuck, Jamie, you're like a…a preprogrammed straight man, trying to be gay."

James gave a disbelieving laugh, hurt beyond belief. "What a crock of shit!"

Ben flinched.

"Gay men can't fall in love, is that what you're selling?" James sneered. "Or *you* can't?"

Ben's expression closed at last. James had finally gone too far.

"I'm sorry," Ben said firmly. "If that's what you're looking for, you're looking in the wrong place." He shook his head with quick, angry frustration. "I *knew* this was a mistake."

And absurdly, even after all that had been said and done, James felt that final, unequivocal rejection like a physical blow to the heart. He'd known it, of course he had, after last night, but having it put into words... The cold certainty that all his feelings were unwanted and unreturned. Useless.

The silence stretched, as if they were both shocked by what had been said, then, on automatic pilot, James stood up and headed for the door.

"Jamie..." Ben called after him, his tone half-alarmed, half-pleading, but James kept walking into the sharp, bright morning.

20

"Yiv a face like a smacked arse, laddie," Scrivenor announced cheerfully, as James sat down at his desk. But James's mood didn't slow him down. "Never mind...here's somethin' to cheer you up. Sameera found a name she recognized in Maria's old case files. Our mate Ricky Burnett. Maria wiz junior barrister when he challenged his restrainin' order. Herself is cock-a-hoop!"

He sat back and waited for James's excitement like a conjurer who'd just produced a large sparkly rabbit from a hat, but James didn't have it in him to oblige. He didn't feel relief or optimism as he should. He felt frozen, but he knew an ocean of regret and recrimination seethed inside him, waiting to pull him under if he let it.

"Hey," Scrivenor went on, gruffly encouraging. "*You* got there wiz a link between Maria and Romilly. You should be chuffed."

"Yeah." James smiled, but he couldn't produce even a facsimile of the elation that pervaded the office. He couldn't take it in properly—

that he'd got the link right, but everything else wrong. He couldn't even feel wounded professional ego; his personal misery swamped that.

Just the day before he'd bragged to Alec and Sameera about his new relationship. His *boyfriend*. He'd have to tell them now he'd never had one.

Fuck, he needed to man up. Forget it. Focus. Just *focus* the way his father had conditioned him to.

The way, he realized, with a vicious, unwanted punch of understanding, his father had focused when his mother died.

Scrivenor had begun to eye him warily, but rescue came from across the office. In the distance he could see Ingham bursting out of her glass box and heading right for them. "You're with me, Jamie," she snapped as she swept past his desk. "We've invited *Mr.* Burnett back for a second visit."

James stood and belted after her, beyond grateful for the distraction.

The Burnett who awaited them in the interview room seemed a different man from the terrified, out-of-his-depth misfit they'd met in PC World. This Burnett radiated bolshie defiance as he sprawled in his plastic chair, and his attitude reflected in the young, equally bolshie solicitor beside him.

"Mark Nimmo," the solicitor introduced himself. He was fair, blue-eyed and public-schoolboy hot, and James couldn't quite judge if his veneer of arrogance added to, or detracted from, his attractiveness.

It was all moot anyway. After everything, James couldn't have felt less interested. But he couldn't fail to notice that Nimmo gave him a comprehensive once-over before concentrating on Ingham. "I expect this won't take long. My client had to request time off from his job for this, and on top of your frankly injurious visit to his place of work, *together* with the specious charge you imposed on him when he lacked legal representation... Well, this is beginning to look like harassment, Detective Chief Inspector."

James raised his eyebrows wearily. It was worth a try, he supposed.

Ingham gave Nimmo her best withering glare. "We *asked* Mr. Burnett if he'd come in to answer a few more questions. To help us with our inquiries. Which he's been good enough to do."

"Under duress, Chief Inspector. You've blatantly placed suspicion on him among his workmates, and intimidated him into this visit. You'd better have some solid grounds for this."

And, yes. All in all, James could see why Burnett seemed more confident. Nimmo was a young attack dog out to make a name for himself. Aggression seemed to be his default method.

But Ingham had walked into the room fired up, and Nimmo would only wind her up more.

James didn't realize how much, though, until the tape had been switched on and the identifications were past.

"Richard Burnett," Ingham said. "I have grounds to suspect you of an offense. You do not have to say anything…" The sounds of shock and protest from Burnett matched the stunned expression on Nimmo's face. And James, who hadn't expected Ingham to move remotely that fast, had to fight to keep his expression neutral. "But it may harm your defense if you do not mention when questioned something you may rely on later in court. Anything you do say may be given in evidence."

"You didn't state that this would be an interview under caution," Nimmo protested. "My client should have the right to decline."

"Do you wish to decline, Mr. Burnett?" Ingham asked imperturbably.

Burnett stared at her like a rabbit in headlights, new cockiness all gone. "I…no. It's all right, I guess."

"What offense do you suspect my client of committing?" Nimmo demanded.

"Offenses relating to the death of Romilly Crompton."

Burnett flushed an ugly, blotchy red. "I didn't…"

"What are you accusing him of…*exactly*?"

"If you'd allow the interview to proceed, Mr. Nimmo, you might find out," Ingham snapped.

"If my client has no idea what you're cautioning him about," Nimmo returned indignantly, "how can he hope to look after his interests in this interview?"

Fair point, James conceded privately, as he watched the show.

"Mark…Mark, it's okay." Burnett tugged at Nimmo's jacket sleeve like an anxious toddler. "I've got nothing to hide."

Nimmo, still glaring at Ingham, let out a heavy breath through his nose, a sound of massive impatience.

"All right, we'll proceed," he said, with great reluctance, as if granting a huge favor.

"We're all very grateful for your forbearance, Mr. Nimmo," Ingham replied, voice sodden with sarcasm. She glanced at Burnett then down at her notes.

"Just for confirmation then, *Rick*. You admit you sent anonymous letters to Romilly Crompton," she said.

Burnett blinked once, twice. "Yes."

"In the letters you declared that you and she 'needed to be together.'"

Burnett peered into the middle distance. Then, "Yes."

"You discovered her home address by following her from her workplace."

"Yes," Burnett said. He seemed, James thought, almost bewildered.

"Did you ever talk to Miss Crompton?"

"No." He frowned. "But she…smiled at me. I'd been waiting outside the studios, and I shouted her name and she looked so pleased to see me. Like she knew."

"What did she know?" Ingham asked.

"She felt our connection. But people kept her from approaching me," Burnett said.

Nimmo shifted in restless agitation. James stared down at notes he'd carried in, more to buy time than anything else.

Burnett seemed to have no instinct to hide his stalking, because he didn't see it as a misdeed. In fact, he could have fit in a textbook: the archetype of an erotomaniac. But more than that, a delusional stalker. And those were the two percent James had discussed with Scrivenor, the ones most likely to become homicidal when they didn't get the responses they wanted.

"Did you know Maria Curzon-Whyte?" Ingham asked suddenly.

A beat of silence. Nimmo sat forward, his expression set in exaggerated disbelief. "You asked my client in to discuss his dealings with Romilly Crompton, Chief Inspector. There was no mention…"

"Yes," Burnett blurted. "I met her when I went to court."

Nimmo flung himself back into his seat in dramatic disapproval.

"What did you think of her?" Ingham asked.

"She was…nice to me. She was nice."

"Just…nice?"

Burnett's small mouth pursed sourly. He didn't answer. Nimmo appeared relieved.

James had a sudden thought. "Did you send any letters to Maria, Rick? Like the ones you sent Romilly?"

He felt Nimmo's gaze fix on him, and Burnett's eyes darted up and met his for the first time since the interview began. To James, Burnett appeared, at that second, to awaken from a daze. As if he remembered at last where he sat, and who they were, and what they suspected him of.

"No," Burnett said urgently. "No!" It sounded almost hysterical.

Ingham saw weakness. "Where were you between three and four a.m. on the morning of the fifteenth of February?"

Burnett's brown eyes flitted back to her. "In bed. I'd be in bed."

"And in the early evening of the tenth of February?"

"I don't know," Burnett said dazedly. "I'd have to think back. I was probably online."

"What do you do online?" James demanded.

He could see Nimmo preparing to intervene, simply, James knew, to break the flow of their interrogation. And—just like that—James's ingrained patience with the game blinked out of existence, and in its place, all his raw, stifled emotion, his frustrated anger and pain, began to swell and bubble like a wellspring inside him. But still, he kept his voice carefully even.

"Do you watch pornography, Rick?" *Are you the insane fucker who left Romilly to die?*

Burnett gaped at him. "No! I mean…"

"No? Or yes?"

"Sometimes. Everyone does!"

"Do you have a girlfriend?"

Burnett's eyes were wide, wild. "No. Why does that…?"

Just another tick in the box, James thought furiously, but his voice showed none of it. "Did you know that delusional stalkers like you often try to hurt the people they think they care about? Like Maria. Or

Romilly. People like you, who try to force and grab at love. Who won't accept they can't have what they want. That the person they fixated on doesn't. Love them. Back."

I knew this was a mistake.

James glowered fiercely, fighting all the unwanted feeling, seething inside.

"No! I wouldn't hurt anyone," Burnett protested. He appeared to be on the verge of tears, scarlet with panic.

"Really, Sergeant. That's quite…" Nimmo began. James had almost forgotten his existence, Ingham's existence. But she was letting him have his head. And James had no wish at all to play Good Cop.

"Most delusional stalkers have a predisposition toward psychosis," James went on conversationally. Always in control. Just as Magnus had taught him. "Did you know that, Rick? Are you receiving medical treatment?"

"I'm not *mad*!"

"I think that's more than enough, Sergeant!" Nimmo barked. "You're harassing my client."

Bluster, James thought with contempt. If Nimmo had grounds to stop him, he would. Burnett squirmed on his chair, one hand clenched in his hair, his agitation an almost visible aura around him.

"I don't think it'd be harassing Rick to tell him how Romilly died, would it?" James mused. "I was there. She lasted a day, all on her own, with two bullets in her brain."

Burnett stilled, like an animal at bay, gaze riveted.

James's voice lowered to velvet intimacy. "At least she didn't die alone though. She died with her eyes wide open, looking into mine."

Burnett let out a sound of distress, a moan of pain. It sounded almost sexual. And James saw what he'd been waiting for—a glint of possessive envy in the other man's eyes.

James smiled at him. Then he glanced at Nimmo, waiting for the bluffing to start. But Nimmo appeared mesmerized too.

"Rick." Ingham sounded brisk, breaking in to the hushed quiet as if the whole exchange had not taken place. "We'd like to get access to your computer. Do you have any objections?"

Burnett and Nimmo both jerked their attention round to her. Burnett's expression became, at once, appalled. "Do I have to?" he asked Nimmo desperately.

"No. You *don't* have to," Nimmo replied. "Chief Inspector, my client has helped you to the best of his ability. If you've both quite finished intimidating and harassing him, we'll be on our way."

"If *necessary*," Ingham snapped. "We can get a warrant to seize the computer. I'm sure we'd all rather Rick cooperate and save us time." And Burnett then wouldn't have the chance to "accidentally" destroy his hard drive.

Nimmo's eyes narrowed; Ingham's café-au-lait skin had visibly flushed.

It reminded James of a game of chicken. Figuratively they were nose to nose. His own surge of rage had evaporated as quickly and completely as it had appeared. He felt cold inside. Hollow. Foolish.

"*Mr. Burnett* is understandably reluctant to have his privacy invaded, Chief Inspector," Nimmo enunciated with insulting precision. "The answer is still no."

It was very obvious to James that Ingham teetered on the edge of calling Nimmo's bluff and arresting Burnett for murder on the spot, thus getting the automatic power to search his house and belongings. But if she did, press hysteria would be unstoppable, and they just didn't have a solid enough case, not yet. Nimmo'd called their bluff, but then he must have had a fair idea of the relative weakness of their evidence, from their line of questioning.

James willed Ingham to back down, though his expression remained impassive.

"Very well, Mr. Nimmo," Ingham gritted out. "Mr. Burnett's refusal to cooperate will be noted."

Nimmo's triumphant smirk told the room that he saw it, very accurately, as retreat, but James's relief that she hadn't let her pride take over felt off the scale. At least one of them seemed in complete command of their marbles.

As he showed Nimmo and Burnett to the door, James got the distinct feeling Nimmo checked him out which prompted a vague twinge of revulsion given he'd just scared the hell out of the man's client. But he didn't have the energy to care.

When he got back to the office, Ingham had begun barking orders. Chief among them: a renewed search of Maria's personal papers for anything resembling an anonymous letter, asking colleagues and family if she'd mentioned a stalker, if she had perceived Richard Burnett as anything other than a client.

All around, officers were taking notes and heading for their desks.

"Jamie!" Ingham called, in exactly the same tone of command. "Good work in there."

James controlled his expression as curious eyes turned to him. He'd expected, if anything, a reprimand, not a public commendation. Ingham constantly surprised him.

While the team got to work, she went straight to her desk to begin the process of gaining a search warrant of Burnett's property from the magistrate's court. When she got back with it at six thirty, she called a briefing.

The mood of the unit in general seemed wired and ebullient now they believed they'd solved not one high-profile case, but two. James though, sat at the back and stayed quiet, a fact which didn't escape Scrivenor.

When they wandered to their desks when the briefing ended, he asked, "Did ye ask Burnett aboot the stones an' chain?"

James shook his head sharply. *No.*

"But...why not? If he did them both."

James's face twisted with frustration. "It was always a mad, fucking call, Alec."

Scrivenor said slowly. "Burnett's the man, then."

James wanted to close his eyes, but he didn't.

"Burnett's the man," he agreed.

21

By the following morning, the MIT had Burnett's computer in custody, but his hard drive had suffered a mysterious and probably fatal accident, involving a heavy instrument and undiluted bleach.

Burnett claimed his flat had been burgled and vandalized while he'd nipped out to the supermarket, and that he'd been about to call the police when they'd arrived with their warrant. He even pointed to a jimmied latch on the door, and various other damaged items, including his phone, bleach splashed everywhere.

Ingham was incandescent, her anger directed mainly at herself for not following her instincts and going for a fuck-it-all arrest in order to seize the computer immediately. Still, the data-recovery consultants used by the Met said the disk could theoretically be pieced back together. It would be like reconstructing a sheet of paper, torn into little pieces—slow and painstaking—but, if all the pieces were still there, doable. It was quite difficult to erase information completely, they said.

The MIT and Burnett remained in that strange stalemate for days, then it stretched into a week and toward two. Nothing incriminating had been found in Burnett's flat, and Ingham couldn't jeopardize a conviction by appearing to harass him. Moreover, none of Maria's family, friends or colleagues knew anything about anonymous letters or fear of a stalker.

For James, the waiting lull at work came at the worst possible time, but he tried to work as many lates and night shifts as he could, and went to his aikido gym more often, and to the pub with his colleagues. Anything other than spend long hours at the flat. The dull regularity of a life lived entirely around work felt both familiar and safe, while time spent at Selworth Gardens had become a kind of penance.

Without ever discussing it, he and Ben settled into an armed peace. Not quite a cold war—they still spoke when they saw each other, and they still divided up tasks like shopping, and worked to a timetable of housework, like good flatmates, but their interactions were stilted and awkward and overly polite. Ben stayed out most nights James spent at home.

Their affair had ended without any more fuss, without even a verbal acknowledgement that it was done. It simply died, without a whimper.

For James, the memory of his own wild happiness, during the weeks in which he'd believed his feelings returned, seemed like some kind of bizarre dream. He couldn't even remember accurately how it had felt to be that happy, he could just remember that he had been.

Scrivenor suspected something, of course, and Sameera kept asking for juicy details about his boyfriend, so James told them both that he and Ben had mutually decided they were better as friends. Kaur seemed to believe him, and Alec allowed him his dignity.

On days he felt particularly depressed, James made desultory searches through listings of rooms for rent to see if anything looked promising, if anything looked attractive enough to galvanize him to leave Selworth Gardens, but just looking at the familiar advert shorthand felt soul destroying. Remembering his last slog for accommodation around central London, he couldn't persuade himself to restart the search with any determination.

Because more than that—more than a reluctance to leave the perfect flat—when he felt tempted to pack his things and get out of the situation, it smacked of running away. Of even more humiliation. An open admittance that he couldn't be adult about a fling.

It felt to him as if his dignity, and his pretense of not caring and moving on, were all he had left after his disastrous first brush with love. They provided the shield he needed.

All in all, he thought he'd been coping quite well. Until the morning when the red football sock made its first reappearance, stuck like a bloody favor on Ben's doorknob when James went to shower, and he felt as if he'd been kicked in the stomach.

He retreated to his bedroom after his shower and left without breakfast or coffee, so he could avoid seeing anyone coming out of Ben's room. And he flagellated himself with memories of his own smugness about being the lover in that room, and how he'd honestly believed he'd never be on the outside again.

Thank fuck for condoms, he thought viciously.

He tried to be reasonable about it. To be fair.

It wasn't as if his old rich friends hadn't been promiscuous as fuck or as if he hadn't shagged around himself, once upon a time, aimlessly, hopelessly, miserably.

But in his heart, he couldn't understand *choosing* it. Ellie had been entirely right about his emotional innocence.

The sock turned up again a few days later, a Saturday morning, as James escaped early to work, and he wondered, as he closed the flat door quietly behind him, why Ben bothered. Did he expect James to knock at his bedroom door if the sock weren't there, when he never had before? Burst in maybe? Or could it be Ben's declaration of independence? A bright red message that he wouldn't change anything about himself, however much James disapproved?

He could only try not to imagine how often it had happened while he'd still been sleeping with Ben. How often it had happened while James fancied they were in love.

He thought, as he walked down the stairs, that he should ask to get a lock fitted on his bedroom door, because who knew if any of Ben's fucks fancied a bit of thievery. But he didn't think that Ben, on the whole, would react well.

He'd almost reached the street door when someone called his name.

He froze, startled, and certainly less than sociable, but manners forced him to plaster on a polite expression before turning round. Steggie leaned against the open door of his flat, clad in a T-shirt and loose, artfully draped sweat pants, ready for anything.

"Hi," James said with pleasant neutrality. "Just heading to work."

Steggie rolled his eyes with pointed violence. "Do you do anything else? Come in for a quick coffee."

James knew, as he'd known since he heard Steggie's voice, that there would be no easy escape.

Settled on Steggie's uncomfortable sofa though, mug in hand, he hadn't quite reckoned on Steggie's direct assault.

"How're you managing?" And before James could even begin to bullshit in reply, "I *was* there. In the pub." Steggie sank down on gracefully onto the sofa beside him. "He kept it going with you for longer than I thought he would, I'll give him that. He's always upfront about what's on offer, even if they don't always believe him." His mouth pursed with distaste as if the words tasted sour. As if he didn't want to say them. "Actually, it's the first time I've seen him do that. Hide what he is, I mean. I s'pose he finally got bored of it."

James blinked hard, nostrils flared. Because even after everything, fuck, that truth hurt. *Bored.*

Steggie sighed. "Aw, c'mon, luv. Ben was the last person in the world a man like you should fall for."

"A man like me?" James sounded bitter even to himself.

"A romantic. You have...a pure soul."

"Fuck. You make me sound pathetic."

Steggie frowned. "No! Jamie, it's a rare thing." Then, he went on softly, "I said he'd break your heart."

And James had nothing to say to that. Steggie, in his own bulldozer way, had been looking out for him all along. Those digs at Ben about true love made perfect sense in hindsight. He'd been trying to embarrass Ben into coming clean.

James contemplated his almost full mug and took a long swig, trying to focus on the nuttiness of the blend, the sharpness of the taste.

"He really did…" Steggie's mouth worked for a second, as if he was again finding it almost as hard to say as James found it to hear. "He *did* plan to keep his hands off. I mean he fucked Olly on day one. I thought he'd learned his lesson. He had a temporary flatmate after, and nothing went on."

James swallowed hard, but the lump in his throat felt large enough to choke him. He'd been the one to make the first move, not Ben. His fault.

"What happened?" he asked. "With Oliver?"

Steggie leaned back onto the sofa, balancing his glass of juice. "He moved in soon after I arrived here. Olly's been around the scene a bit. He knew the score. But he fell for Ben like… Well, Ben's got something, hasn't he? With that charm of his, they all end up loving him in the end in one way or another—his friends, his shags, even people who *should* hate his guts, like Olly and you."

It sounded sour, as if Steggie himself had been burned. James opened his mouth to ask, but Steggie could read his mind.

"Oh, no fucking *way*! Anyway." He took a pointed sip of juice. "Olly. He got a few weeks of flatmate sex…with some threesomes and Ben shagging on the side, of course. Then Ben stopped it. Olly couldn't stand watching Ben's fucks parading through the flat when he'd stopped getting any himself, so he left. Ben was gobsmacked. Totally blindsided. It was hilarious. I mean it was obvious to everyone *else* Olly'd fallen hard, but Ben didn't even notice. So Olly's stuck with the group, hoping Ben'll remember why he fancied him. And Ben pretends he doesn't notice, and tells himself it's gone away. Truth is, he hasn't got the balls to put Olly out of his misery. He doesn't like being *unkind*."

James considered this, depression sinking like damp into his bones. But the copper in him had noticed something else.

"You don't like him much," he said. "Ben, I mean."

Steggie appeared startled, then moved his head back in the universal gesture of *What the fuck?*

"Why would I dislike Ben?" Steggie sounded amazed. "I'm hardly gonna disapprove of shagging about, am I? He's a mate. I mean, I can't say he's not a user, whatever he tells himself, but…that's the scene, isn't it?"

James eyed him for a few seconds, but he couldn't be bothered pursuing it.

Maybe there would be times he'd resent the fuck out of Steggie for all his home truths, but right then, he found himself grateful for the friendship.

"For what it's worth," Steggie added with obvious reluctance. "He won't let the others take the piss."

James cringed inwardly. He just…wanted it all to stop.

"How about you?" he asked in desperation, though he usually veered wildly clear of asking Steggie personal questions. "Are you seeing anyone? Or…?" *Lots of people.*

Shit.

His instincts had clearly served him well, up until then. Steggie stared at him as if James had just launched an attack on him out of the blue.

"No," Steggie snapped. "But I'm not exactly lacking for sex, am I?"

James flushed, appalled by his own ineptitude, after all he'd learned about Steggie.

"Then again," Steggie went on, but now he sounded very much in control. "Maybe I'm holding out for Mr. Right." He grinned evilly. "Like all us girls. *Anyway.* How's work? Any progress in your cases?"

James rubbed a palm over his face and laughed because he couldn't help it. Yet much as he wanted to embrace the change of subject, what could he say about the waiting game with Burnett? He shook his head mournfully instead.

Steggie, touchingly, looked worried. "They can't blame detectives for not solving cases, can they?"

James snorted. "Oh, they really can. But there are…some leads."

"It's good you're so busy anyway." Steggie reached out and patted James's hand like an elderly aunt patronizing an obedient nephew. "You need the distraction."

Perhaps he saw in James's eyes that a limit had been reached. In any case, on perfect cue, as if a light switch had been pulled, Emile appeared—entertaining and flamboyantly unashamed. His new shoot, he announced in some detail, involved a sex swing—and James found himself laughing hard.

Steggie delayed him for no more than half an hour in total. But when he rose to leave, James felt like part of the human race again.

He was almost out the door of Steggie's flat when he turned round. Steggie was right behind him, which seemed quite symbolic when he thought about it.

"Stegs, listen. I've got this thing…a charity event my…father's organizing, and I was wondering if you fancy going along with me?"

It wasn't often he'd seen Steggie speechless, James thought fondly, but for once, Steggie seemed too shocked to cloak his pleasure in ennui.

Still, he rallied quickly. "Is there free booze? And how fabulous would I be allowed to be?"

"Yes. And relatively fabulous," James replied. But he hadn't actually asked Steggie in the hope of shocking Magnus, he'd asked him because Steggie had become the best friend he had outside work. "It's an art-show thing, and then an auction and a ball."

The last of Steggie's arch pose melted away. "Are you sure, Jamie?" he asked shyly. He seemed almost awestruck. "You want *me* to come with you?"

"I'm really sure," James said firmly. "Would you like to come?"

After a second or two, Steggie nodded, and it was settled.

◼◼◼ ◼◼◼ ◼◼◼ ◼◼◼

Just over two and a half weeks after their split, James finally had to face up to more than his own imaginings of what Ben had been doing with his time.

He walked into the lounge one morning to grab a yoghurt on his way out to work and found a man he'd never seen before, sitting in his underpants, reading his phone at the breakfast table, and Ben, also in tight boxer briefs, clattering around the kitchen.

The shock of it left James so murderously angry and hurt that he almost turned round and stalked out. But when the man glanced up, James realized with a jolt that he wasn't a stranger after all.

Jace, with his hair cropped short, looked older and even more handsome. "Hi, Jamie." He grinned cheerfully. "Just passin' through."

And James, for the sake of his own dignity, could only pretend to be pleased to see him. He walked to the fridge in the kitchenette and took out a carton of orange juice, then went to a cupboard for a glass. He refused to look at Ben.

Ben's quiet, "Morning Jamie," though, could hardly be ignored. It sounded tentative, careful, as if he half-expected James to burst into tears.

James felt a muscle jump in his jaw. His pride forced him to turn. His own visceral reaction to Ben's tousled, half-naked beauty didn't help, but perhaps the dark mouth-bruises on Ben's long neck did, the bite mark on his shoulder. Ben managed somehow to exude both worry and defiance, but James could see he was trying for the appearance of normalcy, the kind of relaxation people forced when they actually felt the exact opposite.

"Morning." His own voice sounded neutral, James thought. Calm.

"There's coffee." Ben offered. "And toast."

At last, James met his eyes. He seemed hopeful, James realized, as if he thought this could be the moment James came out of his sulk; the moment, perhaps, he accepted Ben had been right, and allowed their relationship to return to the easy friendship it had once been. A part of James even wanted that, because he missed Ben as a friend, almost as fiercely as he missed Ben as a lover.

But he couldn't go back. Not yet. Maybe not ever. He wouldn't become another Oliver, hanging around Ben's social circle like a ghost that refused to rest, envying and hating the men Ben wanted.

But he recognized too that he couldn't continue to mope like a child who hadn't got his way. Ben was who he was, and James had projected his own need and love on to him. If he intended to stay in this flat, he couldn't continue to behave like the jilted lover he so acutely felt himself to be.

His mouth pushed out into a fierce pout, fighting his own pride, but he nodded, poured himself a coffee and went to sit at the table, followed swiftly by Ben.

With stoicism, James then began to work his way through two symbolic pieces of toast as Jace, bouncy and unselfconscious, began an incriminating chat about James's appearance on TV, his Yorkshire accent doing continual violence to the Americanisms scattered through his speech.

"Sorry I missed you last time I came through, dude. But we watched you on *Crimewatch*, didn't we, Ben? Had the popcorn out an' all. You were shit hot."

James forced a smile, though it felt more of a grimace. That'd been the evening after he'd first slept with Ben, when he'd been in Cardiff happily obsessing about it and building castles in the air. And Ben had been here, fucking Jace.

"Yeah," James said. "Shame I missed you."

Jace appeared to be as uncomplicated an occasional fuck buddy as Ben could wish…a Labrador puppy, impossible to dislike, though James desperately wished he could. Most of all Jace was oblivious to tension, and as he rabbited on, it became obvious by the fact he now seemed to view James as a sexual brother-in-arms that he knew James had slept with Ben.

"Fuck, I'm knackered. I'm just off the plane and I'm hustled straight into bed and it's do this…do that… Put it there, fuck me harder." Jace winked at James and shot a provocative glance at Ben.

James checked the status of his plate. Still half a slice to go.

"Can it, Jace," Ben muttered.

Jace barked a gleeful laugh. "I don't believe it! I made you blush!" He beamed at Ben. "Ah, I'm just yankin' your chain, man. It's worth the bossin'. You're definitely the best fuck around. Isn't he, Jamie?"

James glanced up and found Ben's gaze on him.

His expression conveyed acute embarrassment and apology, as if he were appealing for understanding for Jace, but if anything that made it worse. That he thought James needed to be handled delicately, unlike the other gay men he knew, that he needed to spare James's girlish feelings.

Even if it was true.

James turned back to Jace and smiled into his innocent eyes. "Yes. He certainly is."

"When do you have to get away, Jace?" Ben asked quickly, hand pushing back his dark curls. That set Jace off on a monologue about his day's shoot, interspersed with reminders to Ben that they still had time for another quick shag if they got right to it.

James made himself remember, as he meticulously finished his toast and drank his coffee, how *he* had viewed fucking Ben, and being fucked in turn, as practically a spiritual experience. The way he'd thought they were *making love.* He felt only blazing derision now for his own naivety.

One last swig of coffee, and he stood, viable escape in sight at long fucking last.

He'd passed a milestone, he congratulated himself—he'd managed civil social interaction with Ben, fresh from being fucked by another man. It was progress. The thought tasted sour.

"How's it all going, Jamie?" Ben sounded almost urgent as he asked it, trying to engage him before he walked away. "Are you getting anywhere on your cases?"

"Oh…slow going," James replied vaguely.

"You fancy coming to the pub tonight, then?" Ben asked at once, his voice threaded with that sweet hopefulness that everything could be fine again between them. "Relax a bit?"

"I'll be late again, I'm afraid." Though James hadn't decided till that exact moment.

Ben caught his eyes. "I hardly see you any more," he said.

It took all James's willpower not to sneer. "Well." As blandly polite as if he were talking to a member of the public who'd asked him the time. "Hard case, you know?"

Ben didn't seem happy, but James could hardly be worried about that. He said goodbye to the ever-amiable Jace and left the two of them sitting at the table. And as he drove to work, he forced himself to slog through the jealousy and rejection and near hatred he felt when he thought about Ben and Jace, undoubtedly fucking again, right this second.

He had three choices left—that was what it came down to.

He could find another flat, as he'd considered in his lowest moments. That would be the most sensible thing to do, impossible as it seemed to be to find a place anything like as good as this Selworth Gardens. It's what Oliver had done.

Yet, something in James's psyche rejected it. He'd been brought up not to run away. And openly admitting he couldn't cope with the aftermath of a fling which he'd been stupid enough to mistake for love... That felt intolerable. He needed to grow the fuck up, not flounce out like a spoiled child.

Staying, though, left him just two shit options.

Live as they were living, with James avoiding contact with Ben as much as possible, and bear with the awkwardness and loneliness until he had to admit defeat, or the pain stopped, whichever came first.

Or—he could try to accept Ben's lifestyle and who he was, and begin to interact again. Be adult about it. Accept. Be friends.

There was no right decision. They all reeked of unhappiness.

22

"Dear God! Are you people doing *anything*? Anything at all?"

Anthony Crompton sounded old and weak and hopeless, his voice a sob of impotent rage and despair. There seemed to be only an empty caricature left of the suave, confident man who'd answered the door to Ingham and James on the night of Romilly's death. Grey stubble covering grey, sunken cheeks. Eyes manic and desperate.

Then again, Crompton currently sat on one of the hard plastic chairs of an Accident and Emergency waiting room while his wife had her stomach pumped. He could hardly be expected to seem at his best.

Their FLO had alerted Ingham to the suicide attempt as she'd been about to go home for the evening, and she'd decided to take James with her to the hospital, though James wasn't entirely sure why either of them had come. Out of courtesy? To do penance? Maybe just to absorb the blind aggression of grief.

But Crompton's anger had been a brief, vivid flash that vanished as if he had no energy left to spare.

"We are following some promising leads, Mr. Crompton," Ingham said urgently. "We're currently waiting for the recovery of—"

"We can't get closure," Crompton muttered, as if she hadn't said a word. His exhausted gaze fixed on a health-information poster stuck to the institutional pink wall across from his chair. "What if she knew him? What if he comes to the house? And he's pretending to be kind to us?"

"Mr. Crompton…"

"It was just an accident." Crompton's eye didn't leave the poster. "She misjudged the number of pills, you know? She hasn't been sleeping. Faye would never do that deliberately."

"I know, Mr. Crompton," Ingham lied, though James wondered if Crompton was talking to them now, or to himself.

Watching the man scrabbling for a hold on his old life, James felt both pity and a gnawing shame for his own emotional wallowing. Because there was nothing like the underbelly of a murder investigation to put your unhappiness into perspective.

But they hadn't even a crumb to throw to Crompton.

They were all waiting like leashed hounds for data recovery to come through for them while still trying to dig up anything at all on Burnett. But the longer it took, the less hopeful it seemed that Burnett's PC would provide the magic bullet. The bleach had done a sterling job on Burnett's behalf.

James left the hospital with Ingham and headed back to the station with little will to do anything other than collect his car and go home, praying only to be left alone. But as he pulled into a parking space near No. 22, he could see lights on in the flat, the curtains undrawn.

He peered wearily up through the windscreen at that false golden welcome, then made himself get out and go up the stairs. He loathed the rush of nostalgia that hit him when he opened the front door to the delicious aromas of onions and garlic. But he smoothed his expression to stoicism and walked into the lounge, ready for anything after Jace that morning, for any number of strangers having sex with Ben on the sofa.

Ben though, sat alone, watching TV with a glass of red wine in his hand, pans bubbling on the cooker in the kitchenette, and for a second it felt as if the past weeks of estrangement had been some sort of terrible dream.

James took a deep breath and ventured a tentative, "Hi."

Ben started and turned to look at him. His beauty felt startling as always, though he wore just a faded yellow T-shirt and jeans.

"Oh, hi!" Ben said. "I didn't know if you'd be late…but I tried cooking for you anyway." He smiled uncertainly, as if he half-expected rejection. And that uncharacteristic timidity made James's decision for him.

Ben so obviously wanted to forget everything and make their flat-share work, to get them past this scorching awkwardness. So James had to try to match him, if only for the sake of his own self-respect. He needed to stop making Ben feel he had to tiptoe round his own home, because he hadn't given James what he wanted.

James manufactured a smile in return, wanting at least to remove that sheen of anxiety. "That's great, thanks. Really good of you."

It'd sounded like something stilted he'd say to an acquaintance, and they both knew that once upon a time Ben wouldn't have had to guess at James's schedule, because they used to text back and forth all day. Still, Ben grabbed the olive branch with both hands.

"Well, it's just spag bol, but why don't you get out of that sexy suit and I'll put on the spaghetti?"

James chewed his lip, nodded and left. *Sexy suit.* Ben'd said that before, the night they first slept together.

Just habit, he reminded himself as he changed his clothes. Ben said nice things to people. It didn't mean anything.

But James was glad that this gesture of friendship had come to-night of all nights, when he felt so demoralized about work and his fucked-up private life that he just needed something to change. When he went back to the lounge, the table had been set, and James gave his best try at cordiality as they chatted about Ben's latest job, taking pho-tos for an interiors magazine which apparently involved a massively egotistical designer.

"Actually…" Ben said, as they cleared away the dishes. "I wanted to ask your opinion about something."

James did his utmost not to tense up. He put the dishes in the sink and turned on the tap.

"Sure."

"Well it's… I got an offer. From a big gallery. They want me to do a show." His navy-blue eyes were wide, as if begging James not to mock the idea.

James smiled. "That's fantastic. Congratulations!"

"You think I should do it then?"

"Of course you should do it."

"But." Ben ran his long fingers back through his hair, disordering his dark curls. "It's a lot of pressure. A lot of extra work. I don't know that I'm that standard."

"They wouldn't have asked you if they didn't think you were good enough. I mean, look…" He waved his hand at the photos on the lounge walls, demonstrating. "You're really talented. I told you that the first day I came here."

But Ben didn't look; his eyes remained on James.

"Yeah," he said softly. "You did, didn't you?"

"You'll sign up for it then," James pressed, though his pulse betrayed him, racing in that old Pavlovian response to Ben's attention. "No more low-self-esteem crap."

It shocked Ben into a sudden, delighted hoot of laughter. "If you say so, Detective Sergeant. Can't have any of that namby-pamby low self-esteem."

James nodded decisively, ignoring the teasing, and turned back to the sink. The only sound was the clatter of dishes as he soaped and rinsed, but though he imagined he could feel Ben studying him as he worked, he didn't turn to check.

At Ben's suggestion they retreated to the sofa after that and put on the next episode of *Game of Thrones*—the episode, as it turned out, which they'd been about to watch together, just before they split up. GoT was much more Ben's thing than James's—James had seen too much gratuitous violence on the job to enjoy it as entertainment—but they watched and flinched together until the end, letting the next episode cue up automatically.

They slouched, side by side, boneless with relaxation, like old times.

"D'you have time for another one?" Ben stretched lazily. "Or d'you need to get to bed?"

James rolled his head against the sofa back to peer at him.

"Another one," he decided on the spot, desperate to hang on to this tenuous feeling of peace. "I'm on lates tomorrow."

Ben reached for the remote. "You've been working flat-out since the day I met you. God. Incredible to think that's two months already."

Fuck. Two months. James stared at the ceiling, instantly wrenched out of his fragile state of serenity.

Eight weeks. The unit would begin their next turn on call in a few days' time. Hard to ignore the symbolism of that. The taste of failure.

A hell of a lot had happened in eight weeks—friendship and love, found and lost. But not enough had happened for Maria or Romilly.

"Are you getting anywhere?" Ben asked.

"Yeah," James said. Then, "No." Then. "I don't know." He frowned angrily at the TV screen.

"You really care, don't you?" Ben ventured. "It's personal to you."

James rolled his head to look at him again, still frowning. He sounded like Steggie, as if a copper caring was strange.

But he couldn't deny he'd sunk in deeper with these cases than he ever had before. Maria was personal—his first big responsibility. Romilly felt even more personal. But there they were, stuck waiting for evidence that might not even come.

And always in his quietest moments, something nagging at him—something he told himself *he* should be seeing, except it danced just outside the corner of his eye.

"One of the victims...her mother ended up in hospital today." Because that was the easiest thing to vocalize. "Everyone's trying to pretend she didn't mean to take too many pills."

He held Ben's gaze hopelessly, angry with himself in so many ways.

"Don't," Ben protested, so quietly that James could barely hear him. His face had twisted as if he couldn't bear what he saw in James's expression. "Don't blame yourself. You're such—such a good guy, Jamie."

Good guy. What the fuck use had that ever been to anyone? James swallowed miserably and turned his head away.

Ben made a low incoherent sound, sympathy perhaps, or protest. James wondered if he'd said it out loud.

"Actually, I think I'll just go to bed. I'm no company..."

Ben didn't signal his intention. He simply leaned across the small space between them, turned James's face back toward him and kissed James's tense, unhappy mouth.

James gasped, then froze, like prey.

A moment of breathless stillness, while they both waited, and perhaps they were both as shocked as each other. But James, stunned, didn't pull away, and slowly Ben's mouth began to move on his, tentative, coaxing, hungry.

James shouldn't allow it for one more second; he shouldn't even want it, because there was a principle somewhere he had to adhere to. But he opened his mouth anyway.

Common sense seemed a poor barrier against the naked relief of feeling Ben's kiss again, feeling how much Ben wanted him still. Pride seemed trivial, distant, irrelevant when Ben touched him like this. And so he let it go on.

The kiss deepened to luscious sensuality, and James wondered for a hazy second if Ben had felt nervous at the risk he'd taken, if he'd felt scared—then thought incinerated.

Nothing mattered after that but the blazing touch of Ben's greedy hands and mouth on his skin; James's T-shirt pushed up under his armpits, jeans opened one-handed. And the sight of Ben kneeling upright on the sofa beside him, wrenching off his own T-shirt over his head, his own jeans and pants shoved down his thighs to reveal his lovely torso, his smooth, broad shoulders and the long, strong column of his neck; his big, bouncing erection.

James took him in, mesmerized, because he'd honestly believed he'd never get to see Ben like this again; that this would be only for other men now. And it felt as if he'd been given an amnesty, from nowhere. Or, perhaps, just a reprieve.

His tentative fingertips touched Ben's stomach, feather light, almost timid, feeling the silk of his skin, but that small movement,

James's participation at last, seemed to explode any restraint Ben had left.

He moved immediately to straddle James, still sitting, startled, in place. Then he gripped James's face with both hands to hold him for another ravenous, possessive kiss, as if he'd been famished for all of it, as much as James had.

They were out of control, both of them, writhing and rutting against each other, bare cocks rubbing blissfully, and the only sounds were their gasps and moans and hitching breaths.

When, at last, Ben slithered down to the floor to kneel between James's legs, neither of them mentioned a condom before Ben's greedy mouth fixed on his cock. James's hips bucked up reflexively into the scalding, wet heat, and he slid his fingers through Ben's silky, dark hair feeling the first hungry, gluttonous suckle, an expert bobbing pull, watching Ben jerking himself off roughly as he did it. As if a cock in his mouth—James's cock in his mouth—was the most powerful turn-on imaginable.

James knew he couldn't hope to watch and not come at once, so he let his head fall back against the sofa cushion, closed his eyes and gave himself up to the excitement, the blinding-white sensations.

He was used to self-abnegation—he had excellent control. But it had been weeks, and this was Ben. He didn't stand a chance of holding on for long—not with Ben's technique and determination, not with the smell of Ben's soap and clean sweat and musk all around him.

The tawdry, unwanted realization flashed through his mind, seconds before he orgasmed into that clever, eager mouth, that this was precisely the position in which he'd first seen Jace. Exactly like this— on this sofa, head thrown back, Ben between his legs sucking his cock just as enthusastically.

But his thoughts were nothing. Anemic red flashes in the red haze of lust that burned him whole. There was no way to resist the covetous build in his belly and the pleasure spreading through every molecule of his body.

The relief, when he came, felt so perfect, as if his balls were turning inside out, spurting gouts of spunk into Ben's greedy mouth, groaning Ben's name. Ben stayed with him, swallowing and sucking gently until every spasm had ended and James's muscles had liquefied with blissful relaxation. And after that he could only be dimly conscious of Ben crawling up his body to straddle him again, a knee on either side of his thighs.

When he cracked his eyes open, he found Ben staring down at him avidly, wanking hard but James could manage only a dazed smile, crooked with affection. He heard Ben's breath catch, a moan—"Jamie!"—and semen shot copiously over James's bare belly.

Ben stayed upright afterwards somehow, arm braced against the sofa back, head hanging low, flat stomach heaving in and out like an exhausted racehorse. And James, wits slowly returning, branded the moment, everything about it—smell, sight, touch—painfully on his brain.

He didn't say anything when Ben twisted his body and flopped bonelessly beside him. Not a word when they ended up sitting side by side again on the sofa, as if they were ready to casually restart watching TV, except they were both now half-naked, exhausted cocks out, filthy with spunk.

The dazed quiet in the room drew tight, tense as the skin of a drum waiting to burst, awkward with unwanted reality.

Ben broke it first.

"I'm sorry," he whispered. He sounded it as well. Devastated, in fact. James refused to close his eyes against what was coming. "I shouldn't have done it," Ben went on miserably. And James accepted only then that, somewhere inside, he'd been hoping for a miracle, not apologies.

"I didn't stop you." Familiar humiliation was creeping in at the edges. Loss.

He sensed Ben turning to look at him, so he made himself move his head to meet Ben face on.

"I know, but…" Ben really did look wretched, as if he'd lost as much as James had, and that maddened James.

"But. What?" he bit out and suddenly—suddenly he wanted to push it to destruction. All their *fuck* had done was underline to him how much he wanted and needed a man who didn't feel remotely the same. How fucking lost he was.

"*But*…nothing's different," Ben said painfully. The lamplight caught the gorgeous angles of his face in shades of cream and gold, and lit his eyes to unearthly blue behind his thick, black lashes. It hurt James to look at him. "That was so fucking *selfish* of me."

James swallowed hard and tore his gaze away. He wanted to smash something, scream his frustration and pain to the sky.

He said harshly, "You make me sound like a little girl you took advantage of." He fixed his attention on the frozen TV screen, the menu of GoT episodes, trying to force himself to make sense of it. Read each word.

"No. I don't mean... Fuck. I'm a cunt. I just..." Ben sounded both guilty and hopeless. "I just I hate the way we've been, Jamie. I hate seeing you unhappy. I care about you. I really do. I want you to be able to come home instead of sleeping on some cot at work. I've really...I've just..." He sounded almost ashamed to say it. "I've missed you."

James stilled. At once, a desperate kind of hope rooted and began to grow, eager and ravenous for anything. And though he knew he had to be fooling himself, James clung on to it.

He turned his head back to study Ben and his heart began to pound with instinctive, mindless, reckless elation.

"I've missed you too," he said carefully.

Ben's slow answering smile looked sweet and sad. "Jamie..." He sighed. "I'm not going to change. I like my life how it is."

Their eyes held.

"What if...what if I can accept that?" James hadn't known he was going to say it, and he certainly hadn't thought it out or planned it. But once it was out there, it made an insane kind of sense.

It was the only way he could be with Ben. If *he* compromised.

Ben wasn't going to. Because the problem was his, not Ben's. It wasn't his fault that James felt...too much.

He could have this...sex and friendship, or he could continue to exist as he'd been existing for the past few weeks.

Something, or nothing. Pride. Or Ben.

And suddenly it seemed so obvious—the only solution he hadn't considered to their situation, yet the only one he could find any happiness with. Other people did it. Lots of gay men did it—had open relationships. He could be adult about it.

Ben's expression, though, showed only wariness and worry, apparently for James. He began carefully, "Jamie. I don't—"

"I didn't understand how things were before," James said, voice level. "I get it now."

For a moment, Ben appeared at a loss, almost afraid, then he swallowed and looked away. And James realized that he was about to be turned down, even as he tried to throw his own principles away.

It felt much like Ben's first rejection had felt, like a boulder dropping and settling in his gut. Humiliation. Desperate, clawing, useless love. Hope, raised by Ben, and dashed by him.

His throat ached too much to speak, and he shook his head once, knowing and loathing that Ben could see it all on his face. He began to lever himself up, craving only escape, though there was no dignified way to stalk off with his jeans and underpants around his knees and a belly crusted with drying come. He didn't believe he'd ever felt quite as mortified as he did then, struggling to his feet.

"No!" Ben's hand caught his arm strongly enough to yank him back down with a bounce onto the sofa. "Jamie, listen to me." James jerked his arm free, breathing too hard. "What you're offering. It's not...*you*."

James fixed his eyes on a photograph on the wall, the stream in sunlight. Wishing Ben were different. Wishing he were different. Wishing he could feel something like disinterest, instead of want and longing and mortification.

"I should move out," he said firmly. "I'm making things awkward."

"No! I don't want that. Please. Jamie. Please?" Desperation sounded through Ben's voice. "I just don't...God!" He pushed his hair back off his face with anxious fingers. "I can't believe I'm doing this. I must be out of my sodding mind. Jamie. *Look* at me."

James turned and glared.

Ben braced himself against the sofa back, on one elbow, leaning urgently toward James. He looked desperately earnest, eyes riveted on James's face. He took a deep breath.

"Right. Jamie." He stopped and rubbed his face with his open palm. "If you honestly want this... If you *really* believe you can handle it, we can...we can give it a try, yeah?" They regarded each other for a long, wary moment, then Ben said quietly, a reluctant confession, "I've missed talking to you... I've missed being able to touch you."

James tried to take it in, suddenly as terrified of this Yes as of a No.

It's different to Oliver, he told himself bracingly. Ben hadn't stopped wanting him.

They eyed each other uncertainly, absorbing what had happened, how things had just changed again. The risk they were about to take. That James was about to take. It felt like jumping into the void without a parachute.

Perhaps Ben saw, because he leaned closer, as if to give comfort.

"You're so beautiful, Jamie," he whispered, before his hand slid down to press against James's chest, over his heart. "Here too. Maybe here most of all."

James drew a sharp breath, swallowing hard against the jagged stone in his throat. It felt as if the rug had been pulled from under him in the first seconds of the game. The moment ached like a pause before battle, heavy and real and incredibly sweet. And he understood, if he hadn't understood before, that he really was lost.

"All right then," James said softly.

And it was settled.

23

James's late shift didn't begin until two thirty the next afternoon, but he couldn't stand hanging around the house obsessing.

His mind had been ducking and weaving like a rat in a maze since dawn, torn between the blazing euphoria of having Ben back and the conviction that he'd just made an appalling mistake.

There was no denying that their first night together back in Ben's bed had been extraordinary.

Ben had practically begged to fuck him and James hadn't exactly argued. And it had been…intense, blazingly sensual, as if they'd both been sexually starved, which had been less than true for Ben at least.

Ben had also invited him, afterwards, to come to his bed when he got home off his shift that evening, to return the favor. And James found he'd needed that explicit invitation, unwilling to take anything for granted anymore.

Despite the glories of the night, though, he'd found himself feigning sleep in the morning, rather than facing his lover, and he waited until Ben left the flat to emerge to shower.

James had hung his jacket on the back of his desk chair by twelve. But he'd barely managed to sit down before he and Scrivenor were summoned to Ingham's office.

"We found Burnett's letters to Maria in her office papers!" Ingham said as he closed the door behind them. "The ones he swore under caution that he didn't send."

James took a seat, unnerved to identify his gut reaction as disappointment, still, that Burnett, in all his mundanity, fell into place so perfectly as the prime suspect. His brain could agree that most things added up; he wished his gut would concede.

"You're sure they're his?" he asked.

Ingham waggled her fingers and grinned.

"So he was careless," James said. "Again."

Ingham's smile broadened. "He certainly was."

"But is it…strange he forgets to be forensic aware when he's sending the letters, but not when he's killing the girls?" James ventured.

Ingham's smile thinned at the edges, and her eyes narrowed.

"People do weird things," Scrivenor said quickly. "Stupid one minute, cunning as fuck the next."

"So," James asked, chastened. "Did he threaten her? Maria?"

Ingham's smile had vanished. She knew him too well. And he appeared to have pissed on her parade. "Not in so many words. It's the same sort of stuff as he sent to Romilly. Mirror writing. Soul mates. We'll be together forever. That kind of thing. The menace is implicit."

James wouldn't say it. He'd already played the party pooper. But at some point someone had to give them a reality check. Even with these letters, the case was circumstantial, relying on coincidence, and thin as fuck if a good brief got on it. Mark Nimmo would have that sort of shit-hot, hungry barrister on speed dial.

His phone pinged and vibrated with an incoming message. He thumbed it open automatically.

Ben. It felt bittersweet that the texts had started again.

May be home even later than you tonight. Have to start planning the show with the gallery guys.

OK, he texted back. He'd signed up for this. Time to start playing the game.

"We're going to bring Burnett in for another interview, under caution again," Ingham announced. "I'm gonna schedule it for the day after tomorrow, suggest it's not urgent, to let him think we don't have anything. Data recovery are hopeful they may have something by then. Jamie, wear those really tight black trousers, to distract that thirsty little shit Nimmo." She met his stunned eyes, innocently. "What? Was that inappropriate?"

They all needed the laugh.

There were no lights on when he arrived home after two a.m., but he'd expected that. Ben had warned him he'd be out late with the people from the gallery.

So James drank a beer, stripped off and, after considering waiting for Ben in his bed as they'd arranged, went to his own room and fell onto his mattress. He was unconscious within seconds.

―ꞁꞁ― ―ꞁꞁ― ―ꞁꞁ― ―ꞁꞁ―

Ben hadn't come home the night before.

James didn't realize it until he opened the bathroom door after his shower, only to hear the key in the lock. He stood there, stomach churning, as Ben walked in, unshaven and rumpled, to find him waiting in the hall, clad only in his towel.

Maybe he just went out for something, James told himself. *A carton of milk.*

But the expression in Ben's eyes, as they stood there staring at each other like a couple of uncertain gunfighters, confirmed everything James didn't want to know. Reluctantly guilty. Defiant. Wary, as if he expected James to throw a full-on wobbly, or blank him perhaps, as he had before.

Their new arrangement, tested immediately.

And strangely, that thought steadied James as few things could. He was fucked if he was going to fall at the first hurdle.

He'd agreed to this—asked for it even. So he'd just have to man up. Shove aside his jealousy and pain, and get on with it.

He had to share Ben—that would always be the bottom line—this time with some guy from the gallery. Or some guy he'd met randomly. Who the hell knew?

Something or nothing.

He had to remember that. And he'd had years of experience in hiding how he really felt.

"Hi." He shot Ben a banal smile. "Good night?"

Ben's wariness didn't disappear immediately. It took a few seconds for James's response to be scrutinized and accepted, but James saw Ben's wary tension leach away, like water into soil, and relief spring up to take its place.

Ben pulled off his jacket and hung it up. "Yeah." He smiled. "Great. I'm sorry the gallery thing came up. I'll rustle up some breakfast before you go, okay?"

James took the toast and coffee bestowed on him like the actor he was, dutifully eating every crumb before he left for work. But he felt torn in two.

He couldn't pretend he wasn't giving up something precious, giving up his self-respect, but...in return he would get something that he needed more.

He needed Ben, more than he needed him to be faithful. How fucking sad was that?

Yet the deep, delving kiss he been given on the way out the door... Didn't that show him he'd done the right thing? Ben's relief at his behavior? His own quick pleasure at feeling so wanted?

But then he asked himself, brutally, how wanted was he when Ben had blown off their plans to have sex with someone else?

A blaring horn yanked James out of his distraction to realize he'd come within inches of clipping another car. He'd driven on in a cramped street, instead of stopping on cue for the other driver's selfish maneuver, and he hadn't even noticed.

Fuck. Get a hold of yourself, you stupid arse!

He wrenched his mind to work and only work, and by the time he reached the office, he was sternly in control.

The MIT spent the day trying to get their ducks in a row, ready for Burnett. But everything changed with the preliminary report from the data-recovery people, arriving like the Seventh Cavalry in the late afternoon while James, Scrivenor and Ingham gathered round Ingham's desk trying to work out the best tack to take.

Ingham skimmed the package of papers, and when she finished she looked up at them, beaming giddily with relief.

"It's a two-for-one deal, boys," she exulted. "They managed to retrieve numbers from the bleached-out phone they found in his flat. The SIM's long gone, and it was pay-as-you-go but…"

"It made the silent calls to Maria…" James supplied. Gill had been good for that, at least.

"Spot on." Ingham beamed.

James rubbed his mouth with thoughtful fingers. "Why wouldn't he just throw the phone in the river instead of trying to use bleach? He knew it had to be vital evidence in a murder case."

"Panic?" Scrivenor suggested. "You said it yourself. He's a panicker."

James gave a slow pout of acknowledgement.

"There's more," Ingham said. "On his PC. Violent porn. *Years* of it. Culminating in some particularly repulsive snuff movies."

She went on, listing badly written works of gruesomely violent pornographic fiction, penned by Burnett himself; evidence Burnett had researched methods of killing, including how to cut a throat and how to best shoot a victim in the head. More than that, data recovery had found hundreds of digital snapshots of five different girls, taken in the streets or outside their homes. Maria and Romilly were two of the five.

"It's him," Ingham gloated. She stood up, hand lodged in her corkscrew curls, too wired to stay still, as James and Scrivenor sat primly in their chairs watching her. "Not a single bloody doubt in my mind."

"But it's still circumstantial," James warned as he skimmed quickly through the report. "He's a stalker and a pervert. But without a confession, how do we prove he's a murderer? He fantasizes about women who'd never look at him, and he has a taste for violence, but so do a lot of men who won't ever do anything about it. I mean, he watched things about…building incendiary bombs too." He scanned the list. "How poisons work. He's into every extreme conspiracy theory out there: the Illuminati, alien lizards… Hey, you like that one too, ma'am," he threw in, deadpan. Ingham narrowed her eyes. "9/11, Princess Diana, Jewish bankers, fake moon landings…"

Ingham shook her head impatiently. "So. We scare the living shit out of him tomorrow. Charge him with possessing illegal porn for a start. Maybe, attempting to pervert the course of justice by damaging that hard drive."

"We can't prove that," James pointed out, beyond tired of playing devil's advocate. He far preferred it the way it usually went, with Ingham or Scrivenor trying to rein him in.

"Tomorrow we crack this bastard." Ingham gave James one last quelling glare and shooed them out of her office.

James sat at his desk and tried to understand why he couldn't seem to go with the flow on Burnett. Why he kept raising roadblocks. His copper's brain told him Burnett should be trussed up like a turkey. He just didn't know how to get his copper's nose to stop twitching.

When he got home that night, about nine thirty, a red sock decorated Ben's bedroom doorknob and a dish of beef casserole awaited James in the fridge, accompanied by a cheeky note, another sign of renewed détente. Back to normal, then, after the intermission.

James didn't even try to pretend to himself it was all right, but he was too tired and preoccupied to allow himself to obsess over what was happening across the hall. At least he couldn't hear anything in his room; at least the flat was old enough to have solid walls.

He still hadn't broached getting that lock fitted, he thought wearily as he stripped off for bed. Though he knew he should. From what he'd seen, Ben didn't allow random men into the flat alone, but James had no clue how well Ben vetted his shags; how well he knew the ones he allowed to sleep over.

Though in truth, the security of his own possessions came well down the list of his worries about the dangers of Ben's lifestyle.

James just had to remind himself that Ben's behavior couldn't be said to be remotely unusual for a young guy. Maybe James was the unusual one.

He slid naked under the duvet, but he felt too restless to sleep. So he spread out copies of Burnett's data-recovery documents on the quilt in front of him, trying to find something, anything, that could convince him as surely as Ingham had been convinced.

He didn't realize he'd nodded off over the papers, sitting up, with the lamp still on, until he felt the mattress compress beside him. He startled awake.

"Sssh. 'S only me," Ben murmured. "I didn't mean to wake you. I saw the light still on under your door."

James felt befuddled enough to say, "I thought you were with…" And then he realized the shaky ground onto which he'd advanced. "I mean…you…"

"He snores." Ben yawned. He sat, hair a silky tousled mass, on the far edge of James's bed, the empty side, with one knee up to face him, unselfconsciously naked, and began to gather up the papers spread across the duvet. "And he tries to cling on to me." He handed the sheaf of papers to James. "You'll get a crick in your neck. You have to learn to relax, Jamie."

James felt wide-awake now, despite his aching tiredness. He checked the clock beside him. 2:56 a.m. "Do you want me to kick him out?" he asked shortly.

Ben snorted. "Thanks, *Sergeant*, but I can kick him out myself, if I feel like creating a scene. He's too out of it to make it under his own steam." He paused. "Is it…? Would you…? Is it okay if I stay here? Till he can leave on his own?"

James froze in the act of rubbing a hand over his sleepy eyes, suddenly, acutely aware of his own nakedness under the duvet.

Even with the understanding they'd come to, he could barely believe that Ben had asked. Barely comprehend that Ben would think it a good idea to try to crawl into James's bed, freshly fucked by another man.

He felt a surge of pure, molten outrage, oddly empowering. And yet, underneath it, undermining it…a small, hungry part of him felt stupidly flattered Ben might see him as a sort of refuge. And that made him even angrier.

"Well," he said coolly. "I hope you showered."

Ben visibly stiffened. "I'll go if you want," he said.

And. Yes. He should say yes. It might set them back, but James had every right to draw some boundaries.

Yet, when he concentrated, he could smell the citrus and mint of Ben's expensive soap and toothpaste. And that suggested he'd already taken the time to clean the sex from his body and the taste of that other man from his mouth before coming in. Which meant that this—coming to James's room at three a.m. after a shag—might not have been as casual and accidental as seeing a light under the door in passing.

"Look. Is something wrong?" James asked. "Ben?"

Ben's eyes widened with shock, huge and inky black in the dim light. As if James had flouted some unwritten rule where neither of them ever addressed what might lie beneath the surface.

James thought he wouldn't reply, but perhaps the intimacy of their semi-dark cocoon changed the rules.

"It's… I'm not…" Ben let out a nervous breath. "I just…I've been thinking alot. I feel like…I feel such a fraud. At the gallery. There are these two other photographers planning their shows first…the weeks before me and…their work's amazing. *Real.* Mine's just…pretty stuff for people to hang on their walls. There's nothing behind it. Nothing… nothing about me." He dropped his head, face concealed by the fall of his hair. "Fuck." He gave a low self-mocking laugh. "I can't believe I'm saying this out loud."

James bit his inner lip hard, but he did everything in his power to keep his expression neutral. He realized he'd never seen Ben's vulnerability before. And he felt terrified of saying the wrong thing.

"Well…the gallery people chose you, remember?" he tried. "So *they* don't think your work's shallow. But if you really don't rate it, why don't you try experimenting? Submitting photos that please you? That reflect you?"

Ben didn't raise his head. His voice sounded muffled. "What if nobody likes them?"

James wanted nothing more than to grab him into a hug, but instinct told him to sit still, hands resting loose on the duvet. "You can't know till you try," he said casually. "Why don't you test them on me first? I swear I'll give you an honest opinion."

Ben slowly raised his head until he was peering up at James through his lashes. He looked almost disbelieving. Certainly doubtful. "You'd…do that? I mean…not tell me what you think I want to hear? You'd tell me honestly?"

"Ben." James's laugh sounded too relieved and incredulous for his own liking. Too close to *I'd do anything for you. Just let me.* "Of course I will. But I don't know if you can trust my opinion, to be honest. I'm a bit of a philistine."

Ben blinked, frowning, and cocked his head to the side, studying James as if he hoped to find the answer to some puzzle written on his skin; studied him so intensely that James wanted to turn away, almost afraid of what he'd see.

"Well. I have some photos on my laptop," Ben offered, voice hushed, as if he were imparting a huge secret. "I can show you tomorrow. If you'd like?" Then, more firmly, "I trust you to tell me."

James thought he seemed almost shy.

"Okay," James returned casually. "And I promise I'll tell you if they're shit."

Ben laughed, though it sounded uncertain. "Deal."

They grinned at each other stupidly.

"So..." Ben rubbed his bare arms against the chill, and James realized only then how cold he must be. April had barely begun. "Can I stay? I'll trade you a massage if you like?" he asked hopefully. "To get you to sleep?"

James had been so sure he needed to draw the line and refuse when Ben asked the first time. Before he'd understood. But now?

He sighed and pulled back the duvet. "Get in then. But I don't need the massage. I'm fucked."

"Well..." Ben said with comically waggling eyebrows as he climbed into the warmth. But when James stiffened with instinctive resistance, he added quickly, "Joke."

They settled down, and James reached out to switch off the light.

In truth he felt wide-awake, and sex would have been a lovely way to get back to sleep, but the idea of it, after Ben had just been with another man, made him feel ill. He could do without any more forced signs of reality.

Instead, he chose to revel in their contented silence as they lay side by side in the darkness, listening to Ben's slow breathing beside him, though he knew he should be crushing sentimentality not embracing it. Still, he couldn't help himself.

He'd just begun to drowse again, drift in the darkness, when the mattress heaved, and Ben rolled onto his side, facing him.

"Jamie." He sounded hushed, hesitant, as if he thought James might already be asleep. James made a sound of sleepy acknowledgement. "Thanks. I don't really like sleeping with..."

Your fucks, James supplied internally, with tired bitterness. When he turned his head on the pillow all he could see of Ben was the glint of his eyes.

"I prefer sleeping alone," Ben finished.

"But…you came in to sleep with me," James couldn't help saying.

He waited, a few tense heartbeats, until he saw a gleam of white teeth in the darkness and felt an arm slide comfortably round his waist.

Ben murmured, almost querulously, "It's not the same."

And James lay awake long after Ben had slid into sleep, wondering. Hoping.

━◖━ ━◖━ ━◖━ ━◖━

The sex Ben woke James for, an hour or so before the alarm should have gone off, felt so avid and ravenous that James barely managed to fumble on a condom before sliding inside him for that long-promised screw.

And when they recovered, Ben told him he was gorgeous, before turning the tables and taking him in a slow, sweet, intense fuck that felt to James like making love. But in the distance, as James moaned and writhed and gloried in Ben's dirty encouragement, like a call to reality, he heard the departure of Ben's forgotten shag from the night before, slamming the flat door loudly behind him.

James did his best not to analyze what had happened, not to build castles in the air again as he showered and shaved. So when he walked into the lounge, he didn't flinch at the sight of the yellow post-it note stuck to the arm of the sofa. He wouldn't have read it just a month ago; now he couldn't bring himself not to.

Ben, didn't want to interrupt when you were hard at it (again) so I left. How you got it up after last night I have no fucking idea. See you Thursday. Ned x

James tried not to let it affect him. The idea that the guy believed Ben had nipped across the hall for more sex with James, after fucking him. And that he believed James had obliged. That this morning he'd heard James actually had. At least James would never have to meet him.

As Ben sat down at the table, James plonked the yellow paper in front of him.

"Ned left a note," he said shortly, and sat down too.

Ben scanned it, and James thought he might even have flushed a bit. Or perhaps not.

"He's one of the partners at the gallery," Ben volunteered. "The ones who're doing my show."

James nodded and picked up his cup. He tried for casual.

"Is it wise to…uh…mix business with…? I mean it didn't sound as if you like him that much. Last night." He trailed off. He had no idea what might be off-limits in this new arrangement.

Ben didn't seem so much offended, though, as astonished. "Ned? I do like him."

"He's not pressuring you, then? I mean you don't feel obliged to…" *Fuck, spit it out.* But he didn't need to.

Ben appeared at once very unamused. "You actually think I let people fuck me to get work?" he asked incredulously.

James frowned, but he didn't back down, though he could see it was a touchy subject. He hadn't imagined anything to do with sex could discomfort Ben.

"I don't sleep with people I don't fancy," Ben enunciated in a dangerous tone. Spelling it out. "I don't sleep my way in to jobs. And I'm no one's victim. The other partner, Fabrizio, commissioned me. And he's seventy-four by the way. Ned had nothing to do with it. So the fact that in his case it might be networking too is a coincidence. I slept with him because he's hot, and great company. *And* a fantastic fuck."

A very touchy subject then.

James refused to react to the provocation. Or punishment, he wasn't sure which.

"I thought he snored and clung."

Ben frowned, trying to hang on to his indignation, but in seconds it had shifted to reluctant amusement, and then slid straight to abashed honesty. "Okay. I uh…I might have exaggerated a bit."

He smirked up at James, all rueful charm, through his long lashes. So.

James had confirmation that Ben had indeed maneuvered to come and see him in the middle of the night, to get into his bed, even while the allegedly glorious Ned was an option. It gave him exactly what he needed.

"Well," he remarked. "You work in an interesting industry."

He tried to imagine the Met operating on that type of *networking*—on the exchange, say, of casual blowjobs. Alec would have evaporated into retirement before James could say Costa.

Then again, Maria had worked in the criminal-justice system, and she hadn't exactly held back.

A contented silence fell between them, and James settled into eating his breakfast. But he couldn't fail to notice that Ben became increasingly nervous as time ticked on, fidgeting with his food rather than eating it. James, as he ate, pondered the delicate subject of whether to take the initiative and ask to see Ben's alternative photographs, or wait until Ben decided to trust James with it.

Finally just as he readied himself to go for it, Ben reached that point himself. He blurted, "So would you still like to look at my other work?"

James took in his badly hidden apprehension, his obvious uncertainty, and he felt such a huge rush of affection he wanted to laugh out loud with the joy of it.

"Absolutely," he said with suitable solemnity.

Ben shot out of the room and returned a minute later, open laptop in his arms. He pulled his chair round alongside James, cleared a space, and put the computer on the table, the screen open in front of them.

"Okay," Ben said, though it felt to James as if he were talking to himself. Buoying himself up. It took courage to show his real work to someone else; the work he felt reflected what he wanted to show. James understood that. "I took a lot of these when I was up in the north of Scotland. The light's incredible there… And…right."

He clicked the mouse pad.

The first image made James's breath catch sharply in this throat. It showed a small, snowy white lamb lying on its side among grass and wild flowers in lovely hues of yellow and pink and blue. The light appeared bright, sunny, joyful. A crow, inky-blue feathers gorgeously iridescent, perched on the lamb's small head, pecking at its dead eyes. And beside the lamb's body, a sheep stood aimlessly on guard. Its mother, perhaps.

"Fuck," James said. "That's…"

The photograph felt disorientating. Very beautiful at first glance, then horrible in its reality. James's mind didn't know which way to go. Repulsion or attraction.

"It's too much, isn't it?" Ben said flatly. He sounded as if he'd expected disappointment. He began to close the screen, his expression closed off, jaw tight.

"No!" James protested. "It's like…photojournalism or something. It's got everything. It's beautiful. I mean the colors and the light. The flowers. The feathers of the bird. But then you look closer." He glanced up and found Ben was in turn studying him as intently as a scientist, observing a subject, every tiny reaction cataloged.

James smiled weakly, propped a concealing hand against his mouth, and took over the mouse pad to flick through the other photographs, one by one.

A gorgeous image of intensive pollution: a lake of crude oil floating on water, backlit by the sun, a bird mired in it. A yellow autumn field of hay, contrasted with an astonishing rainbow sky—startlingly pretty, until the eye fell on the corpse of a rook, hanging, wings spread in crucifixion, on barbed wire at its side, a live rook circling above it. A row of cows in golden sunlight; on closer inspection, walking into an abattoir. Cigarette butts rotting in filthy, stagnant water. A close-up of a snail's repulsive head, in perfect focus. A young man with angry, weary eyes, so beautiful that it took a second or two to focus on the thick scar tissue stretching from both corners of his lovely full mouth to his ears in an obscene Glasgow Kiss.

"Fuck." James blew out a loud breath, oddly shaken. "They're…" He dropped his hand back to the table. "I'm not sure I'd want them… hanging on the wall over the telly. I mean, I don't know enough about the market to know if they're commercial. But…God." He tore his gaze from the mutilated man on the screen to meet Ben's anxious eyes. To drive home his sincerity. "Yes. I definitely think you should show them to the gallery. They're incredible, Ben. You're an incredible photographer."

Ben didn't react immediately but then he blinked hard, and instead of speaking, he pressed his lips tight together, as if he was holding everything in. "Thanks, Jamie," he said, bashful and very relieved. His pale skin had flushed a rosy pink.

James found it beyond endearing.

"Beauty in ugliness," he remarked indulgently. "That's what you want to show?"

Ben had begun to close the laptop lid, and James thought he might have imagined a tiny hitch in his movement as he did so, in reaction to the suggestion.

"Something like that." His expression was unreadable. "More... ugliness cloaked by beauty maybe. I think I might show them to Fabrizio, then."

James smiled. Ben hadn't once said, *Do you really mean it?* He seemed to have trusted James's promise not to bullshit him. Strangely that felt like the highest possible compliment.

He leaned back in his chair as Ben stood and pulled his own seat back to its original place across the table.

But as Ben sat again, over his shoulder, James's eye caught a large cream envelope on the breakfast bar. The one containing his father's invitation.

"Aw, fuck," he groaned. "I forgot to RSVP."

Ben turned his head to follow his eyeline and understood at once. "Oh." Then, almost hushed, "Are you going to go?"

James sighed and rubbed a hand over his mouth.

"I have to. It's being held in my mother's name. And, you're right. I have to find out what he's really after."

Ben's subdued mood lifted at once, and he beamed at James as if he'd just given the right answer to a hard puzzle.

"That's great. I really don't think you'll regret it." But then some thought visibly struck him, and his expression slid with comic speed to caution. It would have been funny, if James hadn't known what was coming.

"You're right to accept, Jamie, but you know I can't go with you? I mean... That's not..." He gazed in agonized appeal at James, waiting to be rescued from saying the words. But James, crazy good mood withering by the second, was buggered if he'd help. Ben's voice firmed, though it still sounded kind—a nice teacher having to give out a bad mark.

"Your dad shouldn't get the idea we're...you know. In a relationship or anything."

In a way, given the circumstances, James even agreed. But that didn't make it hurt any less. After the night before, and the sex that morning, the intimacy of Ben sharing his work with him, Ben's reaction dealt a cold slap of reality.

"Don't worry." James smiled with false ease. "He won't. Steggie's coming with me."

He'd been watching closely, so he caught the flash of Ben's astonishment, masked at once.

"Steggie," Ben repeated flatly.

"Yep. I asked him a while ago."

Ben's lips turned up at the corners, but James didn't think he seemed particularly relieved or pleased. In fact, he appeared to think James was having him on.

"That's...an interesting choice," he said lightly. "Are you trying to piss off your dad?"

"No," James replied. "Steggie's a friend. I trust him. And if anyone can make it bearable, he can. Fun even."

A pensive expression ghosted across Ben's face, but after a second, it changed to a wry smile. "Yeah, well. Just don't fuck him."

James absorbed the shock of that in silence, feeling the first tendrils of anger twining through his sick disappointment. He couldn't be sure what wicked impulse made him shrug. "Depends."

Ben didn't appear at all amused. "*Jamie.* He has a thing for you. Don't lead him on."

James stared at him in amazement until Ben dropped his gaze, aware perhaps of his own hypocrisy. But James could hardly fault him for having Steggie's back, even if he'd got it all wrong.

"I wouldn't do that," he said shortly. He stood to go.

Ben studied him, frowning, but he stood up with him though he still seemed preoccupied as they said their farewells.

As James opened the door to leave, though, Ben hooked him into a goodbye kiss that felt almost as hungry and affectionate as James could have wished.

▬◖▬ ▬◖▬ ▬◖▬ ▬◖▬

James forced himself, as he settled at his desk later that morning, not to analyze what had happened with Ben. To forget about it and let it all go, because obsessing over it would be pointless.

He focused fiercely instead on the imminent crucial interview with Burnett.

He'd been castigating himself about it since the day before, trying to compel himself to look at it from Ingham's point of view and silence his own doubts. Because Ingham was right.

Burnett had a motive: well-documented obsession. He also had no solid alibi. As for means—they'd been unable to unearth either of the murder weapons, but they did have the computer, his letters to Romilly and Maria, the photographs and the phone. Yeah, it was circumstantial, but on the right day, with the right jury, the implications of all of that could lock Burnett away for thirty years.

The clock read 15:55 when James and Ingham walked into the interview room to find Burnett wearing a haunted expression and Nimmo working on "theatrically pissed off".

Nimmo launched at once into a protest about harassment of his client, giving a good pretense of viewing Ingham as a barely competent plod. In turn Ingham made it clear that she wanted to rip his balls off. James watched from the sidelines. But as they settled into their chairs after the initial roleplay, James caught Nimmo giving him an up-and-down assessment so blatant that it should have raised his cock.

So he hadn't imagined it, and neither had Ingham. Nimmo *was* interested, and fuck, but James wished, for a rebellious second or two, that he had it in him to fancy the guy back, even if, as a lawyer in a live case, he had to be off-limits.

The sound of the tape machine switching on diverted him. They all identified themselves, and Ingham began.

"Rick, you understand you're still under caution?"

Burnett nodded miserably then darted an anxious glance at the tape machine. He reminded James irresistibly for a moment of a large, hairless rabbit. "I mean, yes."

"We've found something interesting since we last saw you," she said amiably. "It took some work but…" She slid a clear evidence bag containing several bits of paper halfway across the desk. "These are anonymous letters written to Maria Curzon-Whyte. They sound very similar in tone to your letters to Romilly. Did you write them, Rick?"

"There's no requirement to answer unless you wish to." Nimmo sounded prim.

Ingham smiled. "Luckily, they have some identifiable prints on them. Your prints, Rick. Yet you denied writing anything to Maria."

Nimmo pulled in a deep breath though his nose, let it out again. Burnett said nothing.

Ingham went on relentlessly. "We were lucky enough to be able to retrieve data from a mobile phone found in your apartment. It was badly damaged of course in the..." a sarcastic pause, "...burglary. But we were able to identify calls to Maria's number." Burnett's eyes looked huge behind his cheap glasses, gaze glued to Ingham. "Did you make those calls, Rick?"

"There's no requirement..." Nimmo began.

Ingham swept on. "You'll also be glad to know we salvaged information from the hard disk also damaged in the..." She smiled without humor. "Well, you know."

Burnett remained frozen in place, a small animal in a predator's sights. Yet James got a sudden, bizarre impression of shark's eyes, blank and shiny.

Ingham powered on without waiting, a righteous juggernaut. "We found a significant collection of illegal porn."

Very subtly, Nimmo relaxed.

"Snuff movies," Ingham continued.

Nimmo's eyes widened.

"As well as videos detailing how to kill, with a knife to the throat or a bullet to the head. And photographs of girls. A fair number of Maria Curzon-Whyte and Romilly Crompton." Silence. "Nothing to say, Rick?"

Burnett's stare now held unconcealed loathing, all aimed at Ingham, and there sat the man James had forced briefly into the open in the last interview. All the greed and rage behind his mild façade.

"So," Ingham said. "This is my dilemma, Rick. Here I am, investigating the brutal murders of two young women. And then I find this man who's stalked both of them. Taken sneaky pictures of both of them. Researched their manner of death. A man who fantasizes compulsively about killing women after raping them. You can see where I'm going with this, can't you, Rick?"

"You have no evidence my client had anything to do with murder, Chief Inspector," Nimmo intervened, poise regained. "Even if Mr. Burnett were willing to admit to any of this, these are comparatively minor offenses. It isn't a crime, yet, to fantasize."

At that exact moment, Nimmo flicked a wicked, cocky glance across to James, who fought in turn not to gape at the utter reckless inappropriateness of it. The guy seemed so unworried he was showing off for him. But then, Nimmo had isolated their problem precisely. How could they prove Burnett had ever acted on his fantasies?

Ingham reacted as if Nimmo did not exist, and Burnett's attention remained fixed on Ingham.

"Mr. Burnett," she said crisply. "You remain under caution regarding the murders of Maria Curzon-Whyte and Romilly Crompton. I am arresting you for possession of extreme pornographic images…"

And as she went on and read him his rights, Burnett didn't break his psychopathic stare.

"Do you understand?" James demanded. "For the tape, Mr. Burnett."

Burnett nodded minutely, but his eyes didn't move from Ingham, spitting defiance and murderous resentment.

Well…no more rabbit.

"Mr. Burnett has nodded," James confirmed.

Nimmo smirked at him, and James could see again, all too well, that this was not a man who believed his client to be in imminent danger of copping a murder charge.

"I'm going to remand you in custody for the moment, Rick," Ingham said.

Burnett's eyes flickered; Nimmo plastered on an unconvincing expression of righteous outrage.

"Surely that isn't necessary for nonviolent crime, Chief Inspector? Or is this an excuse to continue to hound and badger my client instead of seeking the real culprits?"

"We have to allow our colleagues in the cybercrime unit to talk to Mr. Burnett, and it's not as if this offense doesn't involve victims,"

Ingham drawled. "If we choose to talk to him again, you'll of course be present."

Nimmo smiled graciously, and he could afford to. Burnett hadn't proved as soft an interviewee as they'd all expected. They wouldn't get an easy confession.

Viewing or possessing rape or snuff movies not involving children could get him eight months—maybe less, if he pleaded guilty. It would be in his own interests to cooperate on the illegal-porn charges, and James felt one hundred percent sure that's how Nimmo would advise him.

"You escort the boy wonder to the door," Ingham said under her breath as they walked out into the corridor. "I can't trust myself not to rip off his nuts."

James gazed at her reproachfully but he didn't have an option, though he felt like meat being thrown to distract a hyena. So he waited, arms folded and face straight, leaning against the wall by the inter-view-room door, until Nimmo finished consulting with his client and custody officers took charge of a sullen, white-faced Burnett. Then James led the way to the reception area, far too aware of Nimmo on his heels.

Nimmo remained unexpectedly and thankfully silent as he fol-lowed James down anonymous, beige corridors; so amenable, in fact, that James thought he might get away without speaking to him. But as they approached the secure double doors out to the front desk, he felt a firm hand on his arm.

He turned with extreme reluctance. "Yes, Mr. Nimmo?"

"It's Mark." Nimmo smiled cheerfully. "And you're James."

James nodded, stony-faced.

Nimmo's industrial-grade self-confidence didn't dim. "I won-dered...when the case is finished of course...I'd like to invite you to come for a drink with me." He gave a charming grimace then lowered his voice to a low, confidential tone. "I could hardly believe my luck when a colleague told me you're not...taken." For which James read *not straight*.

James stared at him, then he blew out a breath of air in a kind of you-got-me sigh.

Nimmo smiled warmly, and he seemed a different man from the cocky little shit who locked horns with Ingham. "I know it's wildly inappropriate at this point," Nimmo went on. "But honestly, I didn't want to miss my chance."

His eyes were a lovely green-blue, and he exuded good health and privilege. He was actually extremely attractive.

James could say yes. He could definitely say yes.

But, "I'm afraid I *am* actually seeing someone," he muttered awkwardly. "I'm sorry."

Nimmo finally flinched. His smile faded. "Oh. Well," he mumbled. "I can't say I'm surprised. But bear me in mind if things change, yeah?"

James smiled at last, tentatively, noting how Nimmo stared at him when he did. Seeing the possibility of a nice guy behind the obnoxious front.

Their farewells out in reception were degrees warmer than their previous interactions.

James's second-guessing began at once, and he made his way back to the office on automatic pilot.

Why the fuck had he said no?

He should be trying to bloody move on! Trying to break his feelings for Ben. *What* imbecilic instinct had made him refuse?

It didn't help that a text arrived from Ben informing him he'd be out that evening, though dinner would be in the fridge.

His frustration with himself prompted him to accept an invitation to go to the pub with Alec and a few of the DCs from the unit after work.

That had once constituted his entire social life, before Selworth Gardens—workmates or aikido friends after the gym, and he'd felt trapped by it. Now, though his colleagues talked about work all evening, it felt like a kind of refuge.

▬ǁ▬ ▬ǁ▬ ▬ǁ▬ ▬ǁ▬

Ben, sitting in his robe across the breakfast table the next morning, had a new purple bruise on his neck, but James didn't focus on it. Or the one on his collarbone. Why would he?

Still, he found himself torn between resistance and relief when Ben pushed him to go out with the group that night.

"C'mon, Jamie!" he wheedled. "You never go out any more."

"Work's—"

"I know… But you need some fun. Relaxation."

James looked at him pointedly until Ben rolled his eyes with a vaguely flustered smirk.

"I mean *apart* from in bed. You're gonna have a coronary before you're thirty if you don't let go sometimes."

Frankly, after his last encounter with them at the Trafalgar—the night James had been forced to see the reality of his relationship with Ben—James dreaded seeing Ben's friends again. But at the same time, he felt some relief that Ben did genuinely want him back in his social circle, enough to manipulate him into it.

Maybe he should see it as a test of normality, another hurdle to get over, if he intended to be with Ben like this. Plus, Ben had a point—he could use some escape from the steam-kettle pressure he felt building up inside him some days. Some nights.

"Oh. Hang on." Ben stood and went to rummage behind the breakfast bar, emerging triumphantly with a small plastic bag. As he sat again, he handed it to James. "It was a sample on yesterday's shoot. I thought it'd look great on you, maybe with that Boss suit. Or the Armani?"

James looked inside the bag and withdrew a tie, pure silk, and patterned, when he looked closely, with diagonal stripes in very muted shades of violet, red, blue and grey. The overall effect from any distance showed one intense color somewhere between red and purple, and it was beautiful.

He blinked at it, then up, bewildered, at Ben.

"That's…I can't possible take…"

"It was a freebie," Ben said quickly. "The line won't be released till next spring. And I knew it'd look far better on you than the guys we used. In fact, everything I shot yesterday would've. I told the stylist we should go and get you from work, to model the line."

James flushed and looked back down at the tie.

It occurred to him suddenly that his behavior must appear less than gracious.

"I don't think my boss'd have gone for that somehow. It's beautiful though," he said with genuine pleasure. "Thanks for thinking of me."

And that was considerably more important than the tie.

It seemed then as if he'd handed his awkwardness over to Ben, like an Olympic torch.

"Well. You'll be fashion-forward now," Ben said gruffly. "Impress the other guys at the unit."

James snorted. "They wouldn't know fashion-forward if it bit them on the arse. Actually…what is it?"

Ben laughed, and James made a grand production of removing his previous tie and putting on the new one as Ben fussed with the knot and boasted loudly that he'd called it right. The tie looked fantastic with James's suit.

Ben's gesture lightened his mood on the drive in to the office, even though the day marked the beginning of the MIT's next on-call week, and Ingham set the whole unit onto Burnett like a pack of hounds.

He'd been charged with possessing illegal porn, but bailed. And the instant James settled his bum in his rickety seat, he was swept up in the operation to pick over Burnett's life.

Ingham doled out interviews with Burnett's friends, colleagues and relatives, and Scrivenor and James were set on to tracking the women on Burnett's hard drive. Two were quickly identified, and confirmed to be alive and well. They'd also received letters, it seemed, but not been bothered otherwise.

But one woman remained, and the images stored by Burnett made it clear that she was different. A working girl. A hooker.

To James that seemed a serious warning beacon. Burnett's other targets were well-paid, attractive professional women who would be almost guaranteed to look down on him in real life. But this girl—Burnett had labeled the candids of her, *Loretta*—she would be available to him.

James had a feeling she wouldn't be easy for the unit to find though. If Burnett had left her alive.

By the time he left the office after nine o'clock, James had received three texts from Ben urging him to come out to the pub, and his own frustration with the case had reached critical mass.

As he drove home, he decided to give Ben what he seemed to want so badly that evening. His company.

—||— —||— —||— —||—

Ben's messages had informed James that he and the group were in the Duke of Wellington in Soho. James hadn't been there before but found it easily enough when he drove there straight from work. He walked through the front door, still clad in his suit, at just before ten.

It looked like a bog-standard pub at first, with subdued lighting, a long, dark, wooden bar, beer taps and optics, but it became obvious very quickly that it was primarily a gay bar. He wove through the mainly male crowd, and it didn't take him long to spot Ben's group, settled in a leather booth round a large table. To James's intense relief, he couldn't see Oliver.

But he did immediately spot Ben, who waved at him in happy greeting from his position beside an unknown blond man on the left side of the booth. The guy had his hand on Ben's thigh.

It felt like perfect déjà vu. James sat down on the other side of the table and wished profoundly that he'd stayed the fuck at home.

It proved to be the pattern of the evening: Ben focused and flirting hard with that night's shag; James faking unconcern, wondering why Ben had pushed so hard for him to come. But he knew why really. Ben thought James needed fun, just as he'd said.

And James saw his gift that morning clearly then for what it had been. A token of friendship. No more.

James had no option but to settle down to be sociable, chatting to Graham about football and Naomi about lighting Ben's exhibition—doing his best to forget his conviction that the group saw him now as another Oliver, played with and thrown away, but hanging around in hope.

Just another shit night, he thought bitterly through his fake smile. He remembered when he'd been happy that this had looked like his brand-new social life.

He retreated to the bar to buy a round the first chance he got. Being Saturday night and extremely busy, it would take a lot of effort to catch any of the bar-staff's eye, effort which he had no intention of making. He didn't want to get back to the table quickly.

But as he edged his way through to lean against the bar, planning to stay there for as long as he could eke it out, the man beside him, sitting on a barstool and nursing a beer, whistled sharply through his fingers and shouted, "Chris! Over here." A barman with very curly blond hair trotted over, resembling nothing so much as a well-trained poodle.

"What's your order?" the barman asked James cheerfully, and James realized Chris had been summoned on his behalf. Taken aback, he reeled off his list and asked for a tray. But all the time, he could feel the man beside him watching him expectantly. When James glanced at him, he registered that the guy was handsome, a little older than him perhaps, and also dressed in a suit.

"Thanks, mate," James said, as he prepared to head back to the table. "But I didn't mind waiting."

"I had to get your attention somehow." The man gave a charming smile. "I've been staring at you since you came in. Don't look so shocked. You're fucking gorgeous."

James blushed on cue, beyond grateful for the low light.

This then was how it felt to get picked up in a gay bar. Life would have been so much easier, he thought sourly, if he'd only tried it long ago. This had been his second pickup attempt, in fact, in a couple of days. It must be a sign.

"I'm Paul." The man extended a hopeful hand.

James shook it politely. "James."

"Are you with someone?" Paul glanced toward their table, and James's eyes followed his.

Yes, James wanted to say. He watched Ben laughing at something the man beside him had said, teeth white, eyes sparkling. He was so beautiful.

But, with perfect timing, Ben leaned toward his companion, close enough to whisper something against his mouth. The man grinned and Ben's grin widened, and their grins met in a kiss, which very quickly became dirty.

"No." James turned back to the bar, sick with self-contempt. "Just some mates."

Paul smiled. His eyes were a warm brown, like his hair. His features were regular and neat. He looked like the hero on the cover of a modern romance. Objectively not as attractive as Mark Nimmo, but he'd do.

No one in the group commented when James slid the tray onto the table, took his own pint and left, but he supposed they were all well used to random hookups. He was finally fitting in. Ben and his friend were still snogging.

Paul turned out to be nice enough, good company, an accountant with a boyfriend at home whom he seemed to care about. And he made it very clear what he wanted, and how ephemeral it would be.

They left together after half an hour of increasingly obscene flirting, and James didn't even look at the table, though a part of him desperately hoped Ben had noticed.

They couldn't go to Paul's flat, because while his boyfriend knew what he did, Paul admitted he wasn't that happy about it, which left James fighting not to identify with the poor bastard. This time, he'd landed on the other side of the fence. It was the scene though. Apparently.

They went back to James's room and undressed, and James allowed Paul to blow him, and he jerked Paul off in turn. Then they slid under the duvet, dozed, and James turned down Paul's request to fuck either way round, so they indulged in some heavy frottage instead. Objectively it felt very good.

James hated it. He hated it just as much as he'd hated the anonymous fucks he'd had with girls, which he'd thought at the time had felt so soul destroying because the gender had been wrong. Turned out he was just a hopeless bloody case in general.

Paul passed out after their second orgasm, and James couldn't throw him out. So they slept through until James's alarm woke them, and Paul immediately began to panic.

Worry and guilt were written across his face, and as he dressed in silence, James didn't know whom to feel sorriest for—Paul who couldn't seem to help doing things that made him ultimately unhappy, or his lover whom he seemed to hurt daily.

The perfect shag, James thought acidly as he said his farewells and watched Paul trot down the stairs toward the front door. Good sex. No complications, for him at least. He closed the door, heartsick, and turned to go back to his room.

His shock at finding someone else in the hall with him was not feigned.

Ben was standing motionless outside the bathroom door, watching him. He wore only a towel around his waist, apparently about to go into the shower, and James knew how he must appear himself, clad only in yesterday's underpants and stinking of sex.

For a long awkward beat, neither of them spoke, and James wanted to believe that Ben appeared shocked, that there might be anger in his clenched jaw, resentment in his eyes.

But Ben smiled with his usual friendly warmth, and James knew it had been in his imagination.

"I didn't see you leave last night," Ben said.

"I don't think you noticed I was there," James returned. It didn't sound as light as he'd meant it to. But he wasn't feeling much like pretending.

An undecipherable expression flickered across Ben's face. "Funny," he said. "I thought you might go for Steggie. To…branch out."

And that shocked James out of his mood—possibly as Ben had intended.

"Steggie?" He gaped.

Ben laughed. "That guy looked hot, though," he teased. Then, slyly, "Looks like my tie helped you pull."

James could see nothing reassuring, no discernible sign of jealousy in Ben's expression. And as he accepted that, he allowed himself to admit that the reason he'd had sex with Paul hadn't been simply to prove to himself he could fit, that he could be a "proper" gay man. He'd also done it to give Ben a taste of his own medicine.

Pathetic.

"I hope you remembered to be safe," Ben said, a teacher checking his student had absorbed his lessons. "And I hope you enjoyed yourself?"

No sign of jealousy, no possessiveness, no hurt feelings. Ben might even be relieved. No more need for guilt, no doubt any more that James accepted and understood. Plenty now, as mates, in common. The thought tasted beyond bitter.

"Yeah," James said with a casual shrug. "But shagging around's not really my scene."

Ben's smile slid slowly off his face like an egg in oil.

"Each to his own though," James called pleasantly behind him as he headed down the hall to his room.

When he passed Ben's door, slightly ajar, he caught movement on the bed—a muscular, hairy, naked leg sliding out from under the grey duvet.

At least, he told himself stoically, as he closed himself in his room, he didn't feel like this for nothing. A purpose had been served. He knew now what he was and what he was not. He knew how essentially different he was from Ben. It hadn't been a lack of opportunity or a lack of experience. It was *him*.

And Ben? He didn't care who James fucked or who fucked James, just so long as everyone stayed friends.

As he dressed, he noticed Ben's gift, the tie, lying on the top of his chest of drawers where he'd left it the night before. Deliberately he slid it under his collar and knotted it into place. He knew where he stood, and he'd be fine.

━◆━ ━◆━ ━◆━ ━◆━

Thankfully the MIT's on-call week had been entirely peaceful. So over the next couple of weeks, the investigation into Burnett slogged on.

The unit had managed to ascertain from the background in Loretta's photographs that she'd been working the streets around Shepherd's Bush when the pictures were taken. But though they sent out a couple of pairs of plain-clothed female officers to show her image around, no one seemed to know her.

The new, angry, dead-eyed version of Burnett smirked that he'd taken the photographs of Loretta as an exercise in photojournalism. He didn't deny having the addresses of the other girls. But he claimed he didn't know anything about Loretta. He said he'd made up her name.

James couldn't work out if there was even a glimmer of truth in it, or if the girl had been material to practice on. The first dummy run, for Maria and Romilly.

The more the unit ran into blank walls, the more Ingham's temper frayed with the knowledge that she *had* Burnett, that she knew what he'd done, but she didn't have enough to be sure she could nail the door shut. They still had no direct forensic evidence that linked Burnett to either homicide, and he had a glib answer to everything—staring them out, daring them to stop him. It seemed to James, sometimes, that Burnett had started to revel in the attention.

Despite all that, James tried, as he'd promised, to get home more often, and he did his best to produce a facsimile of his old, pre-sex friendship with Ben, determined to mimic old behaviors that no longer came naturally until somehow they clicked into place again. Ben, after all, hadn't changed from the guy James had known before they started sleeping together, though perhaps he might be slightly more gentle, more careful.

He came home more often too.

Still, it was very clear that Ben would never compromise his own identity. The red sock made regular unapologetic appearances, and there were frequent nights that Ben didn't come back to the flat at all. But when he stayed in, and when James made it home as well, they talked about their days at work and their families and things they had in common.

And there were many…their combat sports for a start. Ben explained why he'd chosen savate—it had been based on extremely brutal street-fighting, and he never wanted to feel as if he couldn't take care of himself in real life, whatever happened. He wanted any potential opponent on the ground immediately, he said, and he'd ask questions when they regained consciousness.

Even better, Fabrizio at the gallery loved Ben's alternative portfolio once he got the courage to show him and wanted to include it in Ben's show. Ben was relieved and thrilled and very grateful to James, and they celebrated with two rounds of memorable, spectacular, champagne-fuelled sex.

As they relaxed into each other's company, James found himself too, for the first time in years, sharing all kinds of insane anecdotes of his life as a jet-setter while Ben mocked him unmercifully. In turn, Ben gradually gave him stories about his parents' big, political, pet-filled home in Hampstead, crammed with souvenirs from their charitable projects abroad. And he told James about their long, happy marriage and their total acceptance of their son.

They'd given him a rescue dog just before he turned nine Ben told him one drunken evening, but he'd never had another after it died. From what James could gather, to Ben, the dog had been a unique and irreplaceable presence. James managed to get out of him that it had been a crossbreed, but Ben wouldn't tell him its name. James got the feeling that Ben saw it as too personal to share.

Through it all, James hoped secretly that the more he got to know Ben as a man, as opposed to a lover, the more mundane he'd become. That James could start to see him as an ordinary bloke, like anyone else. But perhaps he'd known deep down that the insane depth of attraction he felt would be out of his control. And it felt as if, far from getting cured, the more he and Ben talked, the more intrigued and besotted he became, and the more perfectly their characters fit together.

Despite himself, in his idle hours, James chewed over the contradictions of a man with a background as fairytale-solid as Ben's, so intrinsically resistant to the concept of romantic love and happy ever after. In James's experience, that kind of bone-deep cynicism usually came from broken homes. Yet tantalizingly, he knew now that Ben could love—intensely—if only a pet dog.

It got worse one Friday night in mid-April when James arrived home unexpectedly early to find Ben in the front hall of the flat, ready to go out, shouldering into a dark woolen jacket, phone in hand.

"Oh." He looked startled by James's arrival, almost shifty but James knew better than to give any sign that he'd noticed. "I didn't expect you yet."

"The DCI sent me home. She said I looked worse than her grandfather. Who's ninety-two, with emphysema." Ben snorted. "Going out?" James asked delicately.

Ben blinked as if the question was somehow unexpected, then he frowned and glanced at the phone in his hand, back up at James, and back to the phone. His indecision was palpable, and that made James feel as uneasy as Ben appeared to be.

Because he knew Ben worked very hard indeed not to appear awkward about his activities in front of James, even though he must be aware that James suffered through them rather than accepted them.

James suspected they were both operating on a system of pretending it was all right in the hope that it would be. He knew why he did it; he often wondered why Ben did.

"I was just going to call a cab." Ben ran his free hand through his dark hair, one of his few nervous tells. His other hand waved the phone around vaguely.

"Yeah? Going far then?" As far as James knew, Ben used the tube to nip around London, and taxis only when it got very late or he got very drunk. But Ben's jittery demeanor suggested he might be about to do something James wouldn't want to know about. "Or on second thought, forget I asked," James finished smoothly. With a blank smile, he edged past Ben further into the hall, to let him get on with it.

"Actually, if you're not busy," Ben blurted. "Maybe you could give me a lift?"

James stopped and turned, keeping his expression carefully free of any glint of surprise, though this would be the first time Ben ever asked James to drive him anywhere.

James thought about it, about the depth of agitation radiating from Ben, but he didn't hesitate. He dropped his briefcase underneath the coat rack and gestured grandly, in answer, to the flat door.

Ben gave their destination only when they were both buckled into their seats, for James to type into his GPS—Harlesden in Brent. Geographically, not all that far from South Kensington, but in wealth and reputation, they were millions of miles apart.

James forced down all his questions because he was pretty sure Ben would be regretting this already. He could almost see tension vibrating in waves in the air between them, and all his instincts told him to stay quiet, not to attempt small talk, not to try easing the atmosphere. Accept the weirdness of it.

The silence in the car continued through the journey, until James began the crawl along Harlesden's High Street heaving with Friday night life, passing shops and restaurants from multiple cultures—Afro-Caribbean, Portuguese, Brazilian, Columbian. No one could deny Harlesden's vibrancy—but parts of it were also associated with the highest level of gun crime in London. It didn't come within the remit of the West London group of MITs, for which all James's unit felt extremely grateful.

"Stop as close as you can to that…" Ben said suddenly. He pointed at an ornate red four-faced clock placed on top of an equally ornate column in the middle of a three-way junction. "The Jubilee Clock."

James did his best to obey, but the best he could manage was to double-park a few hundred yards along from it, hazard lights flashing in a vague bow to the parking laws.

The moment the car stopped, Ben opened the door and darted out onto the pavement, moving quickly through the aimless crowds. He still hadn't said a word to James about his plans, or when he'd be back, or if he'd be back, but it didn't occur to James that he'd just be abandoned there. He knew Ben wouldn't do that.

James's eyes followed him in his driver's mirror as he walked back toward the clock, hands in his jacket pockets, but he'd moved barely a hundred yards along the pavement before his head turned sharply to the left, and he visibly reacted to something said by a figure peeling out of a shop doorway. James turned round in his seat to watch.

The man wore a dark hoodie, with his head covered, and baggy, low crotched jeans. But James could make out at least that he was Afro-Caribbean and young and he appeared to be extremely jumpy.

And suddenly James had a sick premonition of where this was going to go.

On cue, he saw Ben slide something out of his jacket pocket and slip it surreptitiously to the boy, and the boy handed him something in turn. Ben spoke, the boy nodded jerkily and backed away, melting into the crowds. Ben dropped his head and then turned back to the car, hands once again deep in his jacket pockets, shoulders hunched.

James didn't look at him as he got in. His stomach had dropped to somewhere in the region of his boots.

He felt numb. Betrayed. Barely able to comprehend what had happened. What he'd aided and abetted. That Ben had blatantly used him—a serving police officer—as a chauffeur to meet his dealer? Did he really think James would be that slavish?

On automatic pilot James switched off the hazards and flipped on the indicator. He didn't say a word as he pulled the car back out into traffic, because if he started, if he began to vent the thoughts, the mounting rage in his heart…

But Ben...*wouldn't*. All James's instincts told him that. Ben would never put James in such a position, unknowingly enabling a serious crime. He just... Ben wouldn't.

"His name's Jordan." Ben's voice broke the silence, hushed and nervous. After the long quiet between them, both deep inside their own heads, James almost jerked with shock at hearing it, as if Ben has shouted.

He didn't say anything in reply. Waited, fighting down all he *could* say, the reproachful accusations fighting to reach the tip of his tongue.

"He's in care now," Ben went on after that long, tense pause. "But he used to live with his mum in Stonebridge." And all Met coppers knew that name—the estate which held the dubious record of the most reported gunshots in London.

James shot Ben a sideways glance, uncomprehending. But again something—the instincts he'd gained around Ben—told him not to make a sound.

"I got him a camera. I didn't want to buy anything big enough to draw attention. Just something small but with enough functions to take the shots he wants. D'you think he stands a chance of keeping it safe?"

"I. Uh..." James's thoughts raced in stunned circles as huge, huge relief warred with almost angry bewilderment. Because... A camera. *Thank fuck!*

But why did Ben have to be so fucking cloak-and-dagger about a camera? For that matter, why was he giving a camera to a street punk in Harlesden?

But Ben had asked him a question. Automatically, he went with the copper's practicality that had long since tempered his idealism. "I think he'll flog it first chance he gets."

Ben snorted with humorless amusement. "God. Probably." Then, "I just wanted to give him a chance." He fell silent again.

The moment felt delicate, but James felt it might be all right to ask, "How d' you know him?"

In his peripheral vision, he saw Ben lift his right hand and rub his nose. It seemed difficult for him to reply. But then he said, as if he were confessing a secret shame, "I do this...*thing*. It's only once a month. I mean…it's nothing. It's supposed to…to help kids who've been brought up with violence, to express themselves using art or photography. I *know* it sounds like middle-class airy-fairy shit. And…no one else knows I do it. But…it really seems to help some kids, Jamie." James could feel Ben's gaze fix on his profile as he drove. "Jordan's got real talent. Look. He gave me some of his new work." He pulled the small packet the boy had given him from his pocket, and James wanted to cringe with guilt. "It's from his shitty phone camera, but it'll be good. An' I know it's against the group's rules. But…*fuck* the rules. I just wanted to help him a bit. So, I organized to meet him somewhere the other kids wouldn't see, to give him that. So he can practice on his own, when he wants."

Another fraught silence fell, as if Ben expected James to tell him he'd done the wrong thing. But James's inability to reply came from the tangle of shame and affection and pride that closed his throat as he took all of it in. Most of all, somehow, Ben's endearing embarrassment.

"He won't sell it then," James said definitely, at last. "And he'll make sure no one gets to it."

Ben didn't reply, simply turned to gaze out the passenger window as they drove back to Selworth Gardens. James remained quiet as well.

But when they walked into the flat together and closed the front door, James caught Ben's wrist and pulled him into a tight hug, simply because he couldn't help himself. Because he felt so much love and pride.

Ben stood stiffly at first, startled but unresisting, in the circle of his arms, as if he'd never been hugged before. Or as if he didn't feel that he deserved this reward.

Then as James thought he'd pull away, make a joke of it, he felt Ben reach up to hug him back, just as hard.

24

The next couple of weeks felt for James like an emotional bungee jump—plunging to the depths then rebounding back up and up to the joy of sunlight before, again, the inevitable fall.

His friendship with Ben held up and intensified after the night he took Ben to Harlesden.

But James found the renewed sexual relationship had taken on a febrile intensity, the intensity, he thought sadly, of two people who knew what they had was headed for an end. Ben wanted, more than anything in bed now, to fuck or be fucked—as if every encounter might be their last.

Ben desired him. James never had cause to doubt that, and he could tell himself that in some way he was unique—someone Ben wanted to come back to, someone Ben shared secrets with. Not just now and then, like Jace. Not dumped when he got in too deep, like Oliver. The only man Ben liked spending time with and sleeping with, over and above sex. Sometimes he even let himself believe that if he held his nerve, he could be the one to teach Ben how to fall in love.

But much of the time, Ben behaved as usual: staying out late and bringing fucks home while James slept, or not coming home at all. On those nights, James stayed late and went to the pub with people from work, or exhausted himself at aikido or watched TV or went to see Steggie. Most if all, he worked stoically to accept it. James couldn't call it cheating, or dishonesty. Ben was just being himself.

Even so, James found himself researching "promiscuity" in more depth than his professional forays into psychology had allowed, though he didn't know what he hoped to find. The alternative explanation to hedonism seemed to be "sexually compulsive behaviors with multiple partners to avoid tension and anxiety". That didn't fit Ben at all. So perhaps James had to accept it as the way Ben was wired, the way so many other people he'd seen on the job, and in his own early life, were wired. For all he and Ben were compatible in every other way, in this crucial thing, they were polar opposites—like fire and ice.

At work, Ingham slogged on trying to build her case against Burnett to cast-iron solidity, but to James their efforts to take it beyond reasonable doubt felt like trying to nail jelly to a wall. Their only relief came when the murder of a female MP in London swung press interest, like the Eye of Sauron, away from them and on to DCI Lawson in Peckham.

But they were all aware that spring had turned to early summer, and yet another week on call, and no one had paid a price for the murders of Maria or Romilly.

James forgot about his father's charity ball until Steggie mentioned that he'd have to hire a dinner suit. And once the prospect became real and imminent, it distracted him from thoughts of work or Ben, and compelled him to focus on the horror to come. He'd told his father's secretary that he'd accept the invitation and arranged to work on lates the next day. But right up until he stepped into the shower on the evening of the ball, he still reassured himself he could back out.

He told himself he didn't have to go as he fastened the jet studs on his white shirt, as he flipped his black bow tie into place, as he laced his shiny evening shoes, as the bell at the flat door rang. He told himself that as he walked out into the hallway to find Ben at the open door in his coat, having just arrived home, and Steggie, dressed to the nines on the doormat.

They both stared at James as if they'd never seen a man in a tux before.

"Fuck, Jamie," Steggie breathed. "You scrub up well."

James felt a ridiculous rush of pleasure and fondness.

Trust Steggie.

He and the whole group knew James and Ben were back on, in an open relationship, because Ben, though otherwise pulling men as usual, had drunkenly snogged James one night in front of them. Oliver had looked murderous, and Steggie made his reservations repeatedly clear whenever James spent any time alone with him. But Steggie also knew how James felt, and so in front of Ben, he'd taken to behaving as if James were the sum of all gay desire. Which had obviously led Ben to mistakenly believe Steggie had a crush on him, given he'd mentioned it twice. Embarrassing, yes, but James knew why Steggie did it.

In this case, though, Ben also eyed him as if he wanted to eat him whole.

Then James properly took in Steggie.

"Wow!" he returned, with just as much shocked admiration, because Steggie seemed to have been born to evening wear, like an old-time movie star. "You look amazing."

Steggie's suit didn't appear to be hired; it fitted too well for that. But he'd resisted any scintilla of flamboyance. Everything yelled classic and understated, from his white high-collared shirt to his narrow black bow tie. His wavy hair managed to be both tousled and controlled, and he'd taken great care to look like a man who would fit at a party thrown by James's father. Something tense and coiled in James's abdomen, something he'd hitherto refused to examine, began to loosen and relax. He grinned at Steggie, and Steggie smiled giddily back.

"So. When do the two of you turn back into pumpkins?" Ben asked, voice dust-dry.

"Don't know." James threw a careless glance at him. But his attention turned back at once to Steggie. "Depends how good the free bar is."

━▪━ ━▪━ ━▪━ ━▪━

The event took place at the Dorchester. It began with the art exhibition contained in a small room just off a ballroom, from which James could hear the familiar noises of an event in the final stages of preparation: the clink of cutlery and glass, the tuning of musical instruments.

The art room was compact, white-painted and brightly lit, packed with obviously wealthy people in expensive evening clothes. But when he walked in the door, James didn't register any of the familiar faces around him eyeing the prodigal returned. He could focus only on the enormous black-and-white photograph hanging on the far wall and dominating the space: Rose Henderson, holding her only child, on what appeared to be the day of his christening.

James felt stunned, almost assaulted. But he barely had time to recover from the shock of that previously unseen photograph displayed so prominently before Magnus's personal assistant pounced on him, and hurried him and Steggie up to a podium, around which the board of Henderson Oil were milling.

The moment Magnus saw James, he snapped his attention to him and away from the slightly startled man he'd been schmoozing.

"James," he said. "I'm pleased you came."

James said, "Thanks for inviting me." He kept his expression carefully neutral because, while he didn't have a clue what his father was up to, he did know he didn't trust him.

"It looks very good." He threw a glance up at the huge photograph looming over the podium. Then he remembered his manners. He'd once fantasized about this moment—introducing his father to his porn-star friend—but now it had come, he felt less than heroic. It wasn't fair on Steggie.

"This is my guest, Emile Nicholas. Emile." And God, that felt weird to say. "My father, Magnus Henderson."

He could feel that Steggie, beside him, had begun to tremble slightly. Magnus had that effect.

"Mr. Nicholas," Magnus said with a society smile. James knew his father's handshake to be painfully firm; he just hoped Steggie was up to it.

"Sir Magnus," Steggie managed, his voice thinner than normal, and he'd tucked his flamboyant persona well out of the way. Because Steggie knew he would be summed up as the representative of James's new life, and James felt unexpectedly desperate that he shouldn't be made to feel inadequate.

He flashed back unwillingly to Ben's handling of his father—as if he'd summed up Magnus at once and had a sheaf of suitable reactions all ready to use. And the thought struck James—at totally the wrong time—how successfully Ben changed to fit with different people. Like a chameleon. Or a diplomat. Or a con man.

Steggie in the meantime had rallied and began to ask Magnus about the art show, since James had blanked out.

Fuck. Couldn't he leave his preoccupation with Ben to one side for a single evening?

Almost in reaction, he placed his hand on the small of Steggie's back, feeling his strong, slender frame tense, and then relax, under his suit jacket. It was a tiny gesture, but James caught a slight narrowing of Magnus's grey eyes and knew he'd taken note and probably come to his own conclusion. The wrong one no doubt, but James hadn't thought it out. He'd been motivated by shame.

"Are you in the art business, Mr. Nicholas?" Magnus asked. "Photography, perhaps?"

Steggie didn't pause, though James could sense his nervousness. "I'm in film production." He smiled. "Educational films."

James pressed his lips together, tight.

"How very interesting," Magnus replied, but James saw a tiny gleam of expression there that made it obvious to him that his father knew exactly what Steggie did. "Perhaps you could contact our PR department. We make regular health-and-safety videos and the odd promotional one."

Steggie smiled and James dropped his hand. For whatever reason his father had decided to be kind. Steggie had no clue that he hadn't just fooled Magnus Henderson.

After that his father's motivations became slowly clearer.

Magnus placed James at his right hand while he made his welcoming speech; a tall, auburn-haired man James didn't recognize had the left. And James had to concede that the evening seemed calculated to make sure all the guests knew that Magnus's son was welcome back in the fold.

The art show featured paintings even philistines like James and Steggie could understand. They milled around among the other guests: sleek, self-satisfied men talking business and ignoring the art; uniformly skinny women honed by professional trainers and clustering in groups like languid storks, flaunting their designer dresses and immaculate haircuts.

When the exhibition wound up, everyone adjourned to the adjacent ballroom, a room so dimly lit that James could barely make out the color of the walls—dark green or blue perhaps. But each large round table had its own spotlight shining down its crystal and silverware like a mini-sun. Most importantly of all, James noted with relief, at the end of the room stood a well-stocked bar.

James and Steggie were seated at Magnus's table with a brittle society matron between them, the wife of one of Magnus's old friends. James knew her vaguely—Sophia, he recalled—but his old skills came through as if he'd never stopped making small talk with people who had literally nothing else to do.

Sophia would know about his defection and his sexuality, but for conversation she stuck to mutual acquaintances and extremely expensive holidays. She reminded him strangely of Mrs. Cordiner, the woman they'd interviewed the night of Maria's murder—like an underfed lapdog, indulged and unsuited to the real world. On the plus side, she appeared fascinated by Steggie, who relaxed more with every glass of free champagne into his most outrageous self.

James found himself hoping, though, that his father had checked out of their gasping conversation about the Kardashians, because, somewhere through the evening, his urge to make Magnus feel uncomfortable, to rub his nose in his new life, had drained away.

Neither of them had apologized or talked things through—that wasn't who they were around each other. But at some point, they'd silently put the past behind them.

He understood that properly when Magnus cornered him at the bar as he was picking up another couple of glasses of champagne for Steggie and Sophia.

"I wanted to have a quick word about Charles," Magnus said without preamble.

James kept his expression neutral. "Charles."

Magnus inclined a casual hand across the room, toward the tall, auburn-haired man James had noticed earlier.

"Charles Forsyth. He's taken over your role at the company. If you decide not to come back, he may be my successor."

James glanced at the man in question. He was handsome in a traditional way, hair cut conservatively, with a strong bone structure and an aquiline nose. He'd also begun to laugh heartily at something he'd just heard from a board member James knew to be staggeringly boring. So—he was either very charming, or had a disastrous sense of humor.

"He looks the part," he said, though a part of him, a tiny part, looked at his replacement and resented him. He turned back to the bar, away from his father's new-favored son, to get his drinks.

"He's homosexual, you know," Magnus threw in casually.

James froze in the action of picking up his tray. His heartbeat sped up, though he didn't know what to feel at that moment. Shock. Hope? Or...

He tried to take it in. His *father* had hired a gay man, for one of the highest roles in the company? When he used to pretend that homosexuality didn't exist, until the day James had forced it into his life?

But just like Magnus, James didn't like to admit he'd been wrong-footed either.

"So I gathered," he lied.

Magnus's mouth quirked. Perhaps he recognized his own line.

The atmosphere around them seemed to have grown several degrees warmer, and it hit James then that any chilliness had been coming solely from him.

"I think he'd make a suitable partner," Magnus commented.

Now James didn't even try to hide his astonishment. Perhaps he'd misunderstood. "Are you…talking about the company? Or…are you trying to set me up with your protégé?"

Of course he was. His father had returned to matchmaking, just switching genders. He should feel manipulated. Insulted even. But more than anything else, James felt exhilarated. Because for his father, this came as close as he could manage to announcing his acceptance.

Magnus didn't look remotely embarrassed either at being called. "He's a good man. And single. You should consider it, since you're free."

James grinned and then frowned. "How do you know I'm free?"

Magnus shrugged. "You're obviously no longer in a relationship with Mr. Morgan or you'd have brought him. And Mr. Nicholas is clearly…a friend."

Jamie gaped at him, silenced, which seemed to satisfy Magnus enormously.

"I'm going to have to talk to some investors. It's very tedious. Do have a chat with Charles. And come and see me before you go."

He set off, and James looked, as if compelled, across the room at Charles, to find Charles also examining him with predatory interest.

Oh fuck, he thought. But he found he wanted to laugh more than anything. And after so many years in which thoughts of his father had brought only pain and alienation, that felt like a gift.

＝ii＝ ＝ii＝ ＝ii＝ ＝ii＝

The clock on the taxi dashboard read almost four a.m. when James and Steggie rolled up to the front door of No. 22, sniggering like lunatics. Some of it was champagne and vodka; some was definitely Charles.

When he'd sauntered across to talk to James, Charles had been a bit of a revelation.

Steggie delightedly mimicked his posh drawl, in fact, all the way home: "I knew you had to have *balls* to leave the way you did…but bringing Emile Nicholas as your plus one to Magnus's society party? That's steel cohones."

To James's delight, and Steggie's initial horror, Charles turned out to be a particular fan of Steggie's work, though he remained discreet enough not to discomfort him. In fact, James had been horrified to discover he rather liked Charles.

"You don't think he'll tell your father, do you?" Steggie had already asked James that several times, and James never had the heart to admit that his father, once he discovered his address, would have had everyone in the building thoroughly investigated.

He put his key in the front door and shook his head solemnly. "No way. It might blow his chances since he is *going* to call you. You know he is." Another argument they'd repeated several times, but alcohol always gave it fresh wings.

"He fancied *you*." Steggie insisted, again on cue, as they reached the door of his flat. "He was drooling. Look…" He reached out and brushed something off James's jacket. "There's a bit of it there."

They both sniggered, then James sighed with happy, drunken camaraderie. "Stegs. Thanks for coming. You were brilliant."

Steggie's smile dropped, and he looked surprised, which surprised James in turn because…wasn't Steggie used to gratitude? Or compliments?

Steggie rallied quickly. "No. Thank *you* for asking me, Jamie. Really. I've never been to something like that. I mean porn-awards evenings… yeah. But that's the first time I've seen a little old lady bid thirty-eight grand for the chance to fly a fighter jet. She was eighty two!" Steggie had been staggered by the charity auction, in which very rich people vied with each other to pay the most, for things that were useless to them, and thus prove their status. "It really turned out to be an education." Steggie gave a wicked glance up through his long lashes. "Like my movies."

James laughed. "Oh *yeah*," he said fondly. "Health and Safety." They stood close together, reminiscing. Unnecessarily close, James realized, at the same moment that he also noticed that his cock had begun to fill mindlessly in his trousers.

"You could always come in," Steggie suggested, voice soft. "For… you know…a nightcap?"

James met his eyes, and suddenly it felt as if there were less air in the hall.

The whole evening had been surreal, but it had left James more at ease with himself than he'd felt since he'd first lost Ben...his *image* of Ben. And Steggie had been with him through it all, supportive and discreet as he could manage, just as he'd been since the day they'd met.

He stared mesmerized into Steggie's golden eyes, and he could see desire and vulnerability there as clear as glass. This wasn't Steggie the abused child, or Emile the practiced porn star. It was his friend, who wanted this. Him.

Ben had been right after all.

He could feel Steggie's tension, that he held his breath too.

He began to lean in as Steggie did, and their mouths touched, a brush of soft damp skin. Electric.

"Jamie!"

His name, called harshly in the dim, silent cocoon of the hall, shocked James so much that he gasped before he jerked back from Steggie. And it took him alcohol-befuddled seconds to realize that Ben now stood at the top of the flight of stairs to their flat, wearing only a pair of grey tight-clinging boxer shorts. His hair lay in a tousled mass against his bare shoulders, and from where James stood, his eyes looked like chips of coal in his pale face.

"It's four in the fucking morning," Ben spat.

"Um...sorry?" James said. But he couldn't work out, through his alcohol fog, how they'd disturbed Ben, when his bedroom sat at the back of the flat. Had they been that loud? To make Ben this angry?

"Sorry if we woke you," Steggie said, voice clear and calm. "We'll be very quiet from now on."

But when James glanced at him, Steggie appeared less conciliatory than cold. And when James turned confused eyes back to Ben, he found Ben returning Steggie's glacial stare.

"So. D'you manage to keep your clothes on around all that money?" Ben asked Steggie, so pleasantly that it took James's tired mind far too long to understand what he'd actually said.

Then, "Ben!" he protested, stunned.

"Oh, that wasn't a problem," Steggie returned cordially and gestured with his head to James. "Until now. Then again, *I* don't drop 'em compulsively for free."

James's wide eyes swiveled to Steggie in turn. *What the* fuck?

Ben and Steggie stared at each other with twin expressions of steely dispassion, communicating without words, and James was left as no more than a bewildered bystander.

Then Ben said, eyes still fixed on Steggie, "Jamie, come to bed. It's late."

James glanced at once, torn and embarrassed, at Steggie, and Steggie pulled his gaze at last away from Ben. His expression changed immediately, softened as he took in James's confusion.

James's mad moment of temptation had passed, but how could he just walk away from Steggie now?

"It's all right, Jamie," Steggie murmured. His voice sounded kind and James couldn't read his expression. But he reached up and kissed James tenderly on the mouth, a kiss that could be mistaken as benediction, as just friendship, if James didn't now know better. "It's late. Go to bed."

James watched his retreat, head bent, into his flat, his thoughts a turmoil of regret and dawning, affronted anger. Then he glared up the stairwell to Ben.

James took a deep breath and stormed up the stairs, two at a time, trying to calm his mounting temper. But by the time he reached the flat, Ben had already gone inside, front door left open for James to follow. James made sure to slam it after him.

Ben stood waiting to confront him in the lamp-lit lounge, and James realized with astonishment that his half-naked body actually trembled with rage. And that elevated James's own righteous fury to incandescence.

"What the *fuck* was that?" he demanded.

"You were going to sleep with Steggie?" Ben shouted, just as outraged. "Really?"

James had never seen Ben angry like this, and even through his own fury, he found himself scrabbling for an explanation. Ben felt so protective of Steggie that he'd insulted him, to get him away from James? It didn't calm James down.

"I can't believe you said that to him!" he yelled.

"I told you he's got a thing for you! You can't play with him like that!"

The hypocrisy overwhelmed any composure James had left. "I'm not playing!" he shouted. "And we're both bloody adults!"

It was as if he'd pressed a button. With no warning, not a sound, Ben burst into movement, and in two strides he'd reached James and propelled him back against the wall. The shock of it knocked the breath out of him, reflexes dulled by alcohol and rage.

He tried to say something, but Ben lunged forward and ground their mouths hard together, and at the same time his hand shot unerringly down to cup James's genitals threateningly through his evening trousers.

James stilled like a shop dummy beneath his hands and mouth, eyes startled wide, body rigid with caution. He could barely believe what had happened, because he'd come to expect many things from Ben, but never this. Never this much frustration, expressed physically. But suddenly, he could see the man he'd glimpsed briefly in the savate gym.

"Shut up," Ben hissed. "Just..."

His fingers began to play urgently with the shape of James's soft cock through his trousers, and before James could say anything else, he kissed him again, impatient tongue sliding between his half-open lips.

The slippery, demanding push of flesh in his mouth shook James out of his stunned daze and into resistance.

They were the same height, but Ben had a leaner build. James should be able to manhandle him away. But when he tried to shove against Ben's naked chest, pushing him out of the kiss, Ben tightened his fingers, just to the point of discomfort, around James's balls and it worked as effectively as a gun to his head.

They were both breathing heavily, faces only millimeters apart, and James could feel every one of the panted breaths puffing across his nose and mouth. To his chagrin, his cock had firmed to traitorous rigidity in Ben's hand.

"Bloody hell," he demanded, outraged. "What's wrong with you?"

Ben's mouth tightened. He shook his head impatiently but his gripping fingers began to move, to stroke and manipulate James's aroused shaft, rubbing the material of his underpants clumsily against the sensitized skin of his cock head.

James couldn't stifle his moan, and Ben hustled closer still, until his almost naked body pressed against James's clothed one.

He breathed fiercely against his mouth. "I'm gonna fuck you."

James's treasonous body responded slavishly, even as his mind blazed with indignation.

But at last adrenalin managed to scythe through his haze of shock and arousal and alcohol, and he understood.

Ben was jealous.

He hadn't been worried for Steggie, he'd been worried *by* him.

James had so conditioned himself to accept Ben's bone-deep promiscuity, that he'd looked automatically at every other possible explanation for Ben's behavior, and excluded that one.

That jealousy would be so intolerable to Ben, so unacceptable, that he'd resort to this.

For a moment he felt relief, triumph, but they submerged quickly below outrage.

The huge fucking hypocrisy of it! The arrogance—as if Ben thought he owned him. As if he could use him when he felt like it and turn on him when he stepped out of line.

Suddenly he wanted to see how aikido would do against savate…a chance to unleash all his huge frustration and thwarted, long-suppressed emotion to match Ben's own ruinous anger.

He flashed through all the moves he'd need to make to free himself from Ben's hold, how he'd counter Ben's response. Bring him down. But as he did, even as he pictured driving Ben to his knees, the maxim of his aikido master slid into his mind to prod his inconvenient conscience.

Resorting to domination was failure. Anger was inner pain turned outwards.

Inner pain, turned outwards.

James took a deep, clean breath, deliberately relaxing his body against Ben's, and then, moving slowly, so Ben couldn't misinterpret, he raised his arms to pull Ben tighter against him into a clumsy hug.

Ben's lewd hand froze, startled, on his genitals. James hugged him tighter still.

After a moment, inevitably, Ben began to struggle, his arm and hand mashed between their bodies, but he didn't try to use his grip to hurt James, and James simply held him until his squirming finally slowed and ceased.

He stood limply then, in James's embrace, hiding his face against James's neck, and James could feel his hot, hitching breaths against his skin, and the fine tremors that ran through Ben's body.

James felt a surge of confidence, of rightness, rushing through his veins like an injected drug.

"You still want to fuck me?" he murmured indulgently against Ben's ear.

After a second, Ben's head shook in denial against his shoulder, like a child hiding after being told off.

He tightened his arms despite himself, brimming over with love and new hope.

Because Ben had felt that much. For him. And he couldn't hide it.

"Well…d'you want me to fuck you?" he asked. "Or should we just go to bed? It's four a.m."

He heard Ben give a shaky sigh. This time, when he pushed back against James's hold, James loosened his arms to set him free.

He didn't meet James's eyes, and his expression appeared almost ravaged, as if his own thoughts hurt him. He pushed close again, and his lips parted on a soft exhale, warm air tickling James's skin before he pressed a sweet, short kiss to his mouth.

He pulled back only an inch or two when he'd finished.

"Fuck me, then," he said, voice small against James's cheek.

James swallowed tightly. The tension and unknown emotion swirling around them should have taken all the stiffening out of his cock, but he was aware he sported a nearly full erection, though his mind didn't seem connected to it. His body felt ready for sex, his brain felt minced.

Still, he moved to pull Ben toward the lounge door, to take him to bed.

"No," Ben said quickly. "Here. Please."

He didn't allow James to question or demur but undressed him, hauling off his rented dinner jacket and dropping it in a heap on the floor, though a stupid, well-trained part of James's mind protested the state it would be left in. He pulled loose James's bow tie and unbuttoned his shirt to bare his chest, frowning at it, as if the sight hurt him. Then he leaned in to press an almost reverent kiss to James's skin, below his throat.

"Ben?" James began, unnerved by every subdued, unhappy movement, but Ben shook his head, a quick, sharp movement begging silence.

He didn't meet James's eyes before he turned and walked to the sofa to brace himself against the back of it like an offering. Atonement.

James stood in place, eying him in an agony of hesitation.

He could hardly deny that Ben's behavior seemed erratic, but he could only guess at the cause of it. He could be totally wrong. He'd never seen Ben like this and he felt completely out of his depth, yet his gut told him the worst thing he could do would be to reject him now.

James firmed his jaw and moved behind him, studying his rigidly tense, bare back, his spread legs, his bent head. He bit his lip and slid Ben's underpants down his thighs to bare his round, smooth arse. Ben didn't move.

"Ben?" James asked uncertainly, silently begging for a sign this was the right thing to do.

"Hard," Ben breathed. "Do it hard."

James closed his eyes and welcomed the surge of lust that hustled aside his doubts. Uncomplicated sex seemed familiar, at least.

He pushed Ben's head down by the back of his neck, until he bent fully over the sofa, hands on the seat cushions. One handed, he undid his own trouser clip and zip and his trousers slid to his ankles pushing down his boxer briefs, just enough to free his rigid prick.

He leaned over Ben until his body covered him completely, open shirt and pubic hair scratching, soft, against Ben's skin. His erection rubbing restlessly in the cleft of Ben's backside. And that, James realized, was as far as he could go.

He groaned, but doing just this felt unbelievably erotic. He could finish them like this, and maybe that would be the best thing. He reached round Ben's hips to grasp his cock, tellingly rigid. Ben made a helpless sound and thrust into his grip, and James took another delicious thrust in his cleft.

"There," Ben panted, and pointed to a drawer in the coffee table.

James stopped. "We can…"

"No. Please. I need it."

James groaned, cock pulsing impossibly harder.

He ordered, "Stay!" in the spirit of the encounter and sidled gracelessly round the sofa, hampered by the bunching of cloth around his ankles, to fumble in the drawer. He found a substantial stash of condoms and lube—obviously intended for Ben's sofa shags.

He didn't even feel a pang when he saw them. Not now.

When he looked up again, Ben waited for him, bent over the sofa, breathing hard, face obscured by his tumbling dark hair, legs spread and ready.

James shuffled back swiftly into position and prepared Ben's arse with slippery fingers. Ben cooperated with desperate eagerness, pushing back the moment James's long, thick shaft slid inside him, moving into the rhythm of James's thrusts.

James allowed a moment to worry that Ben might be feeling as awkward as James would probably have felt, bent over the sofa and taking an animalistic fucking, but Ben's enthusiastic participation didn't allow doubt to take root.

Ben didn't submit; he demanded what he wanted, with every writhing, grunting fuck onto James's swollen prick. Braced against the sofa cushion, Ben's hands were shaking and that proved to be the tiny thing that James fixed on as his body slavishly answered Ben's.

In the end, their desperate coupling didn't last long; they were both too wound up. Ben came first, messily, over the back of the sofa, clenching rhythmically around James's deep-pressed cock. And the sight and sound and smell and feel shoved the last of James's restraint off the edge. He teetered on the razor's edge of orgasm, but the thing he tried to hide even from himself—the overpowering primal urge to possess and claim—pounded in his temples and demanded satisfaction.

When Ben finally relaxed, James pulled out of him, fumbled off the condom and jerked his erection until he peaked spectacularly, spurting semen copiously all over Ben's glorious backside.

He wanted so much more. He wanted under his skin. To plant his seed as deep as he could, watch it trickling out of Ben's arse. But this was something.

He had the clear thought as he watched his spunk dribbling between Ben's cheeks and down his splayed thighs that he might as well have pissed on his leg.

Yet, he reminded himself, he'd have been the one taking the fucking if he hadn't turned the tables. Because Ben had wanted to take possession of him too. *Ben* had been jealous.

James, as he staggered backwards on spaghetti legs, more than half-expected some kind of backlash in the aftermath, but Ben seemed still lost in an orgasmic mist.

Neither of them said a word as they stumbled down the hallway to Ben's bedroom and gave each other a cursory wipe down with a flannel. And when James collapsed into bed, Ben climbed in beside him.

They lay side by side in the darkness in an exhausted, waiting silence.

"It was Shep," Ben said suddenly. "My dog's name."

James closed his eyes, trying to control the warmth and excitement in his chest.

"That's the corniest dog's name I ever heard," he said. "After maybe…Fido."

The bed shook slightly with Ben's laughter. "I was nine, hotshot. I didn't do originality. So what did you call your dog? Churchill? Ozymandias, king of kings?"

James snorted. "Ozzy. Not bad. Nah, I never had a dog. Father didn't see the point of pets."

He sensed Ben's gaze on him through the darkness, then a hand reached out to clasp his.

"Your dad. Did it go all right tonight?" Ben asked.

James thought about Charles, and how he'd meant to make Ben laugh about it when he told him. Maybe tomorrow.

"Yeah. It went pretty well."

Ben's hand squeezed tight. "You'll have a dog one day." He sounded close to sleep. "Ozzy the dog."

James squeezed back, thinking about what had happened. Thinking that maybe one day, if he could hold on, it would be Ben's dog too. They fell asleep, still holding hands.

25

James woke alone, but at almost eleven o'clock he could hardly be surprised by that.

He lay there thinking over the events of the night before—and the buoyancy of hope he'd felt when he fell asleep still bubbled away inside him, though he was desperately trying to keep a lid on it.

With Ben it felt a bit like handling a wild animal—nothing should be done to spook him. James mustn't let him see how obvious he'd been.

But James couldn't know whether going on with sex last night, accepting Ben's apparent need for his domination, for penance, or exorcism, had been a good idea or a bad one, in circumstances so crazy and violently delicate. But it had been instinct, and there could be no point second-guessing it now.

He went in to the office at noon, after returning his evening suit, but the daylight part of his shift was as uneventful as every other recent one, save a *How are you? Thanks for last night* text from Steggie.

James stared at it and began to compose a noncommittal reply, feeling like an unmitigated arsehole. And only then, as he tried to find ways to brush off Steggie without hurting him, did he understand how right Ben had been about it.

He still believed Ben had been motivated by jealousy the previous night, but James knew too that, underneath his gilt-edged bravado, Steggie was fragile, and he didn't need to invest in someone already a hundred percent hung up on another man.

He worked steadily on a backlog of form-filling. An hour or so before James was due to leave to go home, Kaur bounced into the office looking bizarrely energized.

"Got her, Sarge! Well, I got a name. Loretta McAulay! One of the guys in Vice finally shared a grass with me. Beverley, her name is. Anyway, she knew Loretta. That *is* her name. It wasn't Burnett's imagination. She came from Newcastle and disappeared from Bev's patch last year. Bev thought maybe she'd had enough and gone home."

James took a moment to absorb it. At last. Luck, and a name.

"Did she say goodbye?" he asked urgently. "Pack up and leave? Or...?"

"Disappeared, according to Bev. But that's not exactly unusual in their line. It's not like they were best pals."

James frowned, then grinned wildly. The point was they had something to go on.

"Get yourself a coffee, Sameera. And put a gold star on your jotter."

Kaur winked and sauntered off, leaving James to trawl for any official records on Loretta McAulay.

Getting the name itself would make Ingham's day, if only because they'd caught Burnett in another lie. But having the name gave no guarantee of finding the actual person.

Despite working at it all evening, James couldn't find a trace of her.

He reached home just after one, expecting Ben to be in bed, after the night before. James certainly knew how exhausted he felt, and he'd had a lie-in. But as he opened the front door into the hall, he heard music from the lounge, and men's voices. And James realized wearily, he really should have expected that instead.

He should have expected Ben to shove back after his display over Steggie.

The door to the lounge lay wide open, and James could hardly fail to see the scene playing out inside.

Ben sat, shirtless, on the sofa, and two muscular, tanned men, also wearing only jeans, were kneeling by the coffee table, snorting lines of white powder off a mirror with rolled-up banknotes.

As one of the men took his hit, Ben stroked his naked back. And it felt as obvious to James as if he'd put up a sign that Ben had already snorted his line. His copper's eye spotted three packets of white powder on the table beside the mirror. He couldn't even call it a small amount of...cocaine, most likely. Or methamphetamine.

He must have moved, because one of the kneeling men—the man whose back Ben had been stroking—glanced up and spotted him. But far from looking worried that a policeman stood in the doorway, he smiled as if he'd just received a special delivery of something delicious.

"Well," he said with blatant delight. "Is *this* the flatmate across the hall?" Ben and the other man followed his gaze. "You didn't mention how fucking hot he is."

Ben eyed James for a long moment. "It never came up," he said, mouth quirking. Clearly neither had James's profession.

The man snorted with mirth. "It's coming up now."

Ben rolled his eyes. "Come on in, Jamie. Let me introduce you." He sounded as unbothered as if nothing more incriminatory than the teapot lay in front of him. He nodded toward the man who hadn't yet spoken, dark haired and carefully stubbled. "This is Liam." Then the man he'd been touching. "And this is Ned. He's moving to New York for six months, so this is his going-away party."

Ned from the gallery. The author of the yellow sticky note, the man who'd heard them having sex.

James assessed him unwillingly. He had spiky brown hair and vivid light-blue eyes. Just as Ben had said—attractive. His gaze, fixed on James, was shamelessly predatory.

Ben, in turn, looked at James like a mischievous child who knew he could wrap adults round his little finger. He lowered his head and smiled up through his lashes, indescribably sexy. "Care to join us?" he asked provocatively.

"Yeah." Ned slid to his feet, showing off gym-honed arms and bulging pectorals, an orangey-brown sunbed tan. "Come and join us, sweetheart."

That *sweetheart* was almost enough to make James pull out his warrant card and arrest them all on the spot. He should do it, and fuck the consequences. But his position was impossible. And Ben had put him there.

He could feel an angry pulse throbbing in his temple. "Ben," he gritted out. "I'd like a word."

Ben met his gaze, and James learned all he needed to know in the underlying defiance he saw there. This hadn't been a mistake. Ben knew James would come home after his shift, and still, he'd done this.

"Come and sit down then." Ben smiled.

James's jaw clenched, granite hard. "In private." A nerve jumped underneath his skin.

"Oooh!" Liam sniggered. "Are we having a domestic? Didn't you ask hubby if you could bring us home to play?"

Ben's smile vanished. "Fuck off, Liam."

He tightened his mouth, but he stood up and edged his way out from between the sofa and the coffee table, to walk toward the door.

"We'll give you five minutes to get started," Ned called. "Then we'll come and join you."

James turned and marched down the hall, though when he reached the end he couldn't decide which door to go for. Certainly not Ben's bedroom. But Ben brushed past him and walked into the bathroom. Neutral territory, then.

The shock of the overhead light felt burstingly bright against the white walls and tiles, and after the dim cosiness of the lounge and hallway, it looked like a clinic, or a morgue.

Ben walked over to the washbasin, turned, and leaned his backside against it, arms folded on his naked chest, legs crossed at the ankle. The whole pose screamed insolence, and James wanted to punch him in the jaw. He pulled the door closed behind him and braced himself, feet wide apart, hands at his sides.

"What the *fuck* d'you think you're doing?" he demanded. "I'm a copper, Ben. That's a Class A drug. What is it? Meth?"

Ben rolled his eyes like a stroppy adolescent forced to listen to an out-of-touch parent.

"Fucking hell. Ned brought it. It's just coke."

James's mouth twisted. "Also a Class A drug."

"So are you going to arrest me, Sergeant?" Ben drawled, smirking. "I wouldn't get more than a caution, even if you did."

James could hardly argue, because using small amounts was no longer a serious offense. He tried not to analyze the fact that Ben knew that.

Yet, irresistibly, he flashed back to the night he'd taken Ben to meet Jordan, when he'd suspected for a few minutes that Ben had implicated him in a drugs deal. His instinctive conviction, then, that Ben would never compromise him. The way that instinct had been vindicated.

At least, he told himself desperately…at least this *was* comparatively trivial.

It didn't help.

"Maybe," he snapped. "Maybe not. Given there are three bags of it on your coffee table. Either way it's a criminal record."

Ben's boredom melted into a scowl. His eyes seemed almost tar-black with contempt, as if he'd been waiting for it to reach this point. As if he'd expected it.

"And that's what this is about, is it? Doing a bit of coke? Or is it the fact I'm going to have sex with two other men?"

James hadn't expected it, though he knew Ben to be both angry and high—because Ben had always stayed well away from his weakest spot.

He knew it was the coke speaking, loosening Ben's tongue. But it had to be more than that too. This whole scene…Ben was lashing out because of the night before, because he'd shown weakness to James. One step forward, James thought wearily, ten steps back.

"Don't try to police *me*, Sergeant," Ben hissed. "Don't think you can own me. Don't even try."

"You fucking *hypocrite*." And just like that, all James's long-suppressed frustration came roaring in, boiling inside him, until he felt almost weak with rage. "What were you doing last night then? You were jealous as hell of Steggie."

Ben's fine-boned face seemed whiter than ever in the harsh light. He straightened up, too infuriated, it seemed, to hold his cool pose any more. His body looked loose, a fighting stance, their second big fight in two days, but this one wouldn't end in sex.

"Don't project your feelings on to me," Ben spat. "You're jealous of every man I touch."

"I know what I saw," James returned. "You couldn't stand the idea I'd sleep with him."

There was a short, dangerous silence. Then Ben began to move, a slow, insolent stroll across the room until he stood toe-to-toe with James.

"Really?" Ben asked sweetly. "Then why don't you come and join us now, Jamie? I can watch Ned and Liam take turns fucking you. And you can see how little I'll care."

Their eyes locked. Ben looked implacable, and James fought with all his will to show nothing at all. He hadn't learned his last lesson, even though it had broken his heart. Now he'd been taught it again, just to make sure.

Without another word, James turned and walked out of the bathroom, went to his room and randomly pulled together clothes for the next day. He couldn't stay in the flat for all kinds of reasons. The fact there were Class A drugs on the premises should be the main one, but it wasn't.

He hadn't stood a chance of winning, fighting someone he cared so much for, who didn't, in the end, care that much for him. Yet he knew how far Ben had to be pushed to be cruel, and James had pushed him on something nonnegotiable...intrinsic to him, whatever James had wanted to believe.

When he pulled open his bedroom door into the hallway, he found Ben standing, eyes closed tight, against the wall beside his bedroom door, and Ned pressing against him, arms looped round his waist, kissing him greedily, hungry hands kneading his arse. Ben had to bend his head down because Ned stood a few inches shorter, and they both seemed blind to anything else. Liam stood beside them, watching avidly, his short, fat erection sticking out of his open jeans.

Liam's eyes followed James as he passed them by, bag in hand, and walked out the flat door. When he got into his car, he sat in the driver's seat for a few minutes, shell-shocked and trying to gather himself. The whole scene, from his entrance to the flat, to his exit, had taken less than fifteen minutes.

What the fuck had he been thinking?

He'd let himself hope again. In fact—he had to face it—he'd been *hoping* ever since Ben climbed back into his bed. He'd even thought deep down that Ben's affection for his dog—the one he refused to replace—might be indicative of some capacity for singular, devoted love. But James had chosen to forget that dogs loved unconditionally. They didn't expect anything back.

What had just happened had been almost as cruel and brutal an awakening as discovering Ben's infidelity in the Trafalgar toilets. Now he wondered if Ben had set up both situations to show the truth to a man who refused to see or believe.

The humiliation and anguish James felt seemed his just desserts.

But he knew what he had to do.

26

James stayed on in the office that night and the next day, kipping on one of the camp beds and starting work again after a few hours' sleep, and by the time he left at around half past seven in the evening, they'd tracked down Loretta's marriage certificate and, finally, her family home. They were waiting to hear back from the local CID when Ingham sent James home. Steggie'd texted him; Ben hadn't.

It was still daylight, and he prayed the flat would be empty all the way through the drive back to Selworth Gardens. Still, he deliberately made a lot of noise coming in, slamming the door behind him just in case.

Ben came, barefoot, to the lounge door, and James knew he should be glad there wouldn't be any reprieve. Glad he could get this over with and make some plans.

Ben wore a loose, collared, pale-yellow shirt and faded, frayed pale-blue jeans. He was still the most beautiful man James had ever seen, and his heart hurt just looking at him.

"Hey," Ben said, smiling. "You made it home."

James manufactured a polite smile in return. "Yeah," he said. Ben didn't try for a kiss.

"I made dinner. I'm..." Ben paused and cleared his throat. Unease peered through at last. "I'm sorry...about the coke. That was...that really wasn't fair."

Just the coke then? James thought bitterly. But of course he wouldn't apologize for the rest. The rest had been the whole point, to incinerate immediately any illusions which might have been created after the ball.

Ben seemed to be waiting for him to speak, but he couldn't think of any actual words he could say out loud that wouldn't lead to a fight, so he nodded. He didn't want a confrontation. He just wanted to pretend, this one last time.

Ben waited a few careful seconds then sighed. "Okay. Well. Why don't you go and get changed?" His tone was still soft. "I'll get the food on the table."

James deliberately didn't think about it while he slid on some jeans and a T-shirt, and when he came back through from his bedroom, they sat down together at the table. Ben made conversation that sounded easy, chattering about his show and Jordan's latest photographs with the camera they'd delivered to him. James made acknowledging noises through a fog of nerves. But it became clear, as he listened, that now the checks and balances were back in place, they were apparently supposed to go on as if nothing untoward had happened.

Ben had made his point, and James had been put back in his place.

But James felt hyper-aware of the tiny glances Ben threw at him when he thought he wouldn't see—nervous, assessing, worried. He could tell Ben felt concerned for him. But then Ben was a decent man who didn't like hurting anyone, though he seemed to make an exception for James. Maybe that was the price James had paid for becoming too close to him, even if only through lust and friendship.

"I'm off to the pub after this," Ben said carefully, as they packed the dishwasher together.

Last time, James thought, and the needle-sharp realization shoved its way into his gut. He wanted to condemn Ben for ruining what might have been, rage at him. But it had never been Ben's fault he couldn't be what James needed.

Ben continued, "D'you fancy coming along? Glynn's bringing some friends. They're models," he coaxed, waggling his eyebrows.

Somehow, James managed a smile. He felt ground to the bone, worn down by months on a case that felt like slogging through treacle, and a love that felt even worse.

"Say hi from me," he said.

Ben's ebullient expression dimmed to a frown, so James tried to produce a facsimile of what he thought Ben wanted to see. Calm, phlegmatic acceptance. No pain.

Ben blew out a slow breath, but he didn't take his eyes off James's face, expression impossible to read. Then his lips tipped up into a tiny smile, and he leaned forward over the open door of the dishwasher and kissed James sweetly on the lips.

James stilled under his mouth, heart aching.

Ben pulled back. "You look shagged out," he said, voice gentle. "I'll try not to wake you when I come back."

And there they were again, speaking in code. Yet James could translate enough to understand that Ben really would let the affair continue on its old terms. They could both pretend the last two nights had never happened.

It felt bizarre to James because he'd felt sure that Ben would be anxious now to get rid of the messy tatters of their paper-thin relationship. That he of all people would be desperate to escape it, because the guilt couldn't be easy on him. Or maybe, as with Oliver, Ben couldn't bear to be the one who delivered the final blow.

Still, that willingness to go on with James, even now, gave him pause.

He retreated to his room and lay on his bed, arms behind his head, staring at the ceiling, listening as Ben got ready to depart. But despite the sadness and turmoil of his thoughts, or perhaps because of them, he fell asleep quickly.

He never knew what woke him.

At first he thought Ben had come to bed with him; then he realized he was alone in the room. But his copper's instincts were aroused.

He crept over and silently cracked opened the door. The hallway was dark, but just before he slipped out into the gloom, he understood what had alerted him. Two men stood by the front door, in the dim glow coming through the fanlight, talking in hushed tones.

As he began to close the door though, a voice rose, not in anger, but almost querulously, and with a shock of recognition James realized the voice belonged to Oliver.

He left the door cracked open. He had to.

As his eyes became accustomed to the gloom, he saw, with a swoop of betrayal, that Ben was naked. Oliver had on all his clothes, even his coat, and he seemed to be leaving. James hadn't even heard them come in, had slept through anything they'd done together. But out of the corner of his eye, he saw the hated red sock on Ben's open door.

It took a while to decipher the words, because they weren't loud, but James tuned in. They were talking about some client they shared, who'd been coming on to Oliver, and Ben advised him to tell the client to fuck off and let him do his job. Not to let anyone make him a victim.

If Ben hadn't been naked, James might have managed to convince himself it'd been an innocent, friendly chat. He excelled at deluding himself like that, he thought with a wash of self-contempt.

"So, d'you feel any better?" he heard Ben ask. "I was worried about you."

Oliver's reply sounded sultry. "Oh, you *seriously* cheered me up."

"Well, that's good," Ben said softly. James heard the smile in his voice. "You cheered me up too. I...really needed a friendly face tonight."

"It wasn't my face that was friendly," Oliver said.

A snort of laughter, then some faint, wet sounds. Kissing.

James closed his eyes.

Somehow he felt more let down by this than anything else since the first shock of reality. He didn't know why, when it didn't even matter now. Why this should be any different to Ben fucking Ned. Or Jace. Because Jace would be classed as sort of a friend too.

Except—Oliver was in love with Ben, like James. He and Oliver were the only two of Ben's "broken hearts" who'd been allowed to stay near him. And only James had been allowed to stay in his bed.

Oliver hated him as a rival in a way he hated none of Ben's fucks. James had instinctively responded in kind. Maybe watching Oliver being kept at arm's length while he could be close had been one of the few things that made James believe he might be Ben's special case. He'd become a kind of symbol, James realized.

He forced his eyes open. He found it hard to focus in the near-darkness, but he thought he saw Oliver's hand slide down Ben's torso. Oliver gave a groan of delight.

"Sssh!" Ben murmured chidingly. "You'll wake Jamie."

Another short silence.

"Look, no offense." Oliver kept his voice obediently low, but his tone sounded sharp. "I just don't get why you kept him around after you got bored. I mean he's like a wet rag. A bit of pity's one thing, but he just doesn't fit."

Fuck. James thought with horrible premonition. *Don't talk about me, Ben. Not to him.*

"Have a heart, Olly," Ben said lightly, pure deflection. "He's a nice guy. He's very...very reliable."

"Reliable?" Oliver sneered with delight. "That's exactly what I mean! He's as boring as…" He stopped as suddenly as if someone had prodded him, as if he realized how he might sound. "Well, I mean you're… D'you love him?"

James didn't want to hear the answer. Yet, he could not disengage.

"I love all my friends, Olly." Ben had moved back a foot or two, so James could see his beautiful profile, recognize that charming, concealing smile. "I love you."

"But you're still fucking *him*."

"And I just fucked you," Ben countered smoothly.

"But." Oliver sounded both distressed and frustrated. "You've kept him around."

"He lives here," Ben said, as if the reason were obvious.

James's eyes fixed on the darkness of the wall opposite him.

"So if it's just that… I mean if I still lived here…" Oliver's need sounded so painfully clear.

"But Jamie does," Ben returned firmly. "You moved out."

And to James, as undoubtedly to Oliver, it sounded like *You gave up your chance at the position, which is currently, regrettably, filled.*

"But…" A fraught pause followed, but Oliver knew when to stop when Ben held all the cards. "Look, we can do this again then though, can't we? Sometime soon? As mates." Oliver had begun to plead, no disguising it.

James bit his inner lip hard, forehead pressed tight against the edge of cold wood. He heard Ben's awkward huff of amusement, indulgent, dissembling, like a parent watching a child who'd been showing off badly. Incredibly, it seemed Ben hadn't understood that Oliver was still obsessed by him. That it wouldn't just be a buddy-fuck. Then again, he hadn't realized the first time either, until Oliver moved out.

"I just wanted to cheer you up tonight, Olly. Because you seemed so down," Ben began the brush-off. "We both needed a friend. I didn't realize you still wanted to…"

"Of course I still want to," Oliver burst out, old pain and new hope laced through his voice like a ribbon.

James thought, repelled, *Christ, do I sound like that?*

He pressed the door shut, quietly, and stumbled back to bed. After a minute or two, he heard the front door close, and then, Ben's door shut too, and he was safe.

No more need for pretense tonight.

No more need for pretense at all.

Ben had sex with him regularly because he was there. James might not be ideal because of his inconvenient feelings, but well, he was...*reliable*. And maybe Oliver'd been right too. Maybe pity had been involved.

After everything, after the split, and James's attempts at an open relationship, and the moments of hope, and the reality that had inevitably been forced upon him... After all of that, at last this felt like the final, merciful coup de grace.

James had gone against his own nature to try to hang on to Ben. Love had unmanned him.

Maybe he'd always had a premonition that the last blow would come through Oliver—the living warning of what happened to someone if they couldn't stop trying.

He lay awake for a long time, blind to the passage to time, plotting and planning, numb to pain. His alarm went off, and he silenced it automatically, but he didn't get up, just lay there thinking until he heard a knock on his door.

"Jamie?" His numbness dissolved like ice in water.

He sat up, bare-chested, as the door opened, and Ben's head appeared round the side, peering into the still-curtained dimness of James's room. "You awake?"

James throat felt closed, choked. He nodded.

Ben opened the door further, letting in more daylight from the hall. "Are you okay?"

James swallowed and tried to find his voice. "Yeah," he managed roughly. "I'm fine."

He could make out Ben's warm, worried eyes. He'd always tried to look after James in his own way.

James said, "Just a headache."

Ben frowned. "Oh. Well, coffee's made, and I'll dig out some paracetamol, okay?"

"Nah." James forced a smile. "I took something already. I'll just lie here till it starts to work."

Ben ran a hand through his hair. He looked worried, uneasy, but then, James hadn't exactly been acting normally the evening before either. "I hope it does. Look I just wanted to say...if you're up for it, everyone's going to the pub tonight."

James smiled wanly. "Again?"

He wondered if Ben understood what he had in store if Oliver turned up, trying to stake his claim. He hoped it'd be cringingly awkward.

"Yeah. I've got a shoot this afternoon. I'll just go straight there afterwards."

"Maybe then," James lied. "I'll see."

Ben hovered for a few more moments, then he walked to the bed and placed a soft kiss on James forehead. "Hope you feel better soon, Jamie."

James closed his eyes, and when he opened them again, the room was empty.

He rolled out of bed at once and sat on the edge, looking down at his hands. He had a lot to do.

The day before, he'd made a begging phone call—out of desperation, but it had gone surprisingly well.

After the ball, James had accepted that his father did indeed want a rapprochement, but when he called, he'd braced himself for some gloating all the same. Yet Magnus surprised him again. He'd asked no questions and simply agreed to let him stay.

So first, he went to the shops, blagged some boxes and bought parcel tape. And back at the flat, he resurrected the remains of the flattened containers he'd used to move in, stored in the unfloored loft. Packing took just over an hour, then he hoovered and cleaned.

When he'd finished, the room looked exactly the way it had when he'd first seen it, the day he'd viewed it—a stranger's room.

It felt almost inevitable that Steggie should emerge from his flat on James's second trip transporting his things down to his car. Like an old gentleman on Neighborhood Watch, nothing got by him.

James froze, arms full as they regarded each other uneasily.

Then Steggie said, tone deliberately tart, "I was *beginning* to think you had no sense of self-preservation at all."

James swallowed hard, unable to speak.

"Come on," Steggie continued. "I'll help."

There were only four more boxes and a couple of cases, so between them they made short work of it.

James left a cheque and a note in an envelope on the coffee table in the sitting room.

Dear Ben,

I think you'll agree it's for the best all round if I move out. I'm leaving this month's rent, plus another, in lieu of notice. I'm sure you won't have any difficulty filling the room. I apologize for leaving this way, but we both know why I have to go and I don't think confrontation and recriminations are in either of our natures. I'd like to thank you for your friendship and kindness. I wish you all success and happiness in the future.

James.

Then, with Steggie waiting beside him in the hallway where they'd first met, James pushed his keys to the flat through the letterbox. It felt ceremonial, symbolic. An official end.

"Thanks, Steggie," he said at last, as they stood beside his laden car. "You've been a good mate."

Steggie's mouth worked for a second, and he looked away sharply.

Maybe, James thought with a pang of shame, calling him a mate hadn't been very kind.

For the first time since he'd met him in fact, Steggie was on the verge of tears. All the shit he'd had in his life, and he was crying over James.

Without second-guessing himself, he reached out and pulled the other man into a hug, feeling his stiff shock, then instant acceptance, arms shooting out to hug him back, hard, far stronger than he looked.

When they pulled back, Steggie's eyes were wet, and he didn't try to hide it. He looked disorientated, as if that simple gesture of affection had shaken him profoundly.

"I'm *still* a good mate." His voice wobbled. He launched a stiff punch at James's shoulder. "And don't you forget it. Keep in touch, Jamie?"

James gave a solemn nod. "I will. Bye, Stegs."

Steggie grimaced. "I'll come to the fucking station to visit if you don't text me. In leather shorts."

James laughed, though he'd rarely felt less like it.

"Is that a promise?" he flirted, and by instinct, he leaned forward to place a soft kiss on Steggie's lips. It was an apology and a thank-you and a goodbye.

Steggie was trembling when he pulled back, as if the kiss had hurt him. James escaped round to the driver's seat.

"Take care of yourself," he called, across the car roof, then sealed himself into his car.

When he looked in his rearview mirror as he drove out of Selworth Gardens, Steggie still stood in the street, staring after him.

◼◼▬ ◼◼▬ ◼◼▬ ◼◼▬

Magnus had already gone to work by the time James dragged his boxes into the Henderson townhouse in Belgravia.

His father's housekeeper admitted him—the same eternally chilly Mrs. Morris he remembered since childhood—as if he'd only spent a night away. And once his car had been emptied, he lay for a few minutes on his childhood bed, looking at surreally familiar walls, torn between gratitude and shame at finding himself back in his old room, with his tail between his legs, at the age of twenty-eight.

Loneliness hadn't driven him back home, but the crushing pain of love had. Still, he had few other options. He needed a bolt-hole in which to lick his wounds while they finished off this case. They had a murderer to lock up, broken heart or not.

Ingham hadn't asked for an explanation when James requested to come in late, not with the hours he'd worked. So when James made it in at ten, no one looked twice.

He switched on his monitor, hoping it might be alive by the time he got back, and went to Ingham's office to report.

As he approached her door, his phone pinged with an incoming message from Ben.

Are you feeling better?

He stared at it, pain and loss stabbing him, a harbinger of so much worse to come. Then it was gone, submerged.

He pocketed the phone without replying.

He felt calm and detached, as he'd felt since he made the decision to leave Ben's flat. He clung to the sense that he might finally get himself back again. He didn't acknowledge the thing crouching in the corner of his psyche, ready to rip and tear at him, when detachment broke.

Scrivenor already sat in Ingham's office when he knocked and went in.

"Loretta's parents haven't heard from her since she went to London," Ingham said immediately. James frowned, trying to force his head back into the game. "She left home seven years ago when she was sixteen to be with some guy they disapproved of. Drugs."

"Did they have her social security number?"

"Yep," Ingham said. "She claimed the dole until last year."

But once she stopped, she'd no longer be on the official radar. James watched Ingham's right hand tapping restlessly on the surface of her desk.

Scrivenor ventured, "If we put out a public missing persons for information, it could alert Burnett that we're close. I mean it's been weeks...an' he's so arrogant he'll have thought we will nae find who she is. If he realizes we know... What if he panics and runs?"

They were silent for a good ten seconds, weighing it up.

Finally Ingham said, "I don't think we have an alternative. We've been looking for her for weeks and this is as far as we've got."

"If we're going to do it, then, we should do it big," James mused. "Nationwide. What about putting her on the missing-persons section on *Crimewatch* tonight? The producers know us...maybe we could get her on."

Ingham rubbed a hand over her face. At least it wouldn't necessitate a TV appearance; it'd all be done with a presenter voice-over. "Okay. Burnett may see it, but it's our best chance of getting her image out there. You make the call then. They're sweeter on you *#hotcop*."

She waved her hands at them in a shooing motion, and they left the office to try to find something to track down Loretta McAulay.

The sense of urgency never left James all that day, and the whole team seemed to feel the same. But he wasn't focusing properly. He knew that.

Still, by lunchtime James had managed to talk Loretta's case onto that night's *Crimewatch* program, and he behaved with careful good humor to everyone.

He ignored two more friendly, concerned texts from Ben, just as he ignored the dull lump of unhappiness in the middle of his chest, heavy and nauseating, pressing against his ribcage. It felt as if it were settling in for a long occupation. He worked hard to hide his misery. He needed it to be private until he could smother it to death.

He dragged out some paperwork, but he spent too much time staring blankly at it unseeing, mind sliding away to rub his nose in personal disaster like a dog being punished. He couldn't help imagining what Ben would feel when he came home from the pub and found James's empty room. Or maybe he wouldn't find it until the next day. How he'd feel when he read the letter, when Steggie told him he'd seen him go.

Hurt. Guilty. Relieved.

"Alec! *Jamie!*"

James's head snapped up in shock as Scrivenor's did, and they stared at each other across their desk. Ingham's sudden howl across the office hadn't sounded anything like a woman hovering on the threshold of career triumph. She'd sounded homicidally enraged.

James and Scrivener shared a last uncomprehending look, then they stood up together and walked fast to Ingham's office.

The found her pacing back and forth behind her desk like a pissed-off cat lashing an invisible tail.

James closed the door before the shouting began.

"We have Burnett! It's him!" she yelled. "It's him! We're this fucking close..." She demonstrated with her fingers. "And they do this! They send us this shit!"

James and Scrivenor eyed each other surreptitiously. Ingham didn't often seriously lose the plot, but when she did, they both knew to stay silent.

"This!" She waved a sheaf of papers at them. "You! You put that shit into HOLMES!"

James blinked at her. Against his better judgment, he tried, "Ma'am?"

"Don't ma'am me! I've just had this couriered from Lawson in Peckham. He's off his bloody head! Or he's not. He wants rid of it, so he's stuffing it onto us!"

"Stuffing…what, ma'am?"

"This! Margaret Calder. *MP*."

"But she wiz offed in Lawson's backyard, on their duty week," Scrivenor protested. "It's front page." And it had taken the heat off them.

Ingham took a deep breath to yell at them again, but she let it go instead in a furious gusting sigh and sank into her chair.

"HOLMES," she muttered. "You heard how she died?"

"Strangled," Scrivenor said, confidently.

"Yeah." Ingham tapped her fingers against the desk, once, twice, three times. "But the papers didn't mention the murderer used a chain."

James's eyes widened.

"And…" she went on, complexion flushed with angry blood. "There were…*stones* in her hand."

"Fuck. Me," Scrivenor breathed.

James could feel excitement gathering in his gut, the triumph of instinct realized. Even his fingertips tingled.

"Lawson says we can have it 'if we want'," Ingham went on, full of disgust. "That lazy bastard knows it's poison. He was bloody gloating…all, 'I just wanna help', the tosser. We don't have the manpower to deal with a huge red fucking herring like this! There's gonna be a fucking takeover unless I can… Fuck!" she yelled again. "I need to try an' explain to the DCS before he gets it from Lawson."

James eyed her uncertainly. Maybe they wouldn't follow it up after all, then, the stones-and-chain link. Ingham could pooh-pooh it upstairs, and she could still get on with Burnett as a triple whammy, if they could just find evidence that he'd done away with Loretta. It had to be, by far, the easiest option.

"Don't look at me like I pissed in your punchbowl," Ingham snapped at James. "I'm a copper. I can see there's a possibility they're all linked, even if I don't want to. I'm not going to ignore it, am I? Barking *fucking* mad as it might be!"

James bowed his head quickly, chastened, and stupidly proud of her.

"Calder's time of death was put at between four and five on Wednesday," Ingham went on. "We need to find out Burnett's exact movements, just in case. But *fuck*, Calder is *not* connected. The stones-and-chains thing is so—" She waved her hand in the air, as if to dissolve the theory in midair.

"Whit aboot Drake?" Scrivenor asked suddenly. "He wiz the first we know of, connected to that signature, if that's what it is. How can he link to Calder? Or Burnett?"

Ingham looked down at her desk, oozing frustration. "If we're making up fairy stories that Burnett has a signature… Celebrity, I suppose. That's a link. Fame. Or in Drake's case infamy. Fuck." She rubbed her eyes. "I suppose we'd better check through the data-recovery report on his online history to make sure. See if he searched the Kelly murders. Alec, get on to data recovery. Jamie, look for Burnett's link to Calder and…Drake too. Now, fuck off, both of you. I'm off upstairs."

James didn't say a word about his revived doubts on Burnett. Ingham still believed in him one hundred percent. Some officers would have charged ahead with an easy collar weeks ago, even without finding Loretta, and taken the risk they'd get it past a soft jury. Ingham had always been better than that. He owed it to her to focus on Burnett first.

He and Scrivenor scuttled out together.

"An' it all looked cut an' dried," Scrivenor crowed as they settled at their desks. "This wiz your genius call, son."

But James didn't feel anything close to a genius. He'd taken his eye off the ball. He simply could not deny that he'd been a far better copper before he'd found a personal life and allowed his feelings for Ben to fuck him up. The ball of tension in his chest had gone, at least, replaced by the churn of purpose, the smell of the hunt.

They studied the photos of Margaret Calder first.

Her skin on her bloated face looked congested mauve, eyes and mouth grotesquely open, and the chain that killed her had dug so deeply into the flesh of her neck it had all but disappeared. A photograph of her lax hand showed the upturned palm full of semiprecious stones—green and black and rusty-red and tiger-yellow against her sad, grey skin.

She'd been found by a security guard in the driver's seat of her Range Rover parked in an underground car park at a suite of offices in which she'd had a meeting, almost a day before. The pathologist's report suggested someone had garroted her from the back seat, and her corpse had been sitting there for over eighteen hours hidden by the heavily tinted windows of her car.

James easily called up her professional details. She'd been an opposition MP for four years, vocal on the Home Affairs Select Committee. Before entering national politics, she'd been a prominent Labor activist and a highly ranked local authority social worker.

James pulled out his old files on Drake and Kelly, with the trepidation and anticipation of a man facing up to an old addiction…hoping that this time it would be worth it. But he felt some of an addict's guilt too, because Ingham didn't want links to Kelly. She wanted links to Burnett.

When Ingham returned from her visit upstairs, she'd calmed considerably, but James thought she looked pared down and grim when he and Scrivenor were summoned again to her office.

"I can't say the DS loves any of us since he can see the very real probability of a massive clusterfuck. But give him his due, he's not turning away from it. So. We have the Calder case too. Lucky us."

Scrivenor blew out a breath that inflated his mustache.

Ingham went on, voice tight, "The good news is, Lawson's not off the hook. He's left with the other angles and he's doing all the press on Calder, so thank God for that. We're left with… Fuck, what are we left with?"

"There's Ksiazek," James put in bravely.

"Who the *fuck* is Ksiazek?" Ingham spat.

"Eve Kelly's only living sidekick. He's the only link to Gary Drake still alive apart from Kelly."

Ingham was glaring at him as if she wanted to tear out his throat with her teeth.

"He has a history of involvement in extreme violence," James defended. "And we weren't able to track him down last time we tried." Admittedly they hadn't searched very hard.

Ingham's jaw clenched and she tapped her pen rhythmically on the desk. It took her almost ten seconds to respond.

"Both of you follow what you're working on for now. But then we need to focus on responses to the call-out on Loretta on *Crimewatch* tonight." She looked meaningfully at James. "We can't afford to lose our focus on Burnett."

Back at his desk, because Ingham hadn't expressly told him not to, James launched anew his search for Ksiazek's official trail—a trail that had ended ten years before.

By midafternoon he'd tracked down Ksiazek's former offender manager, Mary Boone, though in the nineties she'd been called a probation officer. Last time he'd sought her out, she'd been attending a conference in Sweden. This time he got lucky. She was working, and unsurprisingly, she remembered Ksiazek.

"I'm hardly likely to forget someone linked to Eve Kelly, am I?" She had a memorably rich voice over the telephone, like a theatrical grande dame. Not, James thought, the kind of person you'd mess around easily. "Though it has to be said he didn't even remotely live up to the glamour."

James asked, "Did he seem potentially violent to you?"

"No," Boone mused. "I wouldn't say so. I'd say he seemed more…a watcher than a doer. He started to take an interest in getting fit in jail. Self-preservation, I'd imagine. You know he managed to complete three A-levels inside? And he started a part-time degree course when he was on license. No idea if he finished it though. He didn't give any trouble, Sergeant. He said he just wanted to start a normal life."

"You think a normal life would have been possible for anyone linked to Eve Kelly?" James asked doubtfully.

There was a short silence.

"*I* think…all he needed was someone to give him a break. And…" James could hear the sharp tap-tapping of a keyboard down the phone line. "Yes, I thought so. He'd got into employment by the time his license ended. Working in a bookshop. We helped him get the job, and the owner liked him."

She named a shop from her records and the owner's name, and James wrote it down.

"Did *you* like him, Mrs. Boone?" he asked.

Boone barked a laugh. "That's an interesting question, Sergeant. I think that he never let me see enough of who he really was to form an opinion. I'm flicking through his psychiatrist's reports now."

James waited, listening to the faint click of a mouse.

Boone resurfaced a few seconds later. "The pretrial and early-custody ones agree on his obsession with Kelly. He was lonely and isolated when he met her. Immature, overweight, socially awkward, intelligent but not worldly. I suppose she knew a follower when she saw one. She paid him attention, flirted with him, bullied him mercilessly. He worshipped her. You can justify anything, if you love someone enough. You know he tried to take the blame for the murders when they were arrested? He wanted to be her savior. When she went down, he believed he'd failed her."

James said his goodbyes thoughtfully. Then he sat and considered.

Had Kelly's spell faded for Ksiazek, or could her last lieutenant still be out there, trying to please her? Or—he couldn't ignore the other obvious possibility: Ksiazek disappeared from official sight in 2006. Perhaps rather than being the killer, he'd been the first victim. Either way, they needed to find him.

The thing was, James thought restlessly, there were two distinct avenues of investigation, linked only by "stones" and "chain". Maria and Romilly could be tied together—they were young, rich, female and both stalked by Burnett. Drake and Ksiazek were tied as Kelly's disciples. Calder was a wild card, connected, it seemed, to none of the others, yet it had been the signature left on her body that brought them here.

He chewed his lip. Somehow, *somehow*, it all fit together. There had to be a link.

His phone pinged.

If you're home early, could you get milk on the way?

Guilt hit him hard, out of nowhere.

The text sounded so innocent.

He should have waited. Told him, face to face. But he *knew* Ben would have hated that even more than the way he'd done it. He'd have hated being made to face his culpability in a friend's pain, when he could do nothing to ease it.

This had to be for the best, severing everything, without warning or recrimination.

He told himself that over and over as he stared at the text—the surreal anticlimax to a huge string of friendly, flirty, funny messages between them that told the story of their short, sad relationship.

He didn't reply, but he didn't delete the thread of messages. Not yet. He felt detached, as if he'd anesthetized the part of him that experienced emotional pain, just long enough to see this through. But he knew that to be an illusion.

He turned his attention the piece of paper on which he'd scribbled the victims' names, the lines between them pitifully sparse. He glanced back at his phone, and it was all threatening to bubble up through the cracks, like a torrent pressing against a crumbling dam.

He pulled his keyboard roughly toward him, forcing his mind back to this, refusing to give in. There *had* to be something he'd missed. They'd gone down every single avenue they could with Maria and her family, Romilly and hers, Burnett, Ksiazek. What had they got left? Calder? Kelly?

Restlessly, forcing concentration, he called up newspaper reports about Kelly, sensationalized and simplified, but they conveyed the overwhelming revulsion her case had caused. The disbelief that a young woman, beautiful, bright, charming, and a mother of two, had turned out to be a monster who killed for fun. Outrage that evil hadn't had the decency to announce itself with an ugly skin.

He scanned from the top of the list of search results from around the world, looking for inspiration, even if it lay in gossip. Accounts of her past lovers, her accomplices, her own background, her trial, popular psychologists analyzing what had driven her. It was pure luck that, as he scrolled doggedly down the list, he spotted two words among the thousands written about Eve.

He stared at them in disbelief, as if he half-expected them to dissolve before his eyes like a mirage. But even after a second or two, they were still there.

Faye Ralph.

He read the context again just to make sure. But, yes.

Faye Ralph.

Romilly's mother. Well of course. Faye had a career as a criminologist and author. Eve Kelly would have been worth analyzing. But something visceral told him it was more.

He clicked on the link. It brought up a retrospective summary of Kelly's trial at the Old Bailey for a British broadsheet, from a writer who'd attended every day of it—Faye had been their crime reporter. James's mind darted rapidly around the discovery. How could he have forgotten that Faye started out as a journalist? She'd worked with Geoff Leadbetter.

A connection existed. But did it exist for Maria too?

He switched screens quickly and fought his way through the cumbersome police operating system to files of logged evidence, doggedly inputted to their database by the DCs who'd recorded all of Maria's cases and those of her mother.

James typed in two names, hit return and held his breath. And there it was.

Cordelia Whyte QC, Junior Counsel to the defense team of Eve Elizabeth Kelly. February 1996.

He closed his eyes and took a deep calming breath, dyspeptically bouncing between the breath-stealing excitement of a breakthrough like this, out of the blue, and the spastic echoes of his personal distress.

He studied the new information and ordered it in his mind—a connection between three of the four victims. Drake, Kelly's sidekick; Dame Cordelia, on Kelly's legal team at her trial; Faye, a reporter who covered it.

So was this it? Kelly reaching out for a twisted revenge from her cell? If Faye had written something she didn't like...if Cordelia hadn't done as much as she wanted to win her freedom...punish them in the most exquisitely painful way possible by taking their daughters? But why wait over twenty years? And how did Margaret Calder fit? DI Lawson had been searching through her present life for a motive to kill her. Now James felt certain she'd been executed because of her distant past.

Ingham's office door remained shut and the blinds were down, which the unit regarded as her accepted Keep The Fuck Out signal.

James decided to keep going, find something more coherent before he approached her.

He leafed through the photocopied files Lawson had couriered over. In 1996 Calder had been a social worker in Peckham. And as a backbench opposition MP, she'd made a big thing of her past experience in social work, majoring on penal reform, and campaigning against long prison sentences, which she called cruel and inhumane.

James read the details over and over again, fingers tapping a mad rhythm on his desk.

From 1991 to 1996, Calder had been the council's Children and Families officer. He worried at his lip and called up her party biography in the hope it would boast about her lengthy experience. He looked at her photograph—neat brown hair and arrogant eyes—the first time he'd seen her as a human being, as opposed to a ruined corpse. Her biography emphasized her years at the coalface of social work and her special interest in families affected by imprisonment.

He stared discontentedly at the screen. At Margaret Calder. And for no conscious reason, the possibility came out of left field and sat there, looking at him, daring him to prove it. His insane instinct again.

He took a deep breath to clear his head. Quickly he pulled up victims' family records, checked through a raft of newspaper articles, and finally, pulse hammering with exhilaration, he pulled up an internal summary of the Kelly murders.

He stared at the screen for whole seconds when the response came, then he shot to his feet and strode fast to Ingham's office, door closed or not.

27

"There's something," James blurted, the moment Ingham grumpily beckoned him in. He pulled the door shut behind him.

Ingham's curls were disheveled from running her hands through them; she looked on a knife-edge.

James felt almost apologetic as he said, "All four murders are about Eve Kelly."

Ingham closed her eyes. "Astonish me."

The aura around Eve's case had been so shiny with evil glamour that most people didn't bother with the exact details. How had James failed to notice the pattern himself?

"Her victims, ma'am. She finished off Mark Rayburn by cutting his throat, Colin Parrish was stabbed between the ribs and his skull smashed, she shot Jeremy Brand in the head, Jawed Masood was strangled."

Ingham remained silent for a few seconds, then put her head in her hands. "Fuck." She lifted her face again wearily. "A copycat? Burnett's been mimicking her?"

"There's more, ma'am." James wanted to set it all out in a logical fashion, but he felt as if he were on the verge of babbling. "Faye Ralph was a crime reporter at Eve Kelly's trial. Cordelia Whyte was Kelly's junior counsel."

"What?" Ingham breathed. She sounded appalled.

"At that same time Margaret Calder, then Houghton, was a social worker in Peckham, responsible for children and families. One of her areas was adoption. Eve Kelly lived in Peckham when she committed the murders. There was the usual injunction in place for the kids, but I found an American paper that said they were girls. Two daughters."

"Jamie? What are you…?"

"Ma'am. The only reason we know Kelly had any kids at all is through the press. There's no official record of them I can find. We don't even know their names. Prisoners' families…no one keeps a note, as far back as the nineties."

Ingham grasped it at once. "You're reaching to the sky this time, Jamie," she warned icily.

"The Kelly girls would be in the same age range as Maria and Romilly," James said.

"Maria and Romilly weren't adopted," Ingham snapped.

"I know, ma'am," James replied imperturbably. "So I looked at their birth certificates."

Ingham expelled her breath in whoosh of sarcastic disbelief. "Naturally."

"All the things they had in common," James went on. "There was something else. We know they were both born abroad. But when I looked back through the archive of the newspaper where Faye worked, she filed crime reports from the Old Bailey for the entire time she'd have been pregnant. In fact, she filed an eyewitness article about a trial she attended in London the day Romilly was supposed to have been born in Mauritius."

There was a short, tense silence. Ingham closed her eyes and hung her head. "Shit," she breathed.

James should have given her time but, "Do you want me phone Maria's parents?" he pressed.

It took only a second for Ingham to gather herself. "No. I'll do it."

He backed out of the room to give Ingham privacy, but he paced around her door like a confined animal until she opened it again and called him in. Her eyes were narrow, her mouth a tight line of temper.

"I feel like throwing the fucking book at them. Under...*extreme duress* Sir George admitted Maria was adopted, but 'they don't want to talk about it'. That's what *they* think. I'm gonna have a little *chat* with Anthony Crompton as well. Right." She rummaged in a drawer in her desk and pulled out a clear plastic envelope containing a few A4 papers, which she thrust at James. "Permission for an interview with Eve Kelly. I set the wheels in motion a few weeks ago. I did *not* expect to use it. I'll confirm it for tomorrow morning in your name."

It was James's turn to be caught off guard. He stared at the envelope he held in disbelief.

"What about this...Ksiazek?" Ingham asked.

"Um..." James blinked back to attention. "I can't find anything on his location. He went to ground in 2006. Or he's *in* the ground, as the first victim."

"Do you believe that? That the killings started ten years ago?"

James grimaced. "Personally? No. My money's on Ksiazek as the killer. Eve's puppet. I don't see how it can be anyone else."

"Christ..." Ingham groaned. "This is a three-ringed circus. Why the hell couldn't it have been bloody Burnett? A nice, neat, murdering stalker? Mark Nimmo's gonna shove my head on a stick and carry it round New Scotland Yard with an apple in its mouth."

James gave a tentative moue. "You're doing the right thing, ma'am. And...we still haven't found Loretta."

She shook her head tiredly. "If I have a career at the end of this, it'll be a fucking miracle. Tell Alec everything. I'm not briefing the rest till we get something solid. And do what you need to prepare yourself for Kelly."

James nodded. It'd be a late evening, especially with the *Crimewatch* calls on Loretta. But he felt grateful for it.

It was almost midnight in fact when he walked wearily into the grand hallway of his father's townhouse. But he hadn't reached the stairs before the door to his father's study opened, and Magnus emerged with two crystal glasses of what James assumed to be scotch in his hands.

If it had been anyone other than his father, James would have thought he looked awkward.

"James." Magnus nodded. "Would you care to join me for a nightcap?"

James drew in a deep, deep breath and held it long enough to find the calm he needed. Then he let it go in a sigh. James hadn't been invited into his father's study since the night before he left to go to university. And now Magnus had waited up for him with two hopeful glasses of scotch ready to go.

His father was trying his best. It might be entirely the wrong moment in James's life for it, but he didn't have it in him to turn Magnus away.

He followed him inside. The room looked as he remembered it, a classic male study painted in an elegant mid-grey and lined with books. A small fire had been lit in the stone fireplace against the evening chill. Two armchairs flanked it. James wondered, as he lowered himself into the second one, how long it had been since someone had sat there.

They both exchanged a few stilted pleasantries about the day as they sipped their drinks, and James even found himself asking politely after Charles Forsyth.

He had no warning when Magnus asked casually, "I assume you left your rented flat because of Mr. Morgan?" James's glass froze halfway to his mouth. His father shrugged slightly. "Your pride in him seemed rather obvious the day we met. That's why I suggested Charles, at the ball. To help you…move on in one way or another."

James lowered his glass to his lap and took in his father's calm face, fire-shadows flickering over his high cheekbones and shrewd eyes. James truthfully could not have been more astonished if Magnus had suddenly started rapping.

Even now Magnus looked as if he would rather be anywhere else on the planet. They had never talked to each other about emotions, not even when his mother died.

James said thickly, "It didn't work out."

Magnus raised his head in an acknowledging movement. "That's rather a pity. He seemed an interesting young man…anxious to make a good impression on your behalf."

James stared hard at the fire, trying to focus on the shifting, twisting flames.

The teapot. Ben urging him to reconcile with his father. He felt as if his father were prodding and slashing at the huge dull mass of pain in his chest.

"I *would* suggest," Magnus began gravely, "that you focus on work to get over it. But personally, I've found that it can be…" His pause lasted long enough to raise James's agonized eyes to him. "It can be easy…to go too far. With that," Magnus said, as if every word had been a fight.

Their gazes locked.

It was all there for James to see. The things Magnus could never say. Regret. Knowledge. Apology. James felt a lifetime's emotion rising in him like a floodtide, rushing to his eyes.

But that was going too far. He might have just lost the love of his life, he might have finally begun to find his father, but Hendersons did not cry.

He cleared his throat roughly. "I have an interesting interview tomorrow actually," he forced out. "Eve Kelly. D'you remember her?"

His father raised his eyebrows. "Well," he said economically. "That should provide a diversion."

28

James drove to Bronzefield, the top-security women's prison, first thing the following morning, after a brief, dreamlike breakfast prepared by Mrs. Morris and taken with Magnus.

It almost felt to James, as he passed the marmalade to his father, that the past few years had all taken place in his imagination. As if he'd never moved to his own flat, or left the company, or become a detective or fallen in love… Except for the fact that Magnus actually paid attention to him, rather than reading the financial pages. That was definitely new.

He'd just parked his police saloon near the visitors' center when his phone pinged. Every muscle tensed. Steggie's name on the screen.

B found yr note this AM when he made brekkie for the man of the hr. Came by to ask if I knew.

James's stomach clenched. It seemed fitting, he supposed, that a shag had been present.

Even so he couldn't resist asking: *Is he ok?*

He sat and gazed out at the drab, grey June morning, the fantastic grimness of his surroundings, where even the cars in the car park all seemed to be monotone, as if everyone in the vicinity, including God, had agreed to a theme.

He'd given up on a reply, ready to leave the car, when the phone pinged again.

He's always ok.

There had been nothing from Ben, of course, and part of James felt massively relieved by that, just as another, larger, part felt irrationally devastated that Ben hadn't even tried to contact him. But what would there be left to say? James had done the right thing. At least he had that.

And at least he could still do his job, even in this state…an emotional fuck-up, living the bloody end of his first try at love. But what would he do when the distraction stopped?

He huffed a rueful breath as he got out of the car. No need to worry about that yet. They were still running in fucking circles.

There had been more reported sightings of Loretta as a result of yesterday's *Crimewatch* appeal than anyone could shake a stick at. From the north of Scotland to Cornwall. Loretta got about.

Even as a copper, James wasn't spared any of the regular routines for entering a prison—a rubdown, metal detectors, a drugs dog sniffing at his shoes. But the governor took him personally to the room in which he'd interview Kelly.

"Eve's one of our Queen Bees," the governor warned before she left him. "Friends in high places too. Her MP keeps in touch. Or she did 'til someone offed her. Kelly and the other big names in here...they're celebrities, complete with private armies. Eve's..." The woman smiled icily. "You'll see."

After she left, James took a moment to center himself.

The walls were featureless, painted in institutional cream, and the space stank of disinfectant. It contained only a table and two basic chairs. The floor was covered with the same mid-brown resin that stretched throughout the building. Easy to mop up bodily fluids, James supposed.

He sat and waited.

He'd believed himself to be relaxed, but every muscle in his body tensed as a door in the wall across from him opened, and a short, hatchet-faced female guard led Kelly in.

She was taller than he'd expected and reed slim, model slim. Her photographs really had made her appear eerily similar to Audrey Hepburn, right down to the clever period makeup she'd used to emphasize her fine, luminous features and enormous, dark, thick-lashed eyes. But even with a clean face and twenty more years, she was stunning.

Now he knew what to look for, James could see the resemblance, the nagging familiarity he'd felt when he'd gazed at Romilly, at photographs of Maria. They hadn't appeared alike exactly, but they'd shared her dark hair and large dark eyes, her oval face and high cheekbones. And something else...something indefinable and magnetic.

Kelly sat down and took him in with casual assessment, exactly as if he were a visitor to her luxurious office. Then she smiled, quite suddenly, with paralyzing charm.

"Well, this is a wonderful treat. I love meeting new people."

She had a warm, youthful voice and an impeccably cultured accent, which fitted that *Breakfast at Tiffany's* image. Yet James knew that, for all her upbringing had been solid, kind and middle class, Eve had chosen from an early age to run with gangs. Drugs and extreme violence had been her recreations from age thirteen. Her parents had been helpless to control her, and she'd shacked up with one of the gang leaders, a mother of two by the age of twenty-two. She'd been twenty-four when she went down for killing five men, and just failing to kill another. She'd only reached forty-four now. She looked ten years younger.

"I just have a few questions, Miss Kelly," James began.

"Miss Kelly," she said, smiling. Her teeth were even and white. She really had won the genetic lottery. "It's been a while since I heard that. Have they given you tea, Sergeant Henderson? You must have had a long drive. They're dreadful at looking after people here."

She met his eyes, mischievous and conspiratorial.

James's expression remained carefully blank, though being mothered by a serial killer was certainly a new experience. Despite himself, he felt the tug of her charm.

"Are you aware what's happened to your children since you started your sentence?" he asked.

Her mood changed with startling speed, huge eyes filling immediately with shocked tears, as if he'd hauled off and hit her. Her eyes weren't brown, James realized absently: they were a dark grey. Startlingly beautiful.

"My…? My *children*?" she breathed. Her brow creased with an anxious frown. "I've…tried not to think about it, frankly." She regarded him for a moment longer then averted her face, but James could see her full mouth quiver as she fought for control. "I can tell you I miss them. *Every* day. And I pray every day…that they're having…*wonderful* lives, far away from the mess I created for them. If I'd only been…" She turned back to James, and he could see the effort it cost her to keep going. "Oh God. *Sane* enough to know what I was doing. If I hadn't let my pain take over. If I'd tried to get help, not revenge, for the things that happened to me…" She tried a pathetic, watery smile, heartbreak written in every line of her lovely face. "*If.* What is it they say about 'if', Sergeant? Still. It's far too late now. But…they'll always be the only beautiful things in my life." An attempt at a bright laugh, then, sharing her vulnerability. "So I *hope* you're going to tell me that they're…*very* happy." She swallowed and ground to a halt, her Bambi eyes pleading, damp with grief.

James tried not to let it affect him. "Were your children adopted through Margaret Calder, Miss Kelly?"

Though tears had begun to trickle down her pale cheeks, Kelly met James's eyes. "Yes." Her slim shoulders shook with held-in pain and apprehension.

James drew a deep breath, hating what he had to do. Whatever had happened, whatever she'd done, she'd still been a mother. "Unfortunately, Miss Kelly, I may have some very bad news. I'm afraid to have to inform you that it appears your daughters, two young women we believe to be your daughters, have been murdered."

He could see the jolt of shock hit her like a physical blow—it seemed she really hadn't known—and, with no warning, stunned gaze still locked unseeing to his, she began to wail. It started from silence, and rose and rose, noise bouncing obscenely off the resin walls as she writhed like a lunatic in her seat, face twisted obscenely, tearing at her neatly tied hair. It reminded James irresistibly of Dame Cordelia, of Faye Ralph watching Romilly's white coffin, and he could only sit, stunned and guilty, and watch Kelly's full, hysterical collapse. It was so immediate and absolute that even the prison officer seemed frozen in place with shock, but when Kelly began to scream, the officer darted over to her.

"It's my fault! It's *me*!"

"We'll have to end the interview," the prison officer shouted as she pulled Eve, screaming and struggling, to her feet. "She's too upset to go on. Perhaps…" She shot James an evil glare. "It might have been an idea to prepare her."

Without waiting for a response, the woman led Kelly back to the door to the inner prison, arm around her slim waist as Kelly sobbed and limped beside her, cradling her almost tenderly.

Limped?

And just as that registered, and the door opened to swallow them back into the interior of the prison, James caught Kelly's profile.

Fury at himself fueled his reaction. "Stop!" he yelled. The prison officer turned, wide-eyed with outrage. "Bring her back now."

"She's upset!"

"I don't give a flying fuck if she's upset. I'm not finished." Then, "You can turn it off, Eve."

Kelly slowly turned round, and James's flint eyes locked with her agonized ones.

Like a curtain slowly falling and rising again, Kelly's expression drained of tortured grief and grew a huge smile of delight.

"I didn't think you had the balls." She beamed and strolled back to the table under her own steam, the red-faced prison officer now a discarded, flapping prop behind her. "Or the smarts. Not that you aren't decoration enough to brighten the day, but five minutes is enough time to breath the same air as a pig. Even a *really* pretty one." She gave a heavy, false sigh. "Shame you're not a screw though. We could have lots of fun, you an' me." Her accent had changed as completely as her mask. Now it was heavy East London, hard and uncompromising, like a cartoon gangster, as false as her Hepburn-posh accent had been. "Course you wouldn't…necessarily…come out of it with your cock attached. But you can't have everythin'."

She grinned, knowing he'd understand. She'd castrated all her victims before she killed them, including the one who'd survived.

"You had a point to that farce, Eve?" James asked with cultivated, weary disdain, but his heart hammered now with adrenalin buzz, finally facing the true predator she was.

"Entertainment." Airily. "I gave you what you wanted, and you gave me that shocked, sad, little frog face. It's so fuckin' easy to play with people who think with their dicks."

"Like Stefan Ksiazek?"

For a second, she seemed genuinely taken aback. "What the fuck has he got to do with anythin'?"

"You led Ksiazek around by his dick."

She laughed, but James thought her eyes looked careful, as if she couldn't quite work out where he could be going with it.

"Not exactly a challenge. He wanted to lick my feet. He'd have 'eld still for anythin'. He was pond life."

"Was?"

She frowned, obviously irritated. "*Is* then. Fuck what is this? Why're you makin' me waste oxygen on that insignificant piece of shit?"

"Is he still trying to please you, Eve? Killing people you want dead?"

Her momentary astonishment was almost too quick to catch, but to James the glimpse seemed real. He found himself not at all surprised, though, when eager excitement flared in her eyes, because her instinct would always be to claim it, glory in it.

"Maybe." She smiled at him coyly and waited.

"Actually," James said. "Maybe not. Maybe he resents what you did to him. Maybe he's out for revenge."

She appeared considerably less pleased.

"Him? He wouldn't have the guts in a million years! He's in *love*."

James regarded her consideringly. *Yes, I think she believes that.*

"Stones and chains. Do they have particular significance to you?"

He watched her eyes flicker, and he had to wonder if these were instants of genuine confusion or the mimicry of an experienced actress. She pretended to give the question thought.

"Well," she said at last, with a shrug. "I *have* staved in a few skulls with rocks. Chains? Yeah, I've found some use for them in my time." She leered at him and waited, but he gave her no reaction.

"Do you actually give a fuck what happened to your children?" James asked.

Out of the corner of his eye, he saw the prison officer shift uneasily.

Kelly sneered. She didn't look a bit like Audrey Hepburn now.

He should be grateful, really, for the experience. He'd had a front-row seat at a full-on demonstration of the Eve Kelly MO. From the shocking charm to the person she really was. Alec would be agog.

"Actually"—she leaned over the table confidingly—"I really don't." Then she sat back again, waiting for his shock like a tribute.

He declined to pay. She frowned at him. He could see the basis of her method—wielding the facsimile of emotions to wrong-foot and manipulate the people around her.

He waited—Magnus's old tactic. She could, of course, completely stop talking to him at any time. She'd already given him more than he'd expected. But he sensed her to be as greedy for information as he, and she had to know it would be a transaction.

"The bitches pretended I don't exist," she spat at last. "Now they don't exist. They were fuckin' useless anyway. Couldn't learn anythin'."

James cocked his head. "What couldn't they learn?"

"Anythin' useful, Piggie. I tried to pass on my skills. Like you're meant to, yeah? *Useful* skills, not fuckin'…ironin', like my stupid cunt of a mother."

"Tell me," James prompted.

"I don't need to tell you. You saw it. You just fell for it."

"You were trying to pass on how to con people?"

"How to control them, Piggie. You got the looks…ladle on the charm, play sweet and *sad*…posh accent, flutter the eyelashes, an' they're clay in your 'ands." She raised a slim arm and snapped her hand closed. "Even if they know you can hurt 'em, they still fall for it. I mean…if they're that fuckin' stupid, they deserve everything they get, don't they?"

"Is that why Romilly had cigarette burns on her back? Because she couldn't learn?"

"Who the fuck's *Romilly*?"

"Your youngest child."

Kelly laughed with pure, delighted scorn. "That's what they called her? Well, how very fuckin' pretentious. She was Chantelle. Mike wanted 'em—he named 'em." Mike, James recalled, had been the girls' father, who'd left them to their mother's tender mercies. It had been a mystery to investigating officers that he'd got out alive and with his dick still attached.

Kelly grinned, so obviously feeding on any flickers of reaction he gave her. "*Chantelle* was as thick as shit. Only way to wake her up was stubbin' out the odd fag on 'er."

"And Maria?"

"*Maria!*" she mocked. "Gemma. Same thing. So…" She tapped her long, slim fingers on the tabletop. "Someone topped 'em, then. If they did it to get at me…they're fuckin' morons."

"What happened when you were sentenced, Eve?" James asked. "What did you agree about the children?"

She tilted her head coquettishly. "Wouldn't you like to know?"

"Well. Obviously."

She blinked for a second then barked a laugh, genuine amusement. "You're not too bad, Sergeant Henderson. For a…" she snorted theatrically, twice, "…pig. Or should I call you…James? You really are the prettiest copper I've ever seen," she purred. And there she went again.

"So, the adoptions?"

Her smug, seductive grin faded. Had she really expected him to fall for that? Maybe twenty years running her own personal fiefdom in here had blunted her memory of opposition. Or maybe men really had been that stupid around her. Maybe, if he weren't gay he'd be easy meat. Or maybe not.

"You heard Margaret Calder's been murdered."

Eve shrugged with exquisite unconcern, but James thought her eyes sharpened. Her smile was obnoxious.

"What did you ask for in return for not kicking up a fuss about the kids? You had her dangling, didn't you?" He laced in some admiration, just in case.

She laughed again, delighted. "I had her danglin' long before then. She was all about cuttin' sentences an' how people only ever do shit because they're abused. Stupid cow'd 'ave believed anythin'. She thought they'd all raped me. An' my poor kids livin' with the stigma." She shook her head with soulful derision.

"Maybe she's been helping with your appeals over the years. Lobbying the Home Office. Pressuring the governor for privileges."

"Spot on, Biggles."

"She might have ended up in government," James said. "Shame she's dead."

"Can't win 'em all."

"You gave her permission to take the kids so you could convince her you were a decent human being."

Kelly grinned widely. "I like you."

"So by my count that's both your daughters, Margaret Calder and Gary Drake. All picked off in no time. How secure *is* it in here?"

As if he'd found some magic button, her smile vanished.

Suddenly he was staring into absolute coldness—no mask, the real Eve Kelly.

"Do you think I'd care, you arsehole?" she hissed. "D'you think I wouldn't give 'em a fuckin' welcome party, after twenty *fuckin'* years of boredom? Death? What the fuck is everyone scared of?"

He met her hatred head-on and with equanimity, but as he prepared to ask the obvious question, she turned her head sharply away, and just like that, he understood.

She'd been more than happy to push other people over the edge but, however miserable her own existence might become in here, she'd always be too terrified to jump herself.

She glared back at him, and her eyes were vicious, daring his mockery.

"I've finished," he said contemptuously, and got unworthy satisfaction from her tiny flinch as he stood. "We'll do our best to catch them before they get to you, Miss Kelly."

He felt her eyes fixed on his back, until the door closed behind him.

29

"It was very simple," Cordelia Whyte said with frigid, resentful dignity. "Maria had been destined for a life of misery and stigma. No one would have gone near her to adopt her if they'd known her identity."

"So what happened?" Ingham kept her voice calm, but all her gentleness and sympathy had long gone.

James sat beside her, both perched on the edge of a cream silk chaise longue that probably cost his year's salary just to keep clean.

"I happened to be junior counsel. Margaret Houghton attended as the social worker supervising the children. They had no living relatives who wanted anything to do with them. We were...talking, Margaret and I...we met over coffee in the Old Bailey canteen, and we agreed on many things. The repressiveness of the legal system. Its failure to take into account the pressures that could drive a woman to murder."

"Miss Kelly behaved charmingly to you," James said. It wasn't a question, and he made a poor job of hiding his antipathy. "She told you she'd been driven to all she'd done."

"She was demonized, Sergeant," Cordelia snapped. "You didn't know her."

"On the contrary, I just met her."

Cordelia frowned at him, but he went no further. She shifted her focus back to Ingham.

"Margaret told me Eve had struggled raising the children, but they were delightful, and all they had ahead of them would be a life in care, being treated like the offspring of Satan, because of the way the press slandered Eve. They had protection orders, of course. The press weren't allowed to publish anything about them, other than the fact Eve had children. But they were already in care and going through hell. You have no idea what the children of prisoners suffer."

"If you wanted to adopt them, why do it that way?" Ingham asked icily.

Cordelia looked away, aristocratic jaw tense. She'd lost weight since James had seen her last. Now she seemed less elegant than skeletal.

"Because the usual channels would have taken years, and by the time the application would have been accepted...*if* it *had* been accepted, the children would already have been brutalized. Children are abused in care, you know."

James raised his eyebrows, though he wanted to roll his eyes. "You were aware of what Eve Kelly did to her children."

"Her partner hurt them," Dame Cordelia corrected. "Eve did her best, but she'd been under huge pressure...a deserted, abused single mother."

"Go on," James said.

"We discussed it at length," she said stiffly, reacting to his disdain. "Margaret seemed very passionate about it. We both knew the real Eve." She shot a swift glare at James. "So, since we could see that Eve's children would be in an impossible position, and since I could have no more children myself, I realized we could offer a good home to one of Eve's. I wanted a sister for Felicity, and I chose Maria. I've never regretted it. She lit up our lives. The most charming creature I've ever known."

"As charming as Eve Kelly?" James asked.

Maria had lived with Eve for five years. Who knew what her mother had thrashed into her? Cordelia shot him a look of patrician contempt.

"Your prejudices are primitive and offensive, Sergeant." As if she were facing down a KKK redneck about to light a fiery cross. His own scorn at her gullibility made James want badly to glower back. *It's her daughter*, he reminded himself.

"You didn't think to mention any of this to us?" Ingham shot out.

"I'd all but forgotten where Maria came from when she died," Cordelia said defensively. "She's my daughter, as much as my own flesh and blood. And how could it be relevant?"

"You'd cut all ties with Eve, then, if you'd *forgotten*?" James asked.

"Yes."

"And when you heard about Margaret Calder?"

"I didn't see how it could be connected. Coincidence."

"Especially since the adoption she brokered was under the counter," James said. "Illegal, in fact. Right down to the falsified birth certificate and the medical records you bought abroad." No wonder she hadn't wanted FLOs hanging around them.

Cordelia turned to stare out the window. Then she returned her gaze to Ingham to ask with stiff dignity, "Do you intend to make this public?"

"We have yet to decide whether to pursue charges," Ingham replied, giving no ground. "Have you seen or heard anything of Stefan Ksiazek?"

Dame Cordelia frowned at her, clearly unsatisfied with her reply.

"No," she said impatiently. "Wasn't that one of Eve's friends?"

"And you never knew what happened to Maria's sister?"

"I didn't know she was the girl in the press. Margaret only said that she'd be searching for homes with like-minded individuals for all the children. Liberal, intelligent, open-minded people." She glared again at James. "I've always been confident Margaret did right by them."

"All?" James put in sharply. "What do you mean *all*?"

Cordelia raised a disdainful brow. "What I said."

James regarded her for a beat of silence. "*All* suggests more than two. The newspapers said that's all she had."

"Oh, and is that where you get your information from, Sergeant?" Cordelia sneered. "The *newspapers*?"

James took a second to beat down the very plebeian response on the tip of his tongue.

"Since there are no formal records of the Kelly children," he gritted out. "*Mainly* because Margaret Calder expunged the ones her department held to enable your illegal adoptions, we had nowhere else to turn, Dame Cordelia. Which made all this very easy for *you*, of course. But not so easy for us."

Cordelia turned her head away from him again. She looked as if she'd swallowed a wasp.

"Well," she said as if he hadn't spoken. "I have a copy of Maria's original birth certificate if will help you. It's in the name of Gemma Cheryl Sweeney."

James wrote it down.

"This is important," he said. "We know about Romilly. *Were* there other children?"

Cordelia studied him with her large, dark, hooded eyes.

"As far as I know, the only other child was a boy. I never met him, but I believe Margaret said he was the oldest. Around eight or nine, something like that, when he lost his mother. She was concerned he'd be harder to place, though sweet and beautiful, like all Eve's children."

James tried to take it in.

Eve Kelly had a son. A woman who loathed men beyond sanity had controlled and formed a boy for nine years?

She hadn't said a word to James about it. She'd got one over on him after all.

But what had that boy become? Another apprentice?

Or maybe he'd already met his end at the hands of his sisters' killer, and they just didn't know it yet.

Either way, victim target or prime suspect, they had another missing person to find.

30

Their interview with Romilly's mother felt almost superfluous after Dame Cordelia's bullish confessions—cruel, in fact, considering the state of her. But Ingham deemed it necessary, and in truth James was as pissed off as she at the way they'd been played for fools. The silence of both families, even after murder.

If Dame Cordelia had lost weight, Faye seemed half the size she'd been when James first saw her. She remained sheathed in a pall of grief, like a thick veil between her and the rest of the world, but at least she now appeared able to communicate.

Her husband had complained vigorously to Ingham's superiors about the interview, and demanded to do it in her stead. But the revelations in the case had cut away Anthony Crompton's influence. No senior officer would now risk getting in the way of an investigation like this, uncovering maggots under every stone they turned. It had to be Faye, because Faye had been the one to deal with Margaret Calder.

Her husband sat beside her on a sofa in their drawing room, holding her frail hand, glaring his impotent loathing at Ingham and James seated together on a sofa opposite.

Faye confessed immediately to taking Chantelle Bianca Sweeney from Margaret Calder, with an adoption certificate she knew would never stand up to official scrutiny. Her husband had been a willing accomplice, as Cordelia's husband had been.

In the end, after too many dazed, listless replies in which Ingham tried to coax information from her, there seemed no option but to attack Faye's apathy. With a meaningful glance, Ingham appointed James Bad Cop.

"Why didn't you tell us about Kelly, Faye?" James demanded on cue. "Didn't you want to help us find Romilly's killer?"

Faye trained her big, empty eyes on him, but he had the impression she wasn't seeing him at all, rather following the sound of his voice.

"It didn't occur to me," she said. "She was dead. It didn't matter."

"It was essential to our investigation," he countered. "You withheld vital evidence. Margaret Calder could be dead because of your silence."

Faye didn't react. To his left, Ingham sat back, leaving him the floor.

"It didn't concern you at all?" James laced his tone with careful scorn. "Not worried about genetics, adopting the daughter of a mass murderess?"

Crompton made an incoherent sound of protest. Faye appeared bewildered, as if she didn't understand the concept he'd thrown at her.

"You *liked* Eve Kelly," James accused.

Faye gave a mildly puzzled frown. "Of course," she said, as if it was unthinkable that she shouldn't. "She's a victim too. Like the person who killed my little girl."

James found he no longer had to fake impatience. "Is anyone responsible for their own actions in your world, Faye?"

"No one is evil," she returned. "No one can be blamed for what happens to them. I believe in second chances. Rehabilitation. What happened to Eve and the others was wrong."

It was Dame Cordelia all over again. But Faye seemed engaged now, actually in the room with them. Beside him, he was aware of Ingham's assessing silence, waiting for the moment James pushed Faye too far.

"Some people can't be rehabilitated," he prodded. "Some people just like hurting other people."

Faye met his eyes, and for the first time he got the impression she actually saw him. Crompton moved restlessly at her side. "Only because that's how they're taught." As if she were explaining the obvious to a toddler. "People can be reeducated. Look at what Charles made of his life. Anyone can change if they get a chance."

Out of the corner of his eye, James saw Crompton become very still.

"Who's Charles?" James asked.

Faye blinked as if she didn't understand the question.

"Romilly's ex-boyfriend?" James suggested. "Charles...Priestly?"

"Yes." Faye smiled with relief. "Charles."

Her husband gaped at her. "*Boyfriend?*" There was a moment of confused silence, then without warning he shot to his feet. "I'm sorry, I'm afraid my wife's very tired. And you're confusing her." He leaned down, pulling Faye up effortlessly until he could slide an arm round her waist, sheltering her from them, behind his big body. "You can see yourselves out, I'm sure."

"Mr. Crompton!" Ingham protested indignantly as she and James stood too.

"Tell me about Charles Priestly," James demanded at the same time. Crompton stopped his slow progress and turned his head to glare at them over his shoulder.

"He was a family acquaintance. He knew Romilly for a time when she was small."

"You didn't know he became her lover last year?"

Crompton's jaw flexed, muscle jumping with strain. "No, I didn't."

"You wouldn't have approved? Why?" Crompton's breathing sounded heavy, in and out and in and out like an angry bull. James kept going, and Ingham didn't try to stop him. "Was it the age difference? Would you have been worried for her safety?"

Crompton made a sound of pure disdain. "Don't be ridiculous! The man worshipped her from the beginning." He stopped and straightened, expelled another frustrated bull-snort. "See yourselves out."

Suddenly Faye peered round his body, a tiny mouse woman.

"Everyone deserves a second chance, though," she said sweetly.

— — — —

"Nice one," Ingham approved as she started the car. "You could poke sticks at wild animals if you give up on the Met."

"Learned at your feet, ma'am," James said absently, as he wrestled his phone out of his jacket pocket.

"So what d'you reckon to their reaction to Priestly?" Ingham pondered. "I mean was Faye implying he has a record? We couldn't find anything."

"Do you know any Polish?" James tapped the screen keyboard, waiting for his search engine to load.

"Any…what?"

"His family were Polish."

"Whose?" Ingham asked irritably.

James chewed his lip then began to tap more phone keys as Ingham pulled the car out into the road.

"*Jesus!*"

Ingham's hands jerked on the steering wheel. "*What?*"

"Ksiazek. Polish for 'little priest.'"

31

"Stefan Karol Ksiazek."

Charles Priestly sat alone across the breadth of the interview table from James and Ingham. Surprisingly, given Joey Clarkson's connections, he hadn't called a solicitor.

They were using the same room in which they'd interviewed Burnett—dim, grey and featureless. It contained a table and chairs, an observational window and a recording device turning silently beside them.

"Not any more," Priestly said.

It was true on the face of it. He appeared to be an entirely different person; James couldn't even blame any of them for not spotting it. The overweight, bearded, bespectacled young loser now this sleekly muscled, clean-shaven, handsome, middle-aged man.

James began, "You disappeared from official view in 2004. What happened?"

Ingham had told him the interview would be his, before she cautioned Ksiazek. James had found him; he could land him.

No pressure then.

"I'd paid my debt to society," Ksiazek replied. "Isn't that what they say, as if you owe the world credit? I'd done my prison time and my probation, and I'd got myself an education and profession."

"Accountancy."

"Yes. I thought you'd have known that," Priestly said. "I expected you to make the connection, every single day." James could believe that. When they'd arrived to take him in for questioning, Preistly had seemed more resigned than surprised.

"You didn't think to simply volunteer it?"

"Would you, Sergeant, in my position?"

James didn't take the bait. "Why did you decide to hide your identity?"

"I didn't really try that hard, did I?" Ksiazek said bitterly. "Translating my name into English? Not exactly deep cover."

"Oh, come *on*. You created a whole new identity, *Charles*. You expunged your past. You have a new *illegal* passport. A false history. I'd say you tried pretty hard. Who helped you?"

Priestly looked down at the table. A muscle jumped in his jaw. "I'd rather not say."

"Your employer, from the time you arrived back in the UK, has been Joey Clarkson."

"You know I'm not going to accuse Mr. Clarkson of any such thing," Priestly said.

Not if he wanted to keep his bollocks attached, at any rate.

"You broke away from your past. You went to some considerable *effort* to break away from your past," James pressed. "And yet you went and got involved with Eve Kelly's daughter. Explain that one to us, Charles."

"What's to explain?" Priestly ran a hand back over his thick silver hair, the first obviously uneasy gesture he'd made. "It's...Eve. I went to visit her when I got out...just once. She told me about the girls."

"Why? It's not as if she cared for them. Or you."

Priestly regarded him with reproach. "I don't know. But to me they were part of her."

Maybe, James thought, she'd just fancied unleashing him on them.

"Do you think she's a victim too then?" James asked.

Priestly's hands, clasped together and resting on the table, had begun to tremble, and James thought he might be looking at Stefan Ksiazek in that moment, nervous and insecure, rather than the urbane Charles Priestly.

"I know exactly what she is," Priestly said defiantly. "But that doesn't make her any less magnificent."

Magnificent.

"When did you make contact with the Cromptons?" James demanded.

Priestly unclasped his hands and ran the palm of one of them over his face. "A month or two after Eve told me. I...monitored them for a while, then I tried to reach out to their new families. I didn't pretend, I told them my name right away. And Faye was lovely. The other one was a total cow." Almost in passing, James noted Cordelia had apparently lied to them again. "But, Faye, she could see I just wanted to help. I couldn't visit as Stefan without drawing attention to them, though, so I went away and became Charles."

James felt his whole midsection tense with the sudden excitement of a hunter closing in on his prey. Ingham didn't move a muscle beside him, but he knew she would be feeling the same.

"You created a new identity to get close to Romilly?"

Priestly closed his eyes and nodded. Then, aloud, "Yes," for the tape. A seasoned veteran of police interviews.

"So Romilly became...what?" James pressed. "A way to get to touch Eve?"

Priestly's eyes sprang open. "No...it wasn't like that. She was a child. I'm not a pedophile! I was just her Uncle Charles. I wanted to make sure she'd be all right. I saw her maybe once or twice a year, and I loved her. As a child. But I stayed away for years."

He bit his lip hard and tears sprang up in his pale eyes. *Getting somewhere,* James thought with satisfaction.

"And?" he prompted.

"One evening—she'd be in her early twenties by then—I saw her in Tina's. She'd been performing on stage. That's how it started. I *told* you this."

"She instigated it?"

Priestly smiled weakly. "She remembered me. I think it gave her a bit of a kick that I'd known her as a child. She kept calling me that. 'Uncle Charles.' She liked to pretend we were...you know...like...incest. But it was all harmless! And yes," he said with sudden, impatient aggression. "Before you even bother asking, she reminded me of Eve. Happy, Sergeant? Like a sweeter, gentler version of her mother."

The bedroom tapes flashed unbidden into James's mind; Romilly ramming a dildo into Priestly's helpless backside. Just an extra layer of kink to add to the masochism then.

He paused, considering his next question. "Have you been back to see Eve?"

Priestly's mouth thinned. "She told me not to."

"So Romilly had to be the next best thing? The consolation prize."

Priestly shook his head in denial, but he looked tormented.

"Did she try to blackmail you?" James probed. "We saw the tapes she made of the two of you. Somehow I don't think Joey Clarkson would be too impressed."

Priestly's reaction was gratifying. His face twisted with disbelief, which became profound horror as his skin surged with dark, ugly blood. "She told me she wiped them." He sounded stunned. "I didn't want to get filmed, but…she persuaded me. She promised!"

"Did you always do what she told you, Charles?" James asked. "Like you did for Eve?"

"I didn't mean it to be…the way it turned out." Priestly gave a small involuntary sob. "Romilly…Chantelle…she seduced me. She used me."

James swallowed against the nausea in the back of his throat. "You saw what Eve did to her kids. You turned a blind eye. And then you were attracted to the result?"

"No! You weren't there! You can't judge me!" Priestly's expression showed a turmoil of appeal and defiance. "You think Eve treated me like shit on her shoe. I know! They all did…Gary and Billy. But all I only ever wanted was to make her happy. I *love* her. You can't know what real love like that is like! I never got free of it."

And there it was. James felt almost sure of it. They had their man. A man who'd seen Eve Kelly murder and torture innocent people and still wanted only to impress her.

"Tell me about her son," he demanded.

Priestly's head jerked back in a gesture of startlement and suspicion, as if James had blindsided him with an irrelevant question about football. As if Eve's son wasn't worth a moment's thought.

"Well…he was the oldest," he said, with a confused frown, but James could see his relief at having attention turned from himself. "He took the brunt for a while, but he had it easier than the girls. They annoyed her. They were too gentle." He hesitated. "It's ironic, I suppose. Eve hated most men, but she despised anything feminine. And femininity's what she used to ambush people. I heard her saying, once, that her son was going to be her revenge."

James's breath caught. "On whom?"

"I don't know." Priestly shrugged. "*People.* She used to tell him that men were scum. That he was scum. But he was the smartest of all of them at pleasing her. He could be an incredible little shit. Or he could be…" He sighed and let his head fall back for a moment. "Like her. Magnetic. She used to say…he was going to grow up to do damage."

James kept his expression still with effort. "What was his name?"

"Well…she called him *names* all the time to toughen him up. *Shithead.* We all had to call him that. His name though…I think…Stevie? Petey? Something like that."

"Is he dead? The boy?"

Priestly blinked. "Dead? How would I know?"

"You'd know if you killed him," James said. "Did you kill Eve's children for her, Stefan?"

Priestly's mouth fell open in obvious horror. "No!" he said. "No!"

"You said you'd do anything to please her," James pointed out, almost kindly.

Priestly reacted with the wild, innocent shock of a man betrayed, as if he'd believed until then that he and James had simply been passing the time of day.

"I haven't visited her for…for years!" he exploded. "You can't pin that on me!"

"What's the significance of stones and chains to Eve?" James went on relentlessly.

"What?" Priestly appeared convincingly confused. "I don't know!"

James exchanged a moment of wordless communication with Ingham.

"This interview is terminated," she said. "We're going to detain you overnight, Mr. Ksiazek." Priestly seemed too shocked to protest.

"What d'you think?" James asked quickly when he and Ingham left the room. He didn't know himself if he felt more triumphant or uneasy.

"I think…he'd do anything she told him to do. He proved murder wouldn't stop him twenty years ago. And she hates her kids," Ingham replied.

"What about Burnett?"

Ingham glared at him. "I'll send him a fruit basket."

"There's still another possibility," James said slowly. Though, Christ, he wanted it to be Priestly. To be over, finally. "Eve's son. If he's alive. You heard what Ksiazek said about him."

"*If* he's alive." Ingham sighed. "You know what? I think the boy was the first to go. We just haven't unearthed what's left of him."

James glanced reflexively at the closed interview-room door.

They had their killer—Eve Kelly's masochistic puppet. It had always been about her.

All they had left to do was find the last victim.

32

James slept at the station that night, texting his apologies to his father. Ingham, Scrivenor, and most of the unit stayed too, taking turns on the camp beds.

The unit didn't disappoint when Ingham finally felt she had enough to brief them—they provided a full house of unhinged jaws. Eve Kelly, her rediscovered disciple, her murdered daughters and her missing son. A TV soap opera and a half.

"It can't be hard to find out who the lad is," Walsh volunteered. "I mean there must be records. Petey or Stevie Sweeney? Pete or Stevie Kelly?"

But after working through every bit of information they had available to them in unsealed official sources, they learned differently. Margaret Calder had done a sterling job of covering her tracks. All three children had totally vanished from official records.

"This is fuckin' mental," Scrivenor grumbled the following morning as another lead died. "How can someone just disappear from the system in this day an' age?"

"Like this," James said stretching. He felt weary to his bones.

"What'd it take for you tae go for muffins?"

James raised an insulting finger. "What'd it take for Spurs to win the league?"

Scrivenor was also a Chelsea man. "Them? They couldnae hit a cow's arse wi' a banjo."

They beamed at each other in delight, high with exhaustion, while James obediently picked up his mobile, ready to order in.

He had two unread texts on his homescreen which must have come in overnight. One offered a two-for-one pizza deal. The other read:

Come home Jamie. Please.

He considered it sluggishly for a second, until he understood with an insane plunge of shock that it had come from Ben.

Ben at…2:26 a.m.

Two twenty-six on a Friday morning. Had he been in bed with someone else when he sent it? Or alone and lying awake? Thinking of James? Wanting him to come back?

His chest felt agonizingly tight, and he couldn't begin to identify his primary emotion—excitement or fear.

"You aw right, son?" Scrivenor asked. "You look like yer gonna puke."

Definitely fear, because even as his heart began to thump hard with new, blind adrenalin, he didn't have the nerve to text back.

He had to remind himself of the one core thing, which had kept him going: the fact that he'd had no alternative but to leave. That nothing important could change between them. Ben had his life as he wanted, set in stone, and James could not fit in it.

"Jamie?"

"Yeah, yeah. Sorry, Alec… Just zoned out." He smiled and phoned in the order for coffee and muffins as his mind scrabbled for purchase.

He glanced at his computer screen, desperate for distraction.

Distraction.

Eve Kelly. For fuck's sake, he was neck-deep in a case that involved Eve Kelly! As Magnus had pointed out, that should be bloody distracting enough for anyone. He'd even managed to provide a brief distraction for her.

I love visitors.

The thought struck him then, as it should have hours before. If Priestly had visited Kelly, might her son have too, at some time in the past twenty years? It had to be worth a try.

It took five minutes of waiting through elevator music to get through to the governor's office at Her Majesty's Prison Bronzefield, and then to get past the pleasantries.

"I just wanted to check, do you happen to have the visitors list for Eve Kelly?"

The governor's secretary sounded genuinely regretful. "I'm afraid

I can't give out that information over the phone, Detective Sergeant."

James grimaced impatiently, but then he saw it for the gift it could be. "What if I come out to the prison myself?"

A pause. "That should be in order."

He stood and shouldered into his jacket as he explained his idea and destination to Scrivenor.

"Shite. Wish I'd thought of that," Scrivenor said, with disgusted longing. "Gettin' outta here for an hour or two."

James met the boy with the coffee and muffins on the way out which, as he appropriated his share, he decided to take as a good omen.

He realized, though, with unwanted self-knowledge, that his mood had lifted because of that text message. He could remind himself of reality all he wanted, but the truth was he felt happy that Ben had bothered, after all. That Ben didn't just feel…glad to be rid of him.

Fuck, he was a lost cause.

His phone rang as he pulled his car into a space in the visitors' center car park at HMP Bronzefield. Immediately, his heart began to pound and it felt like perfect déjà vu. Last time, it had been a text from Steggie. Now…for all his best efforts to talk himself down—what if it was Ben, following up the text? Did James really want to speak to him?

No. It would be an incredibly bad idea.

But he almost fumbled the button in his haste to press Accept.

"Jamie?" Scrivenor.

James's shoulders slumped, though he hadn't realized he'd tensed up. He felt ridiculous. "Alec," he said shortly.

"News. Sameera unearthed the lad's birth certificate. Different father. Or that's what Kelly put in there. Steven Matthew Brooker—Steven wi' a V. He'd be twenty-eight now. Once we put the name in the system, he turned up in Grantham Close Care Home for a few months. Calder hadnae quite wiped all his records like she did wi' the girls. Then he disappeared."

James stared at the dashboard for some time after Scrivenor rang off. His stomach felt cold.

They had bloody Ksiazek waiting in a cell. They had it all sewn up except for finding his first victim.

There were lots of care homes. Hundreds of them.

But his heart hammered, faster than ever.

Oh fuck off, he scoffed at himself, impatiently. *You bloody drama queen.*

What kind of coincidence would that have to be?

Yet the thought wouldn't lie down. As he walked up to the prison governor's office, his brain couldn't stop reiterating those unwelcome links.

Same age. Care home. No parents. Abused.

Maria'd had the address written down. Maybe…she'd have been able to remember her older brother. It wouldn't be unusual for adopted siblings who'd been separated to try to find one another as adults. Maria'd had the resources. What if she'd decided to try to make contact with Steven?

And what if Steven hadn't wanted to be found?

Shit. He just wanted to get this fucking visitors list and get the hell back to base.

Maybe…maybe he should text him. Arrange to meet up, tonight or tomorrow. He'd like that. James would like it too.

But as he reached the door, his confident denial began to collapse.

*Christ…*he begged fiercely. *Anyone but Steggie.* Bargaining.

Steggie bore no resemblance to Eve, he reassured himself—*or* the girls—but a cold, logical part of James's mind told him Steven had a different father.

He didn't need the same entry procedures this time because he'd be staying in the administrative part of the building. No dogs. No search. The governor's secretary waved him in, and pleasantries automatically exchanged, he signed for a photocopy of the list, several pages long, to cover every visit to Eve Kelly, as he'd requested, for the past twenty years.

He deliberately didn't glance at it until he'd seated himself again in the car—then he gave it a quick skim, to confirm it had been a wild goose chase. That's what he told himself.

He saw the address at once, and it took whole seconds to force himself to look at the name.

So much for bargaining.

33

"What d'you mean, you know him?" Ingham's mascara had degenerated to a sooty smudge beneath her tired eyes, but she remained sentry-alert.

James squeezed his lids closed then forced them open. He'd done all his raging in the car. Duty was all that remained now.

"I mean. He's…" A hard swallow. "He *was* my flatmate. In Selworth Gardens."

"Ben Morgan," Ingham confirmed.

"Yes, ma'am." James stood to attention in front of her desk. He felt as if his guts had frozen solid.

"Selworth Gardens. That was the address you found at Maria's house. You asked permission…"

He bowed his head. He couldn't face her. "Yes, ma'am."

After a short, telling silence, Ingham asked, "When did you move out?"

"A couple of days ago, ma'am."

"Why did you leave?" She sounded distant. As if she were questioning a witness. "Did you have an issue with him? Something you noticed?"

Nothing but the truth. "No, ma'am. We'd become…romantically involved. I left when it ended."

Scrivenor had tucked himself in the corner, as if he were trying to disappear into the wall to give James some privacy.

When he glanced back down at her, Ingham's eyes looked like black holes in her face. Somehow she managed to appear both grave and appalled, and he couldn't blame her.

If it got out, the publicity would be crucifying for the unit. For her. And for him. Not to mention the potential effect on any court case… if it came to that.

But at that moment, he didn't give a fuck. He couldn't feel anything.

Ingham rolled her pen back and forth nervously between her fingers.

"What's he like?" Ingham demanded. No comment on the other thing.

"Nice. He's…nice. Kind." *Charming.*

Christ. No wonder. The eerie familiarity of Maria and Romilly. It hadn't just been Kelly…it had been Ben. None of them really looked alike, but they all shared the same basic, gorgeous bone structure, they all had that striking pale and dark coloring.

And he'd been sneering at Cordelia Whyte for falling under Eve's spell, believing everything she'd been fed, seduced by manipulation. He took a deep breath, forcing calm.

He was jumping to wild conclusions…they all were.

"There were a couple of other visitors' names on the list," he volunteered quickly. "Apart from Ben, and Margaret Calder."

Once he'd seen Ben's name he'd scoured the list like a maniac, in the car, almost weeping with frustrated shock, trying to find some way to deny it. Searching for some magic trapdoor away from the worst possible eventuality.

"Gary Drake went to see her when he got out of prison. And apart from her solicitor, there were…" He produced the names like a magicians rabbit. "Norman Howard, S. P. Underwood. S. S. Connell, and um…George Pirelli. Over the last few years."

James handed her the list, and she flicked through it. Five people over twenty years.

"Morgan's been going every six months for…three years more or less," she said.

James grimaced, emotions floating on the surface like crude oil on water.

"It could be work." He thought he sounded reasonable. "He's a photographer. Maybe he'd been trying to persuade her into a project and…I don't know… They became friends?"

Ingham had the mercy not to shoot it down at once.

"Can you provide him with an alibi for any of the murders since you've known him? Maria? Romilly? Margaret Calder?"

And hadn't that been the first thing he'd tried to work out once the initial shock had passed? Feverishly scrabbling for hope.

"No," he admitted with stiff formality. "I don't believe I was with him at any of those times."

Ingham nodded slowly as if she was absorbing all the implications. Then she asked, in the same emotionless tone, "Do you believe he's capable of murder?"

James stared at her, appalled. But what did he expect?

She wanted him to remember what he was at core. A police officer, in pursuit of his duty. She wanted those instincts of his trained on Ben. It felt like a test.

He face twisted painfully, but he stiffened his spine and began to rap out his copper's observations, all emotion excised from his voice.

"He's physically fit and strong. He excels at a martial art, so theoretically he's capable of violence. He's promiscuous. Impulsive—sexually impulsive—but to my knowledge, he's not reckless. He uses drugs recreationally...on occasion. He's not an addict, or a dealer. He's charismatic. Extremely attractive. Intelligent. Insightful. Resourceful. He's strong willed and determined, but he doesn't strike me as a meticulous planner. Too impetuous. So possibly, unlikely to manage this killer's level of forensic awareness. He's selfish, in defense of his life choices. But, on the whole, kind...to other people. And..." he finished, defiantly. "He knowingly chose a police detective as a flatmate."

And surely to do that, as a murderer, would require insane audacity?

Ingham tapped her pen slowly against the desk, shrewd eyes taking in his imperfectly concealed distress. He heard Scrivenor shift behind him.

"Right," Ingham said. "But you didn't answer my question."

James gritted his teeth and fixed his eyes over her head, staring blindly at the wall behind her. "In *theory*," he said, fighting his irrational resentment. "Anyone is capable of murder. Ma'am."

She'd be well within her rights to pull him off the case, not least because of the possibility, however remote, that his presence could theoretically compromise any court case. Not that it would come to that but...she couldn't know.

Part of him desperately wanted her to remove him now, so he wouldn't have to be involved in hurting Ben in any way. Another part needed to be there, to help him. And yet another—the copper in him—felt only shocked, horrified suspicion that the case had come, with no warning, so close to home. That he might have been played. That he couldn't even function any more as a neutral police officer.

When he dropped his eyes to her, Ingham regarded him with a worried softness that he recognized, with despair, as pity.

"He didn't mention knowing the murder victims? Not at all?"

James shook his head, jaw clenched painfully tight. "He told me he didn't know Maria during the initial interview. He gave the impression of not knowing Romilly."

"Did he show interest in the investigation?"

Did he? How much had James let slip? He couldn't remember ever being pumped for information. Ben had never seemed bothered, beyond worrying about James's wellbeing, with his ferocious schedule. But he'd seen James's depression when they were getting nowhere. Fuck, he'd comforted him. Praised him for caring.

"He watched *Crimewatch* when we were on," he offered. The pain he felt at that moment was unbelievable, remembering all those innocent moments, seeing everything now through such a different filter. His heart felt as if it would melt away soon, like hot solder in his chest, leaving behind a shiny useless mess.

"Well. Ksiazek is still our prime suspect," Ingham said gruffly. "Morgan might have been his next victim, if he's Kelly's son. The only way we can find out anything is an interview. Do you know where he'd be now?"

James took a deep steadying breath and checked his watch.

Four eighteen. Maybe his studio, if he hadn't gone out on a shoot. James didn't even know the address. Ben had told James once that he never fucked in the studio, because it was separate and special to him. His professional space was sacrosanct. Ben had never invited him there, which showed, James supposed, how completely he'd been shoved into the box labeled "sex".

"Fix something up," Ingham ordered. "Something that doesn't warn him. I want to catch him off guard."

She meant to keep James in the investigation then, though it went against guidance. He pulled out his phone.

He took a second or two to brace himself, then he texted: *Can we meet at the flat?*

He remembered, as if considering a character in a book, the trepidation and excitement he'd felt when he got Ben's text that morning.

He could only imagine how he'd have been feeling now, if the reply he'd just sent had been his own genuine response, deciding to take a risk again on something changing.

How pitiful his problems had been. Just unrequited love. Just someone he loved who didn't love him back. Christ, not this.

The silence in the office felt like agony as they waited.

"I'll set Sameera and Barry on tracking down the other four names on the visitors list," Ingham threw in.

When? Buzzed back at almost at once. James dug his nails hard into the meat of his palm, needing physical pain. It felt like treachery.

He typed in: *Can you manage now? Are you working?*

And Ben's immediate response: *I'm leaving now. See you there.*

A few hours ago, he'd have been encouraged by such eagerness, given he'd assumed Ben wanted rid of him. Now he thought... *Why's he making this effort for me? To keep close to the case?*

"We're on," he said.

Ingham rose and pulled her suit jacket from the back of her chair. Scrivenor didn't say a word as he watched them go.

It took far too short a time to reach Selworth Gardens, and it felt like only minutes since James had last come home at the end of a day to this flat.

This time, though, he stood at the front door and waited to be buzzed in by Ben. Then he climbed the stairs to the flat, in front of Ingham.

The door lay open when he reached the top. His stomach had knotted up tight, until he felt as if he were about to spew all his fear and disappointment out like sickness, all over the plush blue carpet.

"You came." Ben stood in the open doorway, smiling cautiously, as if he wasn't quite sure what to say or do. He looked young and effortlessly beautiful, dressed all in black—T-shirt and jeans—hair in loose, tousled curls around his face.

Then he spotted Ingham.

His expression faded to puzzlement, closely followed by a frown of uncertainty before he produced an instinctive social smile. And James felt as if he'd betrayed him, delivered him to his enemies.

James swallowed hard, but still his voice sounded thick. Wrong.

"Ben, this is Detective Chief Inspector Ingham. My boss."

Ben's brow cleared slightly, though he still seemed confused. "Pleased to meet you." Then, "I've heard a lot about you."

Ingham moved to the front to take his outstretched hand. "Can we go inside, Mr. Morgan?"

Ben turned back, confused, to James.

"Jamie? I don't…I thought we were meeting to talk about…about things," he said softly.

James clenched his teeth against the words he wanted to say. Instead, Detective Sergeant Henderson stared stoically over Ben's head into the flat beyond.

"Right. Come in." Ben's voice sounded flat, upset. He led them into the lounge. "So, what's this about? It doesn't feel like a social call."

James felt the accusation like a kick to the gut. But Ben had every right to feel lured here under false pretenses.

"Mr. Morgan," Ingham said. "I understand you've been a regular visitor to Bronzefield prison? To visit Eve Kelly."

Ben's mouth fell open. His focus darted to James then back to Ingham. He appeared both appalled and stunned.

"Could you tell us the purpose of your visits?" Ingham prompted into the shocked quiet.

"I didn't know it was an offense to visit someone in prison," Ben managed, but his voice had no fight in it. It sounded thin, diminished.

"It's not, of course," Ingham went on gravely. "But we're investigating a series of murders. We believe they're linked to Miss Kelly."

To James, Ben appeared so mystified that, his plaintive, "I don't understand," seemed redundant.

"Can we clarify, first, your reason for visiting her?" Ingham asked.

Ben glanced desperately at James, and the awareness came clearly. Ben didn't want him to know.

"We're attempting to track down Eve Kelly's son. A…" James looked down, all theatre, at his notebook and, suddenly, he felt incandescently angry, though he didn't really know why. "Steven Matthew Brooker." Stonily, he met Ben's dark sapphire eyes, huge with distress. "Is that you?"

Ben's lips worked for a few moments, no sound, then his eyes filled with unshed tears. James realized that he'd never seen him close to tears before.

He fought not to flinch when Ben said, "Yes." Ben's attention remained fixed, laser-like on James, silently pleading for…what? Understanding?

He confessed his shame to James alone.

James held up his mask of cold imperturbability. "Could you explain why, since you knew I was investigating the murders of Maria Curzon-White and Romilly Crompton, you failed to mention the fact that they were your sisters?"

Ben seemed to physically jolt in place, as if someone had touched his skin with a live electric wire. He turned in seconds from pale to paper white.

"*What?*" he whispered.

James drew a deep breath, and despite all he'd been denying to himself, he felt brutal relief that Ben hadn't known. Or at least, appeared not to know.

He's Eve Kelly's son, he reminded himself. *He had you in the palm of his hand.*

"Gemma Sweeney," Ingham put in matter-of-factly. "Otherwise known as Maria Curzon-Whyte. And…Chantelle Sweeney known as Romilly Crompton."

Ben's legs gave out from under him. He collapsed backwards onto the sofa, staring up at Ingham, as stunned as if she'd just casually shoved a knife between his ribs.

Like Eve, James thought relentlessly. *When she played me.*

"Are you saying you didn't know?" Ingham continued.

Ben shook his head, dazed.

"I showed you a photograph the day I interviewed you," James reminded him. *The day I met you.*

"But that wasn't Gem," Ben said, appalled. "Was it?"

"We found your address in her home," James accused. *And it led me to you.*

"I don't know why. She didn't come here!"

"You didn't know who adopted your sisters?" Ingham asked.

Ben looked as if he were about to pass out. "No. The lady just said they'd be happy." His hand shot to his mouth and pressed hard against it. Tears began to slip down his face. "I promised I'd take care of them."

"Who did you promise?" Ingham demanded.

"*Them!* I promised *them!* I said…I wouldn't let them be hurt any more. Fat use I ever was to them." His high cheekbones glistened in the thick golden afternoon light as tears coursed over them, unchecked—ascetic, gorgeous, bleeding pain.

"At this point, Mr. Morgan," Ingham battered on. "It appears people who were associated with your mother in some way are being picked off. Both your sisters, one of your mother's associates, and the woman who arranged all three adoptions have all been murdered." Ben stared at her dazedly, as if he couldn't quite keep up. "Is that why you chose to rent a room to DS Henderson. Because you feared for your safety?"

Ben's complexion was ashen. His dark brows and thick, wet lashes; his stricken ocean eyes were slashes of crayon on a white page.

"No." He shook his head again. "I didn't know any of that was happening."

"Perhaps it might be best if you accompanied us to the station in any case," Ingham said. "For your own protection."

Ben paused, as if to control his breathing. "You think I'll be next?"

James hadn't a clue what Ingham was thinking. She hadn't mentioned Stefan or the fact they already had him in custody. The fact that there should be no threat any more.

"It seems a sensible precaution." Her tone sounded calm and reassuring.

"*Christ.*" Ben's hand went back to his mouth, a nervous gesture James had never seen him make before today. "I suppose…all right. I suppose so. I'll… Will I need anything?"

"Maybe an overnight bag, if you decide to stay in protective custody."

Ben stood up. He turned at once to James, but his voice sounded hesitant. "Will you be with me?"

James's pulse leapt. To Ben, it seemed, he remained a friend.

"Detective Sergeant Henderson is part of the investigating team," Ingham interrupted smoothly.

Ben's eyes didn't leave James's face, but whatever he saw tightened his jaw. "I see." He lowered his head. To James, he seemed smaller somehow. "I'll just go and pack a few things."

Ingham didn't suggest James follow Ben to his room, for which he felt immensely grateful. He couldn't have coped with being alone with him, not without trying to comfort him.

The summer sun beat relentlessly through the big Georgian windows as James and Ingham stood and waited in silence. The light left square patterns on the polished wooden floor, and James remembered his first sight of those windows. How quickly he'd been seduced by everything about this place.

The ginger and sandalwood scent seemed totally familiar now. It came from furniture polish Ben had sourced in some pretentious organic shop. The windows stuck sometimes, when they tried to open them. He knew the reality behind the beauty. It had become his home.

His restless gaze fell on the sofa where he and Ben had watched TV together and snogged. The sofa James had fucked Ben against, that last time together. He took in the kitchenette, where they'd washed the dishes and bullshitted and kissed for the first time; the dining table where James had eaten the food Ben cooked for him, and eagerly soaked up his interest and his fussing, and where James had once taken breakfast with one of his other lovers.

Have they given you tea? They're dreadful at looking after visitors here.

Ben had so many people—men—emotionally, sexually enthralled by him. Just like…

He squeezed his eyes shut. He was being unfair. Horribly unfair. Letting Eve taint everything. He was… They were *both* treating Ben like a monster, because as a child he'd been left in the grasp of his mother. James was allowing his own prejudices to wipe away all the beautiful things he knew about Ben—not giving him a fair go without judging him guilty.

And, God, he thought, with a burst of panic, if James'd been doing that, a man in love with him, how could Ben hope for anything more from other people?

Eve Kelly's offspring… They'd all think he must be tainted. That he had to carry her evil like a seed, even if Ben could just as easily have been the next victim.

He jerked his gaze up, eyes fixed on a photograph on the wall. He felt tormented by guilt and indecision, veering wildly from one position to the other. Ben had just discovered he'd lost both his sisters for fuck's sake, and they were both treating him like a…

His heart stopped. For a second or two, the shock stopped it beating. Then grief started it again.

He stared for a few desperate seconds, begging it to disappear, an illusion brought on by too much high emotion. A trick of the light through those fucking windows.

But it didn't disappear. And then he had no choice.

"Ma'am," he choked out. All he could do was gesture with his head, and she turned to see.

He had no idea how he hadn't seen it before. He'd lived here for months for fuck's sake, glanced at the work often enough, admired its artistry. He'd noticed it on his very first visit, but it just hadn't registered until now. There must be some deep reason for that.

A black-and-white framed photograph on the wall, of a stream. Smooth stones covered by water, glittering in the sun. And half-obscured by the reflection of sunlight, a fine chain, lying curled up on one of the huge pebbles. Ben's photograph.

Ingham breathed, "Fucking gotcha."

It felt like the end of the world.

34

"Tell us what happened, Steven."

He glared at her furiously, eyes wet. "*Ben.*"

James and Ingham sat across from him in the interview room, alone. It wasn't an informal, information-gathering chat after all.

When Ben had returned red-eyed, bag in hand, to the lounge, Ingham had ambushed him with a formal caution. And as Ben had stood there, gaping in disbelief, she'd asked for permission for a search of the flat as well as Ben's studio and laptop.

"This is fucking insane," he kept saying, bewildered, and "Jamie! Please! Tell me what's going on!" but James had stayed resolutely silent, face impassive, screaming inside.

Jamie? Please? Why won't you speak to me? Is it because of her? I can't help being her son.

He could hear it still—maybe he always would—that tone of absolute betrayal, until at last Ben quieted and went with them without argument. He'd told Ingham listlessly that a search of the flat would be fine by him because he had nothing to hide. He'd refused a lawyer on the same grounds—that this was fucking insane and there was no need. Perhaps he made the civilian's mistake of thinking a lawyer made him appear guilty, or perhaps, like his mother, he was just so arrogant he thought he could outwit the police without one.

Eve Kelly had refused a brief too, but then she'd been proud of what she did.

Was Ben proud? Or innocent?

Finally James had been driven to blurt as they'd entered the station, "You really should get a lawyer." But it had come out as stiff and cold, uninvolved, as if he believed in Ben's guilt. Maybe he'd meant it to.

Ben repeated sadly, "I don't need one. I haven't done anything."

And so here they were, tape running, two against one. Ingham hadn't been sympathetic enough to excuse James from the interview.

Ben sat with his elbows on the interview-room table, hands clasped tightly in front of him, head bowed, hair half-concealing his face. His jacket hung, discarded, on the back of his chair, and in the chill of the room, he wore only his black T-shirt, clinging to his broad shoulders and displaying his beautifully muscled arms. Even in the unflattering grey light seeping through the high frosted-glass window beside them, he seemed like a model in some stylized artistic photograph—an ideal.

But, unwillingly, James saw too, just as on the night of the ball, a glimpse of the other side to him. The physicality of the savate fighter. Graceful. Powerful. Ruthless.

"Then tell us what happened, Ben," Ingham said dispassionately.

Ben raised his head and drew a deep breath.

"We were taken into care when…when Mum was…" James flinched at that word—*Mum*. Ben's attention flicked to him, distress, then acceptance, written all over him. Maybe this was what he had always expected, if anyone found out. Repulsion and horror. "When *she* was caught," Ben went on. "The lady…the social worker…kept saying we shouldn't suffer. For Mum." He huffed a bitter little laugh. "There were other kids in the home who'd been there much longer than us, and it wasn't as if Mum gave a rat's arse what happened to us. But the lady really believed it."

"You weren't close to your mother?" Ingham asked.

"What do *you* think?" Ben asked with disbelief. He fixed his attention on his hands, still clenched together white-knuckle tight, on the table. "The lady came a few weeks into…Mum's trial and said she'd found Gem a new family. Gem didn't want to go at first. She didn't want to leave us, but no one would take all three of us, and the lady said we were lucky she'd found people who'd give us a chance at all. Being who we were." He shook his head slightly. "I knew she was right too. The people in the home…the kids and the staff…they treated us like monsters. Like *we'd* done what she did. So they used to take it out on us…target us, especially me."

James fought to keep his face blank. "Were you abused?" he asked, though it was hardly pertinent.

Ben's focus returned to his hands. "They didn't rape me, if that's what you mean. They just beat the living shit out of me instead. Chan found a home next, and I was left behind. I was harder to place, I suppose. But after a couple of months, the lady came back, like she promised, and told me about the Morgans. She told me to pack and go with her and… hell…she could have been taking me to white slavers for all I knew or cared. As long as I got out of there. But they met me outside. Mummy and Dad and my dog. And…they taught me… How to be kind to myself, and to other people. And then my life became like something out of a book." He grimaced painfully. "Happy ever after."

There was silence when he finished. James felt as if his heart were breaking.

It made so much sense now—how Ben tried to nurture people, to collect them, while never really investing in them. The insecurity that drove it.

Ingham asked, "Why did you start visiting your biological mother?"

Ben shrugged weakly. "Because I couldn't forget, I suppose. I was too old when I got out. I remembered too much. Maybe I wanted to remind myself…of what I could turn into." He rubbed a shaky hand

across his mouth. "My therapist said it would be a good idea to confront it. Confront her."

"Your therapist?" Ingham mocked.

"Yeah." Ben scowled defensively. "You think I wouldn't need one
after everything? You think I trust *anyone* when I've seen firsthand
how easy it is to convince one man to cut another man's cock off? How
easy it is to lure people away from what they think they love?"

James's breath stilled.

Oh Jesus, he thought sickly again. No wonder.

No wonder Ben sneered at love, wanted only uncomplicated
sex. And the rejections, the lessons James had believed he was being
taught, to keep him in his place... Had those been unconscious tests
of his devotion that Ben had always expected him to fail? To prove to
himself that love had no staying power?

"I wanted to face her as an adult," Ben went on doggedly. "Not...
not a terrified kid. I wanted to make fucking sure she knew that while
she withered away in there, I was out here, living my life as hard as I
could."

"Tell us about your relationship with her," James blurted. "When
you were a kid."

Ben regarded him steadily, but James couldn't decipher his expression.

"I was piss-scared of her, *Sergeant*. All the time. It was better when
Dad was there... I mean he wasn't my dad but...he tried to be kind.
But he was scared of her too, and...he left us maybe a year before...
Well, it got much worse after that. But you know what? She was okay
to me sometimes, if I did things right. Almost...like a mum, and that
fucked my head more than anything else. Chan and Gem though...
She used to teach them the same stuff as me...how to be around people...be nicey-nicey, then, do what you like, when you have them. She
used to set tests...make them try to wheedle things out of people by
being sweet, or flirty if it was a man, and if they didn't bring back what
she asked them to get, she'd really hurt them."

"But not you?" James asked.

"Not so often." Ben rubbed his eye, a child's gesture of tiredness. "I
was good at it."

"You learned how to manipulate people," Ingham clarified. James swallowed the nausea in his throat.

Ben shrugged again, listless. "She used to say she'd cut off my cock or my balls whenever I annoyed her. She had a big pair of kitchen scissors, and she used to make me hold my bits up while she put the blades round. She'd make me beg and beg her not to close them."

James looked down at his empty notebook. *Bits.* Even the terminology was a child's.

"Maybe she'd've done it one day. I think she wanted to turn us all into…versions of her and maybe it gave her a kick that I'd be the male one. She used to tell us how filthy and disgusting men were. How easy to use."

"And is that why you have sex with men now?" Ingham asked, sounding nothing more than academically interested. "Because you know how manipulate them? Is that why you seduced Detective Sergeant Henderson? To *use* him to keep an eye on the investigation?"

James felt as if Ingham had just punched him in the gut. Why had she forced him to participate in this?

Ben's reaction seemed first disbelief, then incandescent fury. Ingham had finally succeeded in provoking him awake.

"How fucking *dare* you? You're suggesting she *made* me gay? That I made *myself* gay as a life strategy? Fuck you! I like men, Chief Inspector. In fact, I *love* men. And as for the rest…" Ben spat. "Detective Sergeant *Henderson* can testify *he* made the first move."

James sat stunned, waiting tensely, sick to his stomach until Ingham turned toward him with exaggerated formality and raised a questioning eyebrow.

"That is correct, ma'am," James said woodenly, for the tape.

Ingham faced Ben again and continued, unruffled. "Have you told your mother you've been having a relationship with DS Henderson?"

James wanted to close his eyes in the short, disbelieving silence that followed, but somehow Magnus's training held. He showed not a glimpse of his huge humiliation. Emotionally. Professionally.

Why hadn't all of this occurred to him before? Had Kelly known, when he interviewed her? Had she been laughing at him all the time?

"*What?*" Ben sounded convincingly outraged. "You're saying I plotted with her to sleep with him? Is that right? For fuck's sake! She tells me every time I see her she wishes she'd ripped off my 'filthy fag dick'! You think I *confide* in her, Chief Inspector? And for the record," he finished savagely, "there was no *relationship.*"

James didn't move or allow his expression to alter.

"The thing is, Steven," Ingham went on imperturbably. "You say you don't collude with her. Or confide in her...yet the fact remains you visit her regularly. I mean...I have to wonder, if you hate her that much, what *do* you find to talk about?"

Ben stared at her with a kind of hopeless disbelief, and then he let his head drop, his burst of fire apparently extinguished by her implacable skepticism. He didn't even protest her use of the name.

"I *told* you... It's like...like exorcism, can't you understand that?"

"Do you remember Gary Drake?"

Ben's mouth contorted with exhausted disgust. "Yeah. I remember. He was pathetic. Just a slave. He'd do anything she told him to do for a smile. Or so she wouldn't be angry with him."

"Were they having an affair?"

Ben shook his head hopelessly. "Who knows? I don't think so. I don't think she did any more than kiss him."

"Were you jealous of him?"

"Was I what?" That brought his focus back up to her. He looked as if he wanted to cry. "No!"

"He took your mother's attention. He kissed her."

Ben laughed, a sound of despair. "For fuck's sake have you listened to anything I said? I wanted people to take her attention...as long as it wasn't Gem or Chan!"

"Drake gave evidence against her at her trial."

"I know," Ben said.

"She must have hated his guts."

"She hates everyone's guts."

"But especially him, I'd think?" Ingham returned. "And your two sisters, who forgot about her. And Margaret Calder, who promised to help get her parole, and failed. She'd want them punished."

Ben stared at her like a mongoose at a cobra. Perhaps he could see at last where this was going. But she threw him again.

"What can you tell me about the photograph on your wall, of stones underwater."

Ben appeared entirely baffled. Not the smallest sign of shock at being caught out, just bewilderment at the change of subject to something so off track.

"The… I took it last year, I think. In Scotland."

"Do you go up to Scotland much, Steven?" Ingham asked.

"It's Ben! And no! I've just been once or twice. For work."

A knock at the door interrupted them, shocking in the intense atmosphere of the room. Ingham made a sound of impatience, but she nodded at James to find out what could possibly be important enough to break into an interview like this.

Scrivenor hovered outside when James slipped into the corridor.

He appeared awkwardly apologetic, and for a second James thought his regret had to be for the interruption. Then Scrivenor held up an evidence bag.

"He wasnae as smart as he thought," he said quietly. "Couldnae resist trophies."

Inside the clear plastic, James could make out two small locks of dark hair, tied with pink ribbon. Another—a silvery-grey lock, tied with red. A lighter mousy-brown one, tied with powder blue.

His heartbeat slowed. There was a buzzing sound in his head.

"It was in a box in his wardrobe wi' dildoes an' the like. Sick bastard," Scrivenor said, then, as he remembered, he flushed and added gruffly sympathetic, "Sorry, lad."

"But why would he be stupid enough to agree to a search?" James pleaded, anguished.

Scrivenor sighed. "They aw fuck up eventually, Jamie. Ye know that. Ego."

James gazed at him, agonized. He could feel tears burning behind his eyes, grief and stress and betrayal.

"Please. Will you take over?" His voice sounded thick.

Scrivenor looked uncertain. "She may not like it."

"Tell her I'm sick. Please, Alec."

Scrivenor sighed again and nodded slowly. "A' right. You go to the bogs then. Till yer feelin' yerself."

James nodded his curt thanks and walked smartly away from the room where Ben was about to be charged with multiple murders. With murdering his own sisters.

He didn't think he'd ever feel like himself again.

35

James sat and stared at nothing in the gents toilets for twenty minutes or so, then he pulled himself together and went back to his desk.

He had a front-row seat for the jubilation which swept through the office when the rumor spread that an arrest had been finally made. And not just any arrest. They'd solved four murders in one genius operation and, as a feather in their cap, taken Eve-Fucking-Kelly's spawn off the streets.

When Ben was led out of the interview room and down to the cells, head down, shoulders curled in, body language screaming defeat, the officers of the unit stood to the side and cheered with relief and euphoria. That a murderer was getting what was coming to him and they'd gotten justice at last for his victims. That a monster was off the streets. Ben walked through that.

Across the office, Scrivenor and Kaur stood, watching, apart from the mob. Scrivenor showed neither disapproval nor pleasure, but Kaur met James's eyes and he could see that her face was carved with sadness. Of course—she knew this was his Ben. The boyfriend of whom he'd been so proud.

He heard Ingham shout, "All right. Settle down," to the applauding, stamping crowd but she didn't make any real move to stop the pandemonium, because, James supposed, she thought the unit deserved the celebration. Maybe he'd have felt the same himself, if his heart weren't broken.

Ben didn't raise his head at all to try to find him in the mass of faces around him. He must have known James had abandoned him.

There was nothing urgent to do after that, James could go home. Hide and lick his wounds. Scrivenor said he should.

But he couldn't bring himself to leave Ben behind in his cell in a building full of people who didn't know him, who despised him. So he stayed.

The lights in the office were both dim and harsh, the most depressing possible combination, but for James, sitting stubbornly at his desk, they suited his mood to perfection. Ksiazek had been released without charge; Burnett would have to look somewhere else for a feeling of importance.

Nine o'clock approached. James propped his elbows on the table and buried his face in his palms, no longer caring to hide that he felt as if he were breaking apart through misery and shame. The lump in his throat was so huge he could barely swallow… Every time he closed his eyes, he saw Ben as he was led, handcuffed, through the mob.

"She's havin' tae let him out."

James dropped his hands from his face and stared dully at Scrivenor, waiting for the punch line.

"Two of his alibis held," Scrivenor said.

"*Two?*"

"Aye. The one he gave you the first time you interviewed him for Maria, remember? The one I checked out for ye. Guy from his gym… Matthew Hollister. Anyway, he's stickin' to the story that they went back to his place for a fuck after trainin'. An' the one for Romilly…a bloke called Carl Loeb…he claims they're sort've friends, met up a couple've times an' had sex, says they were at it most of the night she died."

James's gut swooped with desperate relief, even as the untrusting part of him already questioned, scrutinized, searched for flaws.

He hadn't heard of either man. But then…Ben would have dozens of fuck buddies, all kinds of connections James had no idea about. In reality, how much did he know about him?

"She's letting him go?" James repeated, stunned, because he knew Ingham. She'd be working like fuck to break alibis like that. Shags. Mates.

All the alibis Ben had given, in fact, were men he'd been fucking, which had given James a wry jolt of heartbreaking familiarity.

"His parents got him a brief," Scrivenor announced. "They're off abroad somewhere, but they sent in the best."

And that explained it all, especially when Scrivenor named a lawyer only the very wealthy could afford, a man most coppers despised for his ruthlessness and his effectiveness.

"He's in wi' Herself now, *Mister* Callaghan. Fuckin' bampot. She's got nae choice. Conditional bail. We're still tryin' tae contact the guy he named for Calder... An' he's confused as fuck about his alibi for Drake. Oh, an' the freezer bag he kept the victims' hair in has his prints, but he's sayin' any of the men he had sex wi' could've planted it." Scrivenor gave a long sigh. "Anyway...she's goin' after Hollister an' Loeb. She's bringin' 'em in first thing."

James blindly moved some papers on his desk, trying to take it all in. If he were still involved, if it weren't Ben, he'd probably be advising Ingham do exactly that. Then again, he thought, grabbing at a passing spar of hope, if someone had known who he was...framed him some-how...maybe they should be searching out Ben's lovers.

"So. I was...thinkin'..." Scrivenor said, and the rasp of discomfort in his voice made James glance up at him warily. "I'm meant tae be seein' him aff the premises. Steven." Scrivenor's moustache twitched. His gaze shifted over James's head and his accent thickened. "But...ah thought...maybe...well...maybe if ye wanted tae, ye know, take him oot yersel'."

Scrivenor appeared deeply mortified by his own softness. But that was fine, because James felt equally ashamed by his own obvious need of it.

He took a deep breath, trying to calm the sickness swirling around his middle, like stirred tea.

Did he *really* want to go? To talk to Ben? With all he knew now?

After all James had done to him and still more-than-half-believed about him?

Apart from anything else, professionally it would be a terrible idea.

"Yeah. I'll do it. Thanks, Alec."

Scrivenor sat at his own desk and opened a brown folder, as if he weren't party to James's idiocy.

As he walked calmly down to the cells, James didn't want to examine his own motivation. He didn't look through the peephole before he had the duty PC open the cell door, he simply walked inside and nodded to the officer to leave before pulling the door shut behind him.

Ben sat in the corner, on the floor, even though a bench-like bed lay against one wall. His elbows were propped on his knees, his head lowered, long hair hiding his face. He didn't bother to check who'd come in. He could have posed as an illustration of hopeless misery: Portrait of a Broken Man.

The guilt of his part in having reduced Ben to this hit him like a hammer blow between the shoulder blades. And yet, seconds later, he reminded himself that he still didn't know if he'd been with Ben Morgan, or with Steven Brooker. If anything had been real.

He cleared his throat. "Two of your alibis are holding up," he announced. His voice sounded cold and stilted, though he hadn't intended it that way. "Carl Loeb and Matthew Hollister. They vouched for you, the nights Gemma and Chantelle were murdered. You're free to go for the moment. You have conditional bail. Your lawyer's waiting for you."

Ben raised his head. There were streaks of dried tears and mucus on his pale skin; his eyes bled exhaustion, his thick, dark lashes clumped together like a distressed child's.

James heard him take a deep, clogged breath through his nose and let it out slowly, a despairing kind of sigh.

"You don't believe it, though." His voice sounded low and bitter. "Any of you. Because…I'm my mother's son, right? And the apple never falls far from the tree."

"Mr. Hollister and Mr. Loeb confirmed you were with them," James repeated stiffly, because he couldn't think of anything else he could say. "We're still trying to contact the other men you cited."

"And that must piss you off even more then, ay, Jamie? That my *alibis* are guys I had sex with." He gave a strange, hard, hopeless laugh that didn't sound at all like Ben, but at least he no longer seemed beaten. Rather, seethingly angry. "*Christ*…you'd probably rather believe I'm a serial killer than accept I was fucking other men."

Straight for the throat—the thing Ben had always known but only once used against him, and then when he'd been high. It showed James the extent of his mistake in giving in to the need to come here. All they could hope to achieve was mutual destruction.

He shook his head once, as if he were clearing it, and turned to go.

But Ben seemed no longer interested in avoidance.

"I trusted you!" he howled.

James jolted back round, shocked by the sudden volume and aggression, very relieved he'd closed the door of the cell behind him, because this could give the duty officers gossip to live off for months. "I can't believe I fucking trusted you. And all the time you were just… you only show up to fucking arrest me!"

"I did my job," James managed shakily, barely able to speak through the stab of bright, hot shame Ben's words evoked.

"Your job? And how long were you doing your *job*, Jamie?" Ben's voice shook with mad betrayal and accusation. "When you slept with me? Were you always trying to trap me?"

James gaped at him. "You think I was undercover? That's insane."

"How soon did you know who I was? Before you moved in? When Gem died?"

"No! None of the time I lived there!" James shouted back, and now he didn't give a fuck who lurked out in the corridor, or who heard. "I loved you, you bastard!"

The words hung in the air between them as they glared at each other. The first time James had ever said that to anyone, and it had been past tense. And ammunition.

They hadn't come close to real honesty before this, they'd always been careful with each other, even when they split that first time. But now they were both out there, walking some line of rage and animal disappointment and James felt almost glad of it, that at least they'd both stop being *reasonable*.

Ben's eyes held James's for a long, blazing moment. His breathing sounded heavy and shaky with emotion, or maybe it was just fury.

"Love?" he scoffed. "That's why you crept away without saying a word, is it? Just a note and a fucking cheque? And why you believe I murdered four people… My own sisters? Because you love me? Because you know me? That's love, is it?" In one powerful movement, he stood, levered effortlessly upright by his powerful thigh muscles, and then he was just a couple of feet away, glaring accusation straight into James's eyes. "Or is this revenge? Did *you* plant those clips of hair?"

It took a beat or two to understand, then… "What?"

"You had the access. And I let you down, didn't I? Fucked other men. Wouldn't stop fucking other men. Wouldn't be your boyfriend. Wouldn't go along with your—"

"That evidence was there!" James yelled, outraged. "And I knew nothing about it until SOCO found it! It had nothing to do with me."

They faced up to each other, the air around them thick with recrimination and mistrust, and as much as he'd thought he wanted truth, James could barely believe how bad this had become. How quickly and completely even the ruins of their relationship had been brought to rubble. And how could he voice his own hurt outrage that Ben believed he could be so small and vengeful and unscrupulous, that he would set out to frame him for murder? Because what had he come to believe Ben could do?

Somehow, James forced his expression into a facade of icy stoicism. He'd barely said a word of defense or attack, nothing to ease the furious, ashamed mess boiling inside him—but he had to finish this now.

He just wanted out.

"Your lawyer should be waiting for you." His voice sounded strange to his ears, distorted and far away. "There'll be a taxi at the front door by now. You can't go back to your flat yet. Apart from anything else, if someone planted that evidence, it might not be safe for you. Find somewhere else. In fact…maybe you should be making a list of all the people who had access to your bedroom. For your lawyer. And yes. I know that includes me." He stopped, because there was nothing left. "The duty officer will take you out." He gazed at Ben helplessly for the last time and turned to go. He felt as if all the blood in his body had turned to slush, as if even his heart beat more slowly.

"And that's it?" Ben shouted furiously behind him. "You just run away again? Fuck, you're an emotional cripple! No wonder you chose someone you knew couldn't love you back!"

Somehow, bizarrely, that proved the tipping point, even for a man as well-drilled in burying emotional upheaval as James.

"There's a difference," he gritted dangerously as he turned, "between not being able to love, and not having the guts to try."

Ben's eyes blazed blue in his chalk-white face, almost shocky. They were like two addled prizefighters, James thought sickly, standing toe-to-toe to slug it out to the death, hitting each other with everything they had. The case had been forgotten, this had become all about them.

Ben's mouth twisted. "So you thought if you just tried you could change me, is that it?" His voice cracked with emotion. "I'd turn into some suburban little woman you could show off at your rich daddy's charity functions? And when I didn't, you left."

"Oh fuck off, Ben! It wasn't working for either of us. You know that. I was just there because I was easy…trying to be what you wanted, never turning you away when you fancied a fuck if you didn't get lucky with someone better. Reliable. Wasn't that what you told Olly?"

Ben opened his mouth, eyes wide, apparently more outraged than at any point in their argument.

James surged on, "And yeah, I know. I know. You warned me. You love *all* your friends. I can't blame you, because I went along with it, can I? And you can't blame *me* for bailing out before it ate me alive."

Ben seemed to be about to speak, but nothing emerged. James could hear his breath hitching, the noise of a cell door clanging closed out in the corridor, a voice shouting incoherently in the distance, as reality returned. He'd completely forgotten there were other people in the building.

"You know how I felt about you." James's voice hushed, saying these unsayable things. "But you never let me really know you. You never let me close enough for that. You wanted to prove you could drive me away. That no one's worth it. Well, I'm sorry I couldn't pass your tests. I'm not that strong or that good."

Ben flinched. "You just wanted to punish me," he countered. "That's why you left the way you did."

"No." And James wanted to cry too, for all he still felt and all he'd never have. "I stopped it before we grew to hate each other, that's all." He started toward the door, desperate to get out.

"Wait!"

James stopped and turned around slowly. There were new tears on Ben's face, as if he'd been stripped of everything but his misery.

"Why do you think Gem tried to contact me?" he asked.

James shook his head. "Maybe—because she wanted to get to know you again."

"Yeah," Ben said numbly. "Bad luck for her."

James clenched his jaw. "The officer will take you to your lawyer. He'll explain the bail conditions." He drew a sharp breath. "Good luck, Ben."

As he left, James thought he might have heard Ben call his name, but he didn't look round.

36

The office was still busy when James returned, but the buzz of underlying celebration hadn't diminished.

The others hadn't yet heard the news of Ben's release, he supposed. But they'd see the alibi—as Ingham did—as nothing more than a minor hurdle thrown in their way by a murderer about to be brought down.

He slumped into his chair and stared at the papers on his desk, as if the past few minutes hadn't happened, as if he'd dreamed them.

Across from him, Scrivenor steadily typed up reports, allowing him his privacy, working, like everyone else in the office, to tie up the loose ends on a case they considered closed, bar the formalities.

Ben would be convicted of murder, and these would be his last nights of freedom until he was a very old man.

The argument, the accusations they'd hurled at each other, circled round and round in his head. And most of all—Ben's charge that James had come to hate him so much he'd framed him.

Had he just been lashing out or...did he really believe that?

Uncertainty gnawed at James like an ulcer. Those trophies... According to Alec, Ben had denied all knowledge of them, and he'd seemed so...outraged when he accused James. Had he been laying the groundwork for his defense? Readying to accuse James as a jealous maniac, because… God, that could create reasonable doubt. And ruin him. And Ingham as well, probably.

Or maybe Ben had aimed to achieve exactly this. Manipulating James's feelings for him into doubting the evidence—Eve's MO. Wasn't he just another Gary Drake or Charles Priestly? Another Margaret Calder? Easy to play? Not like Ingham.

Alec said Ben'd kept asking her in the interview, "Why would stones mean anything to Mum? Why would chains?"

Why would they?

He'd never really attempted to work out what meaning stones and chains might have to the killer. Why choose that as a signature? Kelly, on her rampage, had never used a signature at all, but *maybe* Ben had chosen to use one as a red herring, to draw attention away from the parallels in the murder methods of both killing sprees.

James regarded his monitor through aching, sandy eyes.

The Google homepage stared back at him. Defiantly, he typed in: *stones significance.*

Links for *the significance of gemstones* came back.

He added *meaning*—and got *the meaning of gemstones.* Adding *chain* got him no further.

For fuck's sake, what did he expect to find that hadn't already turned up in police databases?

He tried: *stones, chain, Eve.*

Jewelry and a video game came back. Pointless.

Still, he typed in: *stones chain superstition* and then *stones chain symbolism* but nothing worked.

What the *hell* was he doing?

He had to face up to it. Ben had cut his sister's throat. Put two bullets in the other one's head. They had evidence. Circumstantial *and* forensic.

He gazed blindly at the back of Scrivenor's monitor, at Christ suffering on His cross, looking down at the world beneath His nailed feet.

He chewed his lip, fighting desperation. Typed: *stones chain religion.*

Two words caught his eye in the list of results. He deleted *religion* and added them: *stones chain patron saint.*

Results for *St Patrick's medal prices* came up. He tried: *St Steven.*

Stephen is traditionally regarded as the first martyr of Christianity… At his trial he made a long speech fiercely denouncing the Jewish authorities who were sitting in judgment on him, and was stoned to death.

He stared at the screen, horrified. Slowly he typed in *St Stephen symbols.* And at the bottom of the first link he opened: *stones.*

One more brick in the wall of evidence against Ben. Against *Steven.*

He hammered the keyboard again, desperate for a different outcome: *patron saint symbol chain.*

It took him almost a minute to hit Return. He couldn't bear to be the person who found that last nail to hammer into the coffin. But he screwed his face up and pushed the key. He felt sick.

The patron saint of orphans. Symbol…a chain.

But Ben wasn't an orphan, James thought blankly. Then he registered the saint's name.

Gerolamo Emiliani.

And he knew.

━◖━ ━◖━ ━◖━ ━◖━

It would be incredibly stupid to go alone. No doubt about it. But James knew he wouldn't be able to convince Ingham to do anything on the scraps he had, and…he had an instinct that there wasn't much time left.

Ingham would tell him he was scrabbling for any alternative to an unbearable truth. She'd order him not to go. And maybe…maybe she'd even be right.

Scrivenor glanced up across the desk as James rose jerkily to his feet. He clearly saw his urgency at once.

"Jamie?"

James grabbed his jacket from the back of his chair. "I need to check on something I think we might have missed."

"Trouble?" Scrivenor asked, frowning.

"Just a nagging feeling. I'll be back in an hour or so."

He told Scrivenor where he was going and why, just in case, and to keep it to himself for now. Scrivenor didn't hide his concern over James's state of mind.

He drove like a maniac through the dark, half-empty streets, and when he slammed his hand against the front door bell, he prayed feverishly that he'd be in time.

This time, his prayers were answered.

"It's me," he told the intercom breathlessly. "Sorry it's so late."

The door buzzed entry at once. The flat door stood wide open.

But as James walked in, he pushed the snib on the Yale lock and didn't quite close the door behind him. Just in case.

A large, soft overnight bag sat at the end of the hall, bulging and ready.

James drew a deep, steadying breath and went into the lounge.

Steggie stood in his kitchenette behind the counter, back to James, already filling the kettle for tea. The television murmured in the background.

"Jamie!" Steggie beamed over his shoulder. "It's about bloody time." He looked unguarded and flushed. Young. Excited to see him.

James swallowed against the aching lump of emotion in his throat. He desperately didn't want to be right. But dear God—he couldn't be wrong. Either way was loss.

"You heard about Ben?" James moved a few feet into the room.

Steggie turned round at once, kettle in hand, leaving the tap running. His expression had hardened.

"Ben? Fuck, Jamie! Don't you ever learn? You're going *back* to him?"

"He's been arrested."

Steggie's eyes widened comically. Maybe he hadn't known. SOCO would have left Ben's flat by early evening, after all. Maybe from the ground floor, Steggie wouldn't have seen the police tape across Ben's door. Or maybe he was lying.

"For four murders," James went on without emotion. "The murders I've been investigating."

"*Ben?*" Steggie put down the kettle and reached behind himself blindly to turn off the tap. The room suddenly seemed very quiet save for the sound of faint voices on the TV and the implacable ticking of the carriage clock, leading its honor guard of gold phalluses on the side table. James watched every single ripple of expression on Steggie's face, every nuance of movement—a cat waiting for a mouse to jump the wrong way. In the near silence, he thought he heard a tiny screech of hinges behind him.

"Ben," James confirmed. "But he's out on conditional bail."

"He's out?" Steggie asked sharply. Then, "*You* arrested him?"

"He had an alibi for two of the murders," James said. "We're checking to see if they hold up. And how his other alibis hold up."

Steggie looked no less stunned. "Are you all right?"

James cleared his throat and produced a smile somehow.

"I'm fine, Stegs," he lied. "You know, I just realized something on the way over. I've never asked why you got called that. Steggie, I mean."

Steggie frowned in evident bewilderment. "For fuck's *sake*, Jamie, Ben's killed four people, and you ask that now? It's a nickname."

James gave a moue of forced unconcern. "Maybe I don't want to talk about that. Maybe I just want to talk about something trivial. I mean...I don't even know your real name. Isn't that ridiculous? It's not Emile, is it?" Steggie's eyes met his. Fixed. Blanked. He could have been a waxwork figure. "Steggie," James continued, but all pretense at lightness had gone. His voice ached with regret. "That's for Stephen, isn't it? Stephen what? Nicholas?"

Steggie's frozen expression didn't change. James watched him, agonized.

Steggie's lips barely moved as he murmured, "Underwood. My name's Underwood."

Underwood. *Under Milk Wood.* The name of Steggie's company, which Alec had thought to be a double entendre. And one of the names on the list James had been given at HMP Bronzefield. James felt validation and devastation in equal measure.

"Who are you, Steggie?" he asked.

Steggie didn't laugh it off, although he could have. He seemed like a man who'd always half-expected he'd be discovered, though the way things had played out, connecting him to the case had been a freak chance. A blind leap. Even now, James couldn't prove anything. Perhaps no one would ever know, except the two of them.

And perhaps…anyone who might hear the recording he'd been trying to make on the phone in his jacket pocket. It might be inadmissible in a court of law, but it could get the truth across to Ingham.

Or—maybe too, the person James heard lurking just outside the unlatched front door could do that. Scrivenor never could conquer his inner mother hen.

"Underwood is my mother's name," Steggie replied with dignity. He looked lost, achingly sad. "*Parrish* is my father's."

It didn't take long to join the dots. By now all the details were carved in James's mind Names, places, what had been done to whom.

"Oh, Steggie," James breathed. "Colin Parrish. He was your dad?"

The desolate expression on Steggie's face vanished so quickly James thought he could have imagined it. Emile's smooth mask returned.

"Oh yeah. My dad was an actual celebrity for a few weeks. Her second last victim. Part of a very select club."

"What happened, Steggie?"

Steggie looked away, mouth working with distress before he got himself under control. "I told you, didn't I? Or just the edited highlights. It finished my mum, not just knowing how he died—all the sick stuff she did to him… But all the rest of it. Mum couldn't even mourn him properly, because she knew he'd been going to just…leave us for that monster. So she took pills. I found her when I came home from school. Dead as fucking mutton." He waved at the table displaying his gold awards. "That's her clock. It's all I have left of either of them." He made a sound of bitter amusement. "The best thing is, they were both Catholic. Devout. An' Dad was gaggin' to commit adultery, and Mum topped herself. That bitch…Kelly…when I saw her, she said she'd pissed herself laughing when she heard." Steggie's expression ached with memory. "My life…it used to be perfect. My sister an' me… We had a dog an' a hamster. An' a house with a garden."

"You have a sister?" James asked, horrified.

Steggie snorted. "Oh…not so much, luv. They split us up. She got pregnant at thirteen. OD'ed. I didn't find out for years."

"Christ. Steggie…"

"And then there was me," Steggie went on brightly. "In the same care home as him. Kelly's son. The girls'd been adopted already, and I didn't go *near* him. But the others used to tell me the Kelly kids all tried to work people, suck up to the staff. An' then he was gone too, a month after I arrived. I remember Ted...the old fucker who started me...the first one who made me suck him off. He told me about this social worker who came on heavy with the staff. She'd said if any of the Kelly kids complained, she'd get them sacked, because she said they mustn't suffer. And he told me how she'd got them great homes. And I remember kneeling there while he zipped up, with my jaw aching, an' his spunk in my mouth, wondering why she didn't think *we* mustn't suffer? Me and Carol? Why she only cared about the murderer's kids and left us to rot?"

Steggie had begun to weep, but it seemed irrelevant to him, an autonomic response. And James could see that he still lived every second, running on the fuel of what had been done to him. His reddened eyes held James's wildly, demanding understanding, demanding absolution.

"Why did you visit her?" James felt like crying himself. "Eve Kelly?"

"Why? To gloat, that at least she has to live the rest of her life in a cage. To find out what the fuck kind of filth she had to be to do what she did to my family. But...as it turned out...I found out more than that. Ksiazek and Drake. Their names were on the visitors list...and that's how I knew they were out of jail already, and gone to pay her fucking tribute. They weren't even *sorry*. I couldn't find Ksiazek. But I found Drake," he finished viciously.

A floorboard in the hall creaked.

"Steggie," James covered quickly. "You *murdered* four people. How the fuck could...?"

"How?" Steggie seemed honestly stunned by the question. "*Look* at me, Jamie. Look at what they made me."

"But even with what happened, you could've..."

"What?" Steggie hissed. "I could have risen above it? There was no one to catch *me*. Ever tried to get a job with just 'rent boy' on your CV? So I have to make a living doing *that*!" He gestured with furious disgust at his table of golden trophies, and James could not comprehend now that he'd never seen how much Steggie despised them. "Getting fucked on camera, for strangers to wank over. To sneer at. And her kids were given private schools and fucking *ponies*, while I had to beg old men to shove their cocks into me for money! I went to hell, and they got perfect lives because *she* slaughtered my dad!" Steggie rubbed the back of his hand over his eye. He looked very young and very tired.

"How did you find them? The kids?" James kept his voice carefully level, praying Scrivenor would have the sense to stay in the hall and summon help. Because if he came in, how bad could this get? "Of course. You saw Ben's name on Eve's visitors list too," he answered himself.

But Steggie looked surprised. "No. I didn't know he went to see her."

James asked soothingly, "Then how?"

Steggie eyed him suspiciously but he said, "Luck. I finally got some of the luck I was owed. I mean…I thought it was over, after Drake. I'd done all I could for Dad and Mum. I didn't have a fucking clue about…him…*Stevie* when I moved in. Fuck. I could have seen him on the visitors list if I'd just had a few seconds longer. But I didn't have a fucking clue!" He let loose a disbelieving laugh. "But I still ended here, didn't I? I mean, I can't claim we moved in the same *circles* exactly," he said with sudden savagery. "But the circles touched just enough. One of his fucks introduced us. A model. Jace. He did a bit of porn on the side." Steggie gave a hard laugh. "Ben seemed so fucking charming. Put a word in for me about this flat, helped me move in… I actually liked him, even though I had to listen to his rejects crying on my shoulder."

James refused to flinch. "So what happened?"

"Like I said—luck. Fate. That stuck-up cow Maria decided to walk down memory lane. She used some people to dig out information other people had buried. And when she got some details, she came here to find her brother—"

"—and she pushed the wrong buzzer," James finished. Of course.

"Fate," Steggie repeated with absolute certainty. "And if that wasn't my dad guiding me to them, I don't know."

"You invited her in…" James prodded.

"Well, she asked for Stephen." Steggie sounded almost defensive. "And something told me—Dad maybe—that I should let her in. She assumed she had the right person an' I let her talk. And then I realized...who they were. She didn't remember him properly...that was another sign. Just a blur, who'd said he'd look after her. Her *Harley Street psychiatrist* blamed trauma apparently." He laughed reminiscently. "God, she was full of it. I mean, I look nothing like him, but it was easy, because I knew so much about Grantham Close." He drew a deep breath, hatred sparking and burning in his eyes. "She wanted to invite me to her manor house in the country, and she went on and on about her glorious career. She had no...*shame*. I told her I needed time. I needed to think. So I took her card. And I hired a private detective to find out all about her, like she had. You'd be amazed what they can do. He found her sister too, and the social worker. And *Steven*...well, he'd already been handed to me on a plate."

"But Steggie...how could you blame them?" James protested. "The kids. She hurt them too."

"They were her clones," Steggie returned coldly. "She made fucking sure of that. All of them...screwing their way to what they wanted without even being honest enough to charge. Forgetting the shame of who they were because it wasn't convenient. Wallowing in money and *love* they didn't deserve. At least I made it quick for them. Which is more than she did for my dad and mum."

He wiped his nose quickly with the back of his hand and seemed to force calm on himself. "And then there's him. Ben fucking Morgan... cocky as shit, world at his feet, no shame, nothing holding him back. Parents who love him, money to burn, using everyone and throwing them away. And patronizing me, when it should've been *him*. Stevie. If his mother hadn't killed my mum and dad...that's what he'd have ended up. A whore. And I'd have been..." His face twisted, expression brutal with pain, and James couldn't find some magical answer to counter him.

Because there could be no denying the basic facts of the situation, seen through Steggie's eyes. Eve's murder spree had given her own kids a gilded life and condemned Steggie, her victim, to madness and hell.

"I just worked out what they all had coming," Steggie went on.

"The ones who'd already had more good things than they deserved. And him—Steven. He'd had his holiday from responsibility. He should get the same as his filthy whore of a mother. Nothing quick. They can both rot alive."

"The stones and chains you left with each of the bodies. Ben's photograph gave you the idea?"

Steggie shrugged. "Nah. I was always a good Catholic boy. Knew all the saints. When I changed my name for…professional purposes, I thought I'd go with that. Emile for orphans, Nicholas for whores. Did you know that, Jamie? St Nicholas? Santa's the patron saint of hookers."

"No," James replied softly. "I didn't know that."

"When I finished Drake, I wanted to mark him. For my dad and mum. Leave a sign of who brought him to justice. So that's what I did. But that photo on the wall…I mean I'd seen it, of course. But once I found out he was Steven… It had to be another message. It was…him and me. The stones for both of us—Stephen—and the chain for me. The stream for Brooker. It was so easy. Except…I tried to point it out to you, on the wall, get you to pay attention to it properly, but you just wouldn't see it."

James felt ill. "No. I wouldn't, would I?" He'd missed so much.

Steggie huffed a rueful little laugh, still standing behind the kitchen counter as if they were chatting about what had happened at the pub the night before. He met James's eyes.

"I liked you from the start, you know," he said shyly. "I tried to help you, and point you at the clues so you'd be the one to solve it and catch him… Get the credit. At the end, I had to hit you in the face with the symbols—with Calder. I knew *you'd* crack it though. You're smart." He sighed. "Too smart as it turns out."

James pulled a bitter smile. "Not smart enough to see what's going on under my nose. I've been a handy stooge, haven't I, to help you frame Ben?"

Steggie's little smile vanished. "No! I was helping you! When you needed distraction. I was going to leave that old cow *Margaret* for a while, but you were so miserable after he screwed you over so…"

James's stomach swooped with new horror. "You killed her…for *me*?"

Steggie waved a dismissive hand. "I just tweaked the timing, to give you something to concentrate on. But he really had his hooks in you by then. And it'd hurt you anyway when you had to arrest him. I thought…better get it over with."

"Fuck…" James ran a shaky hand over his face.

"I hated what he did to you." Steggie's voice softened. "You're one of a kind, Jamie. I didn't believe men like you existed outside a book. I've met so many sharks—so many cops. You're like something out of a fairy tale. You took me to a ball for God's sake, like fucking Cinderella."

James shook his head, denying it, his throat too tight to allow words to escape. Even now Steggie's twisted, stunted loyalty stabbed at his heart.

He'd known that Steggie had feelings for him, but he'd dismissed them. He'd hurt him like everyone else had hurt him.

And Steggie had taken his revenge on the world.

"I understood why you wouldn't sleep with me," Steggie went on. "I was too dirty for someone like you. But he's no different to me, Jamie."

James stared at him helplessly, and he could feel nothing but regret.

"Steggie," he whispered.

Steggie's mouth twisted. And James knew that whatever Steggie had hoped for, James hadn't delivered in any way.

"Still," Steggie said brightly. "One plus to my career in film—and on the streets, courtesy of Ben's delightful mother—is that I associated with all kinds of interesting people. If you're *friends* with them, they do you all kinds of favors. Like getting you a *sweet* little handgun, like this one, complete with silencer." As he spoke, he pulled his hand casually from behind the counter and placed a small gun, silencer attached, in front of him on the marble top. "See?"

Everything in James seemed to still, but there was a roaring in his head. His blood. His heart beating too fast.

Steggie's smile stretched, but James saw no glint of humor in it.

"I have quite a few useful friends, you know? They can tell you where to place a bullet, how to garrote someone properly, how to pick locks, how to make sure you leave no awkward forensic traces." His head dropped suddenly, an exhausted marionette with his strings cut. But he straightened at once and pushed on gamely. "The thing is, I've no intention of going to jail, sweetie. It's just not me." He lifted the gun and primed it smoothly even as he strolled round the breakfast bar toward James. "I never wanted to hurt you of all people, Jamie, you know that, don't you?"

All James's attention zeroed in on the gun in Steggie's steady hand, pointing directly at his head.

It reminded James of how he'd felt once as a passenger in a crashing car. Time slowed to a stop around him.

So he had plenty of opportunity to accept that he'd seriously underestimated Steggie's willingness to do him harm. Time to hope Scrivenor had the sense to stay outside till help came. Time to hope, at least, that the recorder was still working. That they'd find it on him.

Time violently restarted. The lounge door slammed open, bouncing almost off its hinges. A figure darted into the room. James thought with raging gratitude as he began his lunge forward, *You fucking moron, Alec!* The dead, black eye of Steggie's gun stared steadily back at him, unmoving.

Steggie said clearly, "Stand still or I'll shoot him in the head."

The intruder froze as if he'd been shot himself. And just like that, the gambit was over. James's last hope of saving this, stood helpless in the lounge with him.

He dragged his gaze from Steggie, insane with frustration. But when he did, he saw with a swoop of horror that his would-be rescuer was not Scrivenor, it was Ben.

"Well," Steggie said, massively satisfied. "About time. It's rude to eavesdrop, Stevie. I wondered if you'd ever find the balls to come in."

Ben's expression was wild, desperate. He still wore the same clothes he'd worn in his cell, and James couldn't begin to understand why he'd be suicidal enough to break cover with no apparent defense for himself. He must have heard everything. He must know that he was the person Steggie loathed more than anyone else in the world, save his mother. Of all the people who could have tried to come to his rescue, Ben had to be the worst of all possibilities, and James's fear for him now far outstripped his fear for himself.

"I'm not Steven," Ben said. His voice sounded ridiculously calm. "And I'm not Eve."

The best hope, James calculated desperately, was to divert Steggie's attention from Ben. But Ben had begun to edge toward James, instead of away as he should, holding his hands up in the universal position of surrender.

"How did you know who was in the hall?" James asked Steggie quickly. *Hold his attention. Don't let him...*

"Oh, it had to be a fair bet he'd come to see me. I'm his best friend now, Jamie. Since you left? When he hasn't been trying to fuck you out of his system, he's been down here whining to me."

Ben made a sound of hopeless frustration. "Why didn't you just *talk* to me?" he pleaded. "For fuck's sake, Steggie! I hate her too!"

"Because *you* took my life," Steggie spat at him. "The life *you* have. It should have been mine." He paced closer a step or two until he stood a couple of yards away from them. Point-blank range. But the gun had swung to point steadily at Ben. "Even Jamie. What if you'd buzzed *my* flat first?" he asked James fiercely. "That day?"

James remembered, *I meant to*, but like Maria, he'd pressed the wrong button.

"What if *I'd* met you first," Steggie demanded, relentless. "If I'd had a chance to get through to you, before he got his claws in? I'd never have hurt you."

"Steggie," James pleaded. He didn't want to think about it. "I can get you help. Just give me that gun. This is... It doesn't have to be a gothic melodrama. It doesn't have to get worse."

Steggie made a hard cynical sound, the gun still steady on Ben. "Oh," he said heavily. "I think at this point...it really does." Any false humor in him had vanished to sadness. "I was going to go away for a little, while he got what he deserved. Life without parole with a bit of luck, just like his bitch mother. And then..." His tone became distant, tender. "I would have shown you what it's like to be loved, Jamie. When he'd gone, you were going to *see* me."

James fought not to show his horror or his pity.

"But..." Steggie shrugged briskly and let out a shuddering breath. His full implacable focus returned to Ben. "As it is, I have...limited options left. You shouldn't have told me how much you were feeling, Stevie."

The barrel of gun held its unwavering line on Ben's head. Steggie seemed to be on the verge of tears again, and suddenly, more than anything else, those grieving eyes terrified James.

Beside him, he heard Ben gasp, as if he'd just understood what Steggie'd said.

Ben moaned pitifully: "Steggie. No."

"Please." James's voice cracked as he spoke. "Please. Don't hurt him, Stegs."

Steggie ripped his gaze from Ben to glance at James with a strange confusion of betrayal and misery.

"Steggie…" Ben pleaded again.

In his peripheral vision, James could see that Ben had begun to shake his head, and the movement of denial gained momentum until it looked crazed. Frantic. And Ben began to beg. "Please. *Please* don't. Steggie. I'll do anything."

Tears spilled down Steggie's pale cheeks as he raised his left hand to steady the gun. But the same movement swung the barrel back round to fix on Jamie. And at that moment, James understood how Steggie meant to hurt Ben. Who Ben had been begging for. Strangely, he felt a flash of relief before the world once again began to slow.

He had nothing to lose from diving at Steggie now. Just as he knew that Steggie could not miss.

"Ben," James said clearly. His eyes never left Steggie, and Steggie hadn't stopped weeping. "The moment he does it. Run. Run like fuck."

Two ticks of Steggie's carriage clock.

Ben propelled himself instead into attack. On the ball of one foot he whipped his body round into an extraordinary lashing arc. James had seen it once before in the gym. Savate.

The movement, all power and grace and violence, both shielded James and cut Steggie's legs from under him.

But as he fell, Steggie fired the gun.

It sounded ludicrously anticlimactic: a popping, insectoid whine. James jerked in place, waiting for agony.

He heard a shocked cry instead, though he couldn't process, at first, where it came from. Then, the leaden thump of Ben's body hitting the floor.

Steggie scrambled back to his feet. James fell to his knees at Ben's side.

He moaned with horror and fear and despair as blood pumped into an obscene, red swamp on Ben's black T-shirt. His glassy eyes fixed on the ceiling, disbelieving. James pressed his hands to the wound, attempting to stem the gush of blood but they felt clumsy and numb with shock.

Ben had deliberately taken the bullet for him. He hadn't stood a chance. But he'd done it anyway.

"I wondered what he'd do," Steggie mused as he hovered above them. He didn't even sound out of breath and no more than interested. "Not what I expected, after all." Then in the same conversational tone, "That'll kill him, you know. If he doesn't get help soon. Blood loss. Shock."

James raised his head to glare stunned loathing at him, feeling Ben's hot blood bubbling sluggishly through his fingers as he desperately pushed down on the wound. He could hear his own uneven, panicked breathing. How close he sounded to sobbing aloud.

Steggie behaved as if nothing much had happened. His posture seemed relaxed. The gun dangled easily from his hand. Ben's eyelids fluttered and closed.

"Alone at last," Steggie quipped. "Well? What are you waiting for? Make the call. Put it on speaker."

James stared at him for a seething beat of silence, then he reached into his pocket and pulled out his phone with his free hand. The voice recorder hadn't stopped running, so he had to fumble his way out of the app before he could access the phone keypad. 9-9-9. He put his free hand back on Ben's wound, pressing hard, and waited for Steggie to pull the trigger at any second.

He held Steggie's eyes as he identified himself to the emergency-services operator. He hated that his voice shook.

"Ambulance," he said. "Critical. 22 Selworth Gardens, South Kensington. Ground floor. Gunshot wound."

"Gunshot wound? Is the area clear?" The operator's voice sounded tinny over the phone's minute speaker.

Steggie nodded almost thoughtfully.

James had no idea what the rules of the game were. He barely cared. "No. The perpetrator is still armed."

"You'll need a couple of ambulances, operator," Steggie called out easily into the speaker. "There'll be two victims. The crews will be safe. No need to delay."

Steggie reached over and ended the call.

James returned his hands to Ben's torn chest, uselessly trying to stop the flow of blood. Two victims.

"You'll have to get out fast," he told Steggie calmly, a last hopeless attempt to stop what was coming. "They're on the way."

"Do you want me to get away, Jamie?" Steggie's voice sounded steady, his face looked calm, wet with grief. "Even if I shoot you too?"

And James whispered, honestly, "I wanted you to be happy."

Steggie's mouth curved up into a sweet smile. "I know."

Tears coursed unheeded down his pale face. His hand held the gun steady, and James knew that he'd run out of time.

"I'm so sorry," Steggie whispered as he moved forward toward James's kneeling figure.

James closed his eyes and pressed down harder on Ben's wound. His heartbeat had slowed to an unnatural, ponderous thump in his ears. More than anything, for these last moments, he just wanted human contact. He wanted Ben.

"Jamie," he heard.

He forced himself to look.

Steggie had knelt down beside him just out of reach, pointing the gun at James's heart. James swallowed hard and refused to show his fear.

"Aw, Jamie," Steggie said, with infinite fondness. "White knight to the end."

The gun whipped up stunningly fast, and James tensed to leap. Anything rather than die a passive lamb, waiting for slaughter. Ready.

But Steggie's hand kept moving upward until the silencer pressed behind his own ear.

James took too long to understand.

"No!" he bellowed. "*Don't!*"

Steggie smiled. "Close your eyes, Jamie."

But James's eyes were open.

Steggie pulled the trigger.

James saw his head jerk violently sideways. An explosion of blood and brains burst from the other side of his skull. He toppled forward, but James fumbling hands failed to catch him.

He sprawled beside James on the floor, fingers jerking spastically before they went still. When James dared to look at them, his eyes were golden.

37

"How is he?" Ingham sounded breathless, anxious as she collapsed into a plastic chair beside James. It was after midnight, but the hospital waiting room never seemed to become less than half-full.

"Out of surgery. It missed the shoulder joint. But he lost a lot of blood." The word broke on a kind of croak. "They got him here fast." James took a calming breath. "He saved my life."

"Alec said. Are *you* all right?" Ingham asked. "You have blood on your face."

James raised a hand reflexively to his cheek then dropped it. It wouldn't be his blood. It would be Ben's. Or Steggie's. Maybe a mixture.

"Oh, I'm brilliant, ma'am," he said with bitter economy. Then he registered her expression of miserable uncertainty, and conscience told him to make an effort. "Alec came by and called me names. I'm a bampot and a wee gobshite. Apparently. And I think I'll need a new suit."

They both glanced down at the gruesome stains disfiguring the fine cloth and looked away again.

A few seconds passed before Ingham cracked.

"What the *fuck* were you thinking?" she yelled, then, glancing round at the other shocked occupants of the waiting room, lowered her voice to a purposeful hiss. "I should formally reprimand you. You should have come to me."

But James had already spent hours second-guessing his decision; he knew what would have happened if he hadn't done what he did, when he did.

Steggie would have disappeared; Ben would have gone down for life. Steggie wouldn't be dead. Ben would be whole.

If Maria hadn't pressed the wrong doorbell, they'd all be alive.

"With what?" he asked tiredly. "All the solid evidence stacked up against Ben. That's how Steggie planned it. I had nothing. Instinct. I spent the whole investigation giving you crackpot theories and doubting your suspects."

Ingham surveyed him, face scrunched with frustration, then she let loose an explosive sigh. She hacked a hand back through her curls. "Your bloody intuition, Jamie. I had the wrong man three times."

"It seemed cut and dried, *three times*."

"Except to you," Ingham said.

And suddenly he couldn't stand her self-flagellation.

Leave that to him, after the huge fucking mess he'd made of everything.

"I had the inside track," he said tightly. "I knew them both. I was right in the middle, and I didn't have a bloody clue until the very last second. So don't pat me on the back, ma'am."

Yet—he'd gone over and over everything, compulsively, and he still couldn't pinpoint where he'd missed crucial signs. The points at which he could have worked it all out. He just knew there had to have been some.

"He was clever," Ingham said. "Really formidable."

Formidable. Fuck, Steggie'd have loved that.

He'd sat cradling Steggie's broken body over his knees, uncaring of the brain and matter seeping into that much-admired Boss suit, uncaring of forensics or anything else—all the time pushing on Ben's wound to stop him bleeding out. It must have looked like a Jacobean tragedy when the police burst in.

James studied his hands. He'd scrubbed them raw but they didn't feel clean.

"He was going to kill me and leave Ben just alive enough to take the blame. But he changed his mind. I don't know why."

He loved you, his conscience told him.

"What a fucking legacy," Ingham said with tired disgust. "Another generation of death and misery, thanks to Eve Kelly. She'll be stoked."

They sat in glum, exhausted silence for a minute or two.

Finally, Ingham straightened in her chair. "Your father's waiting for you outside. Well…" Her mouth twitched with something resembling amusement. "*Waiting* is pushing it. He's threatening the staff with legal action."

James squinted at her, as surprised as his shell-shocked brain would allow. Maybe, he acknowledged hazily, he should see the police counselor this time.

"Why?" he asked. Ingham frowned. "I mean why's he here?" James clarified.

"Well…I phoned him. To let him know you'd been involved in a major incident." She sounded defensive suddenly, walking on eggshells. "I didn't know if you'd been injured at the time, and he's still your stated next of kin. And…I hope that's all right."

James blinked at her owlishly then subsided back to listlessness. "Yeah, it's fine."

"Fuck," Ingham said worriedly, ignoring the offended faces around her. "Come on then." She chivvied James upright. "Your father's waiting."

James followed her in a zombie daze, first along the corridor to the nurses station, and then out into the hall where the lifts were situated.

Immediately he spotted Magnus, dressed bizarrely in shabby corduroys, a pajama jacket and an expensively tailored woolen coat, pacing back and forth in front of the lifts like an unfed big cat. James fancied he could almost see a tail lashing, fangs exposed, and Magnus's haphazard clothing didn't lessen the effect.

In his distraction, it took Magnus a few seconds to register the two of them standing watching him, but when he did, he stopped dead in his tracks. James knew the sight he must present: white faced, smeared with blood and gore.

"Father," James greeted. Then, weakly, "It's better than it looks."

In two strides Magnus covered the distance between them, yanked James toward him, and locked his arms around him in a steel-tight hug. And James stared over his shoulder, limp and confused in his embrace, until the reality hit him, that this was his father.

His father was holding him.

On any other day, his disbelief and suspicion, his pride, would probably have held him back. But not today.

His arms crept up until his hands could clench in the expensive material of his father's coat, and with all his strength, he hugged him back.

 ▬||▬ ▬||▬ ▬||▬ ▬||▬

James went to the hospital to see Ben every day, though the hysteria surrounding the end of the case made escape difficult.

Sometimes that's all he did—he watched Ben through the slatted blinds on the hall window of his private room, making sure his condition was improving. But those were the days on which Ben had no visitors.

When Ben's parents were at his bedside, or Naomi or Glynn or Oliver, James popped his head in to ask after Ben's progress to his face.

Ben's response was always the same—subdued, polite, careful— as if they'd barely met. He never pressed James to stay and he never suggested they talk alone and James felt torn between relief and hurt. Relief won every time.

James didn't want to examine his desperation to avoid talking to Ben, one to one. Or the imperative that forced him to the hospital day after day. Maybe he felt he owed Ben a debt. An apology. Or maybe he wanted to make sure he hadn't dreamed that Ben had survived. Either way, James accepted that their story was over.

Concealing Ben's identity from the press had been a complicated business but Ingham, and the Morgans' expensive lawyers, had made quite sure his true role would never be revealed in any account of the case. Even Ben's friends didn't know the truth of why Steggie had shot him, and the press were not told about the existence of Eve's son, far less the man he'd become thanks to Margaret Calder. If they did ever discover it, a handy injunction had been put in place to prevent publication, and official sanction had been given for Ben's change of identity.

In any event, the media were thrilled enough with the story they were given... Multiple murders and suicide, Eve Kelly and the shadow of old sins—all sorted out by the Met.

Ingham's star rose so high that her case against cuts had been waved through and James put in line for a commendation and early promotion. But the DCS, of course, reaped the greatest political rewards.

Loretta turned up, thanks to *Crimewatch*, working in a massage parlor in Newcastle. As it turned out, she'd fled London in fear of her life, to get away from Burnett who'd harassed her, followed her to her rented flat and finally tried to rape her.

Ingham had been quietly triumphant.

The CPS decided to take no action against the three couples who'd broken the law, two decades before, to adopt Eve's children, but there had been no way, as parents of two of the victims, for the Curzon-Whytes or Romilly's parents to avoid public exposure. Dame Cordelia grasped the opportunity to promote her beliefs.

James reluctantly visited the police counselor and kept working, and continued his compulsive, pointless visits to the hospital. But he found he didn't much care about anything, other than his astonishment to find himself in possession of a father who worried about him, and his determination to master his own emotions which veered wildly between self-possession and a tearing, all-encompassing feeling of loss.

When Steggie's body had been released for burial, James attended his funeral on a bright-blue June morning with a handful of other people who James didn't know. He sat through the sparse service and watched his coffin lowered into the ground beside his parents. And how could he hope to explain to anyone that he was grief-stricken over a man who'd slaughtered four people in cold blood and plotted to wall up another?

He repeated to himself, over and over, all that Steggie had done, but he couldn't help it. Sometimes he felt like a sleepwalker.

Then, one evening, ten days after Steggie had died, the pattern changed.

James almost hadn't gone along because of the late hour, but he knew he wouldn't settle until he saw for himself that Ben was still all right.

He emerged from the hospital lift into the small hall outside the ward, planning to peer quickly through the blinds at Ben's window. Just to make sure.

But there, one foot up against a wall across from him, arm in a sling, stood Ben. He looked like an exhausted movie star, cruelly beautiful.

He seemed to be impeccably shaved, his long curls were shiny, and he wore expensive pajamas. But he also had dark circles beneath his eyes, and his pale skin was weary-white.

When he recognized James, he straightened at once, eying him nervously. And James had to face up to the reality of what he'd been avoiding.

Closure. He'd been running and ducking from it like a child. Dread settled in his stomach.

They stared at each other for long, fraught moments, but Ben took matters into his own hands. Without a word, he launched himself off the wall at James, pulling him into a hard one-armed hug. He hugged, and held on.

"Christ," he muttered and squeezed tighter with his good arm. "Jamie." He pulled back far enough to study James's face, his own eyes black with anxiety and emotion.

James forced himself to meet his eyes, to say what needed to be said. "I'm sorry. I'm sorry for thinking, even for a second—"

"*Don't!*" Ben's face twisted painfully. "I can't blame you. He planned it so well. Your DCI said you were the one who put it together—that Steggie would... You saved me, Jamie."

Gratitude. Fuck, he could do without it.

"And you saved my life," he returned.

"No," Ben said with a hollow smile. He dropped his arm and stepped back. "I don't think so. I don't think he could ever have harmed you. He was...in love."

James stared at him, stricken.

"Anyway," Ben said determinedly. "The doctor says I can be discharged tomorrow morning." He rolled his eyes. "Not sure I can stand to go back to Mum and Dad's though."

"Yeah." James gave a weak smile. "Father's fussing too. It's like someone abducted Magnus, and this one's a crap imposter. He phones me twice a day. And he waits up for me."

Ben stilled. "So that's...where you went? Your dad's?"

James nodded carefully.

"Steggie wouldn't say," Ben mumbled.

James swallowed hard. "He didn't know."

"I know I should hate him," Ben said quietly. "I mean, he made his own choices. And he took Gem and Chan away. But I can't. I just feel numb."

James nodded again, throat tight.

Ben went on relentlessly. "When you left...I spent a lot of time with him. I was such a mess. I fucked like a maniac... Then I went to his place to get pissed and talk about you." He gave a watery laugh. "I even tried to persuade him to get you back round to the flat somehow. I went to him because we had you in common. I thought...we were friends."

James closed his eyes, trying to swallow the mass of emotion in his throat that just wouldn't go, just got bigger and bigger instead.

"I worried..." Ben sounded uncertain. "When you wouldn't come here to visit me properly... But then you kept coming every day. And I wanted to be well enough to...to have this talk."

James acquiesced with a final nod. Too much now. Too much feeling. He needed the killing blow.

He allowed Ben to persuade him to have a cup of tea and let himself be led into an empty lift. He didn't really notice his surroundings again until he found himself sitting in what seemed to be the hospital's all-night cafeteria, with other tired, forlorn people. The lighting was harsh, fluorescent white, and the room stank of stale chip fat and overbrewed tea. It reeked of helplessness and desperation.

In the background, over the callous clatter of plates and cups and metal cutlery from behind the counter, he heard a woman's quiet sobbing. It didn't feel like a place anyone had ever been given good news.

James went to the counter and bought a couple of cups of tea, but though he knew he should eat something, his stomach felt like a ball of knotted wire. Just the sight of food made him nauseous. His father said he hadn't been eating enough, and he was probably right.

All they'd done to each other, he and Ben, all the pain and re-criminations between them, seemed pathetic now, like the squalling of children next to Steggie's life, and Steggie's end. And yet, still, this hurt, like a red-hot poker to the skin. He wondered if he'd ever be free of what he felt for Ben.

Ben reached across the table and took his hand. James thought he should pull it away, but he didn't have the energy or the will to refuse his touch.

James met his eyes. He felt empty. Blank. Braced.

"You were right. What you said to me in the cell..." Ben freed James's hand but he leaned further forward over the table, radiating intensity. "It was right. But...please. Please understand? I never had... the guts to let anyone close. Better to never take the risk, you know? Never trust anyone."

"I understand." And James truly did.

Ben's eyes were liquid with anguish. "The thing is...I'm *her*, Jamie. Her genes. Her flesh and blood."

"No." James shook his head, very sure. "You're *not*. You're your own man. A good man."

Ben searched his face anxiously, then his expression resolved into a sad, perplexed smile. He leaned back slightly.

"I knew," he said, as if he were confiding something. "From the first day I met you. I knew you could flatten every rule I had. You even had an added cosmic hazard sign attached... I mean you were a policeman and I had so many secrets." He pressed his lips together. "I knew I shouldn't offer you the place, but I couldn't help myself. And then I tried so hard to keep my hands off you. But when we started... It was something I couldn't give, not the way you wanted. But I was greedy and selfish and...I thought maybe I could *have* you, and keep you at arm's length at the same time. And you'd...learn. Adapt. Or I'd get over wanting you so much. And I knew it would hurt you but...I couldn't let you *go*, Jamie."

"Ben." James raised a hand to rub his aching forehead. "It's all right." He didn't want to listen to any more of this. He wanted it to end now, because it hurt too fucking much. He didn't need Ben to do penance. It was no one's fault they couldn't work.

Ben was relentless.

"I just kept feeling *more*, you know? Screwing around like a madman to keep my distance, making myself ration the times with you. Fucking...gutted, *obsessed* when you broke up with me that first time.

Then so relieved and worried when I let myself start again. Like a fucking *addict.*"

He shifted restlessly, jarring the table, spilling their tea. And James, frowning, began to understand that Ben hadn't said what he'd expected to hear. That Ben's view of their past seemed very different from his.

"It's like…I spent so long being in control of my life, my emotions, Jamie. Making sure I kept myself in check, just in case. And then you. All I felt for you. You made me join the fucking mess of the human race." He gave a short humorless laugh. Then he shook his head hopelessly. "I should have been relieved when you took Steggie to your father's ball. But I sat at home all night hating that he'd gone with you, and hating that I hated it. I even hated that…*Paul.*" Ben's agitation seemed to be growing, if anything, eyes wide with anxiety.

"I felt so…*jealous* and worried, because I knew you liked Steggie, and the two of you might have…I just lost it. And then I had to push you back again. And…fuck I can't *explain!*" He shoved his free hand into his hair, gripping it off his forehead, his expression wild with frustration. "I'm just…so, so *fucked up* over you, Jamie."

James opened his mouth to say something, but he felt so wrong-footed, so bewildered, he had no idea what was going to emerge.

Ben rushed on, as if he was frightened he wouldn't get it all out, frightened James might stop him.

"When you left, I couldn't think about anything, except…I had to get you to come back. I spent hours just…staring at your photos, like the stupid, creepy bastard I am. And I know I didn't think it out. I know I didn't face up to anything properly." He paused and swallowed painfully, breathing audibly disordered. "And I know you…you probably don't want me, after everything. And now that you know who I am. But the truth is…I really want to try, Jamie. If you'd just let me?"

The torrent of words stopped at last. Ben's shaking lips pressed tight together, as if he was making himself wait, making himself stop explaining and confessing. Waiting for James's verdict.

"Well…I…" James cleared his throat, feeling all the crushing weight of his own emotional ineptitude. "Thanks for telling me."

Even to his own ears, it sounded indescribably awkward.

Ben's eyes didn't leave his face, searching for something he didn't seem to find. Then he lowered his head, and James realized that he'd expected rejection from the start. But he could see the huge courage it had taken for Ben to try this at last—and openly, as Steven Brooker. Ben's identity, though, had nothing to do with James's decision.

He dug his fingernails into his palm underneath the table. His heart was a boulder in his chest.

"The thing is, I'm a monogamist, Ben. It's who I am. And you're… not."

Ben's head rose again, skin chalk-white, eyes huge.

"I'm not criticizing you for it," James went on quickly. "It's just… that doesn't work. Not for me. I can't do an open relationship. You knew that yourself. We tried, but we don't go together that way."

"No." Ben shook his head vigorously. "All that's what I did. It's not what I *am*. There were reasons."

James eyed him sadly. "I know. I know there were. But you need… variety. You need—"

"I *don't* need to fuck around! I need you. *Just* you. I need the man I trust." Ben's voice sounded increasingly shaky, desperate. "The man I love. I really fucking love you, Jamie. I've never been in love before. Never even close. I think…this has to be it."

I would have shown you what it's like to be loved, Jamie…

Steggie's echo sprang unbidden into James's mind, an indecent ghost pushing in to haunt the moment.

He wanted you to remember him, he told himself harshly. *And you will.*

Ben's need and misery lay out on display for him, open and generous, all defenses razed. For Ben to say these words, there had to be truth.

There had been so much James had misunderstood in his own inexperience and unhappiness. Hadn't seen at all, in fact, until now.

"Jamie. I swear," Ben said unsteadily. "I swear."

James could feel something breaking loose inside him, something like relief. Like hope.

"I love you too," he said, with total conviction. Uncomplicated happiness felt strange and clumsy to him after so long, like an unused limb. "And I'd like to get to know you. All of you."

Ben stared at him, as if he were unsure whether to believe it at first. But then he began to smile, and the smile widened to wild euphoria, tiredness and fear wiped away in one sweep.

He lurched forward and grabbed a handful of James's tie with his good hand. He yanked it toward him, hauling James halfway across the table and narrowly avoiding upending their cups of tea.

"Jamie," he breathed, grinning crazily into James's startled eyes. "I'm going to show you. And we…are going to be brilliant!"

38

"For fuck's sake, Jamie! Where did you live before? Windsor Castle?"

"You're exaggerating," James said, imperturbably. "There's not that much."

"Jamie." Ben spoke as if he were delivering a necessary and horrible home truth. "There really is."

They were standing, wrapped to the eyeballs in coats and scarves, peering into James's opened storage container, at piled-up furniture and haphazard boxes as far as the eye could see, stuff James hadn't seen for years.

"How the hell did you get it all out in one night?"

James grinned. "Preparation. Paranoia. Extravagant tipping."

Ben rolled his eyes. "We'll have to move to the Outer Hebrides to find a house we can afford that'd big enough to take all this *and* my stuff. My normal amount of stuff."

James chewed his lip as he considered that unfortunate truth. Then he conceded with reluctance, "I can dump some of it."

He should have expected Ben would read him perfectly.

"No…s'alright," Ben said quickly. "Not the things you love. We'll find somewhere."

In fact, Christmas loomed on the horizon, and they'd only just started house hunting, five months after Steggie had blown his brains out in the flat beneath them. Ben's exhibition and James's accelerated

inspectors exams, not to mention establishing their reborn relationship, had combined to persuade them to stay put for the moment,
though they were both keen to move away from Selworth Gardens
and its black memories.

More than that, Ben had become unnervingly eager to make a
commitment, tie James down somehow. And buying a house together
would be quite a big one. And getting a dog. Ben had been pushing
hard for a dog he'd already named Ozzy.

Pooling their resources—their increased earning capacities,
James's mother's inheritance, Ben's own money, they could probably
afford something nice. But possibly not central, if it was to be large
enough to house all of this. Magnus, of course, champed at the bit to
buy it for them.

James peered into the dim interior of the container, trying to identify the box he'd come to find just as Ben's mobile rang. Ben glanced
down at the screen, and the corner of his mouth lifted in a rueful little
smile.

"Just Jace," he remarked.

James sighed.

"It's no big deal." Ben sent the call to message-service. "He's just
hovering. In the hope I slide back into slut-dom."

James's mouth fell open.

"Too soon?" Ben asked innocently.

James shut his eyes and shook his head in exaggerated despair,
turning away to hide his grin.

In reality he had no doubts at all about Ben's fidelity, now he'd
committed himself. Ben wasn't by nature a cheat—he really did value
honesty. James felt very sure of it.

Of course, inevitably, other men still wanted Ben, still came on to
him, but James had almost managed to convince him that he didn't
mind Ben flirting back a bit—that it was okay to be himself.

Oddly though, Ben had proved far less able to cope with watching
James chatting to attractive blokes. Ben, in love, had revealed himself
to be a deeply possessive, jealous man, which James found ingloriously
satisfying. And Ben had been the one to push to stop using condoms.

"Hang on to this?" He tossed his phone to Ben as he clambered nimbly over piled-up furniture to reach the box he'd spotted at the side of the container. It held books and photographs, a couple of things that had belonged to his mum, and the carriage clock his granny had left him, which now reminded him of Steggie. Things he wanted with him, now he had a home. As he climbed he heard his ringtone behind him, but he kept going.

He reached the box quickly and began to reel it in, and as he did, he had a clear memory of throwing everything into it the night before he'd been locked out of his cavernous penthouse. How determined and sad and scared he'd been. And look at how it had turned out in the end. How much, at last, he loved and was loved in return.

But he never forgot how lucky he'd been, and every so often, he went to lay white carnations, for remembrance, on Steggie's grave. Ben never protested, but he didn't go with him either.

James clambered back down, holding the box under one arm, the other helping keep him upright, as furniture and boxes slid around under his feet. But as he hit solid ground he noticed Ben staring at the phone he'd been given to hold, with a peculiar mixture of amusement, frustration and worry.

"Ben? Was that a call-in? Alec again?"

Ben had acquired the habit of "casually" answering James's phone on his behalf if he wasn't in the room, a legacy James knew, of a lifetime of mistrust. James didn't mind; he had no intention of ever letting him down. And he felt certain Ben would soon grow bored of relaying messages from the unit, or his dad.

Ben eyed the phone now, though, as if it had bitten him.

"Magnus," he announced. "He wants you to go to dinner on Friday. With Charles Forsyth." He pronounced the name as if Magnus had invited Beelzebub.

James raised his eyebrows. Inside he was sighing. "Me? Or both of us?"

"He invited me for politeness," Ben said with a frown. "But you *know* he wants you and Charles to…unite to further the Henderson Empire."

"Ben. You've heard Charles has started seeing a Tory MP?" James asked in his most patient tone. "And you know my father likes you."

In fact, though Ben had decided Magnus should be told his true identity, James and his father had never actually discussed him beyond that, just as they hadn't addressed their own past or the future. They focused on sewing down the present. Neither of them had changed enough to become great talkers.

Still, James knew Magnus liked Ben, as surely as if Magnus had given him a presentation on it, complete with slides. Just as Ben believed that Magnus couldn't possibly see a murderer's son as part of his family. Hopefully time and James—and Ben's renewed visits to his therapist—would chip away at his reflexive insecurity.

"You're going to have to face up to it someday, Jamie," Ben said steadily. "You're sole heir to a billionaire, and you can't pretend that's not—"

"No," James interrupted firmly. Because now he had him, he understood exactly what Ben needed—the reassurance that nothing and no one would ever lure James away. "I am a newly fledged Detective Inspector and you're not exactly living in a cardboard box. Nothing's going to change what's between us."

Ben shook his head, but James saw the ghost of relaxation there. "Well," Ben said, almost shyly. "At least Magnus finally saw how amazing you are." He elbowed James in the side, trying to macho-up the moment with jokey affection.

James gave a heavy sigh, but his heart had turned to mush.

"Whatever happens with my father," he repeated. "Nothing important's going to change. I'm always going to be Alec's muffin boy."

Ben snorted a shocked, delighted laugh. "That image... Fuck. I need to bleach my brain."

Together they heaved the doors of the container shut and locked them. Ben still had to be careful of his wound but he'd been able to get back into the gym again, almost back to his old fitness.

"It's important though," Ben said doggedly when they'd finished. "I'm glad you have your dad back."

James pulled him close and kissed him hard.

"Yeah," he allowed, lips so close they brushed Ben's as he spoke. "But some parents…they just contribute DNA. Whatever happens, you and me…we're always going to be more than that. We chose each other."

Ben pulled back to meet his gaze. He was frowning, his full lips pursed in a sad moue.

"It's not that easy though, is it? There's something… Maybe, because they made you, you know? Whatever they do, some part of you always wants to forgive them. To be able to find something to…admire. Deep down, maybe we always crave their love."

James chewed his lip then finally nodded. Because, perhaps it was true. Perhaps it was Ben's tragedy, as, in a way, it had been Steggie's.

"You have mine," he offered.

Ben's eyes cleared. "Suppose I'll struggle through then."

He kissed James softly on the lips, and they walked back to their car together, shoulder to shoulder.

ABOUT THE AUTHOR

Dal Maclean comes from the North of Scotland and has a background in journalism, and a passion for history. Dal has lived in Asia and worked all over the world, but the UK is now home. She dislikes the Tragic Gay trope but loves flawed characters and genuine conflict in romantic fiction, and believes it's worth a bit of work to reach a happy ending. Agatha Christie, English gardens and ill-advised cocktails are her three fatal weaknesses.

ACKNOWLEDGMENTS

This book would never have seen the light of day without the help of some generous and talented people.

I want to express my huge gratitude to Josh Lanyon for her unbreakable faith and friendship. Without her encouragement and belief, I wouldn't even have tried this, and I certainly wouldn't have persisted with it. Her generosity and kindness are unfailing. Thank you so much.

Nicole Kimberling has whipped this book, and me, into shape over long months which have nearly driven us both to drink. Or, at least, to drink more. I've learned an incredible amount (mainly about melons and eyeballs, but that's another story), but it's also proved to be one of the most enjoyable experiences of my life. That's principally because Nicole is Nicole—always open to ideas, patient, very funny, insightful and scarily clever. She's an editor in a billion, and I feel honored and thankful to have been able to work with her.

I'd also like to thank the brilliant Ginn Hale for taking the time to cast a critical and forensic eye over the story and characters, which helped beyond measure. Thanks too to Anne Scott for a super-methodical, impeccable copyedit which significantly tightened my stays. And thank you to Whitley Gray for helping out a perfect stranger with details of forensic pathology. That was really kind and hugely appreciated.

Finally, I'd like to thank my family for putting up with my nonsense, and all the nonsense to come. I love you more.

The Bellingham Mystery Series Volume 1

Peter Fontaine just wants to break a juicy story and maybe win an award for his intrepid journalism. But all too soon his instinct for prying into secrets and his fantastical turn of mind conspire to draw him deep into murder and mystery.

Three novellas from Lambda Literary Award winning author Nicole Kimberling collected in one volume!

blindeyebooks.com

BLADES OF JUSTICE

The scissors are blacksmith worked, crude and blackened, nothing like any other pair in the village. But they've always hung there at the door of Treagove. Through three hundred years of history they have watched over the women who live at the old house—and where the scissors are, justice seems to follow. Who says the tool of justice can't be domestic?

Blades of Justice

HELEN ANGOVE
JESS FARADAY
RACHEL GREEN

EDITED BY NICOLE KIMBERLING

Three novellas spanning three centuries of crime and mystery.
Coming March 2017

blindeyebooks.com

CPSIA information can be obtained
at www.ICGtesting.com
Printed in the USA
FSOW02n1832021116
26839FS